A CATHEDRAL OF DEMONS

JOE TALON

vinci

BOOKS

Vinci Books

vinci-books.com

Published by Vinci Books Ltd in 2026

1

A CIP catalogue record for this book is available from the British Library.
Paperback ISBN: 9781036733995
The EU GPSR authorised representative is Logos Europe, 9 rue Nicolas Poussion, 17000 La Rochelle, France contact@logoseurope.eu

By Joe Talon

Griffin Woodbury Supernatural Detective

Music of the Damned

The Wishing of Trees

A Cathedral of Demons

A Valentine Investigation

For Whom the Willow Weeps

Seven Tears of Heaven

An Agony of Lies

Lorne Turner Supernatural Thrillers

Counting Crows

Money for Old Bones

Dead of the Winter Sun

Salt for the Devil's Eye

Bad Waters Run Deep

The Alchemist's Corpse

The Spirit Glass

The Dead Also Have Secrets

Prologue

Thirty-four years ago

The skin around her belly felt like it would split under the pressure from the shifting lump of human who'd taken up residence. Her back and hips ached all day, and nerve pains were tormenting her legs at night. Everything had swollen, especially her boobs. They were huge and kept leaking this horrid white stuff onto her clothes. She refused to call it milk. It made her sound like a cow. Her mother tutted and muttered under her breath constantly, and her father couldn't bring himself to look at her.

Elena wanted to cry, and each time she felt all that sadness well up, she turned it to anger. The only part of her life she had any control over. Rather than seek comfort in her confirmation gift of a golden cross hanging from a fine chain, Elena now wore a quartz crystal around her neck. She'd removed the simple wooden cross she'd prayed to every night since she was a small child. In its place hung a picture of a full moon over the sea. Bollocks to the damned Church.

Over nine months, her rage had built to catastrophic levels. She wanted to tear down buildings, rip out trees and hurl them at her parents, the teachers, her missing friends. Cowards. The moment they'd found out she was pregnant, they'd fled from her side. Like it was catching, or something. Yet another betrayal.

She sat on her narrow bed in a room decorated with posters of Take That. Her favourite was bad boy Robbie Williams. That crooked smile and blue eyes just melted her heart. Maybe that's why she'd ended up in this state.

He'd had twinkly blue eyes and a cheeky smile. His congregation loved him for it. She'd loved him for it. Those damned tears threatened again.

She yanked open the drawer on her bedside table and removed her diary. The pink, sequined surface looked offensive to her now, like it was for a little girl, not a fifteen-year-old woman of the world. She threw it back in the drawer and pulled open another.

A 'so called' friend had given it as a birthday present. It was a witch's diary and spell book. Elena, heavily into the Church at the time, had shoved it away.

Maybe this magic stuff was something that would never betray her, never force her to make impossible choices? Did she need to follow a new path? Anxiety made her stomach twist again, and the nausea rushed back. She opened it and the first thing she read was: *Your Mother loves you. She is always there for you.*

Below this was the image of a beautiful woman dressed in robes made of butterflies, ears of wheat, birds, squirrels and more. It was beautiful. So different to the misery of Christ's suffering on the cross. So different to her suffering.

Elena wanted to be loved by someone like this. No one in her congregation loved her, that was for damned certain.

She rubbed the huge, round belly. "You're screwed, you know that?" No tenderness echoed in her words. She hated this lump. By the time she realised she was pregnant, she'd already crossed the threshold for a legal termination. So, she'd drunk a bottle of vodie, having stolen the money for it from her mum's purse, and thrown herself down the stairs.

It hadn't worked. In the process, the nurses, then her parents, discovered she'd ruined her life forever. The screaming and blaming had started at the hospital and hadn't seemed to stop for the next five months. She'd basically been a prisoner here, in her bedroom, for all that time. Her mother had refused to buy maternity clothes, just pulling out the old ones from the loft. They dated from the bloody seventies, it was old hippy shit. Elena spent her days in her dressing gown, which just about covered the obscene bump.

When she'd finally confessed to her furious father which bloke had knocked her up, he'd gone deathly quiet. The look of confusion on his face was comical, not that she'd dared to laugh. It took him several attempts to speak, and when he'd managed it, he'd said: "You'll go to hell for lying. You know that?" Despite being Protestant, he was still from Northern Ireland. Hell was a big, and very real place, and the Church mattered. Its reputation was as important to him as his own. It was her fault. She'd been the temptress. Her skirts were too short. Her tops too tight. No girl of fifteen should be in heels or makeup.

That's when he started in on her mother.

Elena knew that just to keep the peace and to stop the fists, her mother would side with her father and she'd have no one to defend her. No protector. In the stupid books she read, there was always a man out there who'd save the heroine. Alas, her fate wouldn't be like that; she was destined to be the bad girl.

Elena snarled. She yanked open the first drawer, removed her old, pink diary, and methodically began tearing out pages. If she was so unlovable, then she'd just have to learn to live with it.

Tears dripped onto the ripped, shredded soft pink paper. Her fingers ached with the effort of tearing each page into tiny pieces. Every time her eyes stopped blurring enough to see the writing, she'd catch sight of her secret name for *him* or a little love heart over a letter. Pages of her signature with her new name. *His* name. That's what he'd promised. Now, he'd gone. The Church spirited him away somewhere else. She'd never see him again. He didn't even fight for her, just did as he was told and left.

Her grief, her shame, her loathing overwhelmed her so much that when the first wave of pain hit, she thought it was just another emotional overload for her body to cope with. Right up until fluid poured out from between her legs to soak her bed and the rug on the floor.

Twenty-two hours later

She lay back sweating, and breathing like she'd just run the school's cross-country at record speed. A joy she'd never felt before filled her exhausted limbs, her fuddled mind, and most of all, her heart.

"Let me hold her," Elena called out to the nurses in the corner of the room. She tried to reach out, hearing the weak wail, and her entire body reacted to the sound. Was this motherhood? This odd sense of connection to another being? A desperation to provide and protect?

The midwife turned back to her with a smile on her face, but Elena realised it didn't reach the woman's eyes. "Just a bit more work to do on her first, dear."

Elena frowned. This wasn't how it worked on the telly, unless there was something wrong with the baby.

Her heart plunged into the agony between her legs. The vodka. The trip down the stairs. The months of hate and shame she'd poured into the lump, wanting it gone. What had she done? Tears filled her eyes again. "Please let me see her. I promise to be a good mum. It doesn't matter if she's not right—" Her shaky voice was ignored.

Elena struggled to sit further up in the bed, ignoring the cooling bodily fluids covering the mattress. If she could move, she might be able to stand.

The weak cry became stronger, and Elena's entire body screamed to provide. "Please," Elena said, making her voice more forceful. "You can't keep her away from me."

The door to the room opened. Elena had hoped it would be her mother. That maybe both her parents would now forgive her, and they could all be a family together.

Instead, an old man walked in. He wore a black woollen coat, black trousers and shiny black shoes. His thin hair was another shade of black never seen in nature, and he'd used some kind of oil to stick it down to his white scalp. Elena hated him on sight.

"Who are you?" she called out, trying to cover herself.

He glanced at her with such disgust, Elena felt like she'd been punched in the face. "You have it?" he asked. This was addressed to the midwife.

She glanced at Elena. "Is this really necessary? We have

the ability to support young mothers. This seems cruel and archaic."

"It's what the parents want. She is underage." He held his arms out.

Elena, who'd never been stupid, foolish perhaps, but never stupid, suddenly understood. She'd glimpsed the man's throat, seen the dog collar.

"No!" she yelled. "You can't!" Curses poured out of her.

The child started to scream. The baby started to scream. The midwife tried not to weep.

Five years later

Elena strode out of the university grounds clutching her degree to her chest with a wild grin on her face and in her eyes. This was the first step on a long journey to make sure no other young woman had to suffer the way she had. With this degree, she could join any medical school in the country, even without her pathetic parents.

First though, she had to go home. Her flatmate had sent a message to her pager, telling her that a recorded delivery letter had arrived. Elena was almost as excited about the letter as she was about the qualification.

Hurrying down Bristol's busy streets, then catching a bus to the St Paul's district, she navigated the area like a native. Despite being white, most of the locals treated her like one of their own, and they'd offered her kindness over the years. She'd always felt safe here.

Breathless by the time she'd run up the three flights of stairs to her flat's front door, she let herself in. Her flatmate would be at work by now, but the letter was on the small kitchen table they used for their essays when not in the library.

Elena grabbed the envelope and ripped it open, hardly daring to breathe. She'd finally uncover the history of her baby girl. When not studying, or learning about her new spiritual path, she'd spent hours, weeks, months, figuring out how to track down what had happened in that hospital maternity ward. Who the man was that took her daughter and where she'd been taken. This letter should tell her who'd adopted her baby without her permission.

She scanned the letter, her entire body fizzing and popping with excitement.

The words didn't make sense.

She read them again. The fizzing turned into nausea. The popping excitement turned into dread.

"No," she said aloud. "No, this can't be right. This can't be true. They must be lying. They're doing it to me again."

The words: *We regret to inform you of your baby's death,* lifted off the page and floated about her head. *Eighteen months old. Sepsis after a short illness. So sorry for your loss. Our deepest condolences. Her burial was held at…*

Elena screamed.

She clutched the quartz crystal pendant around her neck and vowed vengeance on them all. Every fibre in her body would be turned into a weapon. They would all pay. She'd bring down the entire fucking Church of England. And when she had burned it, she would dance on its ashes.

Chapter One

Riding my retro-style Kawasaki Café 800 from home to work used to be an easy pleasure. This being Cornwall and not central London during rush hour. Now, the short ride between Turpin Cottage and the Department of Paranormal Investigations satellite office—or Rural Security, depending on who asked—proved to be a juggling act between the four wheeled traffic and his desire to reach work in one piece. Perhaps that should be a high-wire act while juggling, in a high wind.

I threw my bike lid at the sofa, which caught it. Then I swiped a hand over my sweating face and grumbled, "I swear, even without the school run I'm going to end up a smear on that piece of road."

Sid looked up at me. He drove a Mark III red classic Mini, which was barely more visible on the high wire we navigated every day than my bike. "Tourists," he muttered before turning back to his screens.

This made me chuckle as I headed for the coffee

machine in our small kitchen. "We're worse, we're incomers. Besides, if you want to call tourists anything, it's *emmets*."

My friend, colleague and housemate, grunted. "I drove through a ford in my Mini. I am now a local," he declared in his Peckham accent.

"You might want to discuss that with Megan."

"If she ever shows her face again, I will."

The coffee machine snarled and growled while I stripped off my bike gear. Despite being a Royal Marine Commando and DoPI's spear point in Cornwall against the *paras*, I was not tough enough to be riding my bike without my protective equipment, regardless of the heat. I switched on the fan in the kitchen area and fluffed out the front of my t-shirt, trying to dry it. High summer had brought high temperatures and sudden, sometimes catastrophic, storms. Climate change was giving the UK a nasty slap around the chops, and we were going down, hitting the deck hard. Only time would tell if we got back up and found a way to fight back.

I pondered what Sid had said about Megan's prolonged absences since May. He had it right; we'd hardly seen her. More importantly, I'd hardly seen her, and we were supposed to be in a new, and romantic, relationship. Or at least heading that way. I'd encouraged her to take up the opportunity for firearms training with DoPI. She didn't want to train through the usual channels as a police officer; it would force her into becoming an Authorised Firearms Officer or AFO, and that wasn't part of her career plan. Besides, it would take her away from DoPI, and despite her atheism regarding organised religion, she would now admit to worrying about what might lurk under the bed or in the back of a wardrobe. She was also battling her day job.

I worked full time for DoPI, as did Sid, but Megan was

my police liaison, which meant when she wasn't needed for DoPI work, she had to do 'normal' police work. The summers kept the Devon and Cornwall Police Service very busy. It felt like the rest of the UK descended on the county in such numbers that the narrow peninsula might snap off from the mainland under the extra weight, and drift into the Atlantic. Her role as beat sergeant meant her shifts were long, and she'd taken on overtime to help her parent's farm financial situation. I'd offered to help as well, but despite being family, sort of as it turned out, Conor Ackley didn't want my money. I didn't press the issue. There would be other ways to help, and my sort of uncle would just have to put up with it.

Sid leaned back in his chair, making it groan in protest. "Any news about the ex-boyfriend?"

I grunted. Unused to navigating ex-boyfriends who didn't know when to give up, I'd turned to Sid for advice. He'd told me to leave it to Megan.

"No, she's still being elusive about Adrian *bloody* Hess. All I've managed to glean out of her, is that most of her colleagues think she did the dirty on him with me."

Sid frowned. "You didn't though, right?"

"No. I mean, it was pretty tight between her breaking up with him and us discovering we aren't biological first cousins, but it wasn't like they were living together, engaged or even that serious."

"In Megan's eyes."

I sighed and carried over a mug of coffee for Sid. "Yeah, that's the problem. He doesn't seem to think she's able to make her own decisions. A 'real' man needs to tell her what to do."

Sid laughed. "He never said that to her."

"I doubt it, he's too clever for that, but it's the impression she gave me. Their colleagues are certainly making the most out of the drama."

Police stations were way too much like schoolyards for my liking. We'd never done the dirty, but that didn't stop the fuel being ladled on the fire by good old Adrian.

I leaned one thigh against Sid's desk. "Are you sure I can't just hunt him down?" The desire to do just that burned through me constantly.

Sid eyed me. "I really hope that's a joke, mate."

"It is, I guess. If I do anything like that, I'm going to be no better than him." Even to my own ears, I sounded like a stroppy teenager.

Sid tried to suppress a smirk. "Trying to be the better man?"

I grumbled, "Right now, I'm not sure I want to be. Throwing her over my shoulder and forcing her to stay in my cave while I kill any trespassers feels like a better option."

Sid laughed. "It's tough being a twenty-first century man."

"Don't I bloody know it."

After finding out Megan and I weren't blood relatives everything in my life had changed. It felt like the ties weighing me down had been cut, but equally, being adrift was disorientating. My inappropriate desire for Megan had oddly kept me locked down and welded into a state of self-pity I now thought of as comfortable. I was currently adrift in uncharted seas.

It had also unmoored me from the only real family I'd felt good about. No one knew where my mother had come from, and the little evidence I had left, didn't reveal that secret. Sadly, it seemed Mum had never discovered her origins either.

I finally plonked Sid's coffee down on his desk and received a grunt in response, before heading for my less technically enhanced office area. The box full of my mother's paperwork sat on the floor beside my chair. It whispered its half-disclosed secrets almost constantly, but that's all they were, half of the secrets she'd contained. I knew she'd been adopted by the Tudor family, but no one knew from where, and that nagged at heart and head. My mother was not a normal woman, and whatever genes she'd passed down to me had brought more with them than half my DNA.

Sid had done a deep dive, but all her details were pre-digital, so only the basics were found online. I'd even considered contacting my father, but that would be the very last of last resorts. For heaven's sake, I was a trained investigator; there had to be something I could do to figure out her origins.

Most of my work over the summer, so far, had been down at Madron. Some of the protesters remained, including Leaze and Denny, and we had the unremitting irritation of Anwen's Children, who refused to leave Trystan in DoPI's hands, but plans were moving forward rapidly. Trystan, a very young and gifted natural mystic, had really started to come out of his shell. The woodland and its Druidic circle were gradually taking shape under his guidance.

The Duchy of Cornwall had agreed to the project, as land management wasn't really in DoPI's remit. You can always trust the Royal Family to keep a state secret, and so far, they had been doing a great job at blurring the lines. The press hadn't caught a whiff of the secrets we were hiding down there. Though, it had taken all my diplomacy skills to coax Denny into signing a non-disclosure agreement and the Official Secrets Act.

Rather than think about tree spirits, I pondered where next to take my investigation of the real Hazel Woodbury. Sid had suggested past life regression under hypnotism, though I failed to see how this would help; it was her life I wanted to understand, not mine. Besides, even for an operative of DoPI, this stretched the bounds of credibility. Then he decided LSD might be the answer. This one I closed down fast. After my one and only experience with MDMA, I wasn't going to be using drugs again. I had to be missing something in that damned box.

Just as I bent to pick it up for the hundredth time since May, the phone rang. Sanchez.

"Ma'am," I stated. She'd thawed recently, but not so much that we had pleasantries to share over the phone.

The moment I heard her voice, my office vanished, and I stood in front of her desk, doing my best to ignore her choice in mind-melting artwork. "Corporal Woodbury, I need you and your police liaison to go up to Truro to speak with Bishop James Chadwick. They have a problem that's come to our attention, and we need to keep on top of it." Her inner android was in full control today.

"Of course, ma'am. Are they expecting us?"

"Yes. Today would be best. Details will be arriving now."

I suppressed a sigh. The woman didn't seem to understand that Megan had an actual job and wasn't always at my beck and call, unfortunately. It also meant dealing with August traffic. "Very good, ma'am." Not like I could refuse a direct order.

"Report back once the issue has been dealt with." She paused for a moment. Then: "And Woodbury, try not to make this into another shitshow we have to hide."

"I'll do my best, ma'am."

"Thank you." The call died.

I checked my secure email and found the briefing. "Sid."

"Got it."

We both read the file for a few minutes while drinking coffee. Sid finished first. "Seems simple enough."

"Why do they need us?" I asked, still going through the details. "It's a bloke with a problem, surely they need the police if it's stalking?"

We didn't have many details, which meant I was probably missing something important. The basics were there, though. A man in his forties seemed to be stalking members of the cathedral's staff, both women and men. Several people had complained he'd followed them home and watched their houses and families for a few days, before he moved on to someone else. He'd also been found in the private areas of the cathedral and its grounds. When challenged, after he'd been discovered making chalk marks on the door to the sacristy, he declared he was a demon hunter and wanted to keep the holy items and vestments of the church untainted. That's when the bishop had called the Archbishop of Canterbury, and his office had called DoPI.

The bishop would know me as Rural Security, but the archbishop, the Security Service and the Monarchy know they'd be sending a DoPI operative. At least that's how close we tried to keep the circle of trust. It was proving harder now that the veil between us and the *paras* was thinning so much that the monsters just kept leaking through no matter what we did to stop them. Social media didn't help either.

"I've got a photo of the man," Sid said. "Do you want me to do a background check on him?"

"Sure, dig up what you can. I'll call Megan." At which

point my stomach flipped on its arse. An uncomfortable feeling.

Sid chuckled. "You should see your face right now, soldier boy."

I flipped him the one-finger salute as I speed-dialled Megan.

"Hey, Griffin," she said after three rings. Three. That was a long time. Did she contemplate switching me off, like I'd seen her do to Adrian?

Really? The poor woman is probably out on patrol somewhere wearing more clobber than you did as a Marine, and she'd have to fish the phone out of some Velcroed pouch on her Batman belt.

Good point well-made.

We hadn't reached the endearments stage, so I stuck with our normal routine. "Hey, Meg. I have a DoPI job if you're up for it."

"Really?" She sounded excited. "Oh my God, that would be amazing. I'm due to provide security for a politician doing the rounds while on their summer holiday down here, so I'd love to come with you. Also, the pile of paperwork on my desk is beginning to resemble the Leaning Tower of Pisa."

"Do you want to come up here, or shall I pick you up at the station?" I asked.

"Now?"

"Roger that," I confirmed.

"Erm, bike or car?"

"Traffic to Truro?" I asked.

"Bike."

"My thoughts exactly. So…?"

"Pick me up outside my flat in twenty minutes. I need to change into something practical," she said. I heard a soft shush of fabric moving against a stab vest. Her voice came over more quietly. "It'll be good to see you. I've missed you."

My heart raced like a greyhound on amphetamines. "You too." Though it was sad she had to whisper for fear of being overheard. Megan killed the call.

The grin on my face made Sid roll his eyes at me. I gave him the one fingered salute.

I'd only been to Megan's flat a few times since moving down to Cornwall. She lived over a deserted pet shop on a street made up of takeaway restaurants, nail salons, hairdressers and a tattooist. It was small, cramped and vaguely depressing. Her flat wasn't much better despite her efforts. It'd take me fifteen minutes to ride from the office down to Camborne's less ascetic side. I pondered whether I should go home to change. A shirt, tie and waistcoat combo should be the order of the day when meeting a bishop.

My shoulders slumped at the thought, but it had to be done. A Royal Marine never went out while at work looking like a reject from rent-a-soldier. Not that I was a soldier, but rent-a-sailor had connotations no one wanted.

I sent Megan a quick text: *Need to make it 30 mins, sorry.*

If I waited for a reply, I'd be waiting forever, so I climbed back into my bike gear and headed for home. On a hanger I had two good-quality white shirts from Saville Row, or that's what the Camden Market trader had told me when I'd bought them. They were a nice fit in cotton. A waistcoat of soft blue wool and a tie with the regiment insignia on it, black with a pattern of the red dagger pointing upwards. I checked the mop of untameable brown curls, decided the bike helmet would flatten them with some luck, and left the cottage. Rather than tackle the main drag through Redruth, Pool and Camborne, I wove through the backstreets and made it with seconds to spare.

She stood on the pavement doorstep of the flat and was obviously in a heated debate with a man. Her bike helmet hung from her right hand by the chin guard, and she looked as if she wanted to swing it at the man's head. Quacker, my bike, is quiet, but she's not silent, and this wasn't a busy street, sadly for the businesses that eked out a living. They both heard my approach.

I'd never been introduced to Hess. Megan had made it clear she didn't want me interfering, and she'd worked hard to keep us apart. Now, I had him in my sights. Tall, probably my height, but slimmer. His shoulders weren't as broad, and he had a leaner frame, more like Sid's. His hair was cut close to the scalp, so he looked bald. With a narrow face and hawkish nose, even I could see he was a good-looking bloke.

Whatever Megan said as I rolled slowly up the street, he backed off. When he turned to look at me, I made sure to flick my visor up, refusing to hide. His eyes were blue, sharp, his mouth thin, and he looked to be a good ten years my senior. Megan pushed past him, shoved the helmet over her braided blonde hair, and walked into the street.

She climbed onto the back of the bike without a word. I'd barely stopped moving, so I continued to ride slowly past the bloke.

There may have been significant eye contact.

Her arms went around my waist, and I gunned the engine, heading for the A30 and east to Truro. She leaned into me, and I rubbed her hands over my stomach. We'd have time to talk later; right now, she just needed to escape.

I may have broken several rules of the road to give her a puff of fun. Despite that, it still took us forty-five minutes to make a thirty-minute haul up the road.

Chapter Two

Truro was a small city, with the usual medieval tangle of streets. I'd never spent any time there, but as we waited at endless sets of traffic lights, melting under the punishment of the August sun and our bike gear, I decided it looked nice. Lots of trees. After my experiences in Madron with the woodland, I'd come to see trees in a new light and often found myself pondering the spirits that inhabited them from beyond the veil. The journey up here from Redruth meant we rode past endless fields of dried grass, crops brought in early to try to save the harvest from the sun, and farm animals who stood as if they were just enduring another punishing day, longing for the cold winds of winter.

The three towers of the Victorian cathedral rose over the city like a beacon for the godly, one of them capped with the vibrant green of copper that I guessed came from the local mines. Having done a little research on the area, basically checking its Wiki page, I'd learned Truro began its life under the Norman yoke of Richard de Lucy, but only really became vastly wealthy with 'modern' mining during the industrial revolution. Now, it floundered slightly like so much of Cornwall, trying to hook tourists, and therefore second homeowners, while also being aware it made life difficult for locals.

"Ignore the sign for the multistorey car park," Megan said from the back. "There's a closer car park that'll be fine for the bike."

She gave me directions, and I rode onto Old Bridge Street. Nowhere could I find a place to leave the bike out of the sun. If any such place existed in Britain at the moment. We stowed the gear in the panniers I'd bought now that I had to think about Megan's clothing and mine.

"If the Vectra had air con, we'd be less sweaty," Megan grumbled. She didn't wear her uniform, but a pair of smart navy trousers and a lighter blue cotton blouse, now creased and obviously sticking to her in places. She'd not quite managed to return her curves to where they'd been back in the spring, but when we had managed to eat together, I always made sure we had plenty.

My waistcoat hid the worst of my sweatiness.

She smiled at me. "You look lovely, but lose the tie, you don't need it."

"It's a regiment tie," I pointed out, looking down. Small freckled hands spread over my chest, making my heart pound.

"That's as maybe, but you'll look better without it, and you don't need to advertise what you were." She lifted herself onto her toes and kissed me.

Hunger for her overwhelmed everything else, and before she knew what had happened, I'd lifted her from the waist with one arm. The kiss went on for some time, heedless of passersby. I may have growled at some point.

When I put her down, Megan stumbled a little, and a

grin matched mine. "We're worse than teenagers." She had to straighten her shirt again.

"We're allowed to be," I told her. "How are you?"

Her jaw tightened for a moment, and she sobered. "Tired." She looked it. "Work is…" For a moment she gazed over the car park looking for words. It took a long time, which meant she was trying to find some that didn't cause me a problem.

"Just tell me, Megan. I'm not the sort of bloke to rip the wings off butterflies out of pique."

Yeah, you say that, but you're just looking for the right trigger.

"I'm just tired, Griffin." She rubbed my arm, sending shivers through me. "Don't worry."

I wanted to press, but Megan kept her work life as separate from me as possible. Despite our shared childhood, I'd realised that learning how the adult Megan functioned brought challenges. Not least her desire to keep her life compartmentalised. Not something I was used to in my relationships. Usually, it was me keeping the secrets. It felt odd. She knew everything about my life, just about, and I still knew so little about hers. Combining these thoughts with how few facts I had about my mother's beginnings again left me feeling adrift in some nameless way I didn't understand.

"Well, let's go see what this bishop wants from us, and afterwards we'll find a nice pub for some lunch." I planted a kiss on her head. "We'll have a proper chat then."

Megan smiled, but it looked a bit wan. I wanted her to feel the way I did: as if every sunrise brought the song of nightingale and lark into my day because I'd be having some contact with the most important person in my life. I'd discovered my inner romantic, and I really wanted to share it with her. Megan, however, carried weights I didn't understand yet, and it made me nervous.

We walked into Old Bridge Street, past a 'wealth management' company's office, which felt a bit on the nose this close to the cathedral, considering how many people in Cornwall struggled to make a living wage. A handful of metres further on, we found a helpful sign pointing us in the direction of the cathedral's offices. It would save us from wandering around the building itself. Though I had to admit to being awed by the place.

Despite being Victorian, the architect had revived the splendour of the medieval cathedrals throughout the UK. Stunning high arched buttresses, spectacular stained-glass windows, and the beauty of stone carvings made it obvious how much the period loved to look back with romance on previous centuries.

My inner archaeologist, who rarely had the opportunity to stretch his legs, desperately wanted to know more. What had been here before this building? Why had they chosen this site, as closed in as it was by streets, for the project? How had—

"Griffin," Megan said, tugging me along, "we're here."

I hadn't noticed. She chuckled, amused and exasperated by turns. The shock of the office building left me speechless for a moment. A brutalist nineteen sixties or seventies concrete hellscape squatted over a small parking area.

"How the hell did they get away with building that?" I asked, pointing at the horror story before me.

"Oh my God, you are such a snob. Come on. Let's go find someone to help." She led me up the broad concrete steps. Concrete. Yuck.

The offices were open, and a receptionist sat behind the desk. She had neatly bobbed grey hair, with streaks of pink and blue running through it. Her glasses, with a diamanté chain attached to the arms, were heavy black plastic that swept up at the corners. If the building came from the sixties, she came from the fifties. A row of pearls sat over the collar of a neatly buttoned, delicately floral blouse.

"How can I help?" she asked the moment we walked through the door.

Air conditioning hit me, and I almost stopped moving to enjoy its chilly fingers as it danced over my prickling skin. Megan flicked open her police credentials. I gave up the temptation to remain near the door and offered a smile. It made the woman frown.

I also flicked open my ID. "Griffin Woodbury, Rural Security. I believe Bishop Chadwick is expecting a visit from me? We didn't have a specific time, but I received a call that said it was urgent."

A colourful pile of leaflets on her desk shifted as my arm caught them. She tutted, rose from her chair and straightened them. Apparently, Truro was about to be the 'centre of culture in Cornwall with an art and literature festival', due to take place in the next week or so. I wondered if Megan would like to come up and have a tourist day with me.

The narrow, red-painted lips narrowed further. "The bishop is a busy man." Not a trace of a Cornish accent.

I didn't say anything. It's usually the best way of getting what I want when I meet an immovable object like an overprotective jobsworth.

She huffed, but put a call through to someone else called Anna, who obviously gave us the green light of approval. The woman said, "Take a seat. Someone will be with you shortly."

We both sat as close to the air conditioning unit as possible. Megan leaned against me a little and closed her eyes. "I don't want to move."

I chuckled. "You know we walked past an Indian, and a fish and chip restaurant back there?"

One eye peeled open. "There's me thinking I was supposed to take on the role of temptress."

This made me laugh. The woman behind the desk, harrumphed. I wondered uncharitably when she'd last managed to crack a smile, never mind a chuckle. Ten minutes of feeling Megan doze on my shoulder passed quietly enough, then another woman, far younger than the receptionist, headed in our direction.

"Mr Woodbury? Sergeant Ackley?" she said, approaching with an outstretched hand. "I'm Anna Price, personal secretary to the Bishop. Thank you for coming so quickly."

I scrambled upright. "Griffin, please. It's a pleasure to help if we can."

"Megan," said Megan, also giving a handshake.

"Come this way. The Bishop's official residence and office is down at Lis Escop in Feock, so you're lucky to have caught us up here." She had an accent that was obviously far more educated than mine. Her age would be somewhere slightly north of thirty, but her makeup, skilfully done, would keep her at thirty for many years to come. Her long brunette hair trailed down her back, clipped with careful casualness away from her flawless face. Anna's eyes were as dark as mine, but they had that Bambi look to them, which meant most people would underestimate her. They'd miss the sharp intelligence. Slim, tall and dressed in a demure summer cotton dress that went just below the knee, she also carried an iPad.

In low-heeled sandals, she started to the door, ready to

lead us back into the furnace. She didn't bother saying goodbye to the receptionist. Instead, she said, "Things are cooler in the school building. We can talk in more privacy."

I glanced behind us at the concrete box. "It's not private in there?"

Anna shuddered. "I shall not name those responsible for that building, but I spend as little time in there as possible."

Megan walked beside me, happy to let me lead on the questions. She must be tired. When discussing mundane matters, I usually took the backseat.

We walked around the cathedral building, and I tried not to gawp like a tourist, of whom there were many scattered about like human confetti. Then we headed towards another gothic inspired building.

Anna said, "He's in the school at the moment, discussing some plans with our headteacher. We'll go to the office."

Walking through a school, especially one that aped the medieval period so perfectly, brought back a rush of unwanted memories from my gothic education in Scotland. That building had been more castle than this clean and colourful place, but it still had the grandeur and smell that made my senses twitch in discomfort.

In silence, we passed closed classrooms, the children free for a summer of fun. Or I hoped they were all having fun. At the end of a long corridor, Anna knocked briefly on a heavy wooden door. A muffled voice just about made it through wood thick enough to see off an army of Anglo-Saxons, and we walked in.

"Bishop Chadwick, I have Griffin Woodbury, from Rural Security, and Sergeant Megan Ackley to see you," Anna stated.

The bishop had the soft body I'd always associated with

the clergy of a certain age. He looked like he enjoyed every stereotype in the book. Port and cheese, meat and red wine, cigars and brandy. Somehow, despite being close to retirement age, a boyishness remained in his features, making his smile cheeky as he rose from the chair in front of the desk of the headteacher. The cornet of white hair around his skull reminded me of a monk's tonsure. He wore the purple due a bishop, the short sleeves of his shirt revealing wrists that might be able to pick up the heavy Bible kept on a lectern, but he'd never be able to throw it at someone. He stood only a little taller than Megan.

The thing I instantly liked about the man was his choice of pectoral cross. Rather than something flashy and bling-inspired, he'd chosen a beautifully carved, but plain wooden design with a simple cord to hang around his neck.

"Griffin, Megan, welcome," he said in a pleasant baritone. "Thank you for coming up here so quickly. I've just been discussing security with Mrs Bourne for the children when they return in September. I'd like her to remain, if that's okay?" He had a voice made of Sunday afternoon ice cream and jolly times while fishing for trout.

I smiled. We all shook hands, and chairs were found for Megan and me. Anna remained standing, her pad poised for taking notes on the surface of a filing cabinet. I couldn't help but notice Mrs Bourne had a view of the cathedral from her office window. Megan removed her notepad and nodded to me, indicating I could remain in charge.

Fair enough. "I don't have a huge amount of information about your issues, Bishop. Perhaps you could explain in detail why we're here?"

The bishop ran a hand over his rounded paunch. An obvious tell. The man was about to enter territory he didn't like. He glanced at Anna, then at Mrs Bourne.

"Well, I suppose all three of us have been—I don't want to say victimised because it sounds overly dramatic—inconvenienced by this individual."

"I found it scary," Mrs Bourne interjected. "He followed me home from the school several times last term." She'd give a sparrow a run for its money in the tiny, dowdy category, but the sharpness in her little hazel eyes made me think of a hawk. Her Cornish accent also marked her as different from the others in the room.

Megan asked, "You didn't report it to the police?"

The bishop took a deep breath. Another tell of his anxiety. Were we about to be lied to? I really hoped not.

"It's tricky, Sergeant," he said. "The police and the Church aren't exactly friends at the moment. The safety of women and children in the cathedral is our highest priority. It's one of my most important jobs, and one I bear willingly. I am here to serve our community. Anything that stirs the pot, involving men who do not feel the same way, puts pressure on us in ways that can cause untold damage to our reputation. When I mentioned it to our chief constable, he said he didn't want to open an investigation into allegations about misconduct on cathedral grounds, whether it was an outsider to our fellowship, or a member of our congregation. He suggested I contact the archbishop, who obviously rang your office in London. I'm just glad you were local."

Clearly a man who loved to use more words than necessary to explain his problems.

Megan frowned. "I see." Though, I wondered if she felt as lost as I did right now.

"Well, we're here," I said. "What's the problem?" I sat poised with my own pen and notebook.

The bishop looked to the headteacher, so she took up the narrative.

"The first of us noticed him during the Easter services. As you can imagine, that's a very busy and important time for the cathedral. We have a lot of extra visitors and many displays to manage, not just the complex liturgies. This gentleman attended all of them, as far as we can tell."

Megan said, "So you've been discussing this among the members of staff?"

"Oh yes," said the Bishop. "We've had agenda items about him during our safeguarding meetings. It's very important that we allow people to air any issues they might have with the public. Then we do regular private appointments if people feel a member of staff is behaving inappropriately."

I almost chuckled. The Church of England wanted more than just its reputation back; it wanted gold stars and a parade. Good on them. Though, horses and stable doors also came to mind.

Megan nodded for Mrs Bourne to continue.

"At first, we just thought he'd moved to the area and decided to become a regular worshipper, which is wonderful. However, on several occasions, some of our many volunteers found themselves being asked strange questions."

"Such as?" I asked.

"How seriously did the cathedral take its Deliverance ministry? Did the cathedral have an active outreach programme looking for problems in the community, such as Satan worship?"

I saw Megan bite her lip.

Trying to head off a fit of the giggles, I said, "That's certainly a red flag."

The bishop said, "Well, yes, it is rather. It certainly put him on our watchlist for potential problems. That's when we take a screenshot from the CCTV and issue all members of staff and the volunteers a low-level warning. It's our yellow alert. 'Please keep this person under supervision if you spot them and don't leave them alone with vulnerable people or children'. We can't afford to report all the people who behave oddly to Social Services, or the police, but it's a way of us keeping everyone safe."

Megan frowned. "Aren't you worried about vigilantism? This list could be used by individuals—"

The bishop held up his hand. "Let me stop you there, Sergeant. Please don't worry; we have all the staff and volunteers trained on how to use this list and what it means. In fact, on yellow, we work to get to know the person and often realise they're harmless. They're either fascinated with the building or trying to understand their call to faith, but they're just not presenting themselves in a positive light. Occasionally, it is someone either mentally ill—and we find them help—or someone who needs help because of damage from their past. Churches attract all kinds of people; many of them need our compassion."

That was us told.

I tried to drag us back on point. "This man doesn't fall into any of these categories?"

Mrs Bourne fielded that one. "At first we thought he did, but we soon realised he presented a possible threat. In May, we found him on the grounds of the cathedral with various newspaper clippings spread about him on the lawn. When our member of staff asked him why he was there, he claimed he wanted to prove that demons existed and the Fourth Estate was in collusion with the government to cover it up. It was the Church's responsibility to speak the truth."

Megan and I managed to avoid each other's gazes. I asked, "Can I have the name of the person involved in that conversation?" My pen was poised.

Anna said from behind us, "Archer, Jayne Archer. She's one of our deacons, so yes, you can speak with her if you really think it's necessary."

"Thank you," I said. Then followed up with, "This was the first time you discovered his interest in demons?"

Everyone nodded. Again, Mrs Bourne spoke. "That's when he began following various people home. After poor Jayne said she didn't think it was the place of the cathedral to speak to the press about demons, and he said…"

The Bishop coughed. "He said that's what he was afraid of. We weren't able to deal with the threat of the demonic because we're all liberal pansies and most of us don't understand the Bible or God." The man's face had turned a disturbing shade of red during this short speech. It clashed with the purple of his shirt. "Bloody fool."

"How many people has he followed?" I asked.

"Five of us so far," Mrs Borne said. "Three women and two men. I have a list here." She handed over a file. "In there you'll find their details and emails. I'm not prepared to share phone numbers and addresses. If they want to speak with you, they can. You also have their testimonials about exactly what's been happening."

I handed the file to Megan, and she flicked through it. "Very good. Thank you. This is exactly what we need."

"It's a shame your chief constable didn't feel the same," Anna muttered, hackles up.

Megan twisted slightly to look at her. "I know it's difficult. We can act only as a police service under very strict guidelines when we're tackling stalking. It's a hard crime for us and the victims. The time it takes to gather enough evidential material is long, and the bar is high. With Rural Security, we can take a slightly different approach. Be a bit more hands-on. Stalking is a serious crime."

Anna's body language settled down. "What will you do?"

I said, "In the first instance, go and speak with him, do some background investigations and if we can give the Crown Prosecution Service enough evidence, we'll initiate action with the police. Can you tell me how these events have escalated?"

The bishop now took up the tale. "When it became clear, he was making various members of staff feel uncomfortable, I stepped in to speak with him directly. I tried to explain our point of view. This was…" he looked to Anna.

"Middle of June, Bishop."

"Ah, yes. It turned out all he wanted to do was discuss the importance of mid-summer rituals to demonologists and their ilk. That's when we discovered he thinks he's a demon hunter. I tried to explain that demons…" His voice petered out again. "Well, I explained, and he didn't take it well. That's when the vandalism began. The chalk drawings were on doors, on our beautiful floor, on the paving outside. Salt over the smaller altars, and he was seen taking water from the font after our last christening. It disturbed more than one member of our congregation. Personally, I feel affronted. It's as if the man doesn't think I can do my job."

Time for a little tact and diplomacy. "You're probably right, Bishop, he might well consider himself an expert, but I wouldn't worry. With people like this, if you're doing your job, they can't do *their* job. You have to be the bad guy. Do you have pictures of the symbols he drew?" I asked.

Megan showed me the folder. I glanced at Anna and gave a grateful nod, which made her smile. I flicked through the drawings. They were fairly standard. Pentagrams for protection, the glyphs of angels that are easy enough to find online, and words in Latin, Hebrew and probably Enochian. I'd have to ask Sid to check those.

"Do you have everything you need, Griffin?" asked the Bishop.

"If you know the man's name, that would help," I said with a smile.

The bishop's face finally relaxed. "Of course, how silly of us. He told us his name is Dean Wesson. We don't know where he lives. There's a photo of him in the folder. Are you really going to fix this for us?"

"I'm going to fix this for you." If only I'd hesitated for a moment to think, to consider, how many ways this could go wrong.

Chapter Three

We shook hands with Anna, and reluctantly left the coolness of the old stone building, to return to the furnace outside.

I led the way back to the street where I'd seen all the restaurants, feeling buoyed by the thought of spending alone time with Megan while not working. "Let's find food, and I'll photograph the guy's image and send it to Sid. We might get this one wrapped up today."

"To be honest, it'd be good if we didn't," Megan said, and I didn't miss the exhaustion in her voice. "I could do with a few days away from the station and Redruth."

This felt like an opportunity. "Yeah, well, what if we went away somewhere for a break?" I suggested. "It doesn't have to be far. We could even explore the delights of Truro."

Megan laughed. "Have you any idea what a last-minute booking in Cornwall during August is going to cost?"

I bumped against her. "We'll put it on DoPI expenses." A blatant lie, and she probably knew it, but Megan had the same pride as her father, she'd never accept my money easily.

"That's not a bad…" Her sentence trailed off, and she stopped moving. I frowned, tracked her eye line, and found my body priming for a fight.

Adrian *bloody* Hess was walking towards us with his arm around a woman at least ten years younger than Megan. Barely more than a teenager, the girl wore a short, strappy summer dress and heeled summer shoes. She looked like a willow branch in a way Megan never would, even if she starved herself to enter death's door.

I felt Megan's panic as if we were attached by some invisible thread. "This place looks good for food," I said, turning her towards a large window. The panes were small, the paint a neat and pastel green. Inside the tables looked clean, and they still had a few standing empty this early in the lunch rush.

"Megan?" the bastard bloody man called out. "Fancy seeing you here."

I'd never felt her stiffen like this before. Was it fear or anger?

"Adrian." A statement of fact, nothing more.

"Are you going to introduce your friend?" he asked, staring at me with a smile belonging to a psychotic cobra on his face.

"No, we're leaving. We have work."

I realised far too late I'd trapped her against the window, with Adrian and the girl blocking her easy exit. Stepping back felt like giving ground, and it put a distance between me and Megan that I didn't want.

Time for me to do something dastardly. I held out my hand to the young woman. "Hi, I'm Griffin. It's lovely to meet you."

"Lily," she said, her voice as soft as her big brown eyes.

"Lovely to meet you, Lily," I said, repeating myself. I stepped forwards, took her hand, small and limp as it was, and very gently forced her to take a step back. Adrian had no choice but to lose his grip on her waist, and she gave enough room for me to turn my broad back on the man. I didn't have any fear of him trying something now; he'd plot that for later. I turned to look at my companion. "Megan, we really ought to go. Bishop Chadwick has been explicit in his need for speed and discretion." I smiled at Lily and pretended to whisper, "We're on a secret mission for the Church. All very mysterious and time-sensitive. I hope you'll forgive us. Maybe we can get together for a double date sometime?"

Adrian stood so close to my back, I could feel his loathing trying to coat me. My plan worked though. I'd parted the waters for Megan, and she took the out, walking past me and Lily without a glance.

I kept Megan ahead of me, so Adrian had to watch my backside, not hers, as we strode up Old Bridge Street. The moment we'd returned to the car park, I jogged to catch her up.

"Wanna talk about it?" I asked.

"Not really." Shards of glass came with fewer safety warnings.

"We need to—"

"Not now, Griffin. We have to get those details to Sid."

I tried again. "Lunch would be a good—"

"I'm not hungry," she snapped, almost rounding on me before I stared her down. Colour rose in her cheeks. "Sorry."

"That's okay, but we do need to talk, Megan. He's not going away. Did he know we were coming to Truro?"

She rubbed her head. "I don't remember what I said to him. Maybe?"

I stared at the entrance to the car park. Time for Sid to do his thing on Adrian *bloody* Hess, and I'd try to convince Megan to give our computer wizard her phone so he could check for tracking apps. The man shouldn't have been able to find us so easily. "Okay, well, let's use Quacker as a flat surface and send as much info to Sid as we can, then we'll leave here and find a place to eat. Just do me one favour?"

"Anything," she said, head down, not looking at me.

"Switch your phone off, remove the SIM."

That made her look up. "What if work or the family calls?"

"Work knows you're with Rural Security. If the family can't get hold of you, they'll call me." I gently took hold of her shoulder. "You know it's what you'd tell a woman in your position to do."

She sucked in a breath as if to argue with me, but I held her gaze, and she rippled through prideful anger into defeat. I'd have preferred understanding, but defeat would do for the moment.

Glaring at me, she said, "Fine, but I'll do it after we leave Truro. Right now, we have to gather intel, and I need my phone to do that."

"Fair enough." It made my skin itch, but I pressed on with work issues rather than interrogating Megan. Among the family, she was well known for her stubbornness, and that hadn't changed with time. If I pushed, she'd push back harder. I wasn't so confident of my place in her life that I'd do something stupid to risk annoying her.

Softly, I heard from her, "Why won't he leave me alone?"

I took the folder from her hands, placed it on Quacker's

seat and gently held her wrists. She continued to look at the ground. In an effort not to crowd her, I just said, "He will. You might need to trust me to help you, though. Could you at least think about it?"

Those blue eyes looked up at me. "You think I don't trust you?"

"I don't know, Megan. You barely let me help you with anything as a friend, never mind a boyfriend. It's really hard for me to watch you go through this alone. Especially when I trust you with so much of my life."

Her lips pressed together, thinning them to almost nothing, and the drops of sadness quivering on her lashes caught the sunlight. "I've never thought of it like that. I'm sorry."

Feeling her sway just a little towards me, I wrapped her up and held her close. "We're together, Megan. It means you don't have to face the world alone. Neither do I. It's a new experience for me."

"And me," she mumbled into my chest. "I'll do better. Let's find somewhere outside the city centre to eat."

Kissing her crown, I released her, and we forced ourselves back into the bike's heavy gear. Rather than head out of town, I burrowed us further inside the small city centre and found a bike-sized parking space in front of an independent coffee shop. It looked loved and, most importantly, I saw an air conditioning unit on the wall outside.

"This'll do," I said, parking up.

Megan didn't climb off the back. "I thought it would be best—"

"I'm not running, Meg. We're both hungry and you're exhausted. Let's eat."

She huffed, but climbed off the back, and we walked into the café. As cool air washed over us, we both relaxed. A young woman with long vivid blue hair welcomed us, sat us down at a table near the back, and gave us simple menus. The food looked amazing, and I wanted to order everything. I stuck with a plate of vegan falafels, hummus and various other tasty treats. Things I didn't find in Redruth and missed from London. I also ordered a couple of craft beers and water.

Megan smiled. "Thank you."

"For what?"

"For being you."

I grinned. "Let's sort out the work stuff and get it off to Sid before the food arrives. Then we might have a result by the time we've finished stuffing our faces. I plan on pudding as well."

"I'll end up like a barrel."

"I love barrels. They are very good at holding things."

She smacked me, and her sadness started to slip away. We'd be talking about Adrian *bloody* Hess at some point, but right now I wanted her to focus on something she was good at—her job.

The pair of us went through our various channels to gather intel. Megan phoned in the details we had about Dean Wesson to a colleague. I emailed the photos and details to Sid. We made a bet on who'd find him first; it might have involved sexual favours. I really hoped I'd win, but losing sounded fun as well.

The food arrived, and I finally saw Megan relax. The drawn, slightly pinched look on her face eased as the beer and quality carbs did their job.

"What do you think about this whole demon thing, then?" she asked around a mouthful of pitta bread. "Are they real?"

"Oh, they're real, alright." I went on to describe what happened at Barle's Keep.

She frowned. "If we know they're real, how do we see them in the world and not things like angels? Or saints?"

"We do, it's just that miracles are treated differently from possession or demonic activity."

I watched the thoughts race through her head as she considered this. "You're right. They are reported differently. I guess demons are rarer?"

"We hope so, and DoPI doesn't deal with miracles; that's not our place. Unless they're masquerading as something dangerous. Also, the Church, both C of E and the RC versions, has definite rules about how to handle them. DoPI grew out of Church doctrine during the seventeenth century, giving us a solid working relationship. It's only when we don't know it's happened, like at Barle's Keep, or it gets completely out of hand, that DoPI comes in to contain the problem. We still need priests and vicars to help us. Sometimes, the Church needs the more specialist approach that people like me provide."

She smirked. "Door kickers?"

"Spear points," I clarified with a grin. "Demons are very rare, though. We're far more likely to be dealing with a man who has a lot of problems."

"But the bishop didn't know you're DoPI?" Megan wanted to clarify.

"No, but the Archbishop of Canterbury does, and the Archbishop of Westminster," I clarified, "C of E and RC respectively."

Megan had almost no working knowledge of organised religion.

"What about Islam and Judaism? The other major religions in Britain?"

"Need to know basis only. Like with the Dru coming through the veil, we didn't need to talk to the Church about that—though they'll receive a report—the other major religions are still too small to be much help. Every parish in the UK has a direct link to us if they need it through the Archbishop of Canterbury, and we can call on each diocese in return through the same mechanism. The other faiths are mostly city based, have a different structure to their organisations, they don't have a single point of contact. Also, the veil, if it opens, tends to do it outside of cities. The close press of the modern world keeps it thick and people safe. The liminal places in rural communities are where the veil is thinnest. It's always been that way."

"Do you really think there are demons in the cathedral?" she asked.

I grunted. "No. I don't. I've never met a demon hunter. Not only that, I can't even imagine why you'd want to be one."

My phone rang. I fished it out and grinned. "Sid."

Megan laughed. "You win then."

"Yeah," I said, and I felt my cheeks grow warm. I swiped to accept the call. "What you got?" I asked him.

"It seems Dean Wesson is a conspiracy theorist of the first order, mate."

"Location?" I asked.

"The best I can give you is a possibility. I'm on his social media, such as it is, and it looks like he's living in a caravan near the viaduct, or under it, I guess. He's near the river down there anyway, so that's the place to start."

"Good job, Sid. Anything we should know before we go in?" I watched Megan order a big slice of chocolate cake and two forks. My mouth watered.

"The man's a serious nutter, Griffin. He's a conspiracy hoarder. You name it, he's been into it over the years. I'm following a hole into the dark web that he's fallen into, and it's weird. The bloke's even been to the US to train as a demon hunter under one of the more evangelical churches."

"Fuck."

"Yeah. It's not great. These guys see demons in women and children. They advocate homeschooling to ensure their families aren't corrupted. Women are sent into seclusion during menstruation. Don't even breathe the word homosexual around them. It's pretty hardcore."

"The chances of us getting anything usable are going to be thin."

"I'll keep digging and send anything that might help with an interview."

"Roger that. Thanks." I watched Megan for a moment longer as she stood at the counter chatting to the younger woman. "I want you to do a full profile of Adrian Hess as well."

"Megan's—?"

"Yeah. Something is very wrong there, and I want to know more."

"I'm guessing I'm doing this on the QT?"

"Very QT. If she finds out—"

"Understood."

The call ended.

Megan returned, carrying the cake as if it were a tiara of diamonds. It might as well have been, it was so splendid.

By the time we left the café, the pair of us felt like rolly-pollies, but we were happy. I explained to Megan the location of Dean Wesson, and we headed off to Moresk car park. It took only ten minutes to reach the place, even in the busy summer traffic. Leaving Quacker under the trees, we looked for the footpath we'd seen, which should take us under the Victorian viaduct that was the only thing, other than the huge NCP car park, to rival the cathedral in terms of presence.

There were trees to shade us, and the dry earth made it a pleasure to walk. Ground elder and brambles smothered just about everything else, with ivy wending its way through, and climbing trees with wild abandon. It wasn't beautiful by any measure, but for a city, it felt good, and there were none of the usual signs of homeless occupation I'd grown used to in London. No needles, beer or cider cans, no fast-food wrappers or even dog poo. Rural cities had a way of keeping their streets and green spaces more civilised than the wild urban areas of our metropolises.

"How'd he get a caravan up here?" Megan asked as we walked into the shadow of the viaduct. The area under the towering structure was thick with trees, and only a wide footpath had access.

"Dunno. With great care, I guess."

Then the caravan came into view, hiding amid the shadows cast by the vast brick legs holding up the railway line. The small, once mobile, home had sides that were green with something I couldn't name. Moss covered the rim of its roof, reminding me of Bishop Chadwick's hair. The windows had disconcerting amounts of duct tape holding them in place, and ivy was sneaking up on it, waiting to devour the small, old caravan. This was not a home to be proud of, or even one to move to a better location.

"How do you want to handle this?" asked Megan.

"You take the lead. I'll keep back. Softly, softly, I guess. No mention of DoPI."

She rolled her eyes at me, this being an obvious point. Walking up to the door of the caravan, she knocked and called out, "Mr Wesson, my name is Megan Ackley. I'm with the police, but this is just a welfare check. There are some people a bit worried about you."

Clever. I'd never have thought of that.

"Mr Wesson?" she called again. "My colleague and I will have to see you, maybe share a few words? If we don't, we'll have to force entry. That's within our legal—"

The caravan twitched as someone moved about inside. Megan stepped back, giving the door a lot of room. It opened outwards with some violence, and a big man filled the tiny space. He'd have to turn sideways to fit through the door and bend some considerable distance. Thick black hair covered much of his face. His head had a close shave to the surface. He wore mismatched army clothing, probably bought from the Army and Navy surplus store in Plymouth. A distinct odour of male sweat, fried food, stale cigarettes, and alcohol drifted around him like flies on a corpse. His gaze slid over Megan and settled on me.

"Fuck off."

Oh, this was going to be fun.

Megan moved a little to draw his attention to her. "Mr Wesson, thank you for—"

"Did the fools in the cathedral send you?" His voice came from the depths of the earth. A rolling bass note that held no real accent.

"Passersby have mentioned you to our local PCSO," she clarified for him, "the local Police Community Support Officer. As I said, it's a welfare check. This isn't a legal campsite, and breaching the—"

His glare sharpened to a point that might've intimidated Megan if she didn't deal with people like him every day. It certainly put me on edge. "What the fuck do I care about your laws? It's God's law that matters, and those fools," he waved a hand that'd cover Megan's face and smother her without effort, "know nothing about what's coming."

I ventured closer. "What do you think is coming, Mr Wesson?"

"The End of Days."

If DoPI had a gold coin for every time that pronouncement had been made over the centuries, we wouldn't need a budget from the government; we'd own the damned thing.

"Are you talking about Revelations, sir?" I asked.

"It's the only book in the Bible that can help us now," Wesson said, stepping out of his caravan. I saw tattoos under the buzz cut hair, many of which I recognised as protection wards. This was the poor man's version of a tinfoil hat.

"And how exactly do you think it can help us?" With care, I reached for Megan and pulled her back a little by grabbing her shirt. She came willingly. I think we both wished we'd brought an asp with us.

"Son, if you don't know, it's not my place to tell you. The Lord will show you if He needs your help, come Assumption Day."

He'd given me a date. There was only one of those, and I knew it was the fifteenth of August.

"I understand, Mr Wesson." I dared to approach, desperate to see inside the caravan, though how I'd fit in there with him, I had no idea. It would be like trying to fit two dolphins inside a sardine tin. "That's the Virgin Mary's day? Right? When she was taken to heaven? It's not far away now."

"That's why I'm here. I've seen the signs. You have to let me do my work."

"Your work is scaring people, Mr Wesson," I pointed

out. "Maybe we could talk about it together? Over a cuppa tea? See if we can help?"

He barked a bitter laugh. "Fuck off. What are you? A fucking social worker? I'm not mad. I'm dedicated, something you wouldn't understand."

I felt like explaining my entire bloody life had been dedicated to the Royal Marines, whether I liked it or not, but didn't think it would help.

"Whatever you're facing, I doubt you can manage it alone. Please come and speak with us. Together we can listen to you, and maybe we can find a plan that'll help? We'll be able to speak to the cathedral together." I moved my head, just a tiny bit, to see around the broad back.

He noticed and shifted to cover the narrow space. A sneer crept over his face. "You wanna get in here, don't you? Well, you can't come in. This is my home, and you can't move me on. The railway owns this land, so you'll have to get them to evict me. Good luck finding some prick to answer the phone on that one." He turned his dark gaze on Megan. "And I don't do drugs, so you won't find anything like that here. In fact, I make sure no one does drugs or drinks down here. It's the safest damned place in Truro, which is more than can be said for anywhere else. Especially after the fifteenth. Demons will walk this world and, what's worse, so will the angels. None of you are prepared for that."

I realised we weren't going to get anywhere. "Alright, Mr Wesson. I tell you what, I'll leave my card with you. I'm Griffin Woodbury, with Rural Security, and I know I can help. If you feel you want to talk, or you need my assistance in any way, then just call me, and I'll be here as soon as I can." Without much hope of it working, I held out one of the business cards I carried. "You can check out the website, so you know I'm for real. I can't arrest you, I'm not a police officer, but I can help."

I had no hope of him taking the card, but he surprised me. With fingers embedded with grime, and nicotine stains, he took the small piece of card.

"There's something about you I recognise," he murmured. For the first time in the weakened light that tried to shoulder its way through the tree canopy and sneak in under the shadow of the monolith over our heads, I saw his eyes were very pale blue. He stared at me for a long time. "Yes, I recognise you, son. Beware. You shall be called, and it will be your trial."

Then the massive bear of a man turned, stomped back up his steps, making the caravan shudder in anguish, and slammed the door shut.

Megan and I just stared first at it, then at each other.

"Well, that was different," she said.

Chapter Four

We walked back to the bike, both of us feeling flat, rather than enjoying the day out together. Somehow, the fun we'd managed to inject into the day over lunch seemed like a distant dream. One of those events used to paper over the cracks. We'd had a lot of those today.

We rode back to Redruth, and I took it in a sombre mood. Reaching home, I said, "My place?" Hoping she'd agree.

A long pause made the old heartstrings shudder. "Only if we can sit in your garden, have a few beers and I can listen to you play your guitar."

In the slow-moving traffic, I turned for a moment. "Really?"

She smiled. "I want to do something I can only do with you."

Not entirely understanding, I agreed, and we arrived at Turpin Cottage. Sid was out, so I guessed he'd gone to spend some time with Luce in Portreath. It would be nice to have the place to ourselves for the evening. Megan offered to cook a simple chicken curry and rice, and we did as she wished. The garden was floundering in the unaccustomed heat, but we sat and shared some beers while I noodled through some songs.

She talked while I played. It wasn't easy concentrating on two things at once, but I think it made it easier for her to share her fears. Since Adrian had shown interest in dating her a few weeks before I arrived in Cornwall during the spring, his cronies at work had been pushing this ideal couple vibe onto her. Being a good thief-taker, a reliable man to have in a Saturday night punch up, and one of the guys, Adrian had the total respect of his peers.

What they didn't know was how he behaved at home. Megan, beginning to think the problems lay with her, tracked down one of his ex-girlfriends in desperation. The woman had moved to Exeter and begged Megan to keep her location a secret. That's when Megan realised she was being gaslighted and controlled.

"If only I'd known sooner we weren't cousins. I can't blame Mum, but our lives could've been so different if we'd known the truth sooner," she whispered, wiping at a stray tear.

I had to agree. "It's what we do now that's important, Meg. How do you want to handle things with Adrian?" Though, I had more than a few ideas of my own.

We could drown him in the sea. Drop him down a mine. Feed him to the pigs. I tried to close down the long list of ideas my gleeful inner voice kept providing. I had to concentrate on Megan.

"I need proof. Cast iron. I can't do that alone. Do you think Sid would—"

"Of course he would." I wasn't about to ruin the evening by telling her the truth. "Give him your phone. Let him download it, and he'll sort through the data. We'll be able to get into Adrian's as well."

"That won't be admissible. I can't take that to my inspector."

"No, but we can use it as a place to start. Then we'll know where he's vulnerable, and we can start tracking him instead. Talking of which, and changing the subject completely, I think I'm going to spend a couple of days in Truro watching Dean Wesson. We need to get into that caravan. I can watch him from the embankment behind the viaduct and wait for him to leave, then break in, and we'll know more."

"That won't be pleasant."

"No, but we don't have the manpower for proper surveillance around the clock, and it's time critical. Today is the fifth, so we've ten days before he thinks we're facing whatever his version of doomsday looks like."

"Do you really believe the end of the world is about to happen?"

I laughed, and my Paul Reed Smith guitar resonated with the sound. "No. It won't be the end of the world, but it could be the end of his, or someone else's, which means we need to fix this."

"The poor man is living in squalor. I think he needs sectioning."

"You're probably right, and if that's the case, we'll set the wheels in motion, but you know better than me, it's a difficult process to get started."

As the night grew dark, the air hummed with expectation. For a long time, we stared up at the sky, at the remarkable visual illusion of all the visible planets lining up overhead. They were bright, with Mars's red colour standing out among the others. Seeing the stars, and the planets in this case, had become one of my favourite things since moving to Cornwall. I enjoyed using apps to find the constellations I didn't know. Megan was happy to indulge me.

I carried the guitar back to its stand in my room, and Megan came with me. We still hadn't quite managed to rid ourselves of a mutual shyness, brought on by years of forced longing and forbidden thoughts, but when I finally had her nestled against me, I fell deeply asleep.

The ringing of my phone dragged me up from the dark, and on the way, flashes of dream memories crashed into each other. The layers I moved through were too fast and dizzying. The haunted cloakroom at my school, my mother's grave, the Brane dolmen, the beach on Exmoor and that damned suicide vest I'd been forced to wear. The images blurred and twisted, even as my hand reached for the jangling noise.

"Griff—"

"Help me… Please, God, help me." A deep male voice. It took a moment for me to locate it in my memory.

Megan groaned. I sat up. "Who is this?"

"Wesson… I… I'm dying… The wards aren't working. She's too powerful. It's going to come in and take me."

"You're at the caravan?" I asked, already moving. His panic and fear leaked through me.

"Yes." This came at me too high and loud. I heard a rending noise in the background.

Why the hell was he calling me and not a fucking ambulance? "Call the emergency services."

"No. They won't," his voice was weakening. Hardly more than a croak. "Understand."

Megan turned in the bed, frowning and confused. "What's wrong?" she asked as I rolled onto my feet.

A faint and distant scream came over the line. "Dean? Dean?" I called into my phone. "Shit." The connection was gone. "Wesson's in trouble. He won't call an ambulance. We need to get up there. He thinks he's dying."

Without further comment, Megan was pulling on the jeans she kept at my place. "You want me to call it in? I can get the Truro police to check on him."

"You think it's worth it?" I asked, worried we'd be wasting their time.

"Did he sound like he was dying?"

Did he? "Shit, yes, he did." I pulled a t-shirt over my head.

"Well then." She picked up her phone.

Within ten minutes, we were on the bike and heading east out of Redruth. At three in the morning, it was an easy, fast ride. When we reached the path under the viaduct, we saw an ambulance and a police car in full livery. Lights filled the tight space, slashing through the leaves of the nearby trees, depriving them of all natural colour. With me leading, we ran up the path.

It had taken too long to reach him.

The first responders were trying to do their jobs, but one of the police officers was vomiting in a nearby bramble bush. The other paramedics stood nearby, unable to understand what their powerful torches were telling them. An older police officer spoke into his comms unit, but his voice shook.

"Sergeant Kinch?" called Megan.

He peered into the darkness. "Is that Megan?" The very strong Cornish accent wasn't a surprise.

"It is. Where can we step?" she asked, all business.

"To be honest, my lover, there's so much blood, I don't

know. We need more light." He sounded shaken, vulnerable.

"I can get the bike up here," I offered.

"Who's that with you?" he asked, voice suspicious. Was he a fan of Hess's? Would I have to spend my life in Cornwall dealing with the thin blue line closing ranks around me as punishment? I wished them silent luck if that was the case.

"Griffin Woodbury, Rural Security," I said without moving. "We were visiting Mr Wesson this afternoon." I decided on discretion for this next part. "He called me just moments before I called you guys."

Megan, using a Maglite from the daysack we'd grabbed from the corner of my room, said, "I called it in, Robin. That's why you're here."

Her words, despite the dire circumstances, warmed me. We were officially public.

You're pathetic, you know that? Wow, my internal monologue was a bastard sometimes. I forced myself to focus on work.

"Ah, they said it was one of ours who did that, but not who."

Megan's light tore open the scene for us. Now I wished I'd stuck with the romance angle.

Dean Wesson lay before his caravan. Face down. Arms and legs spread-eagled. Naked. Flesh flayed off his back, buttocks, thighs and calves to the point the organs were exposed and the long line of the man's spine flashed white in the trembling torch beam. Blood pooled around the corpse. A lot of blood. The man's heart had continued to pump for a significant amount of time.

For a disturbing moment, I thought of the arches overhead, mirroring the thick ribs now vivid in the torch's light.

"Oh my God," whispered Megan, mirroring my horror at the scene.

I'd seen men, women and too many children shredded by bullets and bombs to be truly disturbed. Eventually, the mind sees these shocking things and they become normalised. Until it cracks. However, this wasn't some place torn apart by religions gone bad and tribal rivalry; this was Cornwall. Dean Wesson lay amid ivy and grass, not sand and weathered stone. The trees here were green and plentiful, unlike the small-leafed endurance trees in the desert lands of the Sahel.

"Fuck," squeaked one of the paramedics. She'd lifted her torch into the tree line behind the caravan, and there we saw something I'd never forget. None of us would.

The man's skin was flung over a low branch, hanging in the hot night air like a blanket out to dry.

It proved too much for the paramedic, and she broke into noisy tears. Even I had to take steadying breaths. It didn't help much; the air was filled with the smell of blood and worse. Flies were droning. Big, fat and ugly. A warm night brought them to their macabre feast in droves.

This would be a DoPI case. No human could do this so fast and with such accuracy, but I needed local boots on the ground to complete the preliminaries. We had to keep this quiet. A murder like this would set off a panic. The heat of the summer was making everything in the country hostile, irritable, fearful. If we added satanic worship to the mix of illegal migration, tax rises, poverty, fuel prices, food inflation, and environmental collapse looming over everything, we'd have a recipe for civil war, never mind a few protests. This murder had to remain 'normal'.

I started to give orders. Sending the younger police officer back to the car, I asked him to keep people off the path and start a perimeter fence at both ends of the footpath. Dog walkers would begin appearing the moment dawn arrived to avoid the heat of another day. We needed the scene-of-crime people to do their thing quickly and remove the remains before the sun and insects added to Dean's indignity. Then the local Criminal Investigation Department, or CID, needed to be informed that Rural Security had authority over the intelligence gathered by their teams.

All this took time. Megan and I walked around the site, but we remained at a distance from Wesson's body. Time wrapped arms around the scene, slowing it down, then surging forwards, adding to the disorientation. When dawn came, I rang London and gave Sanchez an update. As I described the scene, even she grew quiet.

"Work with the locals, Corporal, but I want to know what did this," she said, her voice even tighter than usual.

"Yes, ma'am."

"I don't need to tell you that if it was demonic, we have a serious problem. One we haven't seen in centuries."

"I know." The weight of her words settled on my shoulders.

The last time DoPI, or its predecessor, had seen a demonic energy strip a human being, it had been during the reign of James II, and almost kicked off another war with the Catholic Church on British soil. The monarchy had lost much of its control in those days, and the government punished those held responsible for the sorcery. It might've been a time for rational thought and logic, but the end of the seventeenth century, just like so many other periods in history, still had those willing to dabble in the darkest of arts. Sadly, the original version of DoPI opted for the simplest solution—it helped to start the witch hunts.

"Keep me updated throughout the day," she added. "I'll send a team down if you need more bodies."

"Understood, ma'am. Thank you. For the moment, let's keep it small. The bigger our footprint, the more likely the local press will become a problem. Never mind the true-crime podcasts."

"Bloody internet," she muttered. "Bane of my life."

I chuckled. It was good to release some of the tension that had built since my phone woke us up. "I'll call soon, ma'am."

"Good luck, Woodbury." The call ended.

If this was demonic, then I had no doubt she'd be sending a team down whether I wanted one or not. The woman wanted a demon or two for her supernatural weapon's programme. Unless some worse event kept the response unit away. Having Markin down here, with the rest of the team, would make my life very difficult. If this was a demon attack, they'd make sure Sanchez finally had her prize, and I really didn't trust her enough to let that happen.

The day dragged on. The heat rose. Megan helped the local police keep the looky-loos out of the area. We'd hardly spoken since we'd arrived, but I'd need her professional eye once the SOCO team had finished processing the body, surrounding area and the caravan.

By midday, we were all hot, hungry, despite the horrors under the white tent, and tired. A support vehicle turned up, and I found Megan taking a turn on the cordon to the north.

"Hey," I said. "We need food."

"You think I can eat after that?" she asked.

"Well, I need to eat. At the very least, you need a break."

She eyed her colleague nearby. "You okay if I go grab us

some water?" she asked a younger woman in a PCSO uniform.

"Of course, Sarg. No one will get past me." The young woman crossed her arms over her stab vest and glared at some teenagers.

Megan patted her shoulder. "Thanks, Debb."

We walked away, back towards the car park we'd used the day before. I wanted to talk to Megan about what had happened, but she didn't look ready. Instead, I said, "You seem to know all the local police up here."

"I've done secondments to Truro, and I've taken training courses with the police volunteers. Debb is one of the ones I've mentored. I'd like her to apply to become a full constable. She's a steady hand despite her tender years." She sucked in a breath now that we were well out of range of the body. "What the hell happened to him, Griffin?"

Experience told me the horror of all this would take time to fade, for all of us. I drew a calming breath and said, "Whatever it was, it wasn't natural. This is a *para-event*."

"You think?" she asked, with a raised eyebrow that told me I was an idiot for stating the obvious.

"When they've finish processing the caravan, we'll need to go through it ourselves," I said. "They'll not understand the details without our perspective."

"That'll be pleasant." She added, "Spoken to Sid yet?"

I nodded. "He's digging deep. He already has the images the teams here are gathering, and the data they've collected so far." Away from the adrenaline of the scene, I felt the tiredness of a disturbed night and the heat sucking at me.

"At what point did Wesson call you?" she asked. "I mean, it must take a long time to strip a human of its skin. It's not easy with a sheep to make a rug, never mind doing something like that. Human skin is like a pig's, softer, far easier to tear."

"There speaks a farmer's daughter."

We reached the makeshift kitchen run by local volunteers who turned up for wildfires, other events needing the support of the emergency services, and it turned out, murder scenes. I feared we'd be peppered with questions from them, but they were discreet. Here to do their job. Behind the second barrier, I saw the press gathered. Locals so far, but when news leaked about the skinning of the body, and it would, I had no doubt we'd be looking at national, possibly international, news. That would be for the team in London to deal with, not me.

Two mugs of tea and cheese sandwiches—neither of us could face the meat options— we retreated into some shade and sat on the tarmac to eat and talk.

"This isn't going to be like the Madron case, is it?" Megan asked. "We aren't dealing with disgruntled tree spirits, or even an incubus with an outsized ego."

I almost choked on my sandwich, thinking of the incubus in that context. "No, no, it's not going to be like those cases. Whatever did this, and it will be a *whatever*, the thing is going to be monstrous."

"A demon?" she asked. The cynic in her finally drowned under the weight of evidence she'd been forced to swallow.

"Probably, but someone must have it under control. The body was skinned with care, but not torn apart. The head and face remain intact, except for superficial damage, and all the organs remain in place. Demons aren't known for being careful, from what I've read, so this is unusual. Which means it might be a warning message."

"Bloody hell, your job is weird," she muttered.

She wasn't wrong. I stared at the few cars in the car

park, closed for the moment to the public. "Someone must've sent something. Wesson wouldn't have summoned a creature and lost control. He was a demon hunter, not a necromancer, or sorcerer, or alchemist."

"We're after a human?"

"That's what I'm thinking at the moment. Unless there's some portal to hell in Truro I don't know about."

"Don't they come through the veil?" she asked.

"That's a matter of some debate. We simply don't know. Are demons a natural part of the netherworld that contains the dryads and the incubus? Djinn and other spirit beings? Or are they separate? Do they come from the opposite place to angels? Does the veil contain the remnants of the human soul after we die? Is it the location of God?"

"Bloody hell, Griffin, I only asked a fairly simple question." She cracked open her bottle of water.

"That's the problem. It isn't simple. Despite centuries of study, people far more knowledgeable than me, real seers and mystics, can't penetrate the veil the way I did with Trystan. Even he can't seem to get back to where we were. The week before last, he talked me into trying it with him, and it's a no-go. He can still hear them, see them, but we can't move through their world. They have to come to us."

Megan frowned. "You didn't tell me you were going to go back."

"I know. You've been busy."

"Griffin, it nearly killed you—"

I put a hand on her knee to forestall the conversational cul-de-sac. "It's the job. That's all."

She frowned and grumbled, "Tell me next time. I'm never *that* busy."

Her worry touched me. It was a novel experience. "Do

you tell me every time someone pulls a weapon on you, or tries to punch you while you're on duty?"

"That's different. I have backup."

"And I have this," I said, holding out the strange witch stone she gave me. "No reason it wouldn't bring me back again."

She shook her head. "Great, you're relying on a stone I picked up out of a random Scottish stream to keep you safe."

"It worked last time." Though, how and why were still a mystery.

We finished eating and headed back to the scene of the crime.

Chapter Five

By 17:40 they'd cleared the body from the scene and forensics had all the samples they needed. Megan and I put on gloves and little paper slippers over our boots, then stood before the caravan. She eyed it suspiciously.

Dark blood stained the grass and leaves. The depressions of the metal footpads, used by forensics to move around without contaminating possible evidence, were obvious where they'd crushed the ivy or brambles. Their scent was pungent on the air, mixing with the aged blood, sticky heat and the near constant drone of flies. My mind wanted to wander off into the long grass again. The defence mechanism overwhelming. In the distance the police tape fluttered, and some of Truro's officers stood barring the way to the press and dog walkers.

"This isn't going to be fun," Megan muttered as she took point going up the small steps into the caravan.

Following her, my stomach lurched at the smell. A powerful mixture of Wesson's remaining body odour, stale cigarettes, spoiled food and rotting caravan. Bodily fluids also filled the air with their miasmic taint.

"How could he live like this?" Megan asked.

I didn't bother answering. The space was cramped with the two of us inside. Wesson had a single-ring gas hob and a tiny grill, but no oven for cooking. The area used for seating had a small table and two foam-cushioned chairs. Next came the bed area, which must also be the living room. Right now, it was made up for sleeping. How a man of his size managed to spend night after night on it, I couldn't guess. I'd never be comfortable unless I lay at an angle and didn't move around much.

Every vertical surface had paper stuck to it. Images, handwritten notes, pages ripped from books, pieces of coloured wool joining thoughts together. It was a glimpse into the man's mind, and I found it deeply disturbing.

Megan opened what could be a cleaning cupboard or a wardrobe to find it full of books. I glanced at the ceiling, and my soft gasp made her look up as well.

"Bloody hell," she whispered.

A series of drawings, probably done in felt tips, lay scrawled over the area. It felt like we were looking at a demented version of the Sistine Chapel. I twisted around trying to understand it, but the meaning escaped me. Instead, I took out my phone and began a recording of everything, giving a running commentary as I went.

Megan kept quiet while I worked, but she began to go through a pile of papers squashed between the books. "Oh shit," she muttered.

I stopped the recording as she pulled a notebook out. "What is it?"

Holding it up, she said, "A list of names, I think it's children because these look like dates of birth." She pointed to the page. "And another of the cathedral's staff. More details about people's movements and job titles."

I took the notebook from her. "There are press cuttings in here as well, and printouts from online groups connected to the area. Not just the cathedral, but other churches around Truro." I frowned. "Or rather, church. It seems he had quite a passion for Kenwyn church as well."

"We'll need to speak with the vicar up here. Bishop Chadwick can help with that." She came over. "It's the list of children that worries me. Do you think he was using all this demonology stuff to hide his paedophilic desires?"

I shrugged. "Right now, I don't know. I really hope not. If he was part of a ring, and they're the ones who skinned him, how bloody dangerous are they?"

Megan looked up at me. "I've never wished for something to be supernatural before, but this time, I think demons might be a relief." She turned in a tight circle. "No one has found a laptop. We have his phone, but no laptop. Considering all this work, why no laptop?"

"Paranoid?" I suggested.

She squashed past me. "In all the room searches I've done, of even the most paranoid of suspects or victims, I've always found some kind of tech. Even if it's in a tinfoil envelope."

Lifting the cheap foam mattress on the bed, the smell of which made us both cough, she had me hold it up while she pulled at the wooden boards used to form its base. That's when she found the narrow space Wesson must have cut himself. Considering what a bad housekeeper he was, he'd made a fine job of creating this hidden compartment. She wiggled the board loose and pulled out a small laptop.

"Told you," she said as I lowered the mattress. Dropping it would only add to the smell in the confined space.

"Why didn't forensics find it?" I asked.

"It's not like they didn't have enough to do with the body and the skin in the tree. Besides, this bit is really our job. They deal with blood, DNA, body parts; we deal with the rest. We need to get this to Sid ASAP." She bagged it.

Yes, we certainly did.

Next, she opened the long cupboard, which I thought should contain food. It didn't.

"Bloody hell," she muttered. "This guy was serious about his work."

The inside was dominated by plastic bottles of all sorts, each full of a clear liquid, which I guessed to be holy water. Jammed in between them were numerous crucifixes with Christ's face twisted in agony from the torture of the cross. The remaining space was taken by several Bibles, tubs of salt, chalk, a knife, and consecration wafers. Pinned to the door were images of Christ, Mary, God, various angels and more. We didn't say anything, just took more pictures and closed it up.

She took the notebook away again and returned to the page with the list of children's names. "We should ask Mrs Bourne if any of these kids attend the cathedral's school."

"That'll please them at the press office."

Megan frowned. "There're all sorts of… Is this astrology?" She held up the page for me to look at.

A neatly drawn circle with twelve clear pie-like triangles in it covered the surface. Inside the pieces of pie were symbols and complex lines connecting each small image.

"Yes, it's a birth chart, I think." I began pointing at different symbols. "This represents Mars, this one Jupiter; the line between them forms part of a square with Uranus and Pluto."

"I didn't think Pluto was a planet anymore?"

"It is for these purposes. Besides, I think it is a protoplanet or dwarf planet now. Anyway, a square like this in astrology means these planets often work in conflict with each other. Then you have the houses they fill."

Megan looked at me blankly.

"Each house represents a different aspect of a person's life. The eleventh, for instance, is about friendships, social networks, long-term wishes, and hopes. With Mars in it, and the opposition to Uranus like this, it'll mean something specific to friendships etc. Maybe, this person will be argumentative and will be inclined to resolve issues with violence. That kind of thing."

"Can you read it?"

"Not really. Though DoPI operatives are meant to have a working knowledge of this, tarot, runes, all the usual."

She muttered, "Yeah, because this is all so 'usual'."

"The date down here is interesting," I said. "It's recent." In fact, it was ten years ago, almost exactly. Or it would be in November. This was a child's birth chart. "We need more Sid magic on this."

"He's going to be busy."

"Keeps him out of other people's servers, don't feel too sorry for him."

Megan chuckled, then sobered. "I'm still worried this is about hiding a pervert's secrets."

I gazed around me. "I'm paid to think differently, but you're right, it's not a good start. Let's begin bagging this lot, and I'll go through the bathroom. I have the feeling it's not going to be a job a woman should have to endure."

This time she laughed. "Such chivalry. Despite my feminist ideals, I'm willing to let you have that one." She bagged the notebook and removed several more from the cupboard.

Once again, we squashed around each other, and I peeled open the narrow door to the bathroom area. Only to be pleasantly surprised. I wouldn't accuse it of being five-star hotel clean, but it would pass the test in any hospital or airport. The man didn't piss all over the seat and floor, that was something.

I rummaged through his wash kit and found the plastic bottles of water he used to wash and clean himself with. I doubted I'd fit into the shower area, never mind Wesson, so he probably cleaned up outside. A smelly towel was hooked on the back of the door.

After searching through a small cupboard under the tiny sink, I stood and my eyes glanced in the mirror.

For a moment, I didn't understand. When I did, my back crashed into the door, snapping it shut.

"Griffin?" Megan's voice reached out for me but slid off without effect.

In the mirror, I didn't see myself. A thick grey fog filled it. Inside the fog loomed a pair of eyes. They weren't red, glowing, or oddly shaped. They were normal, human, greeny-hazel, rounded and made me think: female. I read an expression of anger in them. A pressure pushed against my mind, like hot needles seeking a way into the soft mush of cells and nerve endings. Without conscious thought, I pushed back. There was enough shit going on in my head without this insanity. Sucking in a breath to call Megan, I blinked, and it was gone.

"Griffin?" she asked again, concerned this time.

What the hell was that? Did I really see it, or was it an episode? Was it something more? Could the owner of those eyes have done this to Wesson? Should I have relaxed, let that pain in? Maybe I could've tracked it, found the female behind those eyes. Then something shocking occurred to me. What if we were looking for a woman who sent this demon? I frowned. Was a woman really capable of this? Why? Why would a woman risk everything to summon a demon? Men? Well, their motivations weren't difficult to understand, but women? You'd have to push a woman a long way to turn her into someone able to skin a man alive, even at a distance, using a creature of the damned.

What if those eyes belonged to my mother? I remembered her as having kind blue eyes, but I could be wrong, couldn't I? My heart rate had kicked up a few notches and my skin turned clammy. I felt the looming, inevitable horror that I was about to fall down one of my rabbit holes. In some desperate, hopeful, probably naïve way, I'd expected that discovering Mum was adopted, that being with Megan, it would somehow deprive my subconscious of its trauma, and I'd be free from the nighttime wanderings. That, maybe, I was becoming more normal. This didn't feel normal.

Trying to calm my breathing and control the sudden tremors in my hands, I let myself out of the small bathroom.

"I thought you'd got lost in there," Megan said.

I managed a smile. "Cockroach." Why did I lie?

She shuddered. "We have enough DoPI evidence for the moment. The scene won't be released for a while. They'll want to remove the caravan and take it into storage. I'm sure forensics will need another go."

Nodding mutely, I followed her out of the smelly, hot confines of the caravan, trying to convince myself it was just my imagination. DoPI operatives had the unfortunate tendency to imagine we see the *para* in the ordinary when it's often just plain old imagination taking hold.

Ha, you're a funny man. Yeah, it's just your mind playing tricks after a long day in the sun. Nothing to do with being a freaky weirdo.

The inside of my head is rarely my friend.

Outside once more, I felt, if not better, then less claustrophobic. Though I couldn't prevent myself from looking over my shoulder at the damned caravan's entrance again.

"You okay?" Megan asked. She was loading the bagged evidence we'd taken from Wesson's other possessions.

"Of course."

"You sure? You're all pale and weird. You don't have another of those tag-along things that Sid talked about?"

"What are you going on about, Meg?" I felt itchy and dislocated, and it made me want to snap at her.

She lifted the daysack onto her back and pulled a face. "That's really going to help with the sweating. Yuck." When she looked at me, she clarified, "You know, when you went into the veil and came back with something sucking the life out of you, and we did that weird prayer, smudging thing."

I tried to keep my balance, to remember to be kind. "No, Megan, it's not that. I'm fine." Though my mind was screaming and asking why I kept lying to her. I knew why. I didn't want to seem weak and needy, weird and freaky. "Come on, we should go home. I'm exhausted."

We'd been at the site since before dawn, with the heat under the canopy of trees and the brick of the viaduct, the smell of diesel from the trains and the fumes from Wesson's body. It felt like we'd been down in this dell of ivy and brambles forever, brushing away flies and mosquitoes. My t-shirt clung to my back as I followed Megan down the footpath. We signed out of the crime scene, and Megan reassured the officers now on duty that we were last to leave the site.

The long day, starting in the middle of the previous

night, left us both wiped out. By the time we reached Redruth, the pair of us wanted to huddle down and do nothing but shower, eat and watch TV until bedtime. Sadly, Sid didn't feel the same.

The moment we walked through the door to Turpin Cottage, he called out, "I've made a ham and cheese salad thing. It's on the table. We have to talk." Soft reggae came from the living room, and a waft of something on the air made Megan look at the door sharply before shaking her head.

I groaned. "Bloody hell. Can you ignore the…"

Megan chuckled. "Don't worry. Weed is the least of our problems. I'm just glad he's your geek and not mine."

Sid appeared from the living room and lifted our daysacks and my panniers. "You have evidence in here?"

"Roger that," I said as Megan climbed the stairs to grab the first shower.

I trailed after Sid. On the kitchen table was a feast. He'd made pasta salad, leafy salad, cut slices off a side of ham and put several cheeses on an actual cheese board.

"We have a cheese board?" I asked.

Sid blinked at me. "I'm not a savage, Griffin. Of course, we have a cheese board." He turned his back and said, "I've been going through the photos and videos you sent over. Do you have more?"

"Some. You can take my phone." I handed it over. He could hack the thing without any effort, so I'd given him my access code months ago. With nimble fingers, he sent the rest of the files to some server somewhere, and I headed to the downstairs bathroom to wash up before eating.

When we all reconvened in the kitchen, Megan and I started in on the food. There was even a fresh loaf of bread.

"You've been stress cooking?" Megan asked Sid as he played with his laptop.

Sid looked up, his dark eyes almost black under the kitchen's lighting. "I don't like demons." Just for a moment, I saw something in my friend I'd never seen before—hardness brought on by experience. I'd seen it among the veterans I'd worked with in the Marines. Those guys, who had decades under their belts, not just a few years like me. Something cold, bitter, and angry lived inside Sid. It might not see the light of a lovely day very often, but it was leaking out now. He blinked, and the image was gone. I'd talk to him about it later.

Sid continued, "I've been looking more into Dean Wesson. He spent five years in the US. Goodness knows how he managed to get a visa, but he studied with a specific church for most of that time. My facial recognition software has picked him up in various films from the church, most of them exorcisms."

"It's one of those churches?" I asked.

He nodded. "Very much one of those churches. They take young people who are gay, trans, addicts, and bring them into the light." Sid's anger leaked out. "Bastards."

Megan glanced at me. I gave a small shrug. This side of Sid was a mystery to me.

"So, no actual demons then?" I asked.

"No," he growled. "However, there was a side to this church that went on the road, and this is where things become more interesting. I've found footage of Wesson helping during an exorcism in Kentucky. A young man who'd been treated for schizophrenia. It turns out he was actually possessed. A rare case." Sid looked at Megan. "Possession by a demon is phenomenally rare. You're more likely to come across the kind of thing that happened to Griffin a few weeks ago. Where a spirit clings on, or some negative energy, and you need to invite the light in to banish it, or ask it nicely to leave."

Megan, fork full of ham on the way to her mouth, nodded, but didn't stop eating. Like me, she was probably trying hard to forget the flayed skin of Dean Wesson as she ate.

"Did they rid the lad of the demon?" I asked.

Sid nodded. "It appears so. They have the footage on their servers behind a firewall. A surprising strong firewall. It took me twenty minutes to find a way in. They probably use it as a teaching aid, but they can't afford for it to leak into the real world."

"What happened?" I asked, though I had a feeling I knew the answer already.

"The lad died. They were all hellfire and damnation about it, and his body became dangerously dehydrated."

Megan stopped eating. "He died of thirst?"

Sid nodded. "Wesson and the others were arrested, but some freaky law about proving it was church business… Anyway, let's just say, Kentucky can be a strange place out in the wilds of the mountains, and there are some strange beliefs. It meant Wesson couldn't remain in the country without bringing more heat down on the church, so they sent him back to the UK. He tried setting up a branch of the church in west Wales, then again in Birmingham, but it didn't stick. His brand of hellfire just doesn't seem to do it for even the most radical of British born-again types."

"That's when he ended up in Cornwall?" I asked.

Sid nodded. "The American branch of his church stopped supporting him financially. They ended up in trouble with the FBI over fraud, and other government departments stepped in. The whole pack of cards collapsed. Wesson ran out of money."

"Why wasn't he already on DoPI's radar?" I asked.

"He was, but even we lost track of him about five years back. From what I've been able to piece together, he's been moving from city to city, sometimes homeless, preaching and trying to rid people of their demons."

Megan said, "I'm guessing these are people in the LGBTQ+ community?"

"And addicts, alcoholics, mostly those among the homeless. The only records I really have are some public nuisance arrests, complaints from parish vicars for harassment and a few videos on YouTube of exorcisms he's tried to do alone, mirroring what his church did in the States."

I leaned back in my chair and rolled my shoulders. "The caravan was…" I puffed out a breath. "To be honest, it was a man cave dedicated to demon hunting."

"It was a man cave dedicated to obsession," Megan muttered. "The guy had to be really ill to be living like that. I feel sorry for him. Providing you don't find any nasty porn on his laptop."

Sid pulled a face. "I'll have a look at the office tomorrow. I can keep it safe and air-gapped there. I don't want it searching for nearby Wi-Fi or internet connections around here."

"I don't think demons can come out of computers, Sid," I said, amused.

He scowled. "Don't be so sure, mate. There's a side to the internet, and it's not the dark web shit, that's more than a bit 'ghost in the machine'."

"Really?" I asked.

"Let's just say, there are a few of us in DoPI that are

trying to hunt something down on the web, but we never quite catch it."

Megan chuckled, "Like a Pokémon?"

I laughed, and even Sid managed to find a smile. With food in my belly, I yawned, my body pressing for sleep. "Shower," I said. "I'll clean up after."

Chapter Six

The heat of the night wrapped burning arms around me and sucked the air from my lungs. Woodland stretched out in every direction, but it wasn't alive. Here, the world felt dense and thick. Tender plants reached for light but struggled to fight through the canopy, the pollution, and the high brick arches that spanned even the tallest of trees. If those precious plants won against that triple threat, then they must do battle with the ivy. It snaked and twisted over everything, clinging to the world with tenacious ambition. I drifted along the path.

Until I came to a clearing and a small, filthy caravan.

"Sid! I think I need you in here." Panicked.

Sounds I recognised, but they lacked urgency for me. I ignored them.

I saw him then, sitting on a low stool, beer by his foot, book on his lap and cigarette glowing between two fingers. Drifting closer, I saw… What was the book?

My world shifted, and suddenly I was behind the huge man, looking down at the book. Even if I couldn't read the words, I recognised the print layout. It was a Bible, and the man had it open towards the end. Revelations. Easy to see once I focused.

"How long has he been like this?" Concerned.

"He woke me up almost… ninety seconds ago." Controlled.

"Okay, we need to—"

A sound from the path on the right came to us. The huge man stilled. He didn't even seem to breathe. I tried to pull away, but something had clicked into place and I felt unable to leave his back. We were bonded now. His fate to mine. How was such a thing possible? He rose, and I followed as he took a few paces to see around the caravan, into the dark.

A rattle and hum came from overhead. One of the night trains was coming. It was late by twenty minutes. His mind registered this, and I heard it, knew it.

"Can we pin him down, Sid?" Pressured.

"I'm not sure how. He's too bloody strong. Just keep stuffing blankets around him, so nothing gets broken." Worried.

The train sounds—chunk, cur-chunk, chunk, cur-chunk—drowned out the soft rustling the huge man wanted to hear. The wood changed its passive energy. The trees shrank back. The summer growth quivered. The ivy shuddered. Small animals fled and roosting birds took flight.

The man began to pray aloud.

Fear in the narrow strip of trees spiralled around me, and the air turned cold. The man's breath came out in puffs of mist. The apprehension burrowed into him, wriggled through me, and we were one being.

The huge man cried out, demanding the creature reveal itself in the name of the Lord Almighty. I struggled to pull away, to become independent once more. The Sisyphean task was beyond me. Each time I pulled a part of me loose, another part attached like a super magnet. I was trapped as the blackness roared down the path.

He scrambled to the entrance of his hovel, tumbled inside, slammed the door shut, still praying. Grabbing his phone, he took a small piece of card from the bin. I recognised it.

"Is he coming around?" Hope.

"No, Megan, I don't think so. Christ, he's cold. I'll go find my electric blanket." Tumble of words.

"Hurry, Sid."

Yes. Hurry, Sid. Hurry.

The man made a call. A voice answered. Panic. Panic. Panic and fear. The big man was drowning me in terror. Something hit the caravan, and it rocked hard on wheels that didn't turn. The man tried to banish his dread through shouted demands for a name to the beast. I clung to his body, an unwilling limpet.

The door flew open. The huge man rose to his feet as blackness poured over the footwell and devoured the thin light from the camping lamp he used at night. Utter, unforgiving, cold blackness swallowed us whole. The man screamed. I screamed.

"God, Sid, we need to stop this…" Panic. Panic. Panic and fear.

Something in the black wall grew solid and hit the huge man hard. He went down, cracking his head on the edge of the units. It hurt us. How was I experiencing his physical pain? I wanted to go home. I wanted to go home…

Pain ripped through the man's ankle as an unseen hand, or claw, gripped hard and yanked. He scrambled to hold on to something, anything, to keep him inside the weak protection of the little caravan, but a castle's walls wouldn't be enough. A cathedral's walls wouldn't be enough. The blind anguish of terror made the man forget his prayers. The clawed hand holding him flipped him onto his stomach in the dirt.

Still attached to his back, I looked up and through that utter blackness, I saw something, even if he couldn't. A monstrous shape of beauty and twisted nightmare. How could something that must once have been divine now be so ugly?

I screamed at the evil I saw in its eyes. The unremitting need and hunger for pain and hopelessness. The definition of malevolence. Any hope of salvation vanished in an instant. It stole belief in hope. That's what it took from me. From him.

"He's crying. Why is he crying?" Shrill.

"Just hold him, Megan. Hold him and keep telling him how you feel. I'm going to go find a Bible and a damned cross or something..." Controlled.

"That's it?"

"That's all we have right now."

The pain, when it came, made the big man scream into the dirt. He couldn't move, despite struggling and fighting like a warrior from the Biblical myths of heroes. I howled and writhed as flesh was torn from bone. Marks were drawn over and over into skin and muscle. When the ripping of the hide came, the final separation from the skeleton, the huge man was dying. A whimper and gurgle came from his ruined mouth. He'd bitten through his tongue and lip, trying to escape the agony of his back.

Sirens screeched through the night, shattering the dome of silence on the edge of the killing field. The creature, licking and feeding on us, lifted its beautiful, craven face. It leapt onto the roof of the van, threw the skin into the branches as a warning, and raced back to where it came from. Sated. Passive now. Its mission was complete.

I lay over the body of the huge man and wept. When his soul finally fled the destroyed flesh sack, I found myself drifting once more. Drifting. Wishing for home. Wishing for hope.

Air rushed in, and I tried to curl into a ball, but something was in the way.

"Sid! He's back!" yelled Megan.

Reality hit me like a baseball to the face. My stomach rolled. I pushed Megan away with a cry and scrambled for my bathroom. I made it just in time.

Nothing made sense. Noise and light swirled around me. The cold of the ceramic burned against my sweaty chest.

My right hand dug into the mat next to the shower door. I smelt cleaning vinegar and Pears soap. Not blood, piss and shit, and the fetid breath of something so foul it stained my soul. Even as I puked again, I realised I was sobbing.

A blanket was draped carefully over my shoulders. I heard a quiet conversation, and a door close. A small hand brushed my hair back from my damp face.

"It's alright. You're safe now. I've got you."

Personally, I doubted I'd ever feel safe again. A shiver once more rippled through me at the thought of facing that… that… *thing* again.

Once the worst had passed, I flushed, and laid my head on the seat. The shivering started to calm, and I found Megan's hand and hung on as the tears stopped. She handed me a new toilet roll and, bless her, she'd unstuck the beginning. It's the little things that make you fall in love with someone. Really fall for them.

That thought made my body ripple again. What if it knew I'd been there? What if it knew about Megan?

"Hey, whatever's going on in your head, slow your roll, soldier boy. It's okay. Just breathe. Right now, we're all safe, and you're okay." Megan began stroking my back this time.

"You don't know," I whimpered.

My bedroom door opened, making me flinch. "Here," Sid said. "This should help. Hot chocolate with a shot of whiskey. My Nanna used to give it to me."

"I can't imagine you needing a Nanna, Sid." Megan put the mug down, and I heard my bed creak. The smell of the hot chocolate rolled over me, and the hint of alcohol helped calm my nerves.

"Give me a minute. I'll wash up," I mumbled, pushing the mug towards Megan. "I want that."

She chuckled. "It's okay. You've scared the crap out of

all of us. Sid's made more. Want to talk here, or downstairs?"

"Here," I murmured, struggling on wobbling legs to stand up. She helped me until she was confident I wouldn't collapse in the small shower and either break it or me.

Not wanting to spend long alone, in case my brain melted, I cleaned up fast, brushed my teeth, washed my mouth, and dried off. The mirror felt off-limits. Almost human again, I left the bathroom. A very wobbly, weak human, one unable to meet anyone's gaze, but human.

Sid and Megan had managed to remake the bed. Fortunately, Luce hadn't spent the night. One less victim of my weirdness.

Megan sat me on the only chair in the room, a far too low, old-fashioned thing that smelt vaguely of horsehair every time it grew warm. She tucked the blanket around me and sat on the floor with our mugs. Sid sat on the bed.

"What happened?" he asked.

I shook my head. "I don't…" Sipping the hot chocolate made the world feel safe. "God, that's good."

He chuckled. "Right? She did it for us whenever we had nightmares. Usually because of the bullies at school or on the estate—that included the police. It was the eighties, and I'm black."

Megan sighed. "Sorry."

"Not your fault," he told her. "Shit happens everywhere. She was a wise woman, my Nanna. Very wise. Came from rural Jamaica. She knew some stuff." An echo of her accent came through in Sid's words. It made me glance at him. A sad smile played around his mouth, just a teasing one. "She was a gospel singer. The Lord lived in her house. A living being that knew just about everything I did while I grewed up, man. And woe betide the fool who tried to lie to her," he made a kissing sound. "She'd have a report from Jesus his'elf in the time it took to climb the stairs to her flat. Yes, sir, she'd knowed about it and there'd be trouble a waitin'." His accent made me laugh.

"Now, that's better," he said, reverting to his more normal voice. "What happened, Griffin?"

"Something I've never known before. It was a dream, or not, I don't know." I rubbed my forehead. "But I was there at the caravan from last night. Somehow my spirit?" I glanced at him, and he nodded. "It went there and got stuck to Wesson." I felt the tears sting my eyes at the thought of the pain he'd endured. "I was like a limpet on his back and couldn't get free as the thing—" I couldn't give it another name. Not yet. "As the thing murdered him. I saw exactly what it did. Felt it. Felt him. The terror. The blind and total terror. He didn't stand a chance. Nothing he'd been taught prepared him for this. It just… It devoured him. When the police turned up, that's what made the thing leave."

"This is important, mate, and I don't mean to freak you out, but did it know you were there?" Sid asked.

I shook my head. "No. I don't think so. It wasn't attacking me." Again, the memories brought tears. "He was all alone. Dean Wesson was all alone. He died alone."

Megan wrapped her arms around my knees and tried to hug them. "It was a dream, Griff. Just a terrible dream."

I glanced at Sid, who obviously didn't agree.

"What happened to me?" I asked them.

Chapter Seven

Megan and Sid shared a long look after I asked my question.

"What?" I pushed. "I heard your voices inside the dream, or at least snatches."

Sid shrugged, relieving himself of the responsibility.

Megan sighed. "You woke me up, thank goodness, by mumbling in your sleep about trees. I thought you were dreaming about Madron. I went to wake you, but your body jerked hard, and before I could stop it from happening, you'd fallen out of bed. Then you started to fit, like you did after coming out of the veil. That's when I guessed you weren't really dreaming. Only it had to be a dream." She frowned and shook her head. "How could it have been real? We didn't know about the death. You didn't see it before it happened, or even while it happened."

"Did you have a sense of smell or taste?" Sid asked. "Could you read?"

"I recognised the Bible verses Wesson was reading," I said, feeling clammy. We both knew what it meant. In dreams, you can't read. Visions or astral projection? They could be different. If a practitioner had enough skills, then it was possible to read. I wasn't capable of either. "I smelt the world as well. The blood. The… the thing. It stank of carrion and sulphur."

Sid rose from his perch on my bed. "I think we should try to get some more sleep. You'll need the rest, Griffin. A generalised tonic–clonic seizure like this can tear the body up, exhaust you. We'll talk more in the morning."

"I'm not epileptic," I stated weakly.

"You don't have to be an epileptic to endure a seizure if it's being caused by outside influences," Sid said. "Sleep, then we'll figure it out. Maybe get you up to London for some tests. You might need help." He left us.

Megan looked at me. "It'll be okay."

I rose on weak legs and realised I'd be lucky to make the bed without falling on my face. Scrambling to her feet, Megan wordlessly helped me. Thanks to my nighttime wanderings, we both slept in t-shirts and boxers despite the heat of August.

"I'm sorry," I murmured as we lay down.

"Don't be. I'm just glad I was here, so you didn't crack your head on anything. You were thrashing like a shark on land."

I rolled over and looked at her, tucking some of that blonde hair behind her ear. "I didn't hurt you?"

She shook her head. "No, love, of course not."

Her first endearment in our new life together. Was it out of pity? A reflex? How should I respond?

Ever practical, Megan took the decision out of my hands. "You need sleep." She kissed my brow and rolled over to her preferred sleeping position.

I wanted to trace her shoulder, half seen in the dim light

of my room, but I didn't want her to think I was being a sex pest. Instead, I lay on my back and tried to remain in neutral until, eventually, I did doze off again.

Waking alone, I stretched, muscles sore after the obvious tension from the seizure during the night. My stomach rumbled, and I needed water. Throwing on a pair of cotton trousers, I padded barefoot downstairs. Sid and Megan were hunched over his laptop.

I spoke through a yawn. "Morning. How long have you two been working?"

They looked up and blinked at me like a couple of startled owls. I headed for the coffee machine.

"Griffin, I think we should call the wicked witch," Sid said. "We need someone with more skills for this job."

"I agree," I said. This seemed to surprise them. "We need a team with an experienced Deliverance minister."

"That was easy," Megan murmured.

"Convincing me is easy; it's the boss that'll be difficult. Though it doesn't stop us from taking practical steps today. Megan, I'd like you to reach out to the police pathologist today, see when they're doing the autopsy and if we can attend."

She pulled a face. "Great. All these years I've managed to avoid that particular pleasure."

"I need them to focus on the skin specifically. I think..." My stomach rolled the coffee over at the thought. "I think it carved something into Wesson's back, but in the dream, I was too panicked and the pain was extreme. It was impossible to see clearly." I was trying to be practical, but my own skin crawled at the memories from last night.

She frowned. "You really felt the pain of it?"

I breathed out slowly and kept my eyes on the kitchen window, focusing hard on the blue sky, the burnt grass, the bird table and sparrows washing themselves in the bath. "Yeah, I felt it." Food. I needed to eat. It would help make things more ordinary and rational. Then I'd talk to Sanchez.

"I'll speak with the bishop as well. Explain what happened to Wesson." With a plan in mind for the next hour or so, I set about making toast. Anything else might not stay down. I couldn't remember the last time I'd felt this physically fragile. The implications of the night's events for my mind were on hold. Internalising that horror…

Again, I began conscious breathing.

"Griffin," Sid said from beside me. "You want to talk about it?"

I shook my head, gripping the sink. "No. No, I really don't. I will, but not now. Work now."

"Okay, buddy, but just know, you don't have to carry this alone. We can all help." He moved away, and I heard the stairs creak. Megan was showering.

I ate my toast standing up and pondered how to explain the events to Sanchez.

"This had better not be another welfare call, Corporal," she said the moment she picked up my call.

"No, ma'am. Though, it is a request for a different team to take over events down here. I'm not confident we're qualified." I kept my eyes on the thrush now making use of the bird bath.

"Explain."

I did. Trying to keep my voice neutral. I held nothing back and told her about the seizure. Hiding things from Sanchez at this point struck me as bloody stupid, and pride shouldn't get in my way. I risked the members of my team if I screwed this up.

She drew in a breath deep enough to be audible. "Then

we have a problem, Griffin." The gravity of her voice drew my attention away from the birdbath.

"What's wrong?" I asked, recognising the more relaxed version of my boss that still unnerved me.

"We've an ongoing mission in Wales. Lampeter University. Some of the students there have raised spirits. I'm heading over now."

"Which means you don't have a team to spare," I stated.

"No. Not at the moment. We've a small, rural town full of students, many of whom are studying various religions, and it's turning into a PR nightmare. There is also a strong Pentecostal church in the town. Do you think the demon has a track on you?" She sounded genuinely concerned.

"No. Whatever happened to me, it's linked to the visions and night wanders I'm having. Remember in my last report about Madron, I told you about the burying of the child in the grove? How vivid it was? Perhaps, because I couldn't go to Truro in my physical form, my mind..." I didn't know what it did.

Sanchez picked up on it. "An astral projection, but through time as well?"

"Sounds daft, doesn't it?"

"Perhaps. Though, you've always been different, Griffin," her voice softening.

An idea suddenly shot through me like a crossbow bolt. Before the words could escape me, I swallowed them down. I needed to talk to Sid.

"Do what you can, Corporal. Keep me updated. If you really need me to divert resources, I will, but you'll have to make a damned good case for it. If necessary, rope the bloody bishop in, that's what the Church is there for, and I'm sure he'll know something about Deliverance."

"And DoPI?"

"Explain if you have to. I'll report to the Archbishop and have him talk to Bishop Chadwick about Dean Wesson's death. Though at this point I think keeping the demon aspect quiet will be wise."

"I'm not sure if I agree, ma'am. Surely it's better he knows that we—"

"No, I don't want that happening. If news of a demon summoning leaks from his office, which it will, we'll have more problems to hide. Life's complicated enough right now." That was also new. She was worried. Which made me very nervous.

"Leave the bishop to me. It'll be easier for you."

Surprised, she said, "Thank you, Griffin, and good luck."

"You too, ma'am."

She cut the connection.

I stared out of the window. Working alone down here, being in control of the big decisions, I found it liberating in many ways, but also challenging. Our last two missions had almost ended in death for me, Megan and Sid. We were all vulnerable to the creatures in the veil, or wherever demons came from, and I didn't know if I could take this on and keep us all safe. After all, I signed up to the Royal Marines knowing someone might well shoot me, or blow me up. Not so for Megan and Sid. Yes, there was a faint possibility of Megan becoming hurt in the line of duty as a police officer, but it was rare in the UK for them to be seriously injured. Even less likely for them to die. Sid, he was just a geek. A keyboard warrior. Luce was the same, an academic.

If I could do this alone, I would, but every operator needed a team. If Wesson had someone watching his back, he might've made better decisions. Whatever killed him, and whoever controlled it, needed stopping.

"You can't give up, Woodbury," I muttered. "You really can't. There's a list of names from that caravan, all of them children. Sid needs to start there. Do your investigation. Keep demon lore front and centre. Stay under the radar. Don't make Wesson's mistakes. You have a ticking clock."

Wesson was convinced that the Assumption of Mary, the fifteenth of August would be the end game. I needed to work with that in mind.

My thoughts settled, and a plan clarified, so I headed for the shower. It was going to be a long day.

When I walked into my room, I found Megan dressing in loose-fitting trousers and shirt.

She smiled at me. "What did the wicked witch say?"

"That they have a huge problem in West Wales they're trying to contain, and they can't come to help here."

"Oh, shit. That's—"

"Tricky. So, here's the plan. You and I go to see the pathologist. Sid tracks down the list of children. We do all we can to keep the thoughts of demons at bay."

"You really think it was a demon?" Megan asked. "What you saw?"

"Difficult not to, though I didn't 'see' it. More felt it, smelt it. I had the impression of something angelic that had been twisted, scored with darkness." I shuddered.

"How are you dealing with that?" she asked as I walked into the shower.

"It's not great." I ran a hand over the faint colours of the tattoo the dryad had left on my inner arm as a sign of our covenant. "Knowing what Wesson faced…"

"Yeah. Just the thought of it happening to one of us, or even someone else…"

We were silent for a moment. "Though," she added. "It does mean that Wesson was on to something viable, which made the demon—what? I don't know what to call a person who does this kinda thing."

"Idiot, mostly."

"Helpful."

"Sorcerer."

"Now I have this image of a certain mouse holding a broom dancing around in my head. Okay, let's use that word sorcerer. What made them react with extreme violence. There must be something in that laptop or caravan that'll show us the way."

"I agree." Without evidence, I couldn't mention my thoughts about this being a woman.

Once out of the shower, I rang the bishop's office. Anna answered. She said Bishop Chadwick was in meetings all day. I gave her a brief rundown of events, leaving out most of the gory details and the demon element. Why? Well, convincing these people of demons wouldn't help right now. Keeping it simple and human should be enough to keep them safe. I finished with, "Wesson's death means we face something none of you have dealt with before. This is more than a safeguarding issue."

"You're asking me to tell the bishop he needs to be careful."

"You all need to be careful. Whoever Wesson was investigating is very dangerous. Don't do anything to advance this investigation that might draw attention to yourselves. No press releases, social media nonsense. Nothing. Understood?"

"Of course, Griffin. I understand. Take precautions."

"Good. I'll be in touch the moment I know more."

Megan watched me. "You don't think they need to know about the demon?"

I puffed out my breath. "To be honest, it could've just

been a weird vision. A manifestation of human violence. I didn't really witness the death, just an echo of it through an impression forced onto the veil." That thought had been developing the more I talked, the more time gave me perspective. I'd experienced an imprint, a memory.

"You really believe that?"

"I believe it was an echo scarring the veil, and it called to me." Yeah, that actually made sense. "Was it a demon? Maybe. Let's hope not. Let's hope it was a normal human nutter." I smiled at her, and she rolled her eyes.

"You can't say nutter."

"I can. Anyone dicking about with demons is a nutter. I just need a quick word with Sid." I tracked him down in the living room.

"All good?" he asked.

I nodded. "We're off to see the body."

"Oh, that sounds like such fun." He pulled a face.

"Sanchez—"

"She emailed me. We have point."

I nodded, relieved I didn't have to explain again. "While I was talking to her, something she said sparked a thought. Could I ask a favour?"

He grinned. "Is it going to involve me doing something naughty to DoPI?"

"Kinda."

"Then I'm in." He saw I was about to point out he didn't know what the request was, but he waved it away. "Don't care. Want in."

I shook my head. "Fine. Dig up anything in the archives about Hazel Tudor."

Whatever he'd been expecting, it wasn't that. "Your mum? Mate, I've tried searching, there isn't anything."

"Yeah, I know. Just have another nose. Try some

different angles. It's something Sanchez let slip. It made me feel like she knew my mother somehow. Don't get caught looking. Don't leave a trace. I just…" I bit my lip. "I just have a feeling there is something there and we're missing it."

"You got it. Secret squirrel mission will commence."

Chapter Eight

The pathologist worked out of Truro, so back up the A30 we travelled. This time, we took the car. Megan recognised I wasn't on top form, and it gave us time to talk as we practiced more patience than most of the locals with the *emmet* traffic. Fortunately, we didn't have to go right into Truro, but we did have to park the car at the hospital. An expensive and difficult proposition.

Eventually, Megan led me through the modern building and down into its lower depths. We walked past the patients waiting for CT scans, MRIs and X-rays, the big machines hidden away.

Her pace left me almost breathless as I tried to keep up. "I didn't think you'd done one of these before?"

"I haven't. But I've escorted more than one body in over the years, and I've brought in family members when we've needed identification for the dead."

A small sign on the door announced, *Pathology*, and she pressed a buzzer. "Their security has to be fairly tight. People are weird."

Part of me wanted to ask, but another part just didn't want to think about it. Having to keep dead bodies safe from the living went against the grain of a DoPI operative. We usually had to keep people safe from the dead.

A young man in a technician's white coat came to the door. He looked harassed as he pulled it open. "I'm sorry, members of the—" He ran his hand through his rapidly vanishing dark hair.

"Police," Megan said, holding up her badge. "We're here to see Dr Dennis Brew. I believe he's expecting us. Sergeant Ackley and Mr Woodbury of Rural Security."

I showed the technician my identification. He nodded and allowed us entrance.

Whatever I'd expected of a pathology department, I hadn't expected this level of high-tech labs and offices. The technician led us through a corridor with rooms on both sides. Through the windows in the doors, I saw state-of-the-art laboratory equipment, and on the other side, offices with soft seating, pleasant working environments and more new technology. Sid would love it here. A set of double doors required a separate key fob to the lanyard the technician carried to enter, and suddenly we were being shown into a viewing area.

"Don't faint. Our resident nurse is on sick leave, and we don't have a replacement. I'm not good with fainting people," the technician said. "Dr Brew will be with you in a moment."

We watched him leave us. "That's us told," I muttered.

"To be fair, I'm not sure how well I'll handle this," Megan admitted.

"You'll be fine. After yesterday, you can handle this."

She pulled a face. "Don't remind me. Do you know how

close I came to puking on the crime scene like the poor woman from the ambulance crew?"

"She cried, it was one of the police officers who puked," I pointed out.

Megan chuckled. "I'd forgotten."

Humour gets dark and weird sometimes.

Opting to sit on the comfortable, low-slung chairs the waiting area offered, we both started scrolling on our phones. The national news had picked up on the murder. Suddenly, Cornwall was the country's capital of horrific gang crime. It seemed to be the spin DoPI had put on the flaying. Smuggling was alive and well in the sleepy county. They'd be republishing Jamaica Inn at this rate.

Just as we grew restless, which didn't take long, the door to the viewing area opened and a vivid paisley waistcoat walked in. It took me a moment to notice the man wearing it. Smaller than Megan, and almost as round as he was tall, the man's Christmas elf face broke out in a smile.

"I'm sorry for the wait. It took a few moments to check some preliminary findings. With a death like this, I know you need the evidence the day before the actual crime took place." He chuckled at his joke.

Megan and I shared a swift glance and bemusement.

She said, "Dr Brew. It's lovely to meet you again."

"Yes, that's right. I think we've met a few times, though, without the uniform…"

"Sergeant Ackley. It's been a few months since I was last here. Megan is fine. This is my colleague from the Department of Rural Security, Griffin Woodbury."

"Excellent. Lovely to meet you. I'm guessing Greg told you not to faint?" His small eyes twinkled like a pair of sapphires. I decided then and there that if the demon killed me, I wanted Dr Brew to cut me up. "Don't worry, I've done the worst bits. There'll be no fainting. Lenard likes his pranks. If you follow me, I can show you the photographs I'm sure you really want to see."

I wondered what pranks a person could do when you worked in a department with actual body parts… Football with three legs?

Seriously, don't go there. For once, my inner critic and I were in agreement.

We followed Dr Brew, who whistled the theme music to Mission Impossible as we walked, and he led us into an office. After finding ourselves given coffee and biscuits, he sat us at the long table and cast his laptop's screen onto the larger one bolted to the wall.

"All mod cons," I murmured.

"For too long, the dead have not been taken seriously. Thanks to the popularity of crime shows, I've managed to convince the hospital that I'm worth it." He flicked invisible hair over his shoulder, making us laugh as he mimicked the advert for shampoo. Then his face sobered. "I have to say, I'm probably a little manic in my desire to see the lighter side of life. This one…" He took a deep breath. "He was badly tortured before passing, and it's been hard to work on his body. All very sad."

"We were there, Dr Brew. We know what happened," I said.

"Whoever, whatever did this needs stopping," he said, pressing something on the laptop. The screen on the wall woke up, and we saw the dead face of Dean Wesson. His tattooed scalp and wild beard still looked alive, but the man's face had been scratched and bruised in those last moments as the demon drove his face into the hard dirt of the summer's soil.

"Preliminary findings will be emailed to you. I'm still

waiting for the results of DNA analysis of the saliva we found on the victim, but considering the state of the body, it might not be a clear sample. Other than that, we've found no skin under the nails, no blood other than the victim's and no fibres. The killer, or killers, were either supernaturally lucky, or very forensically aware. How they managed to subdue a man this size without using narcotics or bonds… I have no idea. He obviously tried to fight."

Megan asked, "How do you know?"

I didn't need to ask. I remembered.

Dr Brew took us through the images one at a time. The various bruises sustained by the body were now coming out after the event. It meant Wesson had been alive the entire time, struggling against the creature pinning him down. The man also had various health issues, including early-stage bowel cancer, liver disease, and more. Apparently, he wouldn't have made old bones. It didn't make me feel any better.

"Then we come to the skinning," Dr Brew said.

The next image made Megan grunt. Wesson's large skin was laid out, cleaned and flattened on a steel table. All the flaps and folds had been tidied up, and Dr Brew had tried to marry up the slashes. Megan and I stiffened, the atmosphere becoming charged.

Oh, shit, you're going to have to stamp on this one fast, soldier boy.

Time for me to turn hot and heavy on poor Dr Brew. Megan wouldn't like it either.

The pathologist said, "I know they're saying on the news that this is a gang crime, but I'm not so sure."

"It might not be wise to put that in your report, Doctor," I said. "Stick with the narrative."

Dr Brew pulled his head back and straightened his

spine. "I'm sorry, but I don't lie for a government department."

I rose from my chair and approached the screen. Pointing to what would've covered Wesson's right shoulder, I said, "This symbol isn't gang related, but I guess you know that. It's a sigil that comes from *The Magus*, or *Celestial Intelligencer*. It's a handbook of the occult and ceremonial magic compiled by occultist Francis Barrett from 1801. This is the demon's name in symbol form. I can't read it, before anyone asks, and I'm not going to try."

Dr Brew huffed and puffed. "That's ridiculous."

"It's a calling card. Down here," I pointed to the left buttock. "This one I've seen in *The Lesser Key of Solomon*. I'm guessing it's the glyph used by the demonic master of the demon. The centre one? That's the demon's human master. The one it kills for." I returned my attention to the previous symbol. "This is one I know. Andras, a Marquis of Hell. That's the demon's demonic master." Trying saying that three times after a few beers.

No one spoke. I sat down and ate a biscuit. They were digestives. I like digestives. Though, the dark chocolate ones are—

"You aren't serious," Dr Brew said. "Surely?"

"I am. They are. It's crude, but it's clear. I've read the book. However, this will be a gang crime in your report, and that image has to be doctored."

Dr Brew's eyes shot to Megan. "This is not how the police—"

"He isn't police, Dr Brew. I'm very sorry, but he's right. This can't be leaked or reported through the correct channels."

I leaned over the table, drawing Dr Brew into my

personal space. "I know this is hard, but Rural Security is actually part of the Security Services. We need your help. This has to be kept quiet. We're tracking a very dangerous individual who is doing something that will kill a great many more people if we don't stop it. Can you imagine the widespread panic if something like this demonology escaped into the real world?"

"People have a right to know," whispered Dr Brew.

"No, they don't. Not when it will cause untold damage. Do you want to start another religious war in Europe? Or do you want to be laughed out of your profession? Maybe you'll take door three. If you choose that door, I have to come back here with my people, and we confiscate all your files. You lose your job and your reputation. We'll take your wife's job, and we'll make sure your children—"

"Enough," he snapped, his face flushing. "Enough." He took a few deep breaths. Megan looked vaguely sick.

"I'm sorry," I said, leaning back. "This is not what I wanted to do. I don't enjoy this part of my job, but I do need you to keep quiet about those markings. I can promise you I will get this squared away, but I can only do that with your help."

"I worked on the bodies of those women from Madron," he said in a small voice. "Also the pieces of Sir Alanson and his men. That was you, wasn't it? You're with that woman." He looked at me warily.

Interesting. It didn't take a genius to work out who he meant. "Ms Pilar Sanchez."

He nodded very slowly and didn't hide his fear. "I've been receiving a stipend from something called DoPI, but I don't know what it stands for."

Bloody woman, she could've warned me. I'd have

handled this differently if I'd known she'd taken him, if not under DoPI's wing, then at least into the same nest.

"That's us. That's all you need to know, all you want to know. We work for the government. We work for the Crown. Our remit is wide. Please, Dr Brew, can I trust in your discretion?"

He searched my eyes, then glanced at Megan, who shrugged. Finally, he asked, "Why is this happening in Cornwall?"

"That's a long story."

"I have time." He crossed his arms over his waistcoat and glared at me.

I looked at Megan. Explaining all this to her hadn't made her life any easier. Would she choose to go back into the box? To forget all this horror was real? Remember that the worst thing she could face was a junky on the streets, not a demon…

She said, "Threats aren't the way to win trust, Griffin, and we need his help. I'm guessing there will be more bodies before this is over." She turned to Dr Brew. "We can trust you, right?"

He gave a single nod, his eyes on me.

I shrugged, time to pull the wool away from his eyes. "Cornwall's one of the more mysterious counties in the UK. Like parts of Somerset, Devon, much of rural Wales and the rural parts of the north, Scotland and Ireland. Rich in myth and legend…" I went on for almost twenty minutes.

By the time I'd finished, Dr Brew's eyes were wide, and when he spoke, it was with wonder, not the scepticism and scorn Megan still liked to pour over me at every opportunity.

"Does this mean there really are aliens?" he asked.

I saw Megan roll her eyes, but he made me smile. "I don't know, and that's the truth. I find it highly unlikely that we're alone. Our people would be the ones to investigate, but I'm more paranormal, not extraterrestrial."

"This is amazing," he said a little breathlessly.

"You know you can't tell anyone about this conversation? Your wife..."

He waved a hand. "She doesn't like talking about my work. I can't blame her for that. We have a lot of hobbies, and that helps."

I looked at Megan. "See, not everyone is a sceptic." A refreshing change. The atmosphere in the room had relaxed considerably.

"Whatever," she muttered. "Do we have your cooperation, Dr Brew?"

The waistcoat strained against its buttons. "Yes, Sergeant Ackley, you have my total cooperation. I'll make it clear in the report that these are likely random marks taken off the internet, meant to scare the gang's competitors. That's the best way of hiding this." His attention returned to me. "So what really did do that to Sir Alanson? It wasn't a helicopter explosion. I know that for certain."

I shook my head. "I'm sorry. I can't explain. It's highly sensitive. Keeping the truth about events in that location is going to save many lives, both here and among the *para*."

Dr Brew nodded, and we continued chatting as he showed us out of the pathology department. He pumped my hand with a great deal of enthusiasm, and I wondered why Sanchez had brought the strange man into DoPI's fold. What was she up to? She had a habit of entrapping innocent people and putting them to work while tying them in knots.

Outside the hospital, Megan headed for the nearest area

of shade. "What's next?" she asked. "I'm thinking we need to go through the evidence back in the office."

"I'm worried about those symbols," I murmured, staring out over the heaving car park. "You're right. We can't do any more in Truro for the moment."

Chapter Nine

It took a long time to reach Redruth. Truro was full, the A30 west was busy. Megan drove, and I pondered the meaning of Wesson's murder and what the hell it had to do with my vision. Was this now my fate? That during a case I'd receive some kind of insight into the location, or the crime? Only this time, I hadn't been a passive observer of an event from hundreds of years before; I'd been part of a recent murder. Although I had some distance from the terror the vision caused, with the sun lighting the car and blending with Megan's music filling the silence between us, I still felt that bitter cold of the attack.

My fists bunched on my lap. The helplessness Wesson experienced filled me as well. I couldn't have done a damned thing to save him. All I'd experienced was some kind of vivid memory stuck in that location. Something so traumatic that it ripped reality, and I'd been drawn into the experience. Probably due to being there just after the event and spending too much of the day watching the crime scene people crawl over the location. That made it all sound so normal. Just another night in the life of a DoPI operative. Only it wasn't normal. I'd never done it before, and the fear still bled through my veins. How was I supposed to sleep tonight? I'd already started drinking more on the nights Megan didn't stay over. Was I heading for the dark hole so many operatives fell into?

During my first year with DoPI, I'd known a man called Scott Thomas, a former member of the Parachute Regiment. He'd been Sanchez's bagman in those days. Grizzled, a vet from Afghanistan and Iraq, he was tough, uncompromising and dedicated. He was also alone. Rarely did he talk to the squad who backed him up. We were the faces who filled in the places he needed us. Eventually, he blew his brains out. I was promoted.

Trauma affects people in different ways. I'd been dealing with it my entire life. On the surface, I tried to maintain a positive attitude to life and my work. Slipping into the mire I tightrope walked every day, wouldn't help anyone. Occasionally, I did just that; I slipped. We all did. But I would not allow it to suck me under. I'd known the kind of pain a child of ten should never have to comprehend; this new twist to my psyche's game playing wouldn't take me down.

"You're quiet," Megan said, cutting through my thoughts.

"Yeah, it's been a lot."

She glanced at me. "Everything solid in there?" Tapping her head.

"More or less." I wasn't going to tell her about Scott Thomas. "Wesson dying like that…"

She sucked in a hard breath. "And you seeing it. Experiencing it. That's a lot to process, Griffin."

I stared out of the window and shrugged. "It's the job."

"No, it's you. The job is to investigate crimes like this. You're experiencing them. That's not something you should have to live with. It's like—" she fished for a metaphor, "—like being a sniper, the suicide bomber and the bomb maker, inhabiting all those people at once. It's horrible. Watching you go through that was just as horrible." Her hand rubbed my thigh and gripped my fist. "We have to find a way to protect you from these vision things. Isn't there something DoPI can do to protect you?"

It would mean another gruelling psych eval. Probably drugs and constant monitoring. What I needed was fresh air, clear views of the horizon and peace. "I'll be alright, Meg. It didn't happen to me, and it's important I train my mind to remember that."

She didn't look convinced, and I didn't blame her. "Just remember, talking isn't weakness. If you don't want to talk to me, or Sid, then make DoPI send a bloody therapist to Cornwall for you to use. Maybe for all of us to use. Someone safe."

"All of us?" I asked, glancing at her. "You having problems?"

For a moment, she held her bottom lip between her teeth, obviously wishing she'd kept her mouth shut. "I have flashbacks to seeing the Dru killing Alanson and me trying to save Steve. It's not been easy. It's one of the reasons I've been working so hard over the summer. The distraction helps."

I was stunned. Why the hell hadn't I thought about it sooner? What kind of friend did that make me? I loved this woman, and I hadn't noticed. "Meg… I'm sorry. I—"

"Don't. Not your place, Griffin. I didn't tell you, and I didn't allow you to see it. That's on me. I'm telling you now because I think we both need help. We both need a lot of help with the things we're experiencing, and DoPI has a duty of care. You might want to tell Sanchez that."

I thought back to Scott Thomas. Sanchez hadn't said a word to me about it. One moment he worked quietly next to my cubical, and we trained together as a team, the next he was gone. An old hound put down by a vet. Never to be thought of again.

"We're just expected to suck it up, Meg. That's the DoPI way."

"Well, it's going to have to change." She set her jaw. "I'm part of the team, and I say we need help to deal with this."

"I'm a Royal Marine—"

"I don't care, Griff. You're a human seeing and doing extraordinary things. You'll burn out. I'm here to stop that from happening." She glared at me.

"Okay, Mum." I smiled. "I love that you care. Thank you."

She huffed. "Someone needs to, you won't look after yourself. It's like you're a ghost in your own life, taking up the least amount of space. Turpin Cottage is full of Sid's gear, you barely exist in the house."

"I like Sid's gear."

She made a dismissive sound. "You just don't know how to hold your place in the world. Think about it, okay? I don't want you to change. I just want you to be aware that you have options. You can live a different kind of life."

"I can't leave DoPI."

"Yes, Griffin, you can. It's just a job—"

"Megan, it's more than that. I'm also a command—"

"No, that's just a job as well. I'm a police officer. That's just a job. A vocation that I love, yes, but it's also just a job."

"What brought all this on?" I asked. "You've never questioned my job before."

"I've never had to deal with a thrashing man, who is in fear not just for his life, but his sanity. You scared me last night."

"I'm sorry."

She shrugged. "It's okay. I get it. But I also need you to protect yourself. Protect us and our future together."

"We have one of those?" We were pulling into the space outside the office.

Turning to face me, as she pulled on the handbrake, she said, "We have any future we want, Griffin, that's the point of being in love." She leaned over and kissed me, all too briefly.

The smile that spread over my face made her laugh. "I love you too."

"I know that, doofus. I've always known it. Get out of the damned car and let's go to work."

I wanted to enjoy the moment. Maybe make it romantic somehow, but as I watched Megan stomp up the path to the door, I realised that just wasn't her way. We'd share our moments, no doubt, but they wouldn't be planned. Besides, doing this just outside DoPI, which is what brought us together again in the first place, was probably fitting.

"Come on," she called. "I'm going to melt!"

Once through our ridiculous security system, Megan headed for the kitchen while I headed for Sid.

"What news?" I asked.

He leaned back in his ergonomic chair and stretched. The chair creaked in protest. "Nothing good, hombre. I've been focusing on the children in the list and have *some* news." He leaned back further. "Megan," he whined.

"Yes, I'm making tea," she said. "Despite my fine investigative mind, I'm also the tea lady. Miss Marple, look out, here I come in my domestic drudgery."

I laughed.

She waved a spoon at me. "Don't! Don't say a word."

"I wouldn't dare. Powwow away from the screens?"

Sid groaned again. "Sounds good to me." He levered himself out of the chair and plonked down on the sofa instead. "What news from the autopsy?"

I explained as Megan brought over the tea and found us something to eat in the fridge. Cheese and onion pasties from the bakery. Nice.

By the time I'd finished, not just my tale but also the pasty, Sid's eyebrows almost met over his nose he was frowning so deeply. "This isn't good. Not good at all. We have a serious problem on our hands. A real practitioner is out there somewhere."

"My thoughts exactly. Summoning a creature related to Andras, a Marquis of Hell in the old texts, is bad news."

"It ties in with what I've just discovered." Sid rubbed his face. "Sadly."

"What have you discovered about the children?" Megan asked, her voice subdued.

"Nothing you're going to want to hear. There were four on the final list Wesson made. I started with birth records. Each child was born in the same hospital at the same time."

"What?" I asked.

"Yeah, and it's exactly the same time. Get this, it's 03.33. We have two girls, two boys, all born on 1st November 2016, All Saints Day, All Souls Day, Day of the Dead. You chose. They are all nine years old at the moment. If they're still alive."

"What does that mean?" Megan asked, alarmed.

"Despite being born in the same hospital, which, if we

needed to add more weird into the mixture, is on a powerful ley line, the children didn't stay local. The families moved all over the country. I've tracked each one. The first to go missing is Emilya James. She disappeared at eighteen months. Stolen from the back of the car as her mother loaded the shopping into the house. They lived in an expensive area of Chelsea. Door cam footage shows a dark figure reaching into the car and the child being lifted out. It was late in the evening. The nearby street light had gone out a few days before, and despite a reward, Emilya hasn't been seen since. Her mother committed suicide three months later."

We were all silent, taking in the terrible news.

"No one has found her?" Megan whispered.

"No. There's no father on the scene either. Each baby was conceived via IVF to a single woman. Further adding to the weird quota. Grandparents tried to keep the police interested after their daughter's death, but nothing stuck. The investigation petered out."

"That's horrible."

"Yep. The second child, Philip Kirk, went missing aged three. Snatched from a public park while under the care of a child minder. That was in Sheffield. Again, no biological dad, but Mum was married to Desmond Kirk soon after Philip was born. Mum, Susan, she went on to become a pill head, trying to cope with her loss, and eventually overdosed. Desmond died soon after in a car accident that may or may not have been suicide."

"Fuck," Megan breathed. "Baby three?"

"More of the same. She is or was, called Ann Dawson. Went missing aged five. Taken from the streets after stepdad was beaten up and robbed while walking her back from a playdate in a nearby park. Mum is currently in a secure ward at the local hospital. Dad is paralysed from the waist down and lives in supported living accommodation. He tries to get people to help him search for Ann, but has no money, no hope and—"

"God, that's enough," Megan said, waving him away.

I had nothing to say. The implications were just awful. "What about number four?"

"That's when things get interesting. Number four has vanished. That's mum and son. I have a birth certificate stating his name is Matthew Moore, mum is Naomi Moore, but nothing else. No school records, hospital records, dentists… I've done the lot. They drop off the planet and stay dropped."

"How are you going to find them?" Megan asked.

"I've a photo of Naomi from a social media account she hasn't visited since Matthew was born. She used to be quite active in all the usual places. The IVF was her way of defying the patriarch, apparently. Her parents didn't approve. She's the youngest, wildest and strangest of the four mothers. She wanted the baby at home. It's all over the feed, but they discovered severe pre-eclampsia."

"Which meant she had to go to the hospital at the same time as the other women," I said.

"Bingo," Sid announced. "You win the prize. There's a single post about her receiving a birth chart from her good friend Star, then nothing. She just drops off the world."

"She could be anywhere," Megan said.

"Yes, but Wesson was in Cornwall. I've been trying to understand his notes, but I need help. It's…" Sid took a deep breath. "It's barely intelligible, even to someone who knows ancient demon lore."

"I'll start there," I said. "I probably know more than you do."

"Why?" asked Megan.

I glanced at her. "I've worked on a few cases involving the Church, demons, angels, that kinda weird. It's a fascinating area of study, historically speaking. Unlike something like the incubus or the Dru, the written records are pretty clear."

"Or madder, depending on your point of view," Sid muttered. "I've aged up our missing mother, and have my bots scouring images and footage. If she's out there, I'll find her. The focus is currently Cornwall, as Wesson was here."

"Seems logical," Megan agreed. "I'm going to look into this IVF. All the women having it at the same time? Then giving birth in the same hospital? I'll put together a timeline, find the people involved, etc."

"Sounds good," I said. "I've set you up with a desk." I pointed to the currently empty desk, the other side of mine. A new terminal was there with access to DoPI's databases. She'd have to prove herself a bit more before she gained full security clearance, but Sanchez had allowed this much. We'd give her the protocols for the doors as well.

"Oh, I thought… Wow. Thanks."

"Saves you going to your desk in Camborne," I said. "It made no sense to expect you to work down there on DoPI data."

Megan gave a nod. "A real part of the team. I like it."

Sid and I shared a smile as she went to investigate her new workspace. We'd been worried she'd think we—translate to I—were trying to control her. Especially after everything she had going on with Adrian *bloody* Hess.

Chapter Ten

We set about our tasks, data gathering. I sat pouring over Wesson's notebooks. We'd removed six from the caravan, as well as his phone and laptop, both of which I'd leave to Sid's tender mercies. The notebooks were a window into a troubled mind. A window full of that decorative glass people had in their front doors so you can never see who is knocking, which makes it just as unsafe as not having a peephole. Only this decoration was made up of the ugly scars on the man's mind.

After returning to the UK and his new church failing, Wesson had gone from city to city tracking supposed demonic energy. In Newcastle, he 'exorcised' a refugee from Sudan. In Birmingham, he discovered a nest of demons living among a community from Ghana. Then in Swindon, of all places, he worked with a Pentecostal church among a British community who were convinced their children had been demonised by the refugees from Iraq. I sighed heavily, recognising some fairly unpleasant truths about Dean Wesson. A lot of his investigations revolved around the colour of a person's skin or their sexual orientation. The demon activity never amounted to anything but torture and a 'cure'.

Having been attached to his white skin, it made me feel icky. It turned out, the local kids in Swindon were the ones doing the grooming. They were selling drugs to the youngsters in the refugee hotel, who sold them on to the adults. Megan worked it out after I had a bit of a meltdown halfway through the afternoon.

By 18:00 we'd all had enough. Home and food beckoned.

Megan drove. "Did you find anything useful in the end?"

"I think I did," I said, holding the original notebook she'd found the birth charts in. "The older ones are important, because they give me an insight into his thinking before this began. It shows me how much he did or didn't know. This one is the main one. He's tied the children together, the dates of their births, and I have rough sketches of the four birth charts."

"They'd all be the same, surely?"

"Yep, but still, he's done them separately. Then he did more for the date of each disappearance, and for the mothers. What did you find out about the IVF thing?" I'd heard her on the phone, but tuned her out so I could decipher Wesson's rambling.

"Ah, well, that's interesting. They were all conceived at the same clinic, which has since closed down."

"Private?"

"Yep, I've been trying to track down their records and staff members. I've been speaking with a nurse who they sacked when she became a whistleblower about their unethical practices. She's a mine of information."

We were back at the house, and Sid ordered in from the local Chinese restaurant. With beers in hand, we sat in the garden, and Megan continued to explain about the clinics.

"Amy, who is the whistle-blower, worked at the clinic in Bristol for six months. After three, she realised something wasn't right. They specialised in IVF for women who wanted to use their husband's sperm where possible, or donor sperm. The clinic seemed to prefer women who wanted a child without a partner. According to Amy, this clinic also made decisions about using donor sperm for married women, without consultation. She thinks all four women might've had the same donor. I've asked her to check what records she kept."

Sid's eyes were wide. "That's terrible."

Megan nodded. "It's not great."

"Can we get the records of the donor?" I asked.

"Not sure at the moment. I'll push tomorrow, but I'd be nervous of using any single piece of evidence for this. We ought to have multiple sources before rattling someone's life. Besides, the donor might not even be aware of any malpractice. Would you, as a bloke, like to be told that four of your kids have vanished? Their mothers dying or incarcerated? I'm certain I wouldn't want to know."

"Or the donor could've been chosen on purpose," Sid said. "Everything else was orchestrated. These women must've been impregnated on the same day. Then for all the babies to be born at the same time… The work that must've gone into that alone is massive." He pondered for a moment. "I wonder if sorcery made it possible?"

I hadn't looked at it from that point of view. The implications were scary, and surely impossible to manage. Biology just didn't work on a clock that specific.

"What if it was more than just these four women?" I asked.

Megan shook her head. "I'm not with you."

I explained my thinking. "It's just all too convenient. I think they'd have done this to all the women they worked with, then these four are the ones who gave birth at the correct place and time. That's where coincidence takes over. Every other woman who managed a normal birth, and child, had nothing terrible forcing a nightmare into their lives."

Sid nodded. "Makes sense."

Megan blanched. "You mean we're going to have to tell a whole heap more people that their daddy sperm isn't actually their daddy?" She puffed out a breath. "That's not my job."

"No, we'll hand over the evidence so that a more thorough investigation can be done. It's not our place," I agreed. "Do we know the names of the people who ran the clinic? The doctors responsible?"

Megan nodded. "I'll track them down tomorrow. The company that owned the clinic has dissolved, and Companies House has a record of debt against the directors. They appear to be Eastern European. I've tracked back to Moldova."

"A place well known for its record keeping," Sid muttered.

Megan hummed her agreement. "We'll hit a dead end with that. I'm not sure it's worth the man-hours."

"Agreed," I said. "What about the doctors?"

"Scattered, obviously. Mostly Indian or Pakistani. One British, but I can't find them either. Sid might be able to?"

"I can try," he said.

"We need a common thread to pull at, which will lead

us to the person summoning the demon, maybe kidnapping these children." I opened another beer. The Chinese food arrived, and we busied ourselves with it for a while.

As the evening bled into the night, we remained outside. "Is there anything in the police reports about the missing children? A commonality there?" I asked.

They shook their heads. "It's only Wesson who brought the names together," Sid admitted. "I'd never have seen it. I'm not sure how he did it. The authorities haven't linked the cases. On the surface, there's nothing there."

"I've begun to understand his thinking," I said. "He worked backwards. The way the planets align in the UK skies during the Assumption of Mary and the August Corn Moon told him there would be a Biblical catastrophe. This particular doomsday project comes in the form of four innocents, siblings, separated at birth, being used in a decades-long ceremony. That made him look for the children. He found them, or rather, the traces of them." We all looked up at the night sky. The visible planets were bright tonight. Dancing their eternal dance to form a straight line through the stars. It was a beautiful cosmic sight. Until now, I'd been looking forward to seeing them align perfectly.

"Why Cornwall, though?" Megan asked.

Rather than see the sky with regret in my mind, I played with the condensation running down the glass, wishing it would magically refill without anyone noticing. This mission left me drained, and horribly bleak. "It's where the alignments are truest. We're going to have a super conjunction. That's the full moon, Mercury, Venus, Mars, Jupiter and Saturn all in the same line. Truro is the seat of Church power in Cornwall. It's a rare astrological occurrence, and Truro just happens to be the right place for the perfect view." I pointed at the sky with my bottle.

"Marvellous," Megan muttered.

Sid leaned on the garden table. "Do you think what's happening in Wales is related?"

I shrugged. "Don't know. Beyond our pay grade, Sid. We've got enough of a problem here."

"Wales and the southwest of England have ties that are closer than most of the rest of the country."

"I know, but we can't lose focus. Not now."

Megan rose and began collecting our plates. "I'm going to do the washing up and crash. If it's okay to stay?" she asked me.

I tilted my head back, and she kissed me. "Always good," I told her with a smile.

As she walked away, Sid watched her. The moment she stepped into the kitchen, he said, "We have a different kind of problem."

"What?" I asked.

"You were right. There is spyware on Megan's phone. Someone is watching her movements."

"Someone?" Rage flashed through me. Hot and enduring. I needed a direction for it.

"I can't trace the person responsible. It's sophisticated software."

"I can make an educated guess."

Sid frowned. "Guessing isn't a good idea, Griffin. We need proof. She needs proof. I'll keep digging. I haven't had time to tackle his phone today, but I will."

"I'm going to—"

"No, Griffin, you aren't," Sid said. "I'm serious, mate. You can't do anything. She'd be furious. Sanchez wouldn't throw the book at you, she'd force you to eat the damned thing. As a serving member of the British military, you cannot act without thinking first. Especially in a domestic case like this. Promise me."

I glowered at him, but Sid just sat back and crossed his arms, staring me down. He was right. If I did anything to Adrian *bloody* Hess, I'd be hauled over the coals by every department possible. The Police Service, CPS, DoPI, the Royal Marines, and the Navy. They'd all have their slice of my hide.

Which made me think of Wesson's skin. I suppressed a shudder.

"Fine, I promise."

He laughed. "You sound like a five-year-old."

"I feel like one. I'm going to help Megan. If you spark up out here, remember our bedroom window is open."

Sid waved a hand in understanding. I carried the left-overs back to the kitchen and helped dry the dishes.

It took us – well Sid – two days to find evidence of Naomi Moore. It had been almost a week since our visit to Bishop Chadwick. During those days we'd filed reports, gathered more intel about Wesson, studied his notebooks, made notes of our own, and generally climbed the walls waiting for action. We found no clues about who or what had killed Wesson. After speaking with the archbishop, Bishop Chadwick requested another meeting, so Megan and I endured the traffic up to Truro. We ended up having a lovely afternoon, wandering around the cathedral with the deacon, Jayne Archer. She gave me reams of details about the history of the building and surrounding area. We also went up to Kenwyn Church in the north of Truro, for a short time the Bishop's Seat in the county. It was a pretty parish church, with the usual ancient origins, and rebuilds. Its tower was a sturdy square of stone with crenellations. The stained-glass made colour splash on the flagstones as we walked down the aisle, and the cool interior was a welcome relief from the heat.

From its view above Truro we could see the cathedral. The graveyard was a mass of old trees. It also had a holy well, just like the one in Madron, on the site, but access was no longer safe. Which was a shame. Parish churches always gave me comfort. Their solidness and traditions in the modern world never failed to calm my racing thoughts and they quietened the sadness inside me. This time, it also pushed back the dark. The looming threat over us didn't ease for a moment, but the church made it easier to bear.

By the time Sid finally said: "I have her!" It was 11:34 on the tenth of August. We had five days before the Assumption of Mary. It didn't feel like enough.

"Thank God," Megan gasped from her desk. "Where?"

I chuckled. "Good to know I'm necessary in this process."

She poked her tongue out. "I'm the sergeant."

"Thanks for that reminder," I shot back.

"I'm a bloody genius," Sid murmured as he leaned into his screens. We came up behind him. He pointed to a grainy image from a shop. A small shop.

I squinted. "Is that her?"

"According to the software."

"How can it tell?" Megan asked, peering even closer.

"It monitors what it learnt from the social media feeds before her disappearance, and compares things we can't change about ourselves to this footage."

"Scary," she mumbled. "Where?"

"This is a small shop in a place called St Just. It's the Co-Op's CCTV. They've just had it updated, and it's on the cloud, rather than a hard drive that rewrites and is essentially air gaped."

I looked down at him. "Why do we know this?"

"I read the emails."

"Of course you did," I said with a sigh. I looked at Megan. "We go, we find her."

She nodded and moved towards the bike's gear.

"Well done, mate." I gripped his shoulder.

"Just remember, this woman is paranoid, or we'd have records of her child at a doctor's, or school, or something. Be careful."

"Roger that."

We'd have to go down to Penzance, but rather than take the A30, we chose the old B3280. On a hot day in August, it would be faster. We'd do some shimming to go around the city rather than through it, pick up the road to Madron, of all places, then head out on the A3071, an awesome piece of road. The views were amazing, despite the drought forcing the grass and bracken to brown far too soon. The road took us past old tin mines and abandoned houses, over moorland and down towards the coast. By the time we reached St Just, it was almost lunchtime, and in the centre of the tiny town, we found two hotels offering food, some cafés and a few bakeries. The town itself wasn't overly burdened with tourists.

"I love it down here," Megan said. "There's something very old-fashioned about St Just."

We'd parked the bike in the large central area, Market Square, and I guessed, back in the day, it was where the farmers would gather with their animals and produce…

"Griffin, are you daydreaming?" Megan asked, poking me in the back.

"Sorry. I was just thinking about how ancient this marketplace must be."

She smiled indulgently but pulled me towards the Co-Operative supermarket. If something that small could be called super anything. We walked in, Megan flashed her police ID at the earnest youth on the till.

"Can I speak with you for a moment?" she asked with a reassuring smile.

The young man coloured pink. "This is my first day. Please don't get me into trouble."

Megan chuckled. "You'll be fine, but could I speak with the manager, or a senior staff member? We're looking for someone who needs our help. It's nothing terrible." As always, her soft management worked.

Within minutes, we had all three staff members looking Sid's aged-up images that he'd created from Naomi Moore's social media feeds. They argued among themselves for a bit before the oldest member of staff, who wore the whites of a butcher, said, "That's gotta be Naomi. She'll be livin' in Grumbla. Off grid. She's a good girl." He scowled at us. "You's sayin' she needs 'elp?"

Megan nodded. "I promise you. She isn't in trouble. We just need to know where she is, and to make sure she's safe."

The big man, with forearms so thick I really didn't want to piss him off, especially if he held a meat cleaver, said, "I lives down that way. Given her a lift a time or two. Her and the boy, they're good people."

"I understand, Mr?" Megan asked.

"Never you mind that," said the man. "What I will tell you is this, she'd be livin' on Glendower land. Grumbla Farm. That's right down in the hollows."

"Thank you. I really mean that," Megan said.

He harrumphed. "Well, just you take care. Glendower

don't welcome outsiders. Or incomers." The man eyed me, turned his back and walked away.

The manager of the shop begged our forgiveness for his staff member's rudeness, and we made all the right noises to reassure the fussy woman, before leaving.

The ride down to Grumbla was like stepping back several centuries. It seemed no one knew about the place. A few houses formed a small hamlet with a handful of farms scattered over fields and moorland. Moss grew in the middle of the narrow lanes, and trees formed a long bower over our heads. The light danced, dodging the shade formed by the canopy of beech leaves, and the hills rose around us as the lane sank into the earth. This was a place of mystery and myth. It was one of those odd little hamlets that still existed in Britain, which made you think of witches and tribes.

I grinned like a child the entire ride down into the dingly dell.

Eventually, after a few passes through the tiny village, we saw a battered, faded sign that pointed to Grumbla Farm. The path was deeply rutted from tractors and cattle. I wasn't going to risk the bike, so we parked, left our gear, and walked towards a grey stone farmhouse.

"Have you been here before?" I asked Megan.

"Never. Though Dad reckons anyone who lives down this way is a bit… I believe his word was touched."

I laughed. "It's a bloody strange place, though I can't put my finger on why."

"Close to the edge of the world, and there's no tin down here. It's been a lonely place for centuries." She sounded genuinely disturbed. "Let me do the talking."

"I wouldn't have it any other way."

The fat front of the farmhouse, with its hard grey

colouring, didn't invite approach. No flowers or bushes softened its appearance, and the paint on the windows was peeling. The door itself was navy blue, and I doubted it had seen a lick of paint in my lifetime. The knocker, handle and letterbox might once have been someone's sparkling pride, but now, they were dim and no amount of cleaning would bring the brass back to its former glory.

Megan didn't use the knocker; she rapped with her knuckles.

"What you want?" came a surly voice from behind, startling the pair of us.

"Mr Glendower?" asked Megan, stepping around me.

A small man, who seemed to be mostly made up of tweed and hedgerows, glared at me. He didn't stand straight; his wellington boots were folded down at the tops and swung around his legs. Grey hair sprouted like a mushroom's roots from places on the human face I'd never seen hair sprout before. An old flat cap kept some of it under control. He had a roll-up hanging from his bottom lip.

"Who are you? What you doin' on my land?" he asked.

Megan's accent thickened. "My name's Ackley. Megan Ackley. I'm with the police up in Redruth."

He sniffed, hawked and spat. I tried to remain expressionless, but obviously failed because the old man grinned at me, showing large yellow teeth. They belonged to an ogre, not a dwarf.

"What's you want with me? 'Ruth is miles away."

I had the feeling he didn't leave the valley very often, and it crossed my mind he might never have made it that far up the spine of Cornwall. Never mind out of the county.

Wow, judgmental or what? For all you know, the bloke used to be in the merchant navy and has been to more places than you.

Yeah, and maybe not.

"We need your help, sir," Megan admitted.

"How's I help the police? And I don't know his name." He pointed a finger at me. It wasn't straight, just like the rest of him.

"This is Griffin Woodbury. He's with Rural Security. We work as a team."

"I gets that, girl, but what's he gotta do with me?"

I didn't want to open my mouth. He'd hear my Englishness and dismiss me completely.

"Sir—" Megan began.

The man's deep-set eyes darted to her in obvious irritation. "I'm sure he can speak for hisself, girl."

"Mr Glendower," I said, stepping forward. "We mean no harm to you, or anyone else. We really are here to help someone. The trouble is, they don't know that they need help. We're concerned."

"You's from upcountry."

"I'm from everywhere, sir. I used to be a Royal Marine. As are my family."

"Army brat, huh?"

Well, no, but yes, it would do. Sometimes, explaining the difference just wore me out, and it wasn't important.

"What's it you want, 'ere?" He shook a finger at us. "And I'll knows if you lies to me. I don't trust none of you lot." Here he pointed to Megan. "Not sure about yous, but my uncle was a Marine. Served in the war."

I guessed he meant World War II. "Where did he serve?" I asked.

"Sicily and Normandy."

That meant he'd served with the new regiment that became the SAS. "Then I'll have seen his name on the walls in our mess hall," I said. "Those men were a cut high above the average. It's always been an honour to serve in their regiments." Which it was, because I respected the history, I just hadn't wanted to be part of it. Still didn't.

He sniffed. "What's you doin' 'ere?"

Megan stepped back, and I came forward. "We're looking for someone who might be in trouble. She needs help, and that's where we come in."

The old man narrowed his lips, the ciggie almost vanishing into his mouth. "I don't knows of no girl."

"Please, Mr Glendower, we need to talk to her. Just talk. No one knows we're here. It's not on any official paperwork." I wasn't about to explain how Sid found her; it wouldn't help.

He sniffed again, but didn't spit, thank goodness.

"Let me call her, see if she wants to speak to you." His clearest sentence yet.

Rather than a mobile phone, he removed a two-way radio, and stomped off to make his call. We were not going to be invited into his home. My stomach reminded me it wanted lunch, preferably in one of the pubs we'd seen in St Just.

Megan checked her phone. "No service."

"I doubt they have the internet." I looked up at the farmhouse and saw a small satellite dish. Huh, I was wrong, they had some technology in there.

"A quiet life."

"Hmm. Certainly isolated. Naomi Moore really doesn't want to be found."

Glendower returned. "She'll come 'ere. You can wait in the lane." He stomped past us, opened his front door, and vanished into the black beyond.

Megan chuckled. "Is it wrong I find him really sweet?"

"Probably. Come on. I've water in the panniers."

"Good. I'm parched," Megan said.

We returned to the bike and waited. It wasn't long, and certainly not arduous under the canopy of trees keeping the air bearable. Though, we saw the signs of heat stress everywhere. What should have been plush summer grasslands, ripe for cattle and sheep, looked weary and spent. The trees were dropping their leaves. When I thought back to the spring, and how vivid the world looked in its new mantle, I could hardly believe it was the same year. In just a few months, Cornwall had dried out. Being stuck out into the sea as it was, I doubted droughts hit the peninsular often. It would be a hard year for farmers, and I wondered if rising sea temperatures would affect the fishing industry that hung on grimly in the area.

Chapter Eleven

While I was pondering the fate of British industries, Megan was pacing up and down the lane, silent but definitely prowling. It did occur to me that this might be the time to talk about Adrian *bloody* Hess and her phone, but if Naomi turned up in the middle of the conversation—

"Ah," Megan said. "Here she comes."

I turned to face up the lane and squinted. The trees overhead fluttered, moving the light back and forth over a slim woman of average height. She almost dissolved between the flashes of sunny fingers, as if she were made of the shadows, tree bark and grass.

She stood watching us, out of arm's reach for long moments. "What do you want?" she called.

Still in the shadows, I had a hard time making out her features, but sharp angles and hard brown eyes came to mind.

Megan stepped forward; Naomi stepped back. Megan stopped and held her hands up. She said, "I'm Sergeant

Ackley, Megan. This is Griffin Woodbury, from Rural Security. I have ID here if—"

"What do you want?" Naomi asked, emphasising each word. She eyed me, much like Glendower had only moments before. I had the feeling that mentioning I was a Marine wouldn't work. Her accent certainly surprised me. No sign of Cornish, only educated English.

"We're here because we're concerned for your safety, Naomi," Megan said.

"So am I now you've turned up," she snapped.

This defensiveness wouldn't help. We needed a more straightforward approach. "Naomi," I said, straightening to my full height. "You and your son need us. Someone is hunting you, we are hunting them. We're here to warn you and to help if we can. Your son is in danger, and I believe you know that."

Megan glared at me. "Really?"

"Well, she wasn't going to listen to us," I said to Megan with a shrug.

We both turned to look at Naomi.

"Fuck," she said. Her fingers went to the long, fairly straggly brown hair. "Fuck. You know? How do you know? Since when are the police interested in something—" She shook her head. "You know what? It doesn't matter. We have to move. Thanks for the heads-up, but if you've found me, then they will, and that's just… Oh, God." She suddenly leaned over, hands on her knees, breath rattling through her small chest.

Megan rushed to her side. "Water, Griffin."

I scrambled for another bottle.

"Just breathe. Slow it down. You aren't alone." Megan repeated this while drawing large circles on the other woman's back. I handed her the water. It took a handful of minutes, but Naomi calmed and Megan sat her on the lane's tarmacked surface. It wasn't like it was busy.

"Where is your son?" Megan asked.

"With Reggie," Naomi whispered. I guessed she meant Glendower.

"That's good. It'll give us time to talk," Megan said, settling down in the road as well. I joined them.

Naomi looked at us, and I realised tears stood proud in her eyes. "I've been in fear of this moment for so long, it's almost a relief to have it happen." She clutched Megan's hand. "You really are here to help? You won't take my boy?"

"I've no intention of taking your son," Megan said. "Why don't you let us explain who we are and what's happened? It'll help."

Naomi nodded.

Something about this felt too easy. I'd expected more lioness, less beseeching rabbit.

Megan explained that Rural Security often worked with different organisations, including the Church of England and the Police Service. Then she explained about Wesson's invasion into the life of Truro Cathedral's staff. Next came Wesson's death and our subsequent understanding of his mission.

"We know your son is one of four born on the same day, at the same time, in the same location," Megan said.

Naomi nodded. "I've always been into the alternative scene. I borrowed the money from Mummy to pay for the IVF. I wanted a baby, but I'm gay. It felt like the right thing to do, and the clinic didn't need me to be married. When I had Matty, it felt great, despite having a hospital birth due to complications. I had his astrology chart done because I wanted to understand how to guide his path through life. It's a mother's job."

You're right, this is too easy. Get ready for her to bolt.

We were gathering too much information. This woman was wily. She'd managed to hide from everyone, including the Department of Education, for years. Why surrender now?

Megan prompted, "And that's why you ran? Because of the birth chart?"

Tears came. "Yes, it was terrible. The woman who did it almost refused to give it to me. It talks about demons and a battle with angels, and it's just… It's horrid."

I left Megan to do the comforting thing. Rising off the ground, I looked around, and that's when I saw it.

"Shit, Megan," I said. "We have a problem."

Glendower was hustling a small boy into a battered Toyota Hilux, while trying to lift two large rucksacks into the flatbed of the truck. A pair of small terriers were racing around at the boy's feet.

Megan rose and jogged over. "Bloody hell."

By the time we both turned back to the woman, she was sprinting up the lane.

"They'll have another exit," I pointed out.

"I'll go after her," Megan said. "You deal with him."

"Great, I get the dogs," I said as she began to run after Naomi.

"Seriously? They're terriers," Megan called back.

I huffed. "They still bite." The run up the lane towards the farmhouse gave Glendower just enough time to start his engine and pull away. My speed increased. Just as he changed from first gear to second, I put my hand on the back of the truck and half pulled, half leapt into the back.

Landing with a thud, I set the dogs off, who were inside the cab, and I banged on the glass.

"Pull over, you damned fool, or I'm going to have to shoot your tyres," I shouted over the roar of the engine. I wasn't armed, this was Cornwall, but he didn't know that. "Seriously, don't make me hurt you, or the boy."

The truck made it into third gear.

"For fuck's sake," I muttered. Clinging onto the back as it bounced up a rutted track away from the lane, I fished around in the pockets of my combat trousers and found a little something I'd taken to carrying with me everywhere. A kubatan. They are nothing more than a keyring in most of their disguises. Just a simple shaft of stainless steel, only a hand span long, with shallow grooves in it to help control a potential opponent's pressure points. Some have very complex designs, but like all things, simple is best. They're a bit more legal than knuckle dusters, but it all depends on their use.

In this case, I began rapping on the glass separating the cabin from the flatbed. The sound made the dogs frantic. "You've ten seconds to stop, Glendower, before I start shooting," I yelled. The smell of the old diesel engine filled my head and made me cough. "We have the boy's mother!"

That made the brakes come on hard.

"Shit," I coughed as I smacked into the Hilux's roof and my diaphragm over-reacted. Irritated now, I jumped down and yanked open the driver's door. The dogs flew over Glendower's small lap and straight at me. Lifting my arms, I readied myself for war with them, until I realised they'd gone past me and hurtled off into the field.

"Bloody useless animals," Glendower muttered, glaring at them as their white coats became invisible in the long grass. The farmer's face was a mask of stubborn anger.

I glanced over him to the boy. He sat wide-eyed and fearful in the passenger seat. I noted the seatbelt. It made me smile.

"Come on, get out," I ordered.

"Thought you had a gun," Glendower growled.

"This is England, not New York, you damned fool." I reached into the truck and removed the keys, just in case. "Come on, out."

In the heat of the midday sun, I forced Glendower out of the truck. "Stay there. I'm going to get Matthew out. Do anything stupid, and I'll show you how fucking tough the Royal Marines make their Commandos these days."

The old farmer stood beside his truck. I felt like I'd just threatened a brownie with a good stomping.

"Hey, Matthew, I'm Griffin. I'm here to help you and your mum. We don't mean any harm. Everyone is trying to protect you." I managed a smile for him. The lad was skinny, but clean, with a tangle of white-blond hair and, unlike his mother, big blue eyes.

"Is Mum okay?" he asked, his voice trembling.

"Mum's fine. She's with my friend, Megan. I'm afraid she over-reacted."

He looked down at his lap. "Yeah, she does that quite a lot."

This made me laugh. "Are you okay to come back to the farmhouse?"

The lad nodded. "It's hot in here, the heater blows even in the summer. Reggie says it's fucked, cos it's old, like him."

From outside, I heard, "Don't go usin' language like that, boy. Whats I told you?"

Pure mischief transformed Matthew's face, and he grinned at me. I chuckled and popped the lad's seatbelt.

"Come on, out you get. We'll be walking home. Can you call the dogs back?"

The boy nodded. "I'm good with the animals. Are you a policeman?"

"It's police officer, and no, I'm not, but my friend is. She's not in uniform today, but I'm sure she'll show you her badge."

The boy scrambled out of the truck and began peppering me with questions. By the time we reached the farmhouse, he had more information about my life than any database anywhere in the world.

"So there really are real pirates?" he asked again. The terriers bounced along beside him.

"Yep, and they're proper scary."

We saw Megan, who had hold of Naomi's arm in a none too friendly grip.

The lad looked up at me. "Can I go to Mum?"

"Of course you can," I said. He sprinted off with all the speed of a nine-year-old.

"Wish I could move like that," grumbled Glendower.

"You and me both," I said.

When Megan saw us and Matthew in particular, she released Naomi's arm. The woman ran to her son and pulled him close. He began babbling to her about my fight with the pirates. He made it sound like I'd managed to battle them off single-handedly.

Megan guided Naomi back to the farmhouse, and they walked through the back door. Glendower scowled and said, "I grow weed. She gonna make that a problem?" He nodded savagely in Megan's direction.

"Is it for personal use?" I asked.

He cocked his head. "Aye."

I didn't believe him. "Then I expect it'll be fine. Just

don't mention it. Provided she can't see it, you won't have a problem."

He sniffed and stomped into his home. I followed into the dark interior.

Inside the place was old, and tatty, but clean. I had the feeling that was more to do with Naomi than Glendower. He paced over to the ancient Aga, leaned against it and crossed his arms over his chest. The mighty beast of a cooker gave off no heat, which made the kitchen cool and soothing. I blinked several times, trying to adjust to the dimness. A worn but loved farmhouse table dominated the middle of the large room. An ancient Welsh dresser, which wouldn't fit in any modern home, looked small against the far wall. The crockery on it might be antiques by now, the heavy earthenware familiar, but I wasn't an expert.

The kitchen units were all old, traditional, with handles worn dark from decades of use, all slightly different colours depending on what lived behind them and how often they were opened. The paintwork would be classified as 'distressed' in a designer kitchen. In this one, it just added to the rural charm. Or lack there of.

Naomi went to a small gas hob and put a kettle on the stove. "We only have builder's tea."

Megan and I shared a look and a shrug. "Fine," she said.

While Naomi clanged about, the mugs hitting the old tiled surface of the kitchen units harder than necessary, silence filled the room. The boy watched all the adults with a mixture of worry and curiosity. He knew he was the reason for all this odd behaviour, but he couldn't quite figure out the dynamics. He wasn't the only one.

When the kettle boiled, Naomi filled four mugs and battered the teabags into submission. The young lad and the old man exchanged glances and pulled their 'Uh-ho' faces. Even the terriers were quiet, curled up in their old beds.

"Coming here just draws attention to us," Naomi finally said.

"They already know you're in Cornwall," Megan pointed out. "Wesson was close to finding you."

"He might not have managed it before the fifteenth," she snapped.

I pulled out a chair and sat, hoping to reduce tension by not towering over the other occupants. "Are you willing to guarantee that, Naomi?" I said, keeping my voice soft and intense. "We saw what this person is capable of, that's why we had to track you down. You see, we discovered something else, something we haven't shared." I glanced down at the boy, who sat with the dogs. "It might be wise to talk alone."

"It's Matty's life, he gets a say in it," Naomi stated.

"Alright," I said, not surprised by her decision. Matty's excitement fairly leaked over the floor like a puppy in a ball pool.

Gathering my thoughts, I said, "We've discovered there were three other women in the maternity ward that night. Another boy was born, and two girls. They all used your IVF clinic. They might've used the same donor, we're trying to track that down right now. Sadly, all three children were snatched at various points, and never found. After it became clear their babies weren't coming home, two of the mothers died, one has been sectioned."

"Bugger me," Glendower murmured. "That's bad, that is." He turned worried eyes to Naomi.

Naomi tried to remain emotionless, but I saw the fear

lurking in those big brown eyes. "You haven't found them? The kids, I mean."

Megan said, "To be honest, we haven't looked. Our job is to keep you and Matty safe."

"We've been safe here for years," she said. "When I saw the conjunction in the planets—"

I held up a hand and stopped her. "Look, personally, I don't believe in astrology. However, someone involved in all this does. So, we need to take it seriously. I don't need the details."

"What you proposin'?" Glendower asked. "Nao is right, she and the lad have been safe 'ere for years."

"We can't protect her here. Too many variables. There are multiple ingress points onto your land. You need to be somewhere I can control." I glanced at Megan. "We can control. Somewhere closer to a police station. Personally, I'd cart you off to London and lock you up until the sixteenth, but my team is dealing with something else right now." Though, DoPI's building in the capital was covered in wards that the public couldn't see, so it was an option even if we were shorthanded.

"I'm not leaving the farm," Naomi said.

"No, neither am I," stated Matty from the ground.

The old man shrugged. "It's their home. We've been warned and can take precautions if you 'splain 'em. Whats you think gonna 'appen?"

I stared into Naomi's eyes as I said, "A demon will come. It will attack the adults in the house. It will take Matty."

Silence.

Chapter Twelve

Naomi refused to move. Knowing I couldn't drag her out of the place without a fight, I opted for the next best thing. Education. It took me most of the afternoon to help protect the farmhouse. We salted the doors and windows, and I explained repeatedly that if the dogs broke the salt line as they came in and out, it had to be repaired. Then I had Naomi and Matty make pentagrams, and I drew sigils on their doors as well. I feared none of it would be enough. The thing I'd felt taking Wesson's life was evil incarnate. I'd met evil men, those that enjoy the pain and grief of innocent people, but that *thing* was something else. Its evil was its existence. The way air contained oxygen. It was a strange concept to grasp.

Leaving them felt wrong, but what choice did I have? They didn't want us there, drawing attention, and we couldn't force the issue.

By the time we left Grumbla, we were both tired.

I rode slowly eastward, and Megan leaned into my back, her visor up. "What's next?" She sounded as worried as I was about the gathering events. Whether one believes in demons or not, an elderly farmer, a woman and a child were being threatened by someone who very much did believe in them.

"I think we need to go back to that damned caravan and try to unearth something we haven't yet found." We'd been in touch with Sid during the afternoon, and he hadn't discovered anything which would lead us to the person responsible for Wesson's death. "There's going to be a person at the end of this, there has to be," I said. "Demons can't act without human intervention."

Megan groaned. "I knew you'd say that."

It took us over an hour to reach Truro, and rather than go straight to the caravan, we stopped at the café we'd used earlier in the week and indulged once again.

"What kind of information am I looking for at Wesson's place?" Megan asked. "All the hocus-pocus in there doesn't help me understand what's important."

I'd been pondering this for a while. "We're looking for anything he didn't have on his laptop or in the notebooks."

Megan nodded, knowing I was thinking about our course of action rather than stating the blindingly bloody obvious.

"Where would he keep that information if not in those two places?" she asked.

"That's the thing, isn't it? We just don't know."

Megan frowned while tackling her falafel. "What if we come at this another way? What does the person want to achieve by using this conjunction of the planets on the Assumption of Mary?"

I grinned. "The weird has got to you."

She nodded. "Yeah, okay, I'm in the boat without a

paddle and the river is full of weird. Now, answer the question." She tapped my plate with her fork.

"Wesson thought someone at the cathedral was going to use children in a dark ceremony. That's why he was tracking different individuals. There cannot be another reason. If everyone there is innocent of kidnapping small children, then he made mistakes."

"Okay. I'll bite that one."

"Wesson believed the cathedral was under attack. He kept trying to ward it, protect the bits that are truly sacred."

Megan leaned back in her chair, her hands going to her face. "Oh my God, I know what's happening."

I frowned. "What…"

"It's the children. The Virgin Mary. Motherhood. This is about children and motherhood. That's why Wesson couldn't see the big picture, and we're taking our leads from him, rather than our instincts. Our knowledge." She leaned forward, her eyes bright. "Oh, I love this bit. Seeing the picture. Mary is the mother of Jesus. People prayed to her in that cathedral and the original parish church for centuries. It's dedicated to her, so she'll intervene on their behalf with the Father, the Son and the Holy Spirit. That's right, yeah?"

I nodded, frowning, still not with the programme. "Well, yeah, but it's Anglican. So intervention from saints or Mary isn't really done."

Megan shook her head. " Doesn't matter. Not for our perp. We saw the side chapel thingy dedicated to the Virgin Mary." She rushed on, "Four children are under threat. Whoever is doing this is using them to bargain with the concept of Mary as a lesser deity. I don't think the children are dead. I think they've been hidden somewhere, and I think the person responsible is a mother. Or was a mother.

She's asking for a mother's help. What do we know about the Church of England and motherhood?"

"I'm hardly an expert—"

"I've been following it in the news over the years," Megan said. "The Church of England wasn't that much better than the Catholics over in Ireland. Though there's no mention of the mass graves and the Magdalene Laundries in the UK, women were separated from their babies right up into the 1970s."

"That could include my mother," I whispered. "She might never have known her real mother. That's why she was put up for adoption."

Megan's colour drained from her face. "Oh, yes, it could… I'm sorry."

Shaking my head. "Don't. We have to stay focused. Just file it away for later."

"Okay." She sounded less enthused about her idea. I loved her for that.

Placing her palms flat on the surface of the table, she said, "Whoever is doing this is using children to call on Mary during her special day and the alignment of the planets. Though how Christianity and astrology can mix like that, I don't know."

"Wise men followed a star," I muttered.

"These people have too much time in their lives," she said, shaking her head. "Anyway, if she lost a child to one of these institutional adoption programmes, maybe she wants to…" Megan frowned, testing her thoughts.

"She wants to destroy the institution," I stated. "Whoever this is, she wants the Church of England destroyed. Why summon demons otherwise? Why spend all that time and money creating children who are the perfect vessels for reaching out to Christ's mother?"

"That's how we find her," Megan said. "We track the money. First, we check the caravan again, because we now know what we're looking for, but after that, we start tracking the money. Who set up that IVF clinic and when."

I grinned at her. "You're quite good at this."

"It's the only thing that makes sense. There couldn't be another reason to use single women to create these four children specifically."

She was right. I'd been looking at it from a man's point of view. Thinking it had to be about power, money, influence, but if I saw the crime through a mother's eyes, then it was completely different, and potentially, much sadder.

We finished eating in a rush and sadly decided not to indulge in more chocolate cake. Climbing back onto Quacker, we rode down to the viaduct. Having parked in the car park, we walked back to the caravan with renewed purpose. A police cordon remained, but no one was there.

Megan frowned. "There should be someone here until we take the caravan for final processing, but we don't have the manpower. I guess they're trusting in the good sense of the public."

"Never a wise choice," I said, following her up the path.

We reached the caravan as the long afternoon turned to evening. The tree canopy and the viaduct did a good job of cutting off natural light, so as we entered the small, foul-smelling environment Wesson called home, we used our phone torches to help and his camping lights. Unable to cope with the smells, Megan opened the small windows, and we began going through the place once again. Every book was upended. Every photo was removed from the wall and checked front and back. Next came the newspaper clippings. We put them all into plastic bags we found under the tiny sink.

Our focus remained on digging through Wesson's version of an archive.

Having spent the last ten minutes pulling things out of the cupboards near the floor, I stood and straightened my back with a groan.

"You're getting old," Megan teased.

"I'm getting more than…" I peered out of the window. "What the hell is that?" A flickering light and a shadow appeared in the gloom outside. Someone was holding something that looked like fire. The image confused my senses for long seconds before dawning horror had me reaching for Megan.

The sound of smashing glass and the *whoof* of greedy fire filled the small interior, right where Megan had stood moments before. The door slammed shut, and I heard something heavy bang against it.

Inside the caravan, the heat and smoke quickly filled what little breathing space we had.

"Griffin!" Megan yelled.

"Window," I bellowed, emptying my lungs of clean air. When I next inhaled, smoke and fumes rushed in, and I started to cough.

Stupid, stupid, stupid.

Grabbing Wesson's blankets off the floor where we'd tossed them, I beat at the fire already crawling up the tinderbox walls of the van.

Megan wasted no time. She leapt onto the hard surface of the bed frame and began kicking at the largest window in the back, her t-shirt pulled up over her nose and mouth. "Fuck!" she bellowed, then she began to cough.

The fumes were toxic. My eyes smarted, and my lungs burned. Once that window fell out, the interior of the van would become the centre of a huge candle. Beating the flames wasn't working. I needed a new plan.

Turning my back on the fire, I took the two steps necessary to cover the distance between me and Megan. Wrapping my arms around her waist, I booted the window with all the training of a true Marine door-kicker. The window exploded. I threw Megan into the void.

Fire roared behind me, and I swan dived after her. She'd rolled away. I hit the ground and tumbled over my shoulder. Pain lashed up my right leg.

Looking down, I realised I'd brought the fire with me. Panic took hold. I beat at the flames encasing my leg, and agony flared over my naked arms. Then Megan threw herself at me and tumbled us through the dirt, smothering me with her own body, screaming and cursing and coughing. The flames died.

I pulled Megan close as the caravan flared and an explosion rent the air as the small camping gas stove and light Wesson used shot shrapnel into the night. Fire reached for the viaduct overhead, hands of flame scrabbling for a hold on the tree canopy and brickwork. We covered our faces, coughing, hiding from the intense heat. Just as quickly, the flare died. When I next looked the skeleton of the van shivered in the dancing light. Black and red. It happened in seconds, not minutes. The surrounding trees and underbrush spat and flashed as smaller flames broke out. The land was so damned dry. We needed help and fast.

"I didn't see how it started," she whispered.

I coughed as a slight breeze pushed the acrid smoke towards us again. "Petrol bomb."

"Jesus Christ, someone really wants to stop us," she muttered.

As the caravan's fire eased back just a little more, I

heard something. Turning, I saw a group of people on the footpath. They were celebrating. Three figures jumped around, whooping and cheering, the sounds they made barely human.

Rage took over. "You fucking little shits," I growled.

Megan twisted, already talking into her phone. I'd lost mine in the melee with the fire. "Go," she yelled at me.

I needed no more commands. Scrambling, I made it to my feet, and started to run. My lungs weren't that interested in co-operating. The group on the path—three of them—saw me coming, backlit by the dying fire. They turned away and began to run as well. They were fast, almost unnaturally so, and had more stamina than I'd expect among civilians. Through the darkness under the viaduct I raced, my targets clear ahead of me. The path was smooth after all the feet shuffling back and forth since Wesson's death. Some distant part of my mind asked me what the hell I thought I was doing.

You were on fire, dude!

Yeah, well, that was then, this was now, and I wanted some bloody answers. The three shadows hit the lane, and street lamps overtook the light of dusk. I soon realised I chased teenagers. They were howling and almost play fighting as they ran ahead. My long strides were covering the ground fast. From behind me, I heard a familiar sound. My beloved motorbike roared to life. Ahead, came the sound of sirens.

We pounded down Oak Lane. Traffic screamed to a halt as the pack of teenagers ran onto the busier Moresk Road. I followed. Within a few metres, they hit one of Truro's busy thoroughfares, St Clement Street. More traffic screamed to a halt, and I heard the crunch of metal smacking metal, making me wince. One car didn't stop, and I found myself jumping and sliding over the bonnet before I'd even thought about it.

From behind, I heard the bike. Megan was coming as backup.

The kids ran into the NCP car park. Six layers of cars and concrete to get lost in. Shit. Racing after them, the light inside better than outside, I saw the last of the three hit the open doors of the elevator. Redoubling my efforts, I ran for those doors.

With a sickening inevitability, they slid shut just as I reached them. I pounded on the surface.

"Griffin!" Megan yelled. She sat on my bike without her helmet, I might add, looking like a soot-covered goddess. I ran to the bike. She pushed herself back without a word, well aware I'd be the safer option while controlling the vehicle.

As I gunned the engine and turned the bike in a tight circle using my left leg as the centre point, Megan clung to my back.

"They've stopped at the top," she said, looking over her shoulder at the lift's notifications.

I roared off. Megan yelled instructions, and I raced up each ramp to the next floor. It did occur to me that the teenagers might've just set fire to the caravan for shits and giggles, but they'd have known we were in there. They'd shut the door and blocked it. Also, something about their yells and yips of excitement seemed off.

"Megan, I think those kids are in on this, maybe even controlled," I shouted as we leaned the bike into another corner.

"You think? I haven't seen a teenager able to run like that in years, and I've chased a lot of teenagers. We have to get to them. They'll have answers."

Determination had me squeeze more speed into the chase. We reached the top of the structure. I locked the back wheel and controlled the skid. Megan rose on the foot pegs to see clearly into the darkening dusk and over the parked vehicles.

"There," she said, pointing to the back end, nearest the cathedral. It was the only other building in the area that rose this high and then some. We found the three teenagers in the far back corner, as close to the cathedral building as possible.

Megan almost leapt off the back, just as my feet hit the ground to catch our balance.

"Wait! Stop! Police!"

I wondered briefly if that ever worked. Fortunately, I didn't have to bother warning them. The bike stand took her weight, and I ran towards the teenagers.

Then something terrible happened. A truly awful sight. It would haunt me forever.

The three teenagers — two lads and a girl, all in hoodies despite the weather, climbed onto the bonnet of a nearby Range Rover, then stepped up onto the wall surrounding the car park. They all turned their backs on the cathedral. Their trainers were bright white in the dim light this far from the street.

Each face looked at us. They were so young. No more than seventeen. Terror filled their eyes. The girl mouthed 'Help'.

Megan and I both screamed, "No!"

I lunged.

All three tumbled back without another word or even a sign they'd heard us.

Chapter Thirteen

The sound.

I'd never forget that sound. A wet thud. They didn't even scream on the short trip down.

I scrambled up the big SUV and leaned over the edge. Three bodies lay in a twisted heap. Megan went to do the same thing.

"No, Meg, don't." I pushed her down. "Don't."

The blood, the explosion. Six floors. Concrete. Tarmac. Shattered skulls. Twisted limbs. It's nothing like it is in the films. It is so much worse.

"Don't," I whispered. We clung to each other, breathing hard. My cheeks were wet. The shock of seeing those terror-filled eyes the split second before they fell, it rolled on an endless loop inside my head.

"They knew," Megan sobbed into my chest. "They fucking knew, but they couldn't stop."

"I know. I saw it." My voice was thick.

We both trembled from the comedown. Megan reached

for her phone again, pushing me away a little. "I have to do my job."

I left her to call it in. I couldn't help. Not this time. Instead, I replayed the last few minutes in my mind, looking for something, anything, that could give us a clue. Megan ended her call.

I said, "How'd you get Quacker to start?"

"Sid gave me a spare key he had made."

"What?" That caught me off guard.

"Well, he was worried about you. He knew I'd be able to ride her if something happened to you, but you'd never surrender a key without an argument. He does that, he circumvents people to get things done. Apparently, that's what annoys Sanchez the most."

I didn't know if I should be relieved or stompingly angry. After glancing at the piece of wall again, I decided on relieved. I didn't have the energy for angry.

"We should get down there. Form a cordon," Megan said, obviously in shock. Two people can't make a cordon and we had no police tape on us. She moved as if made of lead.

I nodded. The ride down took longer. The world zipped, then slowed, then zipped. I'd known this sensation to happen after a firefight. My body was trying to catch up with events my brain knew were over. It was shock.

We reached the ground level, and I rode down the outside of the large car park. Fortunately, it wasn't a public road, just a side one for commercial parking linked to the nearby shopping centre. No one had seen the kids hit the ground. The darkness hid them from the street. Small mercies for all involved. I stopped far enough back to prevent Megan from seeing the results.

She laid a hand on my shoulder. "I've seen dead kids before, Griffin."

"I know, but… Not with me. Not like this. This was DoPI work. It was my—"

"This wasn't your fault. Or mine."

Oh, I wish she hadn't said that. It brought with it such a wave of shame. Logically, I knew I couldn't have saved those kids. Whoever did this, had set those teenagers up a long time before we found them. Why use them like this? How did the sorcerer know they'd be needed? None of the last half-an-hour made any sense. It burned hard inside me.

"I need their phones," I said. "Stay here."

"Griffin, I really can't sanc—"

"I need their phones, Megan."

She stood in front of me. "No, Griffin. I'm not letting you interfere with due process. Seriously, I'll arrest you if I must, but Sid isn't having that information until we've done the right thing by the families. Give them some dignity. Please."

"If I don't get to their phones, more people could die." I pushed against her hands, almost unaware of my actions, just knowing I had to do something. I had to move this case forward right now. If I didn't achieve something from this horror story of an event, then what was the point of my being in this job? Finding the person, the woman, responsible for these deaths — that's all I cared about.

A small hand reached up for my jaw. "Griffin, look at me," Megan instructed.

I pointed to the crumbled bodies in the road. "I have to—"

"Griffin, please, look at me," she said again, her voice soft.

I glanced down into those big blue eyes I'd loved since I was a boy. "Meg, they died."

"I know, sweetheart."

"Children died." She wasn't the only one in shock.

"I know. I feel it too, but we have to respect their deaths. Let the professionals deal with their remains. Take a moment. Calm down. You need your burns seen to, and so do I."

"Calm down? We have to—"

"I know, Griffin. I know. But right now, we can't help anyone, and you are not going to raid their bodies for their phones."

I stared into her eyes.

The Marine in me wanted to shove her to one side and get on with the job. That was my training, years of it being drilled into me by my father and then the military. If you're going through hell, you just keep going. We were dealing with demons and a really fucking tight schedule. If these kids were murdered by the same person controlling the monster who'd torn Wesson's skin off his back, then I had to act fast. What would they do next? Were Matty and Naomi on this list for tonight?

The man inside me, the one I wanted to release from the prison he'd been forced into when his mother died, *that* man wanted to mourn the loss of three young people. He wanted to wrap his arms around the woman he loved, bury his face in her hair, and forget the pain in the world.

I made my decision. "I'm sorry, Megan. This is the job." We both knew she couldn't stop me moving towards the corpses. The look of betrayal in her eyes, the tears that suddenly and silently tipped over the edge to tumble down her freckled cheeks, was almost enough to hold me still.

Almost.

Pulling out a pair of disposable gloves from one of my many pockets, I reached the tallest of the male bodies. Swallowing down the bile, trying to ignore the smell and visuals of the surrounding area, I found enough clean tarmac to kneel and rifle through his clothing. His phone was in the front pocket of his tracksuit pants. I pulled it out. The screen was cracked, but not as smashed as the lad's bones. It lit up when I pressed the button. Glancing at the lad's face, I realised it wouldn't be able to unlock the phone. Nothing married up now the back of the skull looked like a spoon-tapped eggshell. Using the broken fingers was the easiest option.

The phone obliged when I realised he was a lefty, just like me. Breathing out slowly, I tapped in Sid's number, then hit the speaker option. I didn't want my ear or mouth close to the thing.

"Hello?" Sid said.

"It's me. I need you to hack this phone and anything else it might be connected to, and the accounts. Get in there, find a fucking link to Wesson's investigation."

"Erm… okay. What's happened?" Sid asked, his concern clear.

"Just do it. I'll explain when I get back." The screen flickered as it was raided.

Talking to Sid made the man inside me want to reach out for comfort. I put the phone back on the boy's chest. Dear God, my throat burned. Clenching my jaw so hard my teeth squeaked, I rose.

"I'm sorry this happened to you. I will end this," I murmured to the bodies.

Turning, I walked back up the narrow roadway. Megan had watched. As I approached, she didn't look at me. We both heard the sirens.

"I'm going back to the office. Are you coming with me?" I asked. We stood like a weird Janus statue. Her one way, me the other.

"No, I'll wait for the teams, try to explain what happened and why you aren't here." The accusations were clear in her voice. She thought my job was on this road, not in DoPI's secret office. My training told me otherwise.

"Will you come home?" I asked.

"I doubt it," she said. "I'll have one of the team drop me back at the flat. I'll have to talk to my inspector tomorrow. We can't just vanish this. The families will have to be notified, but I guess that's not a…" here she used air quotes and looked at me, "Rural Security job, is it?"

I found it almost impossible to meet her gaze.

Almost.

"It's not my job."

"Then you need to go," she said.

I gave a single nod and walked away.

Man versus Marine. The Marine won. He always did. Is that what made my father the man he was? Did the same thing happen to my brother? Was it just easier to deal with the world on those terms? It was simpler to be a Royal Marine than an average bloke in normal society, following indistinct codes of conduct for social cohesion. In the Armed Forces, the higher-ups deal with the grand concepts they tell us we fight to protect. We aren't trained to care about the individuals in the world. Caring hurt. Loving cost. Split loyalties caused confusion.

I reached Quacker and looked down at my hands. They were burned in the fire. I'd lost all the hair on my arms, and the pain in my right leg finally made itself known. The air made my ear sting, and something was wrong with my hair. Less than an hour ago, Megan and I were a single unit. A team. Now, I'd betrayed that, and I hadn't even said sorry.

The first police car turned up.

Who did I want to be? My father? My fists clenched, making the burns screech in protest.

An ambulance arrived, and the police officers left their vehicle.

I swung my leg over Quacker's seat, shoved my helmet on, making my eyes water from the pain, turned the key and rode away.

The entire journey back to Redruth I kept my brain in neutral regarding Megan. I had no idea how to fix it. With anyone else, I'd take it as a death knell and walk away. Doing that with Megan was not an option. I'd have to find a way to make it right. Whatever it took.

For now, I needed to focus on the job. That meant dealing with the consequences of the fire at Wesson's caravan.

When I reached the office and let myself in, the burns on my leg and arms became a real problem. It felt like someone had splashed cooking fat over me. My combats had saved my legs from the worst a fire can do, the thick cotton and pockets acting as a barrier rather than melting against my skin. Still, I had holes where the fire had nibbled its way down to flesh. My forearms were worse; the only place really unharmed was where the dryad had left her mark on my skin. That strange tattoo remained undamaged. The flames had also caught my face.

Sid looked up as I came through the final door.

"Bloody hell, what happened?" he asked, his eyes wide, mouth hanging open.

"Someone threw a petrol bomb at Wesson's caravan. It's been a long day. We found Naomi and Matty, the boy.

They're at a farm in a place called Grumbla." I moved to the kitchen and opened the fridge. We had a small freezer compartment, and I removed one of the muscle ice packs I kept in there for when I needed them.

"Grumbla? Are you taking the piss?" he asked.

"No. Then we went back to Wesson's. We needed a lead. We thought..." I took in a breath, the bodies and Megan's face flashing through my mind. The fire burned her golden hair.

No, that didn't happen. It's just the shock.

"The sorcerer bewitched some teenagers to lock us into the van and set it alight. At least I assume that's what happened, and they didn't do it just because they could. We escaped. I ran after them. We chased them up through the NCP car park. They threw themselves off the top. They died. I called you. Megan's still there, dealing with the fall-out. I'm here looking for answers."

Sid just sat at his desk looking at me. When he didn't say anything, I managed to glance at him. "What?" I snapped.

"You've lost a lot of your hair, mate," he said quietly. "Shall we see to your wounds first?"

"No. I need a sitrep. We have a job to do."

"Not at the expense—"

I slammed the flat of my hand against the surface of the kitchen unit holding the coffee machine. "I have a fucking job to do. Your job is to facilitate that." I glared at him. "I've already had to remind Megan, don't make me remind you."

His expression changed from one of concern to contempt. "I bet that hurt."

He had no idea. I pushed the ice pack into it.

Sid returned to his screens. "I'm still following a thread that I've found on three related phones in the immediate vicinity of the one you called me on. It's pulling me into a website that's hidden from the surface net. I've used a tor browser, and the site is dedicated to witchcraft. Not the Wicca kind. This is more like the Crowley kind, only he'd think twice about some of the shit on this site. It's serious. We'll need to remove it. Until then, I'm chasing down all the IP addresses that have made contact with it, then I'll have to narrow that down to Cornwall. It won't be easy, or quick. I suggest you go home and leave me to it." He didn't look at me while he spoke. "Don't worry. I'll make sure I do my job, Corporal."

Rarely had my rank been thrown at me with such contempt. Maybe my father could top it.

My father again. The benchmark of bad behaviour.

I didn't want to go home. The restlessness of post-action energy filled me. Right now, I could gnaw the plaster off the walls. The office phone rang on my desk.

Pacing over to it, I lifted the receiver. "Woodbury."

"One of the local officers recognised the kids." It was Megan. "You need to come up here. I'm heading over to the squat they've been using."

"On my way," I stated.

The moment stretched. Longer.

Megan huffed. "And I thought you'd be different. More fool me." She hung up.

Chapter Fourteen

I stared at the phone. Different? Different to what?

An image of Adrian *bloody* Hess gripping her arm floated through my head.

You need to apologise. She's the other half of the team, and you disregarded her direct order.

My shoulders deflated, and my spine collapsed. "I'm sorry, Sid."

"Sounds like you owe Megan the apology," he said, voice cold.

I dug deep to find the courage to look at him. "I do, but let's start small, and I'll build up to that one."

His eyes narrowed. "Don't push it, soldier boy."

For the first time in what felt like days, I smiled. It pulled or rather pushed, at the skin around my left cheek and ear. If he was calling me 'soldier boy', his hackles would settle, provided I didn't do anything stupid.

He made a shooing gesture. "Go on, off you fuck. Go be the dynamic duo."

I gave a single nod.

"Oh, and take this," Sid said, opening a desk drawer, reaching in and throwing something at me.

I caught the object. A new phone identical to my old one. "How did you know?"

"Doh, why would you be calling me on a suspect's phone if you still had yours? Don't worry," he said with a martyred sigh, "I cloned your SIM. It's exactly the same as the old one. I've had it for weeks. It'll update the moment you switch it on."

I looked at the phone and looked at Sid. "Thank you." The depth of the thanks made his colour deepen. With a grunt, he turned back to his screens.

I let myself out of the office and rode up to Truro. This time, I didn't keep my brain in neutral with regard to my teammate, I spent the miles thinking through the problem I'd created. Megan wasn't just my girlfriend, she was my *friend*. Probably the closest I'd ever had and my colleague. I'd disrespected her. Being a woman in the Police Service had to be tough. I had little doubt she'd worked twice as hard to become a sergeant and had to work twice as hard to keep everyone's respect so she could do her job effectively.

If I'd been her direct subordinate, she'd have been right to have me disciplined. In the Marines, I'd never have disregarded an order from my sergeant. I had no right to do it to Megan. She'd been right. Watching those kids fall, hearing them die, it flipped a switch that closed me down and cut everyone out. It was the same switch I used when I needed to hunt and kill to protect a target or destroy an enemy.

I was not my father's son. I was better than that. More importantly, I *had* to be better than that, or she'd kick me to the kerb.

By the time I reached the car park, the ambulances had

gone, though the crime scene guys were back. Some press littered the pavement beyond the cordon, but Megan sat on a wall, under a street lamp, eating a large baguette. Another sat beside her with bottles of water and a first-aid kit.

By now, night held the small city in its grip, and on the whole, it was quiet. I climbed off the bike and approached Megan. She watched me, her expression careful.

"I'm sorry," I said. "That was close to unforgivable. I treated you badly in your professional and personal capacities."

Megan cocked her head. "Did you practice that for a long time?"

"Very long."

"Good. Eat your food, have some water. It's going to be a difficult night. You also need those burns to be cleaned, so you're going to stay still and let me tidy you up. Though I fear we'll be taking some clippers to those curls of yours."

"I'm forgiven?"

"Not entirely, but I know why you did what you did. Don't do it again, Griffin." She slipped off the wall and looked up at me. "I could do with a hug from my boyfriend now." Her eyes were too bright. "I watched them having to actually scrape the bodies off the ground."

I wrapped my arms around her, and for the first time I really considered the truly terrible deaths those youngsters had faced. "I'm sorry I left. I'm sorry I didn't listen," I murmured over the feeling of her hot body pressing into mine.

We clung to each other for a long time. The events at the caravan and car park slowly filtered through our minds to settle into the sludge of horrors we'd both witnessed over the years. I had no doubt we'd be sharing our nightmares.

It turned out that despite our emotions needing a bit of

a rest, our bodies needed fuel. My stomach suddenly issued a growl so loud it made Megan laugh. Still touching, we sat down and ate our sad picnic.

"My inspector isn't happy with you," she said.

"I'll call and apologise to him as well, if it'll help," I said around the cold bacon and avocado french stick sandwich, which to be fair, it was amazing.

"Don't, you'll only get an earful. He'll calm down. He's more worried that we have four deaths in Truro to deal with and no rational explanation for any of them. I'm hoping there won't be more."

I nodded. "It's not great. What does he think?"

"We're going with drug overdoses for the kids, which is likely. We found crack in a pocket belonging to the girl. What's even worse is that we found fentanyl in another pocket. You can't run like that on either drug, so maybe they were dealing rather than being high, but…"

"It could be a spell that kept them going?"

She shrugged. "What do I know? I did find this on one of them," she said, opening her hand.

A small leather pouch. I took it from her and wiggled the crude gardening string to open it up. Three small bones, a wedge of something sticky, and some pieces of parchment with tiny writing on it. I couldn't make out the words even under the streetlight.

"A hex bag," I said. "Or a jinx. It's a spell. One full of ill intent. We don't want this on us."

"We can't throw it away either," Megan said.

"Were there more? On the other bodies?" I asked.

She nodded. "They'll go into evidence. I shouldn't have taken this one, but it was too important for our investigation and I didn't want it being packed away in a box somewhere."

"Can you call our tame pathologist, Dennis Brew, and make sure he snaffles the other pouches and does the autopsies?"

"Already have," Megan said with a smile and a lift of her eyebrow. "I'm beginning to understand how DoPI works."

"Thank you."

"I also told him not to touch the bags if he can help it."

"Good plan."

"That blob of stuff smells like blood and animal fat."

"It probably is, with various herbs, and other stuff ground in. The bones are interesting."

"They're bird bones," she said.

I looked at her. "How'd you know that?"

"Because I have two older brothers who are gross, and we grew up on a farm."

That seemed fair. I pulled the hex bag closed. "This probably means the sorcerer always meant the kids to die. She might've told them these would help them fly or something."

"Seriously?"

"They lived in a squat and had fentanyl on them. Who knows how rational they were? I watched them run out into traffic without a moment's hesitation. They weren't long for this world. We'd never have stopped them."

Megan opened a family-sized packet of crisps. "That just makes me even sadder. My lot are having a fit at finding fentanyl in Truro. The county lines smuggling operation is getting so much worse down here. The team in Plymouth has been informed. It'll go up the chain. CID will be at the squat with forensics first thing. That's why I thought we should go in tonight. Look for anything DoPI related."

We sat and ate in silence for a while.

"Where is the squat?" I asked.

Megan looked at me. "I bet you can guess."

A warning pit opened in my stomach, and the sandwich teetered on the edge. "Kenwyn?"

"Gold star for the Royal Marine."

"Fuck."

Megan just sighed and handed me the bag of crisps.

We refuelled for another fifteen minutes, and Megan cleaned the worst of my burns. She'd been given the first-aid kit by a paramedic, who'd left her with salve as well. I owed the person responsible a bottle of something nice. The cooling effect made everything feel better, but the best part was Megan fussing over me. That felt better than anything else had all day.

We rode up to Kenwyn, and Megan guided me into Grenville Road. Nothing on the street screamed money. The first car my headlights picked out was at least twenty-five years old. The second was up on bricks. The houses were set back with front gardens steep enough to need crampons, and good luck if you were pushing a wheelchair. I certainly wouldn't want to carry shopping up from the car if I had a large family. This was the Cornish version of a tower block. We were miles from anywhere nice for kids.

Megan tapped my shoulder and indicated I should pull over. We rolled to a stop outside a house that had more in common with a zombie movie than a suburban love story. I glanced at the house next door in the mid-sixties terrace. It had flowers blooming and a neat lawn, despite the weather. I saw rain buckets under the guttering, and bird feeders hanging from small trees. The paintwork was clean, neat and maintained.

The house we were about to enter had turned into its

evil twin. One of the downstairs windows had a black plastic bag acting as a pane of glass. The wooden door had been replaced with metal, but that obviously wasn't the main entry point for the squatters.

"This way," Megan said. "I received the full report about this place from the officer who recognised the kids. He's called up here a couple of times a week, apparently."

She led me through a slalom of boxes filled with the empties no one wanted to leave out for the recycling, bin bags that probably gave the local foxes and cats heart disease, and her torch glinted off the needles attached to syringes. I'd seen some shitholes in my time in Africa, but nothing as bad as this. It was sad and a terrible image for Kenwyn. The other parts we'd seen had been perfectly lovely. Even the rest of this street was okay, poor maybe, but tidy. This place was a verruca, on a wart in an otherwise lovely Cornish parish.

Around the back, things were worse. Rubbish vanished into the darkness, and small eyes glittered as Megan's torch found them. The back door was also metal, but someone had helpfully built a stairway of uncemented bricks, up to a window. A large piece of wood was propped against it. The smell of the place was overwhelmingly bad.

"What is it about demon-related humans that makes cleanliness impossible?" I muttered, kicking aside a plastic container that held something unmentionable in the bottom. "Let me go first, Meg."

"I'm a smaller target, Griffin. Besides, it'll take you time to fit through that, I can scout it and make it safe while you're still trying to shove your shoulders through the hole."

She had a point.

"Do you know how many people live here?" I asked.

"The three kids plus two others. Of course we don't know if those two managed to make it back from the city centre okay either. They spend their days begging down there." She grunted as she lifted the plywood sheet out of the window and handed it back to me. I propped it on the ground. Or I tried to, the edge rested on various things that squished and crackled at the weight.

With some trepidation, I watched Megan slip into the dark interior, then followed her up and over. She was right, I didn't fit through the small window with any grace or ease. By the time I'd climbed in, I'd realised the smell in the squat was worse than outside. I gagged. The stench was all too familiar.

"Someone's died," I groaned.

Megan reached into a pocket and pulled out two face masks. "These might help. I was warned it would be bad, but nothing like this."

The smell of the dead is recognisable whether it's in Cornwall or the Sahel. The only difference is the threat level as you search for the body. That and the heat. Though this summer had turned the house and its foul contents into a giant petri dish of disease. Using Megan's police-issue torch, another borrow from her colleagues, we toured the small house.

The kitchen defied description. I'd cleaned out latrines that were less of a health hazard. Rat droppings littered pizza boxes and takeaway containers. One of the taps at the old sink had snapped off, which must've flooded the place at some point. It now had plastic bags stuffed down the remaining pipework. Not a single cupboard door sat straight on its hinges. The soles of my boots stuck to the floor with each step.

The living room and dining room had been knocked

through by someone who once cared for the property. In there we saw a sofa which had last lived its best life back at the turn of the millennium and now needed someone to put it out of its misery. The two armchairs felt the same but couldn't be bothered to make the statement. The walls were covered in graffiti, the carpet shredded from use, and probably a few fires from alcohol and drugs being abused in the same space.

I made Megan shine her torch on the walls for some time, in the hope we'd see something familiar, but it was just mindless, and foul scribbling.

Megan went up the stairs first. "I'm not going in the bathroom," she murmured through the mask.

"Not asking you to," I said. More graffiti dominated the remaining wallpaper. The stairs were missing their banister. Someone had probably used it in the fireplace at some point.

A hum reached our ears. Or maybe it should be more of a buzz.

"Oh, bollocks," Megan groaned. "This is going to be bad."

With nitrile gloves on, I reached for the doorknob of the front bedroom. In a house like this, it would be the largest. Megan reached out and stopped me from opening the door.

"This time we deal with the dead together, right?" she asked.

I nodded. "Promise." I turned the knob, a china one with a floral pattern under the grime.

The door swung open, silently.

We found the bodies. Megan and I just stood in the doorway and looked. Not from any reverence for the dead. More out of shock.

Large nails, not the kind they used in modern carpentry,

but the kind they built ships with centuries ago, were hammered into hands and legs, staking out two full-grown men. Both bodies were naked, except for the coating of flies and maggots. The two men were crown to crown; some part of my brain worked out it would be east to west. Their feet almost touched the walls. The graffiti in this room wasn't random scrawls. Surrounding each corpse were thick white circles in paint, and inside these circles were occult symbols. More had been painted with a careful hand on the bodies. Over the groin area, the forehead, the palms of the hands and I guessed the soles of the feet, though I wasn't going into the room to look. Not just yet.

Megan played her torch over the grizzly scene slowly, and it being night, the flies buzzed and lifted, but they were fat and lazy.

Each corpse had suffered more abuse. Throats were cut, ear to ear. Neat and tidy. Then someone had cut from the bottom of the sternum to the groin, pulling the skin apart and displaying the organs on the chests of the men, over more sigils of some kind.

I had never seen anything like it.

"Can't," Megan said, her voice strained, and she backed out of the doorway, taking the torch with her.

My phone began to buzz. For a disturbing moment, I thought the flies had started to feast on me. I pulled it out and followed Megan.

"Sid." I was taking shallow breaths through my mouth.

"I've had a call from the wicked witch. I've given her an update."

"I've two bodies. Who wins?" I asked, blinking back the tears caused by the smell.

"Shit, you do, man. What you got?"

"Ritual sacrifice in what was once a nice suburban

home. We've got to get a crew down here. CID is due in the morning. We can't leave it to the locals. There are occult symbols everywhere. Can you call the boss?"

"Sure."

I gave him the location. No way was I handing this over to Megan's colleagues.

Chapter Fifteen

We left the house. The DoPI cleanup crew would photograph the scene, collect evidence, identify the dead. There was nothing we could do in the house right now except pick up some nasty disease. As we walked down the steps outside, the neighbouring door opened.

"Excuse me, are you with them?" came a voice belonging to an old man.

We both turned, Megan's torch flashing up. The man raised an arm and blinked.

"Sorry, sir," Megan said. "My name is Sergeant Ackley. Can I help?" she asked.

"Oh, thank goodness," came a relieved puff of words. "Well, my dear, I hope so. There is a terrible smell coming from next door. We can't go on like this, my wife is ill."

As he talked, we walked towards him, careful of his flowerbeds. The poor man took in the state of me in particular and backed into his hall.

I held up a hand. "I'm sorry, we've been working a case

that involved a fire, and I happened to be caught on the wrong end of it. That's what led us here. Griffin Woodbury, sir, I'm with Rural Security. I have my ID." I began patting my bike's jacket. Had I lost that as well? Sanchez wouldn't be pleased.

Megan had already flashed her badge.

"Have you just come out of that house?" the man asked. He wore tartan slippers, a different tartan for his pyjamas, and a woollen housecoat, fortunately, not tartan. All this, despite the heat.

"Yes, sir," Megan said. "Do you know your neighbours?"

He sighed. "How much of the story do you need, officer?"

Megan and I shared a look. She said, "Everything you have."

"Then come in and have some tea. I know it's late, but I've just had to settle my wife down again. Her night wanders can be bad. Dementia." He turned his back and shuffled down the hall.

If next door was some post-apocalyptic vision of a hellscape with a smattering of damnation. This was a house to remind the world that some people still believed in the fairytale of living a good life. Family pictures adorned the walls from various generations. Everything was clean and tidy. It smelt of a home. It was bright despite the late hour and made me feel safe. A sensation I hadn't realised I needed until that moment.

In the immaculate kitchen, the old man waved at the chairs around a small pine table.

"I'm sorry, sir, I didn't ask your name," Megan said. She looked pale and wide-eyed, obviously struggling to keep herself professional. I doubted I looked that different. The man certainly seemed worried about us the way his eyes darted around our general area.

"I'm surprised you don't know it if you're police from around here. I'm forever having to call you," he said, sounding bitter.

"We're from Redruth, sir," Megan explained.

He grunted and started boiling a kettle. "My name is Colin Stunt. I've lived in this house for forty years. My children grew up here. They've," he stabbed a teaspoon in the direction of next door, "made our lives miserable for two years. The council won't do anything, and the police can't."

"You're not going to have a problem now," I said. "My team will come in during the next twenty-four hours and clean it out. What can you tell us?"

"What do you mean, clean it out?"

Oops. To be fair, it was late, and we'd had a traumatic few hours.

Colin narrowed his eyes. "Is this why the two of you look like rejects from a film set?" He waved a hand at the side of my face. "I thought it was a fashion statement, what with the dark and all, but now I see you've been in the wars."

I almost laughed. "It's been a night, Mr Stunt."

He waved that away. "Colin, son. That's fine. I have local radio on in my wife's bedroom, it helps keep her calm, but tonight they actually have real news to share. A fire at the viaduct and something about deaths at that car park near the cathedral. Is that why you're here?"

Megan decided that letting me loose with the conversation probably wasn't a wise idea.

"Colin, we have reason to believe that the bodies found in the NCP car park are three of those who occupied the house next door. We're waiting for final confirmation."

"The young ones?" he asked, eyes wide.

"Yes. What can you tell me about them?" she asked.

He leaned back in his chair. "They started out okay. If you discount breaking into someone else's home."

I needed more background. "Who owns it?"

"Squabbling children. Their parents died close together, so they inherited, but there was no will. One of the children was estranged. One did all the caring. The third is trying to be the peacemaker. It's a complicated situation. Two years ago, the youngsters broke in and set it up as a squat. They kept it well enough, and I was touched by their attempts to play house. Kids from a care background have a difficult time trying to establish themselves in the world. They told us they were seventeen, but I never believed them."

"You sound like you understand the system," I said.

He nodded. "Former social worker and my wife was a teacher. We helped them with various things, and they kept the noise under control. Gradually, things began to change. Other people would rotate through the house, drug addicts, alcoholics, homeless guys with serious mental health issues. I worried about the young lass, but soon realised she could look after herself."

"Did you ever see anyone strange there, by which I mean, someone that stood out, different from the usual?" I asked.

Colin took a moment, considering his memories. He nodded. "We had the police and the council around several times, but there was one person who stood out. I thought she might be a parent or social worker, but she never spoke to me."

Megan leaned forwards. "Definitely a woman? And the same one? How many times?"

She must've been just as exhausted as I was. We'd both

been trained in interviewing witnesses, and rule number one was clear: Don't ask more than one question at a time.

"Yes, a woman. The same one. At least once a month for the last year." He watched us both, his eyes assessing. "What's going on?"

"Can you describe her?" I asked. "Did she ever—"

He held his hand up to stop me. "I can do better than that." He rose with a groan and shuffled to the kitchen units. He lifted a tablet off the top and woke the screen. "I've been told to keep evidence of problems. I have cameras set up and a feed to a cloud account that stores all the footage for six months. Once a week I go through it, download the problematic footage, but I never delete anything. I'd rather pay for it than let myself down by deleting something I need."

Megan and I just stared at him.

He grinned. "What? I'm old, not stupid. This is my home, and I want to protect it. I can learn, and I used to write code, long before computers did it for themselves."

"Colin, I think I want to be very unprofessional and give you a hug of complete gratitude," Megan said.

"You don't even know if my information it's useful or not." He sat back down with a smile on his face.

"Right now, considering what's at stake, I'm sure this is the break we've been looking for," she said.

I was itching to get Sid into the account.

"Give me a minute, and I'll show you what I have on the woman, or at least some of it," Colin said. "She was here the day before yesterday. I shouldn't spy, but I don't have much to do all day, and it's hard to concentrate on much when Shirley is up. She's very active." He hummed and hawed for a bit as he went through the footage but showed no signs of confusion as to how to navigate his app.

I was impressed. Most of what Sid put on my phone I hadn't opened, never mind tried to use.

"Here she is," he said after only a minute.

He gave the tablet to Megan, and I leaned over to view the screen. There, in colour no less, was a woman in a long summer dress with short sleeves. She had long brown hair down her back, and it contained streaks of silver. The image was so clear we could see the wrinkles in her elbows as she walked up the path and around the back, just like we did. I'd put her in her late forties, early fifties. She moved easily. Not fat, not thin, though hard to tell any more than that with the shapeless dress. She carried a bag for life in each hand and a small bag on her back. One of those handbags that's designed to be a rucksack. If they had a name, I didn't know it.

The camera only caught the side of her face, and that was in shadow from the large sunhat she wore. Megan and I watched.

"You'll want to go forward. She stayed a very long time that day," Colin added.

If she was the one responsible for the sacrifice we'd seen in that room, then I wasn't surprised she'd taken her own sweet time being there.

Megan pressed the relevant icon, and the screen jumped forwards. We scanned three hours of footage. The woman came out and there, as she came around the corner of the house, we caught the perfect shot of her face.

I will admit, a part of me was disappointed that she didn't have a hooked nose and chin, with a huge wart. It was a perfectly nice face. Large eyes, lightish but not clear under the hat, strong brows, a straight nose, but not overly dominating, a wide mouth with full lips. The creases in her skin were now permanent, but couldn't be described as wrinkles. She stood straight, and no longer carried the bags for life. I saw a quartz pendant on her chest as it caught the light.

"Did you see those bags in the house?" I muttered to Megan.

She shook her head. We watched the woman walk down the path and vanish off the camera's screen. No obvious signs of the carnage covered her clothing or body. She must've worn protective gear, or a robe.

I looked up at Colin. "Do you have footage of the road?"

He shook his head. "It's enough of a legal black hole filming over the fence. I'm not filming public roads."

"There could be other neighbours with doorbell cameras, right?" I asked Megan.

She nodded. "But wait a second."

The camera might be set to capture the movements of Colin's neighbours, but in the distance, it did catch the road. "There, that's a Nissan Micra. A blue one," Megan said. "I can track that if it went through the nearby ANPR cameras. We can use that image of her number plate to get her details."

We both took a deep breath. An end to this horror was in sight. We had a real lead.

"We don't know it's her," I said. "She could be a parent or something. It could be food in those bags."

Megan grunted and glanced at me. "What are the chances of that, Griffin?"

"Slim, I'm just making sure we don't waste time jumping in the wrong direction."

She looked up at Colin. "Can we access your footage?"

He smiled and handed over a piece of paper. "Sometimes analogue is safest. I don't want electronic evidence of my passwords in email or text messages. Don't lose that." He tapped it as he handed me the login details.

"This is beyond helpful, Colin. Thank you." I thought about the cleanup team I'd be calling in for the bodies next door. "I would ask another favour, though. Could you switch the cameras off for a few days? You really won't be having anyone else staying there, and my team will not want to be recorded. Things next door are worse than you can imagine."

He nodded slowly. "What's really happening?" Age had caught up with him again, and he suddenly looked vulnerable.

"Don't worry. By the time they've finished, the house will be clean, clear and you won't have a problem."

"I'm sorry the kids are dead. They were okay people originally. It makes me sad. Whatever got them into that state, whoever is responsible, they need stopping."

"That's our job, Colin," Megan said. "And you've really helped us tonight. Thank you."

We left soon after.

"Do we need to go back in and find the contents of those bags?" Megan asked eyeing the miserable house.

I shook my head. "I don't think so. Not at this stage. Our job is to find this woman. If that doesn't pan out, then we'll come back." Before we left the area, I called London. Sanchez wasn't there, but the clean-up team took the details I gave them, and said they'd arrive in Truro the following morning. With luck, Colin and Shirley wouldn't have to live with that smell for much longer. I had a quiet hope that maybe the energy from their neighbours now leaving the premises would mean Shirley could settle down and both of them would feel safer. People with mental health issues often picked up on disturbances in the veil or with the occult. The energy agitates their condition.

The ride back to Redruth was easier with Megan on the back of the bike. By the time we reached home together, she was dozing, leaning against me, her arms wrapped around my belly.

I rubbed her thigh. "Come on. Bedtime."

"We need to do something about your hair," she muttered as I half-lifted her off the back. "God, I'm exhausted."

Sid was asleep. The little house, dark. We went in through the back, stripped off our bike gear, and I let Megan go to the shower first. I headed to where I kept the whiskey, pouring us both three fingers worth. When I reached the bedroom, Megan hadn't finished, and I began unpeeling my clothes. They stank of smoke and my sweat. It was not a pleasant combination. I was amazed Colin had let us into his house in this state. He must've been desperate. With it now being past midnight, my brain was too tired to think about the woman in the security footage. We needed a few hours of downtime.

As I removed my black fatigues and the Snoopy socks, I'd chosen that morning, I saw the extent of the damage to my skin. Sore and blistered, the open wounds weren't pleasant, but they could've been so much worse. Surface damage only. Time would heal them, so long as I kept them clean. So far, I hadn't done a good job on that score. It would be necessary to dress them before bed. In a small mirror on my old chest of drawers, I looked at the damage to my face and hair.

"Ah, fuck it," I muttered. I'd been pretty much scalped by the fire over my left ear. It was raw and pink, which explained why the bike helmet hurt going on and off. The flesh over my neck, jaw and cheek was red, but the fire hadn't caused blisters. I'd been damned lucky. The skin might peel off a bit, like a sunburn, but there wouldn't be scarring. I rummaged in a drawer, moving my socks and underpants around until I found my clippers.

Glancing in the mirror again, I muttered, "Back to a military haircut, I guess." It made me feel sad.

"It doesn't have to be," Megan said, coming out of the small shower room. "I can trim it so you have longer hair on top, longer than you'd be allowed in the Marines."

"You'd do that for me?"

She smiled up at me, rose on her toes and kissed me. "I'd do just about anything for you," she whispered with a glint. "Go get in the shower. Keep the temperature down, or you'll annoy your skin. Then we'll dress your wounds, and you can say 'thank you, Megan, for looking after me'. How does that sound?"

I may have growled at that point.

Chapter Sixteen

The phone woke Megan before me, and she grunted, "Wass up?"

"Sergeant Ackley? It's Naomi Moore. I think someone is watching the house. He's been here all night. Can you come down? You said you wanted to help."

I rubbed the palms of my hands into my eyes, which made them sting enough to drag me the rest of the way into consciousness. After we'd made love, Megan had wept in my arms about the youngsters living in that squat, the deaths of the two nameless men, the horror of what we'd found. We hadn't talked much. What could we say? There wasn't a health care system in place to catch any of the people involved in that house on Grenville Road. They'd all slithered through the cracks and fallen out of the bottom, only to become victims of this… this sorcerer.

The fact that she'd—and I was sticking with our theory of our perp being a woman— had planned each event meticulously for years, that she'd trained these kids up over months to perform some horrible ritual, made it monstrous.

What the hell had happened to her to make her behave like this? Why use those teenagers so cruelly?

For me and Megan, the argument we'd had, the sex, the tears, all were reactions to the violent deaths, the sinister findings, the horrors we were uncovering. It would leave scars. Megan was an experienced police sergeant. She'd seen the terrible and sad ways people died, but unlike me, she dealt with them in the context of a wider society. She had to go home at the end of the day and be 'normal'. Those of us in the Armed Forces, we had a different burden to carry. Mass casualties among our own. Mass bloodshed among the enemy we killed, but we didn't have to go home every twelve hours and be normal people. We didn't have to deal with the events of the crimes we witnessed on our local communities. It was strange, the differences between our vocations, and I realised I now lived in Megan's version, not the one I'd grown used to in the Royal Marines, or while working with DoPI. I was part of the story of Cornwall. I had a place in a society of 'normal' people. That came with responsibilities.

"We'll be there as soon as possible," Megan was saying as we rolled out of bed. "Don't leave the house. Do not let Glendower shoot anyone." Silence for a bit. "No, don't bother phoning the local station. We'll be faster. If you're that worried, lock yourself inside a room and barricade it. Bathroom is best, you'll have water. Yes, I'm serious." A moment, then a thud. "Fuck."

"You alright?" I asked.

"Just fell over trying to put on my socks," Megan muttered. "What time is it?"

"Six-ten," I said with a groan.

We rushed through dressing, headed downstairs and took some energy bars from my food cupboard. I grabbed my daysack and handed it to Megan. It contained all kinds of goodies that could be essential if the farm was being watched. Next came a long drink of water each, and we were good to go.

This early in the morning, the ride to Grumbla was amazing. The roads were quiet, dawn was now in full retreat as day took over, and the sky once again became a colour welcomed by tourists, but not by the farmers this year. By midday, it would be hot enough for me to curse the lack of air-con on the bike, but for now, it was perfect, and fast. Very fast.

When we reached the tiny hamlet, made up of a few houses and a series of farms, I slowed the bike. Rather than ride down into the dell that contained the old farmhouse, I pulled over.

"What you doin'?" Megan asked.

"You take the bike down. Make sure they're okay. I'm going to come in on foot from the fields."

"Naomi said there's been someone parked in the lane a bit further along. They've been there almost since we left yesterday. A man. He gets out, walks around, gets back in the car. She says he's been all over the farm during the night. Both the fields and the yard. He seems to be talking to himself, but he's also on the phone a lot. He's taken pictures as well."

The moon was almost full, so those in the house would've clearly seen anyone moving around nearby. "Why didn't she ring earlier?"

"Dunno. I'll be asking."

While we'd been talking, I'd gone through the daysack. "Take these," I said, handing her an asp, some plasti-cuffs, a bottle of holy water, and a small tub of consecrated wafers. She looked at them with a puzzled expression. I explained,

"You can crumble them over a threshold. If there's a possessed person down there, it'll slow them down."

Megan shook her head. "This is mental. Your life is mental. My life is now mental."

I had more stuff in the bag, but I'd need it.

Megan took over the front seat of the bike, and I watched her slowly pull away from me. After she'd disappeared from view, I jumped up and over the nearest gate, and began my run to the highest point on Glendower's farm.

It didn't take me long to find the ideal spot where I could disguise my wait, while I viewed the yard, garden, house and lane. Though the latter would be tricky, with the leaves dancing like they could hear the music of the universe. For all I knew, they could. I should ask the dryads if they ever decided to speak to us again.

Taking out my compact but powerful monocular, I slowly and methodically quartered the farm. If I saw something, great, but spending this time viewing the location that the target used meant I'd become familiar with the space and its changing shadows. This also meant my brain should pick up on anomalies before I consciously recognised them.

I spotted the car. A fairly new white BMW 3 Series. Its sleek lines were out of place near Glendower's farm. Whoever was down there had just left it in one of the gateways the tractors used. A crazy thing to do with a vehicle just two or three years old.

My phone buzzed in my pocket. I had my Bluetooth earpiece in. I tapped to accept the call.

"Griffin," I said, without looking at the screen.

"It's me," said Megan. "The car belongs to Adrian."

I removed the monocular from my eye. "What?"

"It's his, Griffin. I know it."

This blindsided me. "I don't understand." Why would Hess be here?

"I'm going to find him. Try to talk to him."

Everything inside me recoiled at the suggestion. "No."

A pause. "Griffin, this is not your call to make alone. I judge it to be safe. You're on overwatch, right?"

I felt my jaw bounce. "I am."

"Then I should be fine."

"I only have a handgun, Megan. From this location, I'm no use."

Another pause. "You're armed?"

I snorted, it should be bloody obvious at this point in the investigation.

She ignored me. "You're just going to have to live with it. Where is the best place to stand?"

I wanted to snap and snarl, but I knew it wouldn't get me anywhere. "Between the house and Glendower's tractor in the yard. I've a clear line of sight and I can get down this field in about ninety seconds if necessary."

"Sounds good. I'll call him."

"This is such a bad idea."

"Noted. Keep back until I say otherwise." She killed the call.

"Bloody stupid," I grumbled. If I sprinted down the hill now, I could be there for the meeting.

And what exactly would that accomplish?

Probably nothing, but I'd feel better.

Ah, your feelings would feel better. Well, that's okay then. A justifiable reason to go making a nuisance.

I found myself grinding my teeth in frustration. Taking a deep breath, I considered Megan's options rather than mine. Hess was a serving police officer at her station. She was trying to navigate a difficult breakup with a man who was obviously controlling, possibly dangerous. We needed proof of his coercive behaviour, but she also needed to be able to watch her own back while on call. I wasn't going to be there with a round from a 9mm Glock at every moment of her working life outside DoPI. She needed backup from me, not another dick-swinging oaf in her life. I hated being rational.

The monocular returned to my eye, and I focused on the spot she wanted to use for the meet. I may have removed the Glock and belt holster from the daysack and clipped it to my hip. Just in case.

Five minutes later, Hess came into view. I frowned. The first time we'd met face to face outside the cathedral, Hess had appeared well put together. Older than me by about ten years, and not as big, but a confident, good-looking bloke. The version I saw now did not look the same. In a week, he obviously hadn't shaved. His clothing wasn't just grubby, it looked dirt-stained. His face was thinner, and when I managed to focus on his eyes, I saw a wildness there that had me aching to run down to the farmyard.

Megan approached. I watched her body language and saw the open concern in her cautious movements. Hess paced. I couldn't hear them, but I watched Megan's hand go to the back of her jeans. She'd have the asp on her belt back there. He began gesticulating wildly.

"Come on, Meg, why is he here?" I muttered, watching them. From my viewpoint, it looked like Megan was placating the damned fool. She reached into a pocket, pulled something out and with a gentle underhand throw, chucked a cloud of something at the man.

Suddenly, he rushed at her. Megan tried to sidestep, but she'd allowed him to get too close. They went down. I was already up and running at full speed, firearm in my left hand. Even as I watched, Hess thrashed to free himself of Megan's grip, seemingly unconcerned about injuring her. Knowing I'd miss my target if I aimed at the combatants, and possibly hit something or someone of importance, I fired two rounds into the air.

Hess jerked his attention towards me.

I vaulted the gate, landed in the yard and took aim. "Stop," I bellowed.

In the doorway, I saw him, the boy Matty. His eyes were larger than dinner plates. Hess lunged at the lad, and I swear I saw him foaming at the mouth.

"Don't kill him," Megan yelled at me.

I fired again. Sound cracked through the farmyard, startling the birds into flight. Dirt sprayed up from the ground between Hess and the boy. Naomi appeared in the doorway. She grabbed the boy, pulled him back, slamming the door shut. I heard the bolt sliding home.

"Give it up, Hess," I ordered.

He turned his head towards me, and I looked into his eyes. My hackles rose. Instincts, long dormant in many people, had me aching to pull the trigger. His gaze was… Christ, it was empty of everything that made him recognisable.

"Give it up," I repeated. The idea of touching him to arrest him was repellent.

"She will win," he snarled. With the speed and power I'd never have suspected possible, he threw a handful of farmyard dirt at my face.

Of course, I blinked, covered my eyes and turned away. The Glock forgotten in my hand. Rather than tackle me, I heard footsteps pounding away down the track.

"Griffin?" Megan was beside me, removing the gun from my hand.

"Bastard," I muttered, blinking.

"Don't rub them. Come on, there's a hosepipe." She led me to the end, put it in my hand, and went to switch it on. After cleaning my face and eyes, I felt better. At least physically, I'd also heard a BMW start up and roar away, which did not improve my mood.

"What the hell happened?" I asked her.

She shook her head. "I don't know. It's like he's someone else completely. I don't recognise him."

"I saw the state of the bloke from the hill," I said. "What was he doing here?"

"He just kept telling me that the boy belonged to his real mother. That I was keeping him illegally. We had no right to separate mother and son any longer. He was barely coherent. I tried talking him down, said we could get him help. When he insisted on seeing Matthew, I told him that would never happen. Naomi had convinced me to carry a handful of those wafers."

"You threw the consecrated wafers at him?"

She nodded. "That's bad, isn't it? The way he reacted."

"It's not good. We need to move Naomi and Matty. Get them packed up. I'll call Sid."

Megan's worried expression bothered me. Was she concerned about Hess? Or the mother and child?

I pulled out my phone, still blinking from the dirt. "Sid, we have a problem."

"I wondered where you were? Did you make it home at all?"

"Yes. I was going to catch you up this morning, but Naomi Moore rang Megan…" I went on to explain what had happened. "We need to move her, keep her safe. I was wondering if Luce's place has a spare room. Ours isn't big enough for a mother and child. Besides, Hess will know where we live. It's not like Megan visits Luce on her own time."

"Won't it be putting her in danger?" Sid asked, obviously concerned.

I rubbed my forehead and closed my eyes. The sun was being obnoxious. "Well, yes, possibly, but she also understands the stakes. I can't put them in a hotel. We'll have no control over their environment. Could you at least ask her?"

"I'm not comfortable with this. After what happened with the Dru, she's been wary."

"That was a positive outcome for us and the Dru. Why does that bother her?" Though, come to think of it, I'd hardly seen her the last few weeks.

"A positive outcome? You had to blow up a helicopter to hide the mutilated corpses of a billionaire and his goons, Griffin. Nothing about Madron was normal, and she loved that place."

"It wasn't me who brought the wood to life." Why was I arguing with Sid about this?

He sighed, probably realising the same thing. "Alright, I'll ask, but no promises, and I'm not pushing. She doesn't have to be a part of this."

"Okay, well, if not there, then it'll have to be ours." Silence for a beat. "Sid, I thought you'd disabled the tracker he had on Megan's phone?"

"I did, but maybe I didn't go deep enough. There could be something else, spyware I didn't notice."

"So, he knows everywhere we've been in the last week?" I asked. My temper was not improving. This information would seriously affect our investigation.

"Yes," Sid admitted. "Maybe. I don't know. Until you get Megan's phone back here, and I go through it in more detail."

"How did you miss this, Sid?" I tried not to bite out the words. I failed.

"Oh, I'm sorry, Mr Perfect, I'll fix her phone, track Hess's, delve into the nasty world of devil worship online and all the myriad other things you've asked for this week. As well as bailing you out with Sanchez and making sure your moody arse still has a phone when you turn one into a fire hazard. I'm one man doing three people's jobs back here. I'm good, but I'm not God. Not yet anyway," he added. "I thought you were being paranoid about her ex. I didn't know Hess would be involved in the investigation."

He had a point. Well, to be fair, he had several.

"Alright. I'm sorry. Let's just get her phone debugged."

"I'll look more deeply into Hess." Sid paused, then said in his 'serious' voice. "You know what this could be, right?"

"Yeah, though, how we explain this to Megan, I'm not sure."

"Well, I'm afraid that's your job."

I saw Megan walk out of the house with Naomi, Matty and Glendower. They stood in the yard, looking like lost refugees being forced to separate.

"I have to go, Sid. Can you get onto Luce?"

He grunted and ended the call.

Approaching the group, I saw the odd struggle Naomi and Glendower were having at their parting. Leaving them to their farewells, I tugged Megan gently to one side. "I've spoken with Sid. He's going to give Luce a call, see if they can stay with her."

"Is that wise? She's been pulling away. Sid stays with her, but she's not coming to the house much."

Was I the only person oblivious to this? *Yes, yes, you are.*

"She can always say no, in which case they'll come to ours."

Megan blinked. "You mean your place and Sid's?"

My temper was not coping with the day. "Yes, alright, mine and Sid's." Biting words like tiny wasp stings. "He'll need your phone back. Apparently, he might not have gone deep enough to rid it of Hess's presence."

Megan's mouth dropped open. "He's still tracking me? He knows everywhere we've been?"

I nodded. "Which might explain why he looked so odd."

"What's that mean?"

"Can I explain a bit later—"

"No, Griffin, now." She crossed her arms, widened her stance and glared at me.

"Fine, let's go sit in the shade. Those three are going to take forever," I said, nodding at the strange little family.

Megan and I sat on a wall still covered by the house's shadow. It helped with the rising temperatures of the day. She said, "How did Sid miss Adrian's interference?"

"He thought I was being a jealous prick. Which, to be fair, I probably was."

Megan spluttered. "Probably? You've been wanting to rip his face off for months."

I opened my mouth to argue. She just gave me a penetrating look that said: I dare you.

"Fine, whatever, the point is, he's been tracking the investigation, which means he might well have been at Wesson's place."

"You are joking."

"I wish I were. Something happened to me the first time we were there, but I figured it might've been one of my weird episodes." I was staring into the distance, thinking about the first time I'd stood in that tiny bathroom. I'd looked into the mirror and a pair of eyes stared back, and they weren't mine. Being an experienced DoPI operative, I figured it was all in my head, pushed it away and didn't think about it again. But what if Hess saw the same thing and didn't push it away? "Megan, did you ever tell him about what DoPI is?"

"No, of course not. He's never been in the circle of trust. He hated my work with Rural Security. Hated you because of it. That's one of the reasons we couldn't make it work, and he became controlling so fast. It's why he wanted me to move to Bristol." She picked at a plant and smelt the leaves. "He always wanted to know what you did, what we did. I just kept to the Rural Security patter. He never believed it."

"Do you think he's been investigating what we do?" I asked.

"It's possible. He's a police officer. He's a control freak, and he hates losing." She looked at me. "He really hates losing at anything."

"And he lost you. To me." Our fingers interlaced.

She nodded. "That's a bad thing, isn't it?"

I decided it was time to confess my worst fears. "Did you ever read Dracula?"

"What?"

I couldn't blame her for being confused. "Did you?"

"Erm, well, yes, of course. It was probably my first foray into horror."

"Okay, um, in the story there is a character called Renfield. He becomes enslaved to Dracula. Although we never discover how the vampire enslaves this man, despite the miles separating them, it's a form of possession. Renfield acts as Dracula's daytime emissary. He's in a madhouse, making him easy to influence—"

"Where's this going, Griffin?" Her impatience and worry made her harsh.

"It's become a name we label those who are under malign and *para* influence."

She frowned. "You think Adrian is under this influence?"

I shrugged. "It's the most likely explanation for his appearance, his manner, the obvious need he has for Matty. If he'd gone to the caravan, he might've seen what I did, and it would've been enough—"

"Wait. What? What did you see?" she asked, standing and walking in one of her tight circles.

I explained the mirror, the eyes, the feeling that something was pushing into my mind, seeking, wanting control. Then I confessed that I thought I'd had another of my episodes. "If he went into the caravan after us, but before it was burned to the ground, she could've ensnared him through the mirror."

"You're not serious."

"It depends on his personality type—or that's the theory. We've never had a Renfield survive for long."

Megan's jaw dropped. "You're not serious?" she repeated.

"Very. We need to bring him in if we can. DoPI have facilities that can care for him, try to bring him back."

"Jesus, Griffin, this is terrible. Whatever Adrian is, whatever he's done, he doesn't deserve this."

"I know." *Liar, liar, your pants*—Yeah, whatever.

"I can call him. Get him to meet me. We can take him down. Get your team here, they'll be in the squat by now, and they can take him away."

"It's a cleaning crew, Meg, not a commando unit. Besides, if this woman has trapped him, he might've helped with what happened at the squat."

Fear darkened her eyes. "This is scaring me."

"Demons are scary." I looked at the strange little family again. "We need to move Naomi and Matty. Adrian can't be our priority right now, but maybe Sid can find him. If I can take him down without you involved, that's got to be safer. The longer he's under the sorcerer's spell, the more deranged and driven he'll become. That puts you in significant danger. He'll also become stronger than normal. The hormones in his brain will be shifting."

"How do you know all this?" she asked. "You didn't know this much about the incubus or the Dru."

"Demons are different. We have required reading about them and the human fools who've summoned them over the centuries. They are very dangerous." The other thing, which I'd forgotten to worry about until now, was Sanchez. She really wanted a demon under DoPI's control. Oh, I did not want to be fighting this war on two fronts. Fighting a sorcerer and Sanchez's drive to have access to someone powerful enough to summon and control a demon this powerful would be bad news for everyone. And I didn't just mean all those working for DoPI, I meant *everyone*.

Chapter Seventeen

Megan drove Naomi and Matty in Glendower's old truck. He said that if he needed to go shopping, he'd take the tractor. I had the feeling St Just was probably used to this kind of behaviour. I followed on the bike. Sid had called and said Luce was happy enough to help. We'd wrapped Megan's phone in tinfoil to create a kind of Faraday cage, even after switching it off and removing the SIM. It pays to be paranoid, and I hadn't been paranoid enough recently.

It took almost two hours to reach Portreath in the old truck. Between the tourist traffic and Megan trying to keep the truck under fifty, even on the main road, for fear of it rattling itself to pieces, we were all hot and frustrated. Naomi and Matty looked worried, bordering on scared. I saw Sid's Mini parked outside Luce's house and felt relief. He'd help smooth over the cracks.

When I pulled up, they came out of the house, and Sid offered me a fist bump.

"I figured you could do with some solidarity. You

sounded on edge." He watched Megan introduce the other women and child.

"Yeah, it's been a morning. Still, we're here, they are safe and Hess doesn't know about this place."

"We hope."

I grunted, struggling out of my bike gear before I murdered someone in a state of overheated frustration. The burns were really beginning to hurt, and I needed water, some painkillers and a nap. The first two I might manage to find, the third was probably going to be a distant dream for some time to come. We went into the house and cool arms wrapped around me, dialling back my temper by several notches.

Luce and Naomi seemed to hit it off and started talking about the myths related to astrology almost immediately. Megan joined us. The kid, Matty, just hung on his mother's hand. I guessed he didn't leave Grumbla all that often. He seemed nervous of all these strange adults and watched Sid with big eyes.

"I've brought Luce up to date with events. She's not really interested in demon lore, so doesn't have much to add to our knowledge. I think you're our resident expert on this one," Sid said.

"I figured. This is very kind of her."

"She wanted to help once she understood. Listen, I might have a lead on the sorcerer's whereabouts."

Megan, yawning, managed to say, "Brilliant. Where? Wait, might? Why might?"

"I've managed to get into Hess's phone. From there, I hacked his laptop, and I've been in his search history." Sid looked at me. "He's done a deep dive into Rural Security, found the cracks and followed them to get into DoPI. The man has skills."

"Shit," I muttered.

"That's not the end of it, sadly. After he broke into Wesson's caravan, he started his own investigation, but he doesn't have our background knowledge. He went straight onto the dark web and found the same chatrooms Wesson was using. Anyway, possibly because the sorcerer connected with him in the mirror, like you told me, she reached out to him in the chatroom. I couldn't find her, but she found him. They've met IRL."

"What?" I asked, not recognising the acronym from the Marines.

Megan laughed. "In real life."

"Oh, right, okay. Sure. Does all this mean you have a postal address?" I asked Sid.

"Kinda. I have an IP address, but it's been pushed through a VPN. The location looks to be a place called Dodman Point. I can't seem to pin it down exactly, but there is a village called Penare. It's just a handful of cottages on the coast in the middle of nowhere."

I grunted. It would be easy to see us coming in a remote location. Far better for this to go down in a town or city where we can track people. Mind you, we'd have less collateral damage in the countryside.

"I've checked the tax records for each house in the area."

"Of course you have," Megan murmured. "Sid, you're a whizz."

With a sly look at me, he said, "Thank you, Megan. I'm glad my skills are appreciated."

I sucked in a noisy breath. "Yeah, alright, just get to the point."

"There's one house registered to a woman who just happens to have three children, all attending the local primary school. I've checked their records, and all three are the same age and have the same birthday."

Megan's eyes widened. "The children are alive? Oh, my God, those poor women."

We all took a moment to ponder the horrors that must've plagued the mothers who'd lost their babies. Two deaths and one in a mental health facility.

I leaned back and stretched, closing my eyes for a moment. "We have to talk about Adrian Hess as well."

A pregnant pause, big, fat, round and daring someone to break it. Might as well be me.

"If he's gone full Renfield, we aren't getting him back in one piece."

Megan stared at her hands. "He really doesn't deserve this." The words were quiet and heartfelt.

I tried to be sympathetic. "I know I'm sorry." Though I wasn't sure what I was apologising for, none of this was my fault.

When Megan looked at me, I realised I'd not pulled off the kind and compassionate blather I was aiming for. Her expression hardened. "I'd appreciate it if you could treat Adrian with the same compassion as anyone else in his situation. Keeping this shit secret from the world means people stumble into it blindly. It's like asking a Victorian police officer to raid a fucking crack den."

I was tempted to mention the Opium Wars but figured it would earn me a smack at best; at worst, she'd start yelling before walking out on me. Still, she had a point. If it were anyone else, I'd be trying to figure out how to save them, not kill them.

Did you just think that out loud? You naughty boy. No killing the irritating twit.

Yeah, okay, I needed to scrub the killing idea for the

moment. "We have to find him, keep him contained. That's all we can do for the moment. Sid, do you now have the evidence necessary for Megan to take it to her superiors for an arrest?"

"Yes, that's a definitive yes." He looked at Megan. "I can put it together in a packet and email it to you."

"That'll help. If I can get a warrant, then we have some hope of bringing him in. I'll make some calls, explain his mental health has collapsed. Ask a team to do a welfare check at his address." She rose, pulling out her phone on the way.

Sid chuckled. "I've never seen you scowl before."

I dragged my eyes from where they were trying to track Megan through the walls. "Am not."

"No, of course you aren't, Mr Rain Cloud."

"He's a shit. Why does she care so much?"

"Because she's a human being with grown-up feelings and a compassionate nature. That's why she's good at her job. Griffin, do yourself a favour, help her bring in Hess safely. Hurt him, and she'll be angry enough to do something you'll both regret."

I stared at the small gas fire Luce used as the focal point of her living room. "How am I going to catch the bugger?"

"That's why I've put together the dossier of information about him for Megan's people. You don't have to catch him, they do. It'll be better that way. She's our liaison, Griffin, let's make use of that. He's a Renfield, and we're running out of time."

"He couldn't be turned into a Renfield without being halfway there already."

Sid frowned at me. "Mate, we don't know that. DoPI has never had a Renfield survive long enough for us to save or test how they were converted." He glanced at the door, making sure Megan couldn't overhear us.

I said, "The sorcerer tried it on me, probably tried it on Wesson as well. When he rejected her, she sent a demon to kill him. When I did, the kids were turned loose. She knows someone is coming for her, and she keeps preparing opponents in the hope we'll be killed before we reach her. I wonder how many more traps she's laid."

"What she did to those kids is terrible." His grief for them was palpable.

"It took her a long time as well. She spent months converting them." I stared at my feet. The socks were Woodstock, Snoopy's best mate, today. I liked his yellow outlook on life. "You should've seen that house, Sid. It was a fucking horror show all on its own, and what they did to the other people sleeping there in the final rituals…" I shuddered. "In all the reading I've done, all the things I've seen myself, I've never witnessed anything that grim. Whoever those men were, I hope to God their souls aren't trapped in some ritual. I hope they have peace."

"I'm sorry you had to see it."

I felt the creeping dread of the vision I'd had with Wesson. "It's the smell I can't get out of my head."

My phone rang. I glanced at Sid. "It's Sanchez."

"Good luck." He rose and left the room, probably to find out why the women were laughing in the kitchen.

"Ma'am?"

"Things have escalated?" She sounded tired, a very rare occurrence.

"Yes. We have several deaths, two of which are part of an occult ritual. I called in a cleanup team. They'll have more of the details."

"Quite right. We'll feed back any pertinent intel."

"Thank you, ma'am."

A pause. "How are you?" She sounded like the question came with a side order of nails she had to choke down. I almost chuckled.

"Fine, ma'am. Job to be done."

"Good. I'm glad to hear it. I have someone coming down to help with the interpretation of what's happening. An expert in the field."

"That would be helpful, ma'am. Thank you. We're currently relying on my expertise in the area."

"Don't sell yourself short, Corporal. I believe you spent some time studying arcane demonic rituals after the events in Somerset."

"I did, ma'am, but this is something different. It would be good to have the additional guidance." Though, having a stooge working for Sanchez in our company didn't feel wise. I'd have to talk to Sid about keeping whatever, whoever, was behind this out of DoPI's grasping hands.

She said, "Well, keep him out of trouble. He's useful. I don't want him dying on us."

I smiled despite myself. "Understood, ma'am. The missing children—they're alive. Sid's possibly managed to locate the sorcerer."

"Don't act until we know for certain what we're dealing with, Corporal. I want those children alive if possible. If we can capture any *para* involved, that would be useful as well. Am I understood?" I didn't miss the hardening of her tone. The wicked witch wanted her new toys to play with.

Yeah, but no. Boss lady ain't getting any new toys. Right, soldier boy?

Damn straight. "Understood, ma'am," I lied.

She ended the call. A good thing, or a bad one? Who

could tell? I wasn't surprised I'd received a call sending a warning shot across my bows. The woman wanted her pet demon, and if we could capture one, it would be a prize.

I walked through to the kitchen. Lunch seemed to be happening, and Megan handed me a plate full of sandwiches and a packet of crisps.

Sid said, "All good?"

I just grunted and dug into the food.

"I've spoken to my inspector," Megan said. "Sent him the evidence packet Sid produced for me. He's going through it. To say he's shocked is an understatement. I've described Adrian's behaviour as a sign of severe mental health issues. He'll be rounded up by our teams."

"That's a start. I don't want us having to check our backs for him as we're trying to move forward."

Her face clouded. "Don't be too sure of their help, Griffin. They're a loyal bunch, and their loyalty isn't to me right now. I'm not too sure they'll believe anything coming out of your office."

"That's not fair," Sid protested. "I worked hard on that lot." His look of affronted dignity made Matty grin. Sid had been giving him a lesson on his phone about computer games. Matty was entranced. Naomi, less so. Well, she couldn't keep the kid locked up forever.

"What are you going to do about the person responsible for all this?" Luce asked me.

"I've been told to hold off until the expert has arrived."

Sid looked up from Matty's attempts to win. "What expert?"

I shrugged. "Don't know. Apparently, it's important I keep him alive. Which makes me think he's not going to be much use in the fighting department."

My fellow DoPI veteran shook his head. "She's up to something again, isn't she?"

"Probably." I glanced at Naomi, and Sid nodded his understanding. No talking in front of the civilians. "Listen, since we can't act on our intel yet, I suggest we all go home and leave these good people to get settled."

"You and I could go down to Dodman Point and check the place out?" Megan suggested.

"It would alert the woman," I said. "We aren't close enough to the ritual to risk exposing our knowledge, or endangering the children. Remaining in a holding pattern is the safest option right now. Naomi and Matty are here. I'll go back to Redruth, catch a few more hours downtime, then return and take watch overnight. I think that's best for now."

So, that became the plan. For the next few hours, I'd rest, recharge the failing batteries, and return to Portreath after dark. Until then, Sid would remain in place. I rode back with Megan, dropping her at the police station in Camborne so she could explain in more detail what was happening with Hess. If he did show up at Luce's, then I wasn't going to hesitate in bringing the bastard down. People didn't become Renfields by accident. Something inside them attracted the darkness of human possession. I also needed to write up the notes for my report to DoPI about what we'd experienced at Wesson's caravan, the NCP car park, how we'd visited the squat and all I'd seen at that location. As well as the neighbour's observations. We now had a visual on the woman, and a physical address. Sort of. We were getting there, and it meant a few hours of peace could be vital to my functioning.

The moment I walked into Turpin Cottage, I knew the

report writing would have to wait. Exhaustion swept over me. I stripped off, showered, and crashed into my bed. At some point, I found Megan next to me, but it was too hot to cuddle. We just drifted through the afternoon and evening. It was good. A moment's pause.

Chapter Eighteen

Megan and I decided to take shifts doing overwatch on Luce's property. I took the bike down and parked away from the street. Luce had spoken with a friendly neighbour who proved happy to have me, then Megan, sit in her upstairs bedroom window watching the street. It was the best obbo I'd ever done. Tea and cake for four hours. Megan let herself in. The elderly lady had left her sandwiches and another flask with biscuits in a tin.

Megan grinned and whispered, "I bloody love Cornwall."

I left her to it and returned home to catch up on the paperwork and gain another couple of hours' of quiet time.

We all convened at Luce's by 08:00 hours. Nothing had happened overnight, except for some unpleasant dreams about car parks. On the way into Portreath, I'd ridden around the narrow streets for a while, looking for a tail, but again nothing seemed out of place. It made me twitchy. Where had Hess gone? Renfields weren't known for sleeping, eating, and being normal. In DoPI's records that I'd read they just kept going until their master called them off, gave them a new objective, or they just dropped—dead. I worried about how that would affect Megan.

I'd brought a makeshift breakfast with me, so set to work cooking with Sid while the women chatted. The strain was easy to hear in Naomi's voice, and Matty was quiet.

"Mum, when can we go home?" he asked as I placed a small fried breakfast in front of him. Those big eyes watched us all, and despite his tender years, he seemed to understand that he was the reason their world had changed so radically. The excitement of the day before had long since worn off.

Naomi looked at me, her expression hard. "Well?"

I backed up, not wanting to loom over the table. "We've help coming from London. I'm hoping that'll give us some more information, and we'll then have a safe plan moving forward." Yuck, what a lot of mealy-mouthed nonsense.

Megan shook her head, exasperated with me. "We don't know, Matty, but I promise, the moment it's safe, we'll let you go home."

"Is Grandpa safe?" he asked, meaning Glendower.

Naomi's colour flushed. "I know we aren't related, but—"

"You don't have to explain," Luce said. "We understand. Families aren't always biological."

Megan added, "He's a lot safer with you here." She rubbed the back of Matty's hand.

"Are we safe?" he asked.

"Are you kidding? I'm a police sergeant, and he's," she pointed at me, "a Royal Marine Commando. He's also a corporal. Do you know what that means?"

"I know he fights pirates," Matty said, with a look in his eyes that might've made me stand straighter.

"Well, yes," Megan said with a smile. "He's done that, but only as part of a team. I'll explain…" It took the rest of breakfast for Megan to give a potted history of the British Armed Forces, making up an awful lot of stories along the way, but it worked, the lad forgot his fear. By the look on Naomi's face, she wasn't overly amused.

Once we'd cleaned up breakfast, I was aware that keeping Matty occupied with Netflix for the day might not be his mother's idea of a good time. She seemed more restless than the kid. Fortunately, before she could start making life difficult, the doorbell rang.

Everyone looked at me. With standard caution, keeping my centre of mass away from the usual line a shooter might take and moving almost side-on to the door, I peered through the spy hole from a distance. A medium-sized man appeared to be standing there. It definitely wasn't Hess.

"I feel like I'm in the Exorcist," I muttered, opening the door.

The man took off his trilby hat. It matched his smokey grey mackintosh, which was not only buttoned up but also belted, despite it being almost thirty degrees in the sun. His small-featured face was pink from the heat.

"Corporal Woodbury?" he asked, his voice polite, genteel and Scottish.

"Yes," I replied, slightly bemused. As always with DoPI, those of us on the front line were only introduced to specialists when it was necessary. I'd never met this man.

"I am Donal Blyth. I am here to help." He held out his hand.

When I took hold, smiling and giving a greeting in return, I realised I held four pink and sweaty sausages attached to a pink and sweaty uncooked burger. Resisting the urge to wipe my palm on my trousers, I showed him into the coolness of the house.

The man was entirely bald, with almost no facial hair in evidence except for his eyelashes and very pale, thin eyebrows. Despite the soft and spongy hand, he wasn't overweight, but I doubted he'd ever done more than taken a stiff stroll once a day for his health. Age hung around him, but it seemed like a cloak he could take off when necessary. There were very few lines on his face. His shoes were highly polished, and he bent to take them off when I explained this was a no-shoe household. His socks were black. I had my rainbow ones on today. I wondered if that would go into a report for Sanchez, it made me self-conscious.

"I'm sorry it's taken me so long to get here. With the incidents in Wales, we've been busy, but Pilar felt it wise for me to attend in person."

Pilar? He was on first-name terms with the wicked witch? How did that happen? Maybe they were part of the same coven? Sid and I would be speculating.

"Thank you for coming," I said, showing him down the hall. "Meet the team and the family we're protecting. Then perhaps we can discuss the events and formulate a plan?"

He carried a small leather bag, one that might've been used by a Victorian medical professional.

"You can leave your hat and coat," I suggested. Just looking at him made me feel panicked with heat exhaustion.

"Thank you." He put the bag down beside his right ankle. Undid his coat in a meticulous fashion, and I realised he wore a three-piece suit underneath. His only concession to the weather seemed to be that this suit was linen, not wool, and no tie hung around his neck. Again, it was grey, the shirt white. He bent and picked up his bag.

We walked into the kitchen. Everyone looked at him. I made the introductions.

"This is Mr Donal Blyth from our Rural Security office in London. He's going to be helping us with next steps," I said.

"Does the family in question not understand our full role?" Donal Blyth asked me.

I glanced at Sid, who offered a shrug. "No, not yet. I didn't want to complicate matters."

"I see. Well, it's time we read them in, or it will be impossible to keep the child safe. Perhaps we can sit somewhere more comfortable? Then I can explain my role to you all."

Luce's house was so small that I doubted anywhere would be comfortable with so many of us present. However, we moved into the living room. Donal Blyth took an armchair, and I stood near the window, feeling the need to keep an eye on the road outside. Matty and Megan sat on the floor, the other adults just about found room to make themselves comfortable. Luce muttered something about putting the kettle on again and made her escape.

"Should we wait?" I asked Sid.

He shook his head. "I think it's best we don't. She's happy to help Naomi, but doesn't want the details. I think it's the vicar's daughter in her. Demons are well off her radar."

"I wish they were off mine," muttered Naomi.

Megan looked as if she agreed.

Blyth leaned forward, his small leather bag once again at his right ankle. "Let me explain who we really are, then we'll discuss the problem."

When Naomi discovered we'd been lying to her about

the nonexistence of Rural Security and the reality of DoPI, she was not happy.

In an acerbic voice, she snapped, "Why would you keep this a secret? We all have to know the dangers if this stuff actually exists. Why can't our government treat us like grown-ups?"

Sid huffed, "You have read the internet, right? Can you imagine the chaos if the world discovered demons were real? If we could prove witchcraft really worked if the practitioner had access to a certain talisman, or book? The insanity if people started to prove which god was the real one? Remember how well that goes down? We keep it quiet because we have to. I used to believe something different. I worked hard to expose DoPI, but keeping it quiet is by far the best policy. It's something I really believe now."

Coming from Sid, that was quite the confession.

Naomi made small braids in her long hair, her fingers restless. "I'm not happy you lied to me." She glared at me, then at Megan. We both tried to look contrite.

"Now we have that over with," Blyth said, "perhaps we can discuss the matter at hand. I've read the reports, but I would like to hear everyone's experiences firsthand. Naomi, if we could start with you and how you came to know that Matthew's very existence put him in mortal danger?"

Her eyes became distant, reliving her decisions. "I wanted a child, but I didn't want a man in my life. I'm gay. Becoming pregnant with a stranger seemed unnecessarily complicated. I borrowed some money from my mother and decided to invest it in my future. The one I wanted. The IVF clinic in Bristol offered a service to single women, provided we had the financial security to care for a child. Despite living in Grumbla, I'm actually an astute financial adviser. I work from home and always have. That's how I support us and the farm." She laid a hand on Matty's tousled head.

"During routine tests, the hospital realised I had severe preeclampsia, so my plans of a home birth had to be scrapped. I had Matty in the hospital, quite alone. When I realised three other women were giving birth at the same time, it felt safer somehow."

I had to admit, Naomi Moore was an impressive woman. Fully self-contained, even at a young age.

"Everything went well. A friend offered to do Matty's birth chart, knowing I'd be interested in seeing what his future might look like, and that's when the trouble started. She drew it up and called me immediately. It became clear he was in terrible danger from an unknown force. His early years would be governed by this force, and it threatened my life as well."

Blyth, his fleshy pink colour now gone, and his soft skin quite white, nodded. "I have seen the chart, double-checked it myself, looked deeper than most, and you are quite right. You would have died from grief, or gone mad, as the other mothers did. Running and hiding from his fate has kept him with you." His smile was kind, and I felt gratitude at that small demonstration of his humanity. We needed her to trust us.

He looked at me. "What do you have to say?"

"It all began with the visit to Truro Cathedral." I went on to explain the events of the past week. Our gradual discovery of the complex plan set in place so many years before. How the IVF clinic might've used the same sperm donor for all four children. How the children went missing and what happened to their families.

Blyth nodded. "Sadly, it's important to the sorcerer that the child's roots in this world are severed. If the mothers hadn't died by their own hands, or been driven mad, they would've been killed. These children need to be cut adrift from social bonds and any biological ones. Using IVF babies is clever and shows a level of planning I've never seen before. It's better than orphans. You can control the genetics, the timing of the births—"

Naomi shook her head. "That's the bit I really don't understand. How could someone control when I gave birth? Then do the same thing for three other women?"

"There are conjurings that can be employed for such biological manipulation. The IVF clinic would allow the mastermind of all this to collect samples from each mother. She has your blood, probably quite a lot of it, and probably your placenta. Things like this would give someone like me a great deal of power over someone like you."

I had a hard time believing Blyth could do anything more dangerous than conjure a rabbit out of a hat, but I didn't say anything.

"What else have we learnt?" he asked.

I went on to explain about Wesson's death, leaving out the gory details with Naomi and Matty in the room. Luce had returned, and we all had cool lemonade to drink. She remained in the doorway, not wanting to be part of the discussion. Briefly, I told him about my experience of Wesson's death. I tried to make it factual, but I think everyone in the room heard my fear.

Blyth nodded and tapped his fingers against the armrest. "I suspect you are right, Corporal Woodbury. Your connection to the veil drew you to the memory it has of the demon's savage attack. We'll have to consider how to protect you in the future. From what I can gather, you are vulnerable to more than just demons."

"That's not what's important," I said. I went on to explain about Hess becoming a Renfield.

"So, she still wants her fourth child," he said. "That's a necessary part of the process, and she now knows you're in Cornwall." He looked at Naomi.

"I have no internet presence. We use Glendower's details for all my tax documents, company records, everything. I'm not on any pieces of paper down here. As far as the world is concerned, I dropped off the planet when Matty was born."

"And yet, DoPI found you," Blyth pointed out. "Well, perhaps we need to talk about what's happening now. Overhead, we have a strong conjunction of planets. For the right practitioners, it will provide a level of energetic connection to the veil, or the multi-verse, or hell, depending on your way of thinking. We at DoPI prefer veil until science can prove it's something else."

Having been inside it, I doubted science would find an answer to that conundrum any time soon.

He said, "Personally, I am unsure as to why Truro Cathedral is so important in your reports."

Megan fielded that one. "We had a long chat with the deacon, Jayne Archer. The original St Mary's Church had a holy spring on the site. Although the church was sixteenth century, the site would've been a place of worship for much longer. The cathedral has its claims to fame as well. The first to be built after the Reformation, it is one of only three with three spires. Three is important in occult practices, right?" She looked at me, then Blyth.

I nodded.

He smiled. "Very good, we'll make you a DoPI operative yet."

Over my dead, cold body. She's safer in the Police Service. However, Megan looked pleased at the compliment.

"There's another church to the north—the one in Kenwyn. That's far older and was once the seat of the bishop. Its significance shouldn't be ignored," I said.

"And yet, you claim the cathedral is the most important location?" Blyth pushed.

"We know from the children's birth charts that the fifteenth of August is important in their lives. That date is also the Assumption of Mary. Mary is the patron saint of the cathedral. We can't rule that out as significant. Also, Cornwall is the best place to view the coming conjunction of the planets. Truro is the capital city."

Blyth nodded. We were confirming his thoughts, but I needed action to end this chaos.

Chapter Nineteen

We fell silent, the small room growing hot despite the fans and open windows. Blyth held still, considering all we knew so far. He gave a single nod, agreeing with himself over some internal dialogue.

"There are a number of possibilities as to where this is heading, but considering the evidence and the deaths involved, we can discard the softer options. The time spent putting this together demands our attention. I would ask one more question of us as a group, and then I will give my conclusions, which I think will match up with your own. My question is this: What is the point of all this death?"

I had the feeling Blyth was asking this question to test the group, to find the different personality types that would answer, or not. He'd then gauge those answers, giving him a different understanding of us. He was behaving more like a profiler than a sorcerer or exorcist. Then again, perhaps those lines were thinner than I thought.

Maintaining my stance by the window, I looked at the others. Being so still had caused my brain to start focusing on the burns, and my right leg pinged and tingled as if ten-thousand needles were burrowing under the skin. Once I'd consciously registered the pain, my hands started to join in. Forcing myself to remain still, I focused on the others. Megan watched just as I did, and we shared a quick grin. Conspirators in our expertise. Luce and Sid were uncomfortable under Blyth's gaze, and Naomi kept her expression blank, a woman used to hiding her thoughts in public.

All eyes landed on me in the end. "Fine," I muttered. "I'll stick my neck out. From my understanding, which Megan discovered, the heart of this problem lies in motherhood. Mary, the mother of the divine made human in the form of Jesus, is going to be called on to do something at the cathedral. That's another reason why this is happening here in Cornwall."

Blyth smiled, but still his face didn't give any real indication of his age. "Very good, Corporal. This woman, our sorcerer, is ruthless in her pursuit of her goals. She has caused the deaths of mothers, children and the vulnerable. There is little to no conscience behind these acts. This would indicate a long-held and very cold rage."

"Revenge," Megan said.

"I believe so. It's important that we understand her motives."

Sid stirred. "Give me a second." He vanished back towards the kitchen. "Won't take long," he called.

"Do we think she's going to try for Matty again?" I asked.

Blyth nodded. "She has to, or this won't work."

"Then I need to move," Naomi stated. "You can't possibly keep me safe from whatever she's going to send after us."

"Let's just wait," I said. "We're safe here for now. It's time for planning, not panicking."

"It's not your son that's being hunted by a lunatic with demons as besties," Naomi snapped.

"No, but it's my job and my duty to protect him," I stated. "That's my role, and it's one I take very seriously. I'm trained for this, you aren't. You may have spent years trying to untangle why Matty's birth chart scared you to the point you dropped out of your life, but I've been trained for this. I can protect him." Memories of my failures began to flitter through my head. I had to hope they didn't show on my face. Then the stink of Wesson's death sparked up. No, I wouldn't allow that to happen here, to these people.

Matty looked up at me, and I wondered again about the wisdom of including the lad in the conversation. He said, "If demons are real, does that mean God is real as well? Won't He protect me? I've never done anything really bad." He twisted to look at his mother. "Right?"

She stroked his hair, eyes filling with tears. "No love. You've never been really bad."

Leave it to a kid to point out the bleedin' obvious, while also leaving us wide open. "It's not quite as simple as that," I said.

Blyth held up his hand. "Actually, it is." He looked down at Matty. "It's a very good question, young man. You would think so, wouldn't you? If demons can come and murder people, why not angels come to protect us as well? Many people believe they do. Many see their angels and believe they interact with them. It's part of the human experience to suffer pain, and to know joy. Some of us suffer more, some of us abandon joy and her sister hope. Perhaps when we abandon hope, we deny angels, and it gives leverage to the enemies of hope. I think demons walk in this world, and I think angels come as well. What this woman is doing is using one to call the other."

Matty frowned, thinking through the logic. "Then I'll be protected? If she does get me?"

"She won't," Megan stated.

Blyth ignored her and kept his focus on the boy. "I don't know. Sometimes God calls us to Him even when it seems to defy the meaning of life. Children suffer where there should be nothing but peace and plenty. We live without His direct interference, but with His guidance. Sometimes, the minions of demons and angels interfere in that covenant, but we don't know why. We don't know if it's caused by humans or if it's God's will. Then we have to think about which version of God we're talking about."

Matty's eyes widened. "There are different versions?"

We all chuckled at that one. Naomi obviously didn't give him any religious education lessons.

Blyth said, "Yes, Matty, there are almost as many versions of God as there are religions that represent Him. People—"

"Men," Naomi muttered.

The strange man glanced at her. "As you said, mostly men are very good at arguing over which version is right. Meanwhile, an entire group of people has stopped believing altogether, and another group wants to avoid the term and believe in nature as their deity."

"Which is right?"

Blyth shrugged. "Who knows? I think we hear what is right in our hearts." He tapped his chest. "Then we can choose what to believe. God whispers to us all, we just have to listen."

I watched the tension ramp up in Naomi. She really was not a believer.

"Maybe we just have to accept that some people do and others don't," she said.

Matty frowned. "But that means demons are real, or not real, depending on your beliefs? So, if I don't believe, they can't get me."

That logic made me chuckle.

"People have spent centuries trying to figure that out and fought many wars over it," Blyth said.

The lad shook his head. "This makes no sense. Can I play with Sid's phone again?" he asked his mum.

That made Megan laugh. "The kid's got a point. Don't worry, Matty, it makes no sense to me either. I don't believe in anything, but I do know something out there is making people act crazy, and we need to keep you and your mum safe."

Matty made a small grunting sound. "I get crazy."

"Got it!" Sid's footsteps pounded up the hall. "We have a possible name from the research I've done, and I think I might've been able to track her back. She's known as Dr Elena Grove, previously, Cooke. She was married for a brief time in the late nineties. Anyway, if she's the right woman, then I've found a report on Elena Cooke. She had a baby at fifteen in Newcastle. There's a record of the birth, but no death certificate. She had a girl. That was back in the early nineties, before she was married, obviously. Any social care records aren't available, but the Cooke family do turn up in church records, her father was a deacon for the cathedral."

Megan hissed. "You think they took the baby and put it up for adoption? A forced adoption?"

"It would be a strong motive. Especially if she couldn't

find the child, or something terrible happened to her," Sid said.

"She did all this because the Church took her baby away?" Naomi whispered. "All these people, my son, the IVF clinic, all of it? Oh, fucking hell, my IVF doctor was called Grove. She's been there right from the start." The colour drained from her face.

Blyth nodded. "Now it makes sense, and we have the final pieces. The Virgin Mary, mother of Jesus, is going to help these four children survive demon possession or attack. This is what Dr Elena Grove must believe. The Virgin Mary will send her angels to do battle with the demons hurting the innocent. Dr Grove will then capture the angel as she did the demon and use it to destroy the Church of England."

I frowned. "That seems like a very complex plan. Surely, just coming forward with what happened will add another nail to the coffin the Church of England and the Catholic Church have already made for themselves? A nice, normal, mundane, legal proceeding."

"It's not enough," Megan said, shaking her head. "If she's filled with that much pain, the law will never be enough. I should imagine we'll find more deaths related to the people involved in her life at that point. For all we know, it was her local vicar who made her pregnant. She'd be angry enough to force anything to happen after that betrayal."

"She's clearly intelligent if she's become a medical doctor," I said. "There's no reason why her hatred of the Church wouldn't spiral her down into dark magic."

Blyth held up his hand. "Magic is neither light nor dark, Corporal. Dr Grove isn't evil, she's desperate and using any tool necessary to achieve her goals. Don't forget, she is appealing to a mother to help her seek revenge. She is fully committed to her version of reality. By summoning demons into the pure of heart, created by her, she believes she can call on Mary to intercede on her behalf to destroy the patriarchy of the Church by summoning an angel, or four."

Luce stirred from her place in the doorway. "Maybe she doesn't want to destroy the Church, maybe she wants something else. Perhaps her child died after she was forced to give her away?"

None of us had thought of that. It made the entire scenario even sadder. Sid said, "I'll do some research. If the child died after the adoption, I'll need time."

"Does any of this help?" I asked Blyth. "It's all supposition. Especially the bit about the possible father." I glared at Megan. She just shrugged, unrepentant in her low opinion of men in the Church.

Blyth said, "Motive can help. It will show us how determined she is."

Megan stretched her legs out, probably needing action as badly as I did. "I think we know how determined she is, Mr Blyth. She's killed three teenagers, and three adult men already. We need to know how to stop her. When it's going to be safe to pick her up from her hide-hole down in Dodman Point. If Sid's right and it is her down there."

Sid defended his skills.

Blyth held his hand up to stop him. "A woman with these skills will have warding stones on the roads and footpaths to her home. When these are tripped, she will be able to use a scrying mirror to see who is coming. Sneaking up on her will be near impossible."

"I was planning a full-scale invasion," Megan said. "We might not have physical proof of it yet, but she has three children there who aren't biologically hers, that'll get me the warrant I need."

Blyth shook his head. "You cannot approach her like that, Sergeant. She is far too skilled, and she has this Renfield out there. It might put your people in danger in ways we cannot predict. What can you tell me about this Hess chap?"

Megan's colour heightened, and she glanced at me. "We dated for a while. He's not a stable man. Before he joined the police, he was in the Parachute Regiment."

"Another highly trained individual," Blyth said. He glanced at me. "You will have problems with that one."

I didn't say a word. Fuck Hess. I'd take him down.

"It's time to act, Mr Blyth," I said. "I want this wrapped up before the fifteenth."

"Understandable, Corporal, but now is not the time to rush. We should go to the DoPI office down here and prepare you for what you might face, both at Dr Grove's home and the cathedral, if things go that far. Although I still don't fully accept the building has the ancient power she'll need to use. I'd like to visit the site as well. We have a day to prepare."

"That brings us dangerously close, Mr Blyth."

"A necessary judgement on my behalf. Sorcerers need time and understanding in order to affect the natural world. We cannot just wave a wand and make brooms dance." He smiled again.

Megan and I shared our exasperation, but I had to respect his knowledge. Blyth was the expert here, not me. I was relegated to being the doorkicker.

Sid offered to stay with Luce and Naomi. I wanted Megan to stay as well, but Blyth said he needed her with us back in Redruth. It seemed unlikely that Hess would attack during daylight, and provided Matty remained in the house, no one could easily snatch him. I gave another firm lecture on safety.

"Just pretend you have the flu," I said to Matty. "It'll be boring, but you'll cope."

Luce said, "We can cook cakes and biscuits. Decorate them. Watch telly. Have a duvet day." She smiled with an indulgence I'd never seen her display before.

Matty looked bewildered by this, and I guessed Naomi and Glendower kept him busy with lessons and farm work. The kid didn't have friends his own age, so their behaviours weren't his. I doubted Naomi believed in 'duvet days'.

Blyth would ride back to Redruth with Megan, and I walked to the bike, knowing I'd be doing an obbo again that night. At some point it would be wise to catch a couple of hours downtime. I needed to stay sharp. As I walked back to the bike, my brain churned over all we'd discussed so far, until I looked out over the houses of Portreath. Luce's house was on one of the hills surrounding the original fishing village. The views from the road were just enough to make me wish we were doing anything today other than demon hunting.

The sea, the clean blue of Megan's eyes, teased me with its presence on the air. I could just see the horizon over the roofs, and it met the pale, misty blue of the sky. Today we had high clouds, thin and veil-like, easily torn by the vagaries of winds we didn't feel, earthbound creatures that we are. The gulls, however, used their playground to full effect. I paused and closed my eyes. Some instinct I'd honed over the years made me aware that we were on the brink, things were changing and the time to act was soon.

Right now, Megan and I were coasting on the wave of the investigation. When it was over, we had the deaths of three teenagers, Wesson, and so much more to fill our idle moments. Both of us had learned to compartmentalise the things we witnessed, but that wouldn't make our lives any easier when those images started to haunt us. Very few people would be able to forget such scenes. I just had to hope nothing worse happened as we brought down Dr Elena Grove.

Chapter Twenty

I arrived back at the office before Megan and Blyth. Rather than faff about with security, I propped open the doors and allowed a little natural light and air into the stuffy concrete box. We had air conditioning, but the longer I stayed in Cornwall, the more I wanted natural light and real oxygen in my workspace. It's what this case needed most—more light.

The desire to charge down to Dodman Point and raid every house in that location looking for Dr Elena Grove almost overwhelmed me. Blyth had his reasons to make sure we were prepared before an incursion, and he had to be our guide on this enterprise, but for a commando, it is the waiting that is often the toughest part of the battle. The most important thing for me was making certain we had those three children back in one piece. Also, to make damned sure we didn't lose Naomi and Matty.

I heard Megan's car pull up and started making us all some tea. I wondered what the conversation in the car must've been like for her, what the softly spoken Scot had shared about our work with DoPI.

They came in quietly, and I sensed no hostility from Megan. Blyth was once more in his buttoned-up coat, carrying that old-fashioned leather bag on his right side.

I handed over her tea, and she smiled with gratitude. Next, after a firm instruction of 'black, no sugar', I handed Blyth his mug.

Time for the questions. "Why did you separate us from the others?" I asked.

Blyth sat on our sofa and looked around. "You've made this place your own."

"Is that a problem?" Code for, 'are you about to report us to Sanchez for having an X-Files poster on the wall and a sofa?'

"Not for me, Corporal. When I first mooted the idea of satellite offices, I made sure to tell Pilar she would need to loosen the reins. She's always been controlling, ever since she was a girl."

Well, colour me pink. "You've known Ms Sanchez that long?"

Blyth looked over the rim of his mug, his little grey eyes twinkling. "I'm the one who found her in Mexico and brought her to England. I was researching an Aztec myth that had grown a little out of hand. Pilar was caught up in it, much like your Matty. It seemed wise to keep an eye on her future, considering…"

I wanted to poke, and prise out information from this strange winkle-like man. "You're not going to share any more than that, are you?"

He grinned. "No. Just reminding you that she's human. People forget that. *She* forgets that. It pays to have someone she trusts remember it. I won't be around forever."

"Are you asking me to be her conscience?" I asked. "If that's the case, you have the wrong man."

"I have the right man, laddie. She trusts you, or she'd have chosen someone else for this role. You defy her when necessary, despite her threats and stampy-footed temper. My girl can see monsters where they don't exist. Sometimes someone has to stop her."

Was he talking about the *para-nuke* theory we'd created in our quiet moments? I watched him, but nothing came from that bland exterior that I could read.

"Maybe we'll talk about this later," I muttered. "You still haven't told me why you requested to talk to us alone."

"I didn't want to upset the mother and child. I also had the sense that your Dr Carmichael—and I know from experience—that Sid would not appreciate what I'm about to say." His intense gaze settled on Megan. "I am hoping you have the good sense to see the bigger picture."

"Why me specifically?" Megan asked.

"In my experience, women can struggle with some of the decisions necessary to prevent a demonic presence from spreading."

"I'm a professional, Mr Blyth," Megan stated, her colour rising.

"I know that, Sergeant. That's why you're here. It's just a practical observation, nothing more. Now, I will explain. It is my assumption that our Dr Grove will summon four demons into the children. The rite I believe she must be using as the basis for this conjuring predates Christianity. It comes from Babylon. We have some writings about such things in the papyruses of the Egyptians, who weren't above similar practices themselves. If we manage to stop her before the ceremony is started, then the children will be safe. However, if even part of the demonic sacrament takes place, then the children must not survive."

Silence.

Megan's eyes flickered to mine, and I saw her panic. She must not be seen as the weak link.

"I'm not sure if I understand, Mr Blyth, and I think it's important we are completely clear on this," I said.

He nodded. "The children must die, Corporal. If the spell is cast, if the demon summoning has begun, then the souls of those innocents will be so corrupted that we cannot allow them to live. They will never be free of the demonic taint. Only through death and prayer will they once more return to the state of purity all of humanity has deep down."

Megan huffed a breath. "You haven't met some of the bastards I've arrested."

"The wicked things people do to each other are not demonic, it's just human evil. It's very sad, horrible even, but it's human. What I am talking about is demonic evil."

"What, like Nazi concentration camp evil?"

"That was human evil, not demonic, despite what many in the world think. The same can be said of what's happened in hotspots all over the world. Human horrors, not demonic. These four children could become the harbingers of the apocalypse. The four horsemen. That's demonic. Can you see the difference?"

Megan wiped her hands over her face and growled. "Yeah, I can see it, if you believe in it."

Oh, shit, she was retreating. Though I understood her denial, I found it frustrating.

Trying to divert the conversation a little, I asked, "What do you want us to do?"

"If we, meaning you as the spear point, cannot prevent

this event, then you will need to kill the children." He reached down and picked up his small leather case. Opening it, he removed two cloth cases with something long and solid inside. He put one down and released the small toggle on the flap of the other. The cloth was velvet, and blue, it reminded me of churches and nuns. Carefully, he withdrew a dagger.

It was black, the blade and the hilt. The crossguard was plain, like two ancient nails held together at the point by the tang of the blade. The double edge of the weapon, even from a distance, was sharp and covered in script of some kind.

"You have to be fucking joking," Megan said. "You expect me to stab four children with that?"

"You are a DoPI operative, and this is a last resort."

"Fuck off," Megan said, pushing herself out of her chair with such violence the soft man flinched.

I tried to remain calm, though Megan's reaction made perfect sense to me. "We'll stop this before it happens," I stated. "Those won't be necessary."

"I hope not, but you understand my need for discretion. We at the Department of Paranormal Investigations have to make the larger sacrifice for the whole of humanity." He watched Megan turning in tight circles as she tugged on a lock of hair.

The moment she stopped, her eyes held mine. I saw it, she'd never be able to kill children, she just didn't believe deeply enough. It didn't make enough sense. It was my duty to protect her as well.

After a long silence, Blyth made a small cough and said, "There is something else we need to discuss."

Megan sat down, her eyes hard, lips thin. "Of course there is."

"If we are unfortunate enough to allow the demons into our plane of existence, then we should work together to capture one."

A small bubble of hysterical laughter burst from Megan. "This is insane." She rose and left the office completely, the doors still open.

I remained in my seat, long practiced at remaining still in the face of DoPI's perceived insanity. "I don't think that's wise."

"We will just need one child—"

"No, Mr Blyth. I will be stopping this before it happens. Children are not going to be used by DoPI. This is a dangerous distraction. It will make us vulnerable." Besides, even if we did catch a demon, I'd be heading up to London to bang some heads together until I destroyed it. Sanchez's sorcerer was *not* having a demon.

"Corporal, I don't think you understand what we're facing out there. Our service to our nation means we have to protect ourselves using any means necessary. Don't dismiss what the Nazis tried to do with their secret rites—"

I held my hand up. "That's where you lose me, Mr Blyth. The moment anyone invokes an idea that came from that regime, it means we're skating on the ice of morality that's so thin, it will crack and demons will be the least of our problems. If DoPI wants a demon, they can conjure it, I will not be involved. We should be forming alliances with the creatures inside the veil that could be allies, like the dryads and Dru. That ought to be our future."

"The demons won't come to our summonings. They know who we are."

"Then that should give you all the answers you need. You capture one of these things, try to use it as a weapon, it'll turn on you like a savage dog." I rose. "Now, if you'll excuse me, I need to discuss things with my partner before she decides to arrest you for child abuse or something similar." I walked out of the office.

Megan stood in the full sun, leaning against her car, shaking her head as if having a debate with herself. "I can't do this, Griffin."

"We aren't taking a child with a demon inside—"

"No, I mean, I can't do DoPI. Blyth wants me permanently. He says you need a full team behind you. They're talking about giving you a response unit, expanding this office to deal with more than just Cornwall and Devon. He thinks having an experienced police officer working with you will help smooth some of DoPI's more extreme behaviours." She turned to look at me. Tears stood proud in her eyes, but they were of fury and hurt. "Children, Griffin. He's talking about children."

"I know."

"I'm not taking part in this, and I'll go to the fucking press if I have to."

"We can't do that, Megan. They'll have you locked away faster than I can reach out to touch you now. Please don't say that aloud." I meant it. If DoPI even caught a whiff of her betraying them, it would end in a shitstorm for all of us, and I'd lose her forever. "Just take a minute, okay. You and I both know we won't be letting this happen. Just as I sent the incubus away, rather than finding a way for DoPI to capture it, I'll be preventing this problem with the demons. If something happens and DoPI end up with Grove or one of her pets, then I'll be going to London to finish this." Her expression softened, and I reached out to grip her hands. "Trust me. We will protect these kids. That's what is important."

"Promise?"

"Easiest promise in the world."

"What if they do get possessed?" she asked.

"We'll be in a cathedral, what better place to ask for help?"

She searched my eyes, looking for a lie, but there wasn't one. I'd protect those children with my life. It was my job and duty, just as I'd told Naomi.

Megan rubbed her face with her hands. "I just don't think I can do this. I thought I could, but some of this shit is just too much. Seeing those kids, the men in the squat... It's a fucking nightmare. Like I'm trapped in a Wes Craven film and I have no escape."

I understood. The time between assignments was like a distant memory. Suddenly, when we were in the thick of the chaos but not fighting for our lives, or the lives of others, we were able to see our work clearly. The madness of DoPI's remit. The horrors it prevented, the others that it caused.

"I understand, Megan. This is why we recruit from the Armed Forces, not from the Police Service. It's a different mentality. A different kind of person is recruited and trained. When I'm given an objective I'm far more of a machine than you will ever be. That's why you're important. A balance, a different way of working. You and I, we're still trying to figure that out. When those kids threw themselves off the car park," I gazed past her, seeing the moment so clearly, "I shut down. Became the Marine I'm trained to be, but that's not what's needed. Not any more. We're dealing with real people. Vulnerable people. We have to be the ones who see the trees inside the wood, each individual tree, and our responsibility is to protect it. Or rather, them." Just as well I torture metaphors and not people.

Megan sniffed and swiped at her eyes. "I thought I

wanted to be part of DoPI, of what you do, but I'm really not sure, Griffin."

"All it takes for organisations to make huge mistakes is to lose the people who will scream at those in charge when they make mistakes." I held out my little finger, like I did when we were kids. "I promise I'll stand with you and scream when necessary. DoPI needs you. It needs us."

Megan sucked in a lungful of hot air and stared at my little finger. "You're an idiot."

"I know. Just do it."

She managed a brief, cynical smile, but she hooked her little finger around mine. "Okay. I'll accept your promise and trust you'll stand by me."

Relief flooded through me.

You know you just manipulated her, right? You get to play spooky ghost shit with your girlfriend, even though she'd be unhappy. That's manipulation.

Was it? Megan could just say no and leave DoPI. She could leave me. Couldn't she?

"Come on," she said. "We'd better stop the mad munchkin in there doing something stupid with your kit." As if preparing her weary self for another battle, Megan sucked in another lungful of the hot air, squared her shoulders and walked back into the office.

I followed, but I have to admit, I was questioning more than just *my* life choices.

Megan stood before Blyth, who blinked at her owlishly. "Alright," she said. "Why's this all so complicated? Griffin doesn't really know, he's just guessing, so am I. Why would a woman do this? Plot like this for over a decade? Become a doctor, a sorcerer, and steal other people's children. Raise them as her own, then sacrifice them? What the hell is going on?"

"It is as you've said. She wants her revenge on the Church that has done her great harm." Blyth leaned back in his chair. "Please, Sergeant, I know you are angry with me, and I understand, but please sit. I will explain." He held his hand out towards her chair, offering peace.

Megan sat, but her body was primed for a fight. I took my chair and kept quiet, still trying to see a clear path.

Blyth leaned back into the cushions, clearly considering where to start. Eventually, he said, "This Dr Grove, she doesn't want to use demons to destroy the Church. She knows they don't have the power necessary, no matter which Marquis of Hell she summons into the children. What she can do is call on the Virgin Mary, as the mother of Jesus, to help save the innocent from demonic possession. When she is answered, Mary will send angels to battle the demons. I believe Dr Grove wants the children to be possessed by angels. They will push the demons out and take over the innocent bodies of the children. They can also be trapped inside the children. Take a moment to think about that."

Megan glanced at me. "He's saying the children will have angels inside them?"

"If it works, yes." My agreement felt leaden.

Her eyes narrowed as they returned to Blyth. "Why do you want the demon and not the angel?"

He managed a smile. "Controlling angels is not something DoPI feels is wise. Leave them where they are."

"Why? Loads of people believe in them," she said.

"Angels are dangerous. Far more so than demons." He glanced at me. "Have you explained what happened at Hinkley Point? Does she understand the doctrine of the Nephilim?"

I shook my head. "Didn't see the point. I thought the

angel aspect of this was us pushing the bounds of credulity too far even for a DoPI operative."

Blyth clasped his hands together. "Think about this. If a demon is summoned and used against the Church, the organisation will use all its might to destroy the creature, the host, and the summoner. People will see its mighty battle, and their faith will be ignited. They will flock to the religion in numbers not seen since the Middle Ages." He held out one hand, his left. Then he held out his other hand. "However, if angels are summoned into the bodies of the innocent, and kept there, what will those angels see of our mighty religious institutions?"

"That's how she plans to destroy the Church? She's going to prove how corrupt and wicked it can be?" Megan asked. "Bishop Chadwick isn't like that. He's a good man."

"He might be, but there will still be people who aren't," Blyth said. "Who knows what the angels will think of as wicked? What would their definition be in the modern world? Their Lord's representatives on earth might well find themselves vulnerable when faced with the commandments, or the deadly sins. What if the major religions of the world have it all wrong?"

I thought of Bishop Chadwick's portly belly. Would he suffer an angel's wrath because he liked red wine and cheese a little too much?

Megan was shaking her head, and it didn't look as if she realised she was doing it. "I just don't understand the logic. Go to the press. Go to the law. Speak up about your abuse. Summoning angels and demons is…" Her loss made sense. We were trying to understand a labyrinthine mind, and we had no map.

"For some, it isn't enough," Blyth stated. "You must know this, as a police officer."

Megan sat back, and I watched her begin to consider the victims she'd interviewed over the years and how the law had let them down. "If you're inclined to believe in this stuff, I can see how it can happen." She sounded so sad.

Blyth nodded. "If Dr Grove felt she had no choice, and her faith had been abused, something she held in her soul, not just her heart, then it could twist her into a Gordian Knot so tangled she'd never find a safe way to freedom from her grief. Angels are powerful beings. We at DoPI will do anything to keep them from reaching our plane of existence. We have no way of sending them back, and they do not want to be here. Their role is to guide through visions and with tender words in our minds. Private. Safe. They are only made manifest through God's will, to do His bidding, not ours. We are not gods."

Chapter Twenty-One

We spent the rest of the day planning. I drove Blyth up to Truro. We walked around the cathedral and Kenwyn's church. He asked to see Wesson's murder site, and the car park. Both were still covered with police tape. The remains of Wesson's caravan and the surrounding area were a soggy mess after the Fire Service put out the flames. The trees were scarred, the ivy brittle and apt to disintegrate when you brushed against it. I could hardly believe the events that had happened over the last week, all based around this one small spot.

When we went to the site where the youngsters had died, I let Blyth walk the lane alone. I'd behaved badly here, and I knew some part of me was still trying to process the horror of what we'd witnessed. I found myself bending my head and, yes, I offered a prayer for them. They hadn't been possessed by a demon, but much like Adrian Hess had become a victim of the sorcerer, they'd been manipulated and used. I wondered what the experts would make of the ritual sacrifice we'd found in that sad excuse for a house.

Doubtless I'd be sent a report at some point. Right now, I wasn't sure I cared. I just wanted this over with.

When we started on the journey home, I said to Blyth, "Why can't I go in tonight and just kill the woman? You must be able to give me something that can hide me from her wards."

"I wish it were that easy, Corporal," the strange man said. "Sadly, it isn't. I cannot anticipate what you will face if you meet her on home ground. I will be spending tonight scrying, trying to see what she has done and where. It's important I ensure that neither of you ends up being attacked in the way Mr Wesson was murdered."

I glanced at him in alarm. "You really think that's possible?"

"Probable, Corporal Woodbury, if we get this wrong."

The thought of Megan being sliced up like that made my stomach churn. What I'd seen in that vision, brought on by the trauma to the veil and my connection to it, was beyond any kind of cruelty I'd seen in this world. Whatever Wesson's faults, and there had been many, he hadn't deserved such terror and violence.

"So we just go home and do what?" I asked.

"Nothing. I have lodgings, so you can drop me there. Then, I will call you when I know more. I suggest you and Sergeant Ackley do as you did last night, watch the house in Portreath for the Renfield."

Sadly, it didn't work out that way.

I stretched my neck and rolled my shoulders. It was 04:07. Megan had gone back to Turpin Cottage with strict instructions to keep all the doors and windows locked, despite the heat of the night. Naomi and Matty weren't the only people likely to fall victim to Hess. It made me nervous that none of us had seen him, and that included his police colleagues.

The report from the cleaning crew, who'd been at the squat, was succinct. I'd opened it with a vague feeling of dread. Initial assessments made it clear that the men had been sacrificed by the teenagers. Their fingerprints were everywhere. Even in the blood. It had been nothing more than a summoning of raw power. They'd taken the life essence of the men and shared it between them. That's why they'd behaved as if on some extreme stimulant, and why they'd believed they could fly. Grove had used her knowledge and given them just enough of it to turn them into weapons. I had no doubt she'd been in that room, giving them instructions, as they'd sliced those poor bastards up. She must've seen me in the mirror, known we were on her track, and decided to juice up her groomed teenagers. Hess would be her fallback, her safety net. He'd be coming for us.

It was sad and left me feeling depressed. Blinking and trying not to yawn again, I poured more tea from the flask Mrs Dennis had left for me. I had lemon drizzle cake and homemade pasties on plates nearby. Homemade pasties! I wanted Mrs Dennis to adopt me.

The lethargy just wasn't going away. It sapped my bones. I rose, walked around the room, did some squats, press-ups and more stretches. Each one made the muscles burn with exhaustion, which shouldn't be possible. I just wanted to sleep. A little snooze. Nothing could happen. The sun would be up soon. Life had to return to the small community, and people must leave for work. Children would come out to play. Naomi and Matty didn't have to face danger for another day, then we just had to get through the fifteenth and this would all be over. Just a few more minutes of sleep…

My eyes closed and my breathing deepened. I still wore the witch's stone around my neck, and it felt hot, but then, everything felt hot, and snuggly, warm and safe. We were over-reacting. I just needed a few more minutes of dozing time.

"Mum!" The scream was an arrow through my heart, despite being muffled by the double glazing.

I jerked awake, caught a glimpse of movement in the street below, fell off the chair and hit the floor hard. "Shit." Scrambling, I made it to the window.

Hess.

He had a hold of Matty. A small woman, Naomi, lay in the street, a crumbled heap. Matty was fighting like a terrier against a bear, trying to escape Hess's grip. Sid rushed out of the house. I was already tumbling down the stairs, Glock in hand. How had I missed this? What the hell was wrong with me?

No, now isn't the time. Focus, soldier boy.

The switch inside me flipped, and all thoughts other than stopping Hess vanished. I rushed outside.

"Hess! Stop!" I yelled, lifting the Glock's dark barrel as I ran into the street.

Sid yelled, "Don't, Griffin. He has a knife."

Hess was dragging Matty towards his sleek BMW.

"Let him go, Hess," I ordered. "You know this isn't right." Panic gripped me.

In the yellow light of the street lamps, I saw Hess clearly. Or what was left of the man Megan knew. His eyes were hollow, big and wild. The careful stubble the man obviously spent time managing had turned into a beard. He looked almost skeletal under the hard white lights.

"I hear her," he said through cracked and bleeding lips.

"Her demands. My reward will be great. She needs me. You all need me. The boy is hers."

Sid moved slowly behind me, and I hoped he was going to Naomi.

I continued to walk with short, balanced steps around the car. "I understand, Adrian. I know what it's like to be out of control of your thoughts, your actions. To have someone else in your head. I get it. But you need to fight back, Adrian. You need to come back to yourself before it's too late. You haven't hurt anyone yet. This can be fixed. We can bring you in. Megan can help you. I'll help you." I was babbling, but he had his back to the open door of the car, and I couldn't risk a random shot.

Firearms in a public arena like this can go wrong. A stray bullet will do horrific damage, and Matty's scream for his mother had caused doors to open in the quiet street. I had civilians appearing in my periphery. Calls were being made.

"Please, Adrian, let me help you," I repeated, trying to maintain eye contact. Matty had stopped struggling, and I feared he couldn't breathe. "Let the boy go."

Sid called from behind me. "Griffin, she's not breathing."

Matty lurched in Adrian's arms. The man twisted, putting the boy right in my line of sight. He dropped into the open car door, Matty on his lap, and the still-running engine, lurched into life. The man was a trained operative; he'd parked nose to the exit on a sharp hill. The car began to roll. If I shot into the moving vehicle, I could hit Matty. Or a ricochet would strike him. This wasn't a car full of enemy combatants.

"Griffin!" Sid repeated. "I need you here."

I was fairly sure Naomi would willingly die if it meant I

could save her son, but I couldn't, I'd never reach him in time. I'd failed. Again. I'd fucking fallen asleep.

Don't think about it now. Save the woman.

For once, a useful piece of advice. I ran back to Naomi. Adrian had stabbed her in the chest. Sid's arms, up to his elbows, were covered in blood. Luce was rushing towards us with towels.

I grabbed one. To Sid, I barked, "When I tell you to move. Move." Folding the small towel down as much as I could, I said, "Move." Sid lifted his hands. Blood squirted. A good sign. Her heart was working. I shoved the towel into the large slice and hole, then pressed down. "I need more," I ordered.

Luce knelt beside me and handed over more towels. We both pressed down.

"Sid, I need her feet elevated. We have to keep the blood she has in her brain and heart."

He scooted around her, lifted her legs and dropped them onto his shoulders.

"Well, that's one way of doing it. Luce, do you know how to check her airways?"

"Yes, yes, I can do that." Luce tipped Naomi's head back and opened her mouth, moving her tongue. She then pressed her cheek to the woman's nose. "She's breathing. Just."

I glanced up at the crowd. "Can someone give me an ETA on the medics?"

"Five clicks," someone said.

I located the voice. A young man, military haircut. "You serving?" I asked him. Dawn was nudging at night and telling it to roll over, its time was done.

"I'm just a grunt."

"Get here, I need more hands," I ordered.

He knelt beside me, and together we pressed on Naomi's small chest. I worried we'd stop her from breathing, but Luce kept talking to her and gradually, the rolling eyes focused. Her hand fluttered, and Luce held strong.

"Chest cavity," the soldier muttered.

"Yeah, I know. We can't do anything. Unless you're a medic?" I asked him.

He shook his head. "Infantry. You?"

"Royal Marine. I've had some training, but not enough, and no equipment."

"You have a sidearm on domestic soil, how's that possible?" he asked, as well he might. "What's going on?"

"Obbo went wrong. I'm seconded."

He whispered, "Terrorists?"

I gritted my teeth. Naomi's blood was cooling on my hands. It felt awful. "No, he's the father. Wanted the son, but has no rights. Violent offender. She's been here in hiding after threats. He's linked to terror groups. That's why I'm here." It was a tired excuse, but one DoPI had come to rely on since the IRA started bombing the mainland. The domestic abuse angle would help us keep the focus on Matty.

Naomi started to struggle for breath, and she tried to ask after her son. Luce looked at me. The anguish inside me just wanted to rage at the world.

"I'll get him back, Naomi. I promise. I'll get him back."

The hate in her eyes burned my heart. Still, it might keep her heart pumping, so I'd swallow it down. I deserved it.

Sirens echoed around the sleepy village, and a paramedic on a bike arrived.

"Stab victim. Severe blood loss," I reported. "Large

gash and deep penetration into the chest cavity. Breathing rapidly, heart rate fluttering."

The paramedic began barking orders at us. "Domestic?" he asked, his eyes hard on Sid.

"Yes," I said, covering him. "The father has run with the boy. This was supposed to be a safe house. I was on watch. I failed."

"Well, she's alive, so that counts," the paramedic said. An ambulance rolled up.

I moved on my knees out of the way, blood covering my clothes. The young soldier retreated into the arms of his mother. Was I ever that young when I signed up? He still had acne, for goodness sake.

Sid moved to the kerb to sit next to me. "What happened, Griffin?"

I shook my head. "I don't know, mate. Just couldn't stay awake. It was impossible. I've never fallen asleep on an obbo. Never." My hands were shaking, my brain telling me it was important to keep pushing on the frail body.

Mrs Dennis stood in the doorway of her house and watched, deep concern on her face. Could she have drugged me? No, that made no sense. Mrs Dennis was Luce's friend, and she was a kind lady. Not everyone in this world had malign intentions.

Suddenly, Sid gripped my left hand and held it hard. "What are we doing? This is all wrong. We're the good guys. She shouldn't… I never thought…" He burst into noisy tears.

I'd seen this happen in the field. Something deep inside me, broken while still a child, made it hard for me to let go enough to do this, to weep my grief and shame all over a friend. Pulling Sid close, I wrapped my bloodied hands around him and held him as he sobbed.

Luce came out with a blanket. She whispered, "When he was a teenager, he was present when his cousin was stabbed during a gang war in London."

I'd had no idea. What a terrible thing to witness. Luce and I managed to lift Sid out of the road. The police had arrived, and there would be a lot of questions. Several people had witnessed Adrian Hess fleeing the scene with the child. I needed Megan. It was time to end this.

Standing outside with two officers who'd already attended the scene in Madron, I called Megan.

"What?" she bleated. "I just managed to—"

"Hess stabbed Naomi. He's taken Matty. I need you and Blyth at Luce's. Naomi's alive. She's heading to Truro hospital, apparently."

"On my way. What happened?" she asked, her phone now on speaker. I could hear her pulling on clothes.

"I fell asleep, Meg. I failed everyone."

A pause. "Somehow, I doubt that's true. I'll be with you as soon as I can, with Blyth. Who's attending the scene."

I looked at the officers. "Jennings and McLean."

"Hand me over to McLean."

I did as instructed.

Chapter Twenty-Two

It took long into the morning to sort out the issues we faced. Megan looked exhausted after just two hours of sleep. I was so stunned by my failure I could barely bring myself to look at anyone, let alone speak. Sid was in pieces and not functioning. Luce put him to bed with some sleeping pills. When she came down, she explained that Naomi had threatened to run earlier in the evening. They'd talked her down, but short of tying her up, they couldn't stop her from bolting with the child.

The police finally took Hess's involvement in a child kidnapping seriously. They didn't want to admit one of their own was rotten, but Megan found herself receiving more than one muttered apology. It didn't help. She was furious with them, and with me. When I finally began washing Naomi's blood off my hands, I couldn't look at my reflection in the mirror.

During all this, Blyth had kept his mouth shut, just sitting and waiting. Once the police left us alone, and I'd cleaned up enough not to stain the furniture, he requested I sit with him.

"Griffin," he said in his soft brogue. "I can see the pain in your heart and your fear for the boy."

Megan closed her eyes. "Great, more bollocks. Just what we need. I want coffee." She rose and left.

My heart left with her. Our future was crumbling, just like the dried blood did before I managed to reach the washbasin.

Blyth hummed. "She'll come around."

I didn't have the energy to tell him any differently, but I certainly felt it.

"Griffin, you didn't fall asleep," Blyth stated.

That made me look up. "What? I did. I fell out of the chair when I heard Naomi scream."

He shook his head. "I've been watching you and, if I'm honest, smelling you."

I frowned at him. That would be an unpleasant experience. I stank of sweat and blood. It had dried on my black combats so was almost invisible, but I could see it, feel it.

His expression became sympathetic. "Not like that, dear boy. I can smell the spell on you. See the colours wriggling through your aura. You've been badly used, I'm afraid. The sorcerer has you firmly in her sights. The skill it takes to ensnare someone with your will is impressive. I would say this Renfield has something that belongs to you and has passed it over to her. Would that be possible?"

I frowned. "I don't know. I don't think…" Wait, hold on a minute. I'd given Megan one of my old t-shirts. She'd worn it home to her place, it hadn't yet been returned to my place. In one of her more romantic moments, she confessed she liked sleeping in it. I knew Hess had been in her flat since they'd broken up. "Yeah, maybe. Megan will know."

"Could you go and ask her?"

Great, DoPI's tame sorcerer was scared of my girlfriend. Though I was as well after screwing up so badly. Knowing I faced ridicule or worse for it, I braved the kitchen. She wasn't there. I found her and Luce outside, in the small garden, sitting in the calm and Zen-like space.

"Sorry for interrupting," I said as both women frowned at me. "But, Megan, do you remember that Porcupine Tree t-shirt you borrowed?"

"What? Don't tell me you want it back now?"

"No," I said, waving my hands in an attempt to keep the situation calm. "No, of course not, but have you seen it recently?"

She blinked. "Why are you asking me that?" Never ask a police officer a question without providing a full explanation. They don't like it.

"Blyth believes the sorcerer has something of mine that could've helped her put me to sleep last night, so Hess could take Matty. Naomi's willingness to leave the house just made it easier for him. As he had a knife, he might've been planning to break in and kill the adults." I'd been considering this as Hess's likely plan for several hours. Naomi's fleeing really was a bonus for him. Me managing to stay awake for so long must've kept him waiting on the okay to go in, and he hadn't done it under Megan's watch because, well, maybe he really did care enough to stop himself going after her.

Hess would sacrifice me to the sorcerer without a moment's thought, but not Megan. Even Renfields could form bonds too strong for their masters to break, until their minds shattered completely. Some part of the man remained.

Megan's expression closed down. "That's your excuse?"

"Pardon?"

"Your excuse for sleeping on the job is that you were the victim of a spell caused by something in my flat?"

"Hess could've taken the t-shirt. You've had it for months, even while you were together, he might've taken it—"

She rose so fast her thigh hit the cast iron table, making it wobble. Luce lunged for the mugs before they tumbled. Coffee slopped, filling the air with its aroma.

Megan spat, "This is now my fault?"

"What?" I glanced at Luce, begging for help. She didn't meet my pleading gaze. "No, Meg, no, I didn't mean that at all. Please, I'm sorry, I just want to get Matty back."

"Then why the fuck are you still here? You're the one with the ninja skills. Go," she waved a hand in the general direction of the south coast of Cornwall. "Go find him, kill the bad guys. It's what you're here for."

Stunned, I just stood there, like a complete lemon.

"I think that's enough, young lady," Blyth said from the back door.

I turned, stunned that he had the temerity.

Megan rounded on him. "Don't you bloody dare. For all your talk and cleverness, you failed to protect an innocent woman and child."

"Or, I have provided us with a way to track them more efficiently," Blyth said.

Her mouth dropped open for a moment. "You… What a dreadful thing to say. How dare you! If that was your intention—"

"Not my intention, but I can use the spell placed on Griffin to track the sorcerer. It will work for everyone involved."

"This is insane." Megan paced around the patio area,

then went up the garden path. "You can't seriously think that a spell—"

Blyth muttered something under his breath while rubbing his fingers over a small pebble in his hand. Megan's eyes glazed over.

"Catch her," he ordered.

I lunged, and just before she hit the ground, I managed to put myself in the way. Her body flopped onto mine, knocking the wind out of me for a few seconds.

"What did you do?" I asked Blyth. Luce was on her feet, rushing towards us.

"Just give her a moment," he said. "She's perfectly all right."

I struggled upright but kept Megan in my lap. Stroking her hair from her face, I found myself wanting to count the freckles on her lightly tanned skin. She looked more peaceful than I'd seen her in days.

Slowly, she blinked and yawned. "Wha' happen'?" she asked, taking her time to focus.

Blyth appeared above us. "I sent you to sleep, dear." He held out a small rock. "I found this in your car and took it. I suspect you use it to calm yourself while in traffic. It certainly contains a lot of your energy. A small demonstration that the man who loves you very much did *not* fail you or Naomi. If she'd remained in the house, she would've been safer. Hess had to wait for her to leave because I had placed various wards around the property yesterday. Not just to keep demons out, but mostly to prevent him from breaking in." Blyth reached into his suit pocket and removed a disk of wood, with a rune or glyph on the surface. "I left this under the doormat.

"Why didn't you tell me?" I asked, helping Megan sit up.

"Why would I?"

"Because we're a team?" Megan suggested. "Jesus, I feel like I have a hangover."

"Drink some water, you'll be fine," Blyth said with no sympathy whatsoever. "Can you see how easily Griffin was influenced? From what he's told me, it took her considerably longer to force him to sleep than it did for me to trap you. Perhaps you could remember that next time." His gaze fell on me. "I need you in the sitting room. We have to find the child."

He seemed angry at Megan. Though it was hard to tell, only his eyes and voice hardened just a little. For her part, Megan didn't know what to do with herself. I certainly didn't know what to say to her.

I followed Blyth into the house.

"Is she really going to be okay?" I asked.

"Of course. It's not the first time I've had to prove to an operative that the impossible is perfectly possible if you know how." He managed a slight grin. "She'll make a good soldier for DoPI if she can just let go."

"I'm not sure I want that future for her. It doesn't tend to end well for us at the sharp end."

"That is her decision, Corporal. Now sit down, this isn't going to be pleasant for either of us." He waved at the sofa.

"Why?"

"Scrying isn't easy, for a start. Trying to scry through another person is very difficult, but I'm willing to make the effort if it helps. I want you to take both my hands and in a minute, you're going to look into my eyes, and you are not going to look away. You will feel pressure, then pain, behind them. I will be using them as I would a bowl of water. The water is malleable, you are not. Expect nausea as well. Please do not break contact."

None of that seemed the least bit reassuring, but I'd commit to anything if it meant I could find Matty before the sorcerer hurt him.

"Take some deep breaths. Calm your mind. Relax as much as you can, and trust me," he said, keeping his voice soft and even. I held the squishy hands, slightly clammy from the heat, and tried to still the bubbling tumult of my mind.

It didn't work. Every time I relaxed, I saw the dead teenagers on the service road outside the NCP car park and felt the horror of the demon killing Wesson. The two were blurring in my mind. With Blyth staring into my eyes, I began to feel dizzy. His were grey with blue flecks and a dark ring around the outside of the iris. His pupils were gradually expanding to take up more of the grey. It's rare you stare at anyone this closely for any length of time, and it made me feel like I was inside a grey tunnel. A swirling grey tunnel that had immense pressure inside it, pushing down on my brain, squeezing it.

I began to pant, struggling for breath, and my heart raced. Weakness filled my limbs.

"Not the teenagers," Blyth whispered. "Try for the wee boy, Griffin."

I had to abandon those kids again? Just like everyone else had in their lives. Apart from the sorcerer, Dr Elena Grove, who had used them. Where were the souls of those forgotten youngsters? Who would rescue them from the horrors they'd created in that house of nightmare and damnation? Who was there to save them?

The panic began to rise as the pain in my head increased. I wanted desperately to move away from the power in those grey eyes. It was all-encompassing. Utterly dominating. A shifting kaleidoscope of grey and blue, green and black, so much black, more black. I tumbled downwards, trying to escape the grip this strange man had on my mind and body.

"Griffin, do not fight me. Relax. I am using your connection to the veil—"

No, no, no, I'm not going back into that blackness with you. I am not walking that fucking rainbow again. I'm not—

"Griffin, I'm right here. I can help." Megan's words were soft, but her hands on my shoulders were strong. Where I'd leaned forward to hold Blyth's hands, Megan had tucked herself behind me on the sofa. I felt her heat down my spine, her thighs tight to my ribs, her knees under my arms. "I'll not let you go. I promise, Griffin."

We were no longer a family. If Megan cut me out of her life, I'd have no one. The world would be a lonely place. She'd been my anchor since the day we'd first met as children. That cheeky smile, those bright blonde curls, she'd been the right of me forever.

My anchor.

I gritted my teeth against the pain. With Megan at my back, I rode Blyth's grey vision and let myself tumble into the veil once again.

The blackness swamped me. This was not like it had been with Trystan. I tumbled, unmoored, despite Megan's hope. End over end, falling, falling, like those poor benighted teens. Tumbled through a nothingness so vast, it was incomprehensible to the mind, like the distance between the stars. We understand it logically, but our souls cannot truly grasp the endless nothing separating those tiny pricks in the black of night.

"Hold fast."

I heard Blyth's words from a great distance.

"I have… You are not what you seem, Griffin Woodbury."

The world swam into focus before I found my feet in the veil. I roared over territory I did not know. A patchwork of fields, small areas of heath, stranded woodland, tiny villages connected by the narrowest of capillaries. Cliffs, mighty high, clothed in green, spangled with yellow from summer flowering. Then, the sea, a deep and endless, ever-moving mass. Another world. The harmony of something so alive, each wave an inhale and exhale as it completed its cycle. Forever moving, forever breathing, a place we could never comprehend in all its glorious facets.

"Come back, Marine. The sea is not for you today," Blyth's voice sounded amused. "Focus now on the boy. See him clearly."

Matty. I did this for him. The pain pressing against my eyes had come to encompass my joints. They burned like the skin on my leg. I groaned.

"He can't do it," Megan said. "Let him go."

"He can," Blyth said. "I know it." He, too, sounded as if he suffered. "Come on, laddie, find the boy. Focus."

Breath shuddered into me and out. I saw Matty then, with the blond hair, the blue eyes, the cheeky smile, just like my Megan at that age. A tumble of boy and terrier as they raced around the farmhouse in Grumbla. His lonely life with so few people in it and all of them adults. Young families couldn't afford to live down there — too isolated, too expensive, Glendower hanging onto his farm because of Naomi's money. The boy.

My vision swooped with such violence, I felt my gorge rise, but the vision stopped over a small cottage close to the coast.

"Down, laddie, down," murmured Blyth.

I sank lower, lower, like someone trying to force Google Maps into a place it was never designed to go. I groaned with the effort it took to approach the house. It hurt so much. A great mesh sat over the place, full of hate and rage. It pricked and stabbed at me as I tried to see through it, to the tiny garden surrounding the isolated cottage. It wasn't possible, I couldn't…

"Come back, find a landmark," came the order.

With relief, I rose. Drifted, and saw what I knew to be Sid's location. Penare.

I think I managed to growl, "West of Penare. I know the house now. Release me."

DoPI's tame sorcerer let go of my hands, he leaned away, and the scrying snapped between us. A huge elastic band whipped back into my head, and the pain made my senses close down. The world went dark.

Chapter Twenty-Three

I came too, lying down on Luce's sofa. Nausea rolled through me, and I felt like I'd been on a three-day bender. Not that I'd ever had a time in my life for such an event, but if I had, this is how it would feel. I ached everywhere. All the places the fire from the caravan had hit me tingled and burned.

"Here," came the soft voice and reassuring hand of Megan. "Blyth said you'd feel sick." A bucket appeared beside me.

"He's not wrong," I muttered. "How long?"

"Ten minutes—that's all. He said it might take an hour for you to—"

"We don't have an hour." I rolled onto my side and found the floor with my feet. Megan helped me upright, and yes, I puked. Wonderful.

Megan gave me a glass of water, then went to refill it once I'd finished the first. I replayed the night's events. Adrian Hess. Naomi Moore. Matty. What a fucking mess.

Though, finding out I'd been caught in a spell at least saved me from some of that shame.

"Action plan," I muttered aloud. We had to get down to Dodman Point. The Assumption of Mary was the fifteenth, but if Dr Grove knew we were on to her, there was no reason for her to wait. The conjunction of the planets overhead would still be relevant even now.

"How are you feeling?" Sid asked from the doorway.

I turned my head, meaning to say fine. Instead, the world tumbled around a bit, and it took a while to focus. "Like shit," came out instead.

Sid came into the room and sat. He looked glum.

I remembered what Luce had said about his friend dying in Peckham from stab wounds. "I'm sorry you had to help Naomi. It wasn't your job."

His eyes flicked to mine. "No one else there, mate."

"I know, but it's not easy. The blood, the shouting, the terror from the victim. It sticks with you. Washing the blood off is easy. Not seeing it—that's far harder."

"Macbeth, right?"

I nodded. "Yep. It's just like that."

"How do you process it?"

A small chuckle escaped me. "How do you think? I shove it in a box, mostly. If Naomi dies, that'll be different, but if she lives, then I did my job. It's all I can ask of myself."

His hands moved restlessly over each other. I reached out and stilled them. He glanced at me and managed a wan smile.

"You'll be okay, Sid. Talk about it. Don't bottle it up."

"That's not what you do, is it?"

I managed a small, more cynical smile. "No, not really, but I'm trained for this stuff. It's different for me. Megan wants DoPI to provide us with a shrink of some kind. She might have a point. We only have each other to talk to, and that's not enough. We need to be able to be angry, sad, confused. Over the last few months, we've had some shit to deal with and our team needs a safe environment to vent."

Sid chuckled. "You millennial, you."

"Fuck off," I said with a smile. Trying to bring my body back online, I started flexing the smaller joints. "Can you get me street view up on a laptop?"

Sid nodded, left, and retrieved his pad. Megan returned with him, bringing more water and tea. Damn, I loved this woman.

"Thanks," I said with a smile, taking the mug. It had seagulls on the sides. They were making one helluva racked overhead. "Find Penare," I told Sid. He did and handed the device to me.

I dumped the little human icon Google helpfully supplies onto a road and wandered up it for a bit before I found what I was looking for. A chill raced over my skin. It felt like I'd already been there. "That's the cottage. It's right on the edge of the beach. Really isolated. There is very little cover for us to use to get close. The next nearest house is about a quarter of a click away up a steep hill. It's possible I can use this small woodland as cover to get within safe firing range, but it still leaves me crossing the lane in daylight and going down to the cottage. We don't have time to come in from the sea, and the beach is wide enough to make us visible. There is no back garden, just bracken and brambles, but going through that slowly will take me hours we don't have."

Blyth walked into the room, Luce in tow. They brought more tea and this time, food. My stomach told me it was time to refuel. Sandwiches and cake. Happy days.

"From what you've told me, laddie, you'll not be able to reach the cottage without her knowing you're there. As I explained, she's warded the area. The moment you trespass, she'll feel you."

Megan frowned. "How can she do that if it's a tourist spot? I mean, it's never busy down there because there are no facilities and it's miles from anywhere down tiny roads, but it always has walkers, wild swimmers, even surfers sometimes."

"You know the area?" Blyth asked.

"Not well, but yes, I know it," she admitted. "Griffin's right. There is no easy access without being seen."

"That's the point," Blyth said. "She's picked the site on purpose. Her wards will be tuned to intent. If people trigger them just walking past, she'll sense they are harmless."

"Does that mean we can approach if we think 'tourist' loudly enough?" she asked, her cheeks pinking at what she thought of as a silly idea. It made her look so cute.

"None of you has that training or skill. If you were a practitioner with enough skill, then possibly, but no, you can't make that happen."

I swished about on the pad, forming a plan. "I can come in on the coast path. Megan can come down the lane. She'll trigger this warding and can distract whoever is in there, hiding my approach. If I can get into the house, I can take out Grove and Hess, if he's still there. I'm pretty sure he won't hurt Megan, but he will kill me."

"Pretty sure?" Megan asked with a smile.

"Well, yeah. It's the best we have. A distraction. We'll kit you out."

She frowned, and her eyes flickered to Blyth. "Surely, they'll know you're coming as well, Griffin."

"If they do, Hess can't attack both of us if we're separate. Just keep out of his reach long enough for me to put some holes in people."

"We're shooting them?" Luce asked, her alarm clear.

I glanced at her, wishing I'd kept my mouth shut. "I'm not going to parlay with them, Luce. They are dangerous people, and children are involved."

"I know, it's just…" She glanced at Sid.

"He's right, Luce," Sid said with a shrug. "We can't mess about with these people. It's too dangerous."

Luce left the room, muttering, "I'm not being a part of this. Not again."

Sid watched her go, his anxiety clear. It made me sad for him, they both deserved to be happy.

"We're clear on the plan?" I asked Megan.

"You don't want more recovery time?" she asked.

"You're driving, it'll help. We can't carry my rifle on the bike easily."

Megan rose. "I'll get our things from over the road, explain to Mrs Dennis we won't be back, then we'll leave. Be ready. If we're doing this, I want it over with."

I nodded in agreement and watched her go. Picking up some carrot cake, I said to Blyth, "Is there anything you can do to minimise her effect on us? Or can you tell me what to expect?"

Blyth shook his head. "There are ways I can protect you. Things you don't need to worry about. It won't be much, but it should offer some protection. If I were with you, perhaps I could do more, but I can't manage fieldwork these days."

"You used to?"

Blyth nodded. "I've been known to enter into a fight or two in my time." His accent had broadened as he'd become more comfortable with us. It was odd hearing Scottish this far south.

"What I can tell you," Blyth said, interrupting my unhelpful train of thought, "is this: Hess will be a weapon in her hands. That's all he is to her. Sacrificing him will cost her nothing. Her goal is the children. His job is stopping you at all costs. If your lassie has any feeling for the man, she needs to forget them. There won't be enough of him left for her to recognise. He might, and I mean this, Griffin, he *might* hesitate to pull a trigger if it's Megan in front of him, but equally, probably, he won't."

I frowned. "You should've said that sooner, I'd have come up with another plan."

"There isn't another plan. If we bring down a team, and surround the house, she'll try to do the ceremony in the cottage, and we're back to four dead children. This is the only way to get the wee ones out before it's necessary to finish them with the knives I've prepared."

I'd forgotten the knives. That burden would be mine alone. I wasn't putting a blade in Megan's hands. The thought of it, after feeling the heat of Naomi's blood on my hands, placed a weight on my heart I knew I'd never shift if I had to kill Matty and the others. Their names drifted through my head like smoke: Emyla, Philip, Ann, Matty. Nine years old and slated to become sacrifices from the moment of their birth. What a horrible, cruel world we lived in sometimes.

It put me off the carrot cake. By the time Megan returned from Mrs Dennis, carrying my daysack, I had my boots on and waited by her car. "I'll take the bike back to Redruth, but I'll follow you. I'm still a bit wobbly," I admitted.

She handed over the bag. "There's a storm coming in."

I glanced up at the blue sky. The endless blue sky. "Seriously?"

"From the southeast. Mrs Dennis just warned me."

"She hasn't got one of those stones that predicts the weather, has she?" I asked.

Megan laughed. "No, idiot, she's heard it on the radio. Poor woman's really upset about Naomi and Matty. I promised to visit to let her know we have the bad guys."

"Let's hope we don't make a liar out of you," I said, waving to the older woman. She waved back.

"You have flapjacks in your daysack. I would say she made them for both of us, but somehow, I think I'd be lying."

"I'll come back and tell Mrs Dennis we saved the day."

Megan huffed. "She'll lock you up in that room and keep you hostage, feeding you cake."

"I can think of worse fates." I walked off to find Quacker.

When we met at the office, we geared up. Megan would be in full tactical kit, including helmet, despite the heat. I'd match her, but I'd be in the camo version. It gave me a chance to change out of the black fatigues I wore that still had Naomi's blood stiffening the fabric. From the gun cabinet, I removed two Glock 17s and two clips for each weapon. I handed one set to Megan.

"I know I've done the training, but it just doesn't seem right." She checked the weapon, loaded the magazine, and checked it again. "It's weird." She holstered it, and I made her go through the routine several times. Her draw was slow and measured but confident. That would do for now.

"Just think of it as your taser," I said.

She frowned, but didn't reply. Next came the pepper spray, the asp, and the plasti-cuffs. My addition to the pile was my L119A2 C8 carbine and the rounds to match. I stripped it down so that it would fit in the bag. With my knowledge of the weapon, I'd have it ready to fire in under a minute. Finally, I headed to my desk, where I'd left the knives. Megan watched me wordlessly as I placed one in the place I'd usually carry a tactical knife.

"It's only for the end game. We'll stop them before this happens," I said.

"I wish you could make that a promise," she murmured, heading towards me.

For a moment, despite the bulk of our gear, even without the ballistic vest, we hugged. It felt good to have her nestled in my arms. I'd have given a lot at that moment to be a normal person, coming home from working on a building site or an office to a family.

Megan pulled away first. "Let's go and make sure we don't need to kill those poor babies."

Chapter Twenty-Four

As we drove down to Penare, I rang Sid and asked if we had an update on Naomi's condition. She was still in surgery. It meant the damage was bad. When I relayed this to Megan, we both slipped into silence. I don't know exactly what she was thinking, but the long list of friends I'd lost to violent death, rattled through my head.

Megan decided to ignore the satnav. We took the A30 east, then down on the A39 to avoid Truro. Despite this, traffic was a nightmare, and it took almost two hours to reach the narrow roads of Dodman Point.

The roads here were sunk deep between banks of bracken, hawthorn, hazel and rosebay willowherb. Elderberries, sloes and blackberries filled the hedges, ripening for the summer and autumn harvests. Ash trees held the line of the lane as we approached Hemmick Beach slowly. The road, with the Vectra's wing mirrors touching both sides, plunged towards the small beach that peeked out and vanished again depending on our angle.

"This is close enough," I said as we neared a wooden gateway.

We were now at 15:34. I did a time check with my teammate, and we checked our comms units. "Leave the line open, Megan. I need to hear what's happening."

She nodded, her nerves making her jaw bounce. "How long do you need to get in position?"

"I'll cut across this field, come back in on the coastal path. Give me ten mikes."

"Are you sure that's long enough?" she asked.

"I'll be double-timing it. I need the run."

We were both tense. The thought of this going wrong, of the children having to die by my hand, it left us… Yes, it left me scared. Facing Hess didn't bother me. Even going for a kill shot with Dr Grove didn't matter. Not after what she did to Wesson and those poor families.

I moved to leave the vehicle until Megan put her hand on my arm. "Don't underestimate Adrian. He's ex-Parachute Regiment. He's had extensive firearms training. The man is a monster in a fight. Please, Griffin, if you have to face him, be really bloody careful."

A cocky smile lit my face. "Yeah, but I'm a Marine and years younger."

She shook her head. "Don't do that. Seriously. I've seen him take down bigger, harder criminals than you can imagine. I hate to say it, Griff, but he's tougher than you are and far more ruthless."

Nice to know she had faith in me.

Really? Come on, dickhead, she knows him, and this is a warning, one team member to another.

Yeah, but I'm the cleverer, younger model who understands the supernatural. I almost felt my internal voice give me an eye roll.

I gave her a brief kiss, which felt weird as we were on a mission, and left the car. Megan popped the boot, and I rebuilt the assault rifle before clipping it in place over my tactical gear. Then I put on the helmet and did up the chin strap. As I vaulted over the gate, it wobbled, and I might not have landed with the athletic grace I was hoping for. Megan lowered the window and called, "You're a bloody idiot."

"Love you," I called back, running backwards through the grassy field.

As I jogged through the green field, under the blue sky, hearing and smelling the sea so close, I wondered at myself. Since arriving in Cornwall, my life had changed beyond all recognition. If we could save these children, have an ending as positive as the one at Madron with the Dru, I would be a truly happy man.

Seriously? Did you just think that? Are you a crazy person? You've just jinxed the entire mission.

No, we fought demons and sorcerers. Surely, with the Church behind us, we were on the side of the angels. Righteousness would prevail.

Oh, my God, stop it. Stop it now before you provoke the Law of Sod into doing something terrible. Blind optimism does not suit you.

My feet hit the South West Coastal Path. I heard Megan over the comms unit. "I'm approaching the house."

"Roger that, I'm on the path," I said, running up a small incline. The sea sparkled to my right. I noticed two bright umbrellas on the small beach. Civilians. "What do you see?"

"All quiet. No lights in the house, which is odd because it'll be dark in there even on the brightest of days. Her Micra is in the parking space outside. I don't see any children's toys in the front garden. I'm approaching now."

"Hold, Megan. Wait until I'm in position to cover you."

I talked and jogged, scanning the horizon. Something about this felt… off. "Megan, did you receive last?"

"Received. I'm exposed out here, Griffin."

"Then go back. I don't—" Dirt sprayed up an inch from my right foot, pattering against the leather and hitting my burns. Two rapid heartbeats later, a loud *crack* echoed over the beach. I threw myself sideways, into the tall bracken, and shouted into the comms unit. "Shots fired. Shots fired. There are civilians on the beach. Megan? Received?"

"Received. Heading to the beach."

"Negative. That's a negative. He wants us. He isn't going to shoot—"

"It's my job, Griffin," she yelled while panting.

"Shit," I muttered. This is where our teamwork always cracked. Her priorities were different to mine. She trained to protect civilians at all costs, I trained to achieve the mission objective at all costs. I had to cause a distraction and draw Hess's fire. Where had the shot come from? With great care, I unclipped my assault rifle from the webbing, and keeping my head down, I fired a shot towards the sea. Just the one.

The thunk of another round hitting the ground near my location enabled me to see the muzzle flash. The *crack* of the explosion gave me an estimated distance. Hess was on the opposite headland from mine. I heard screaming from the beach and Megan's voice echoing through the comms unit and from her location. She was ordering the civilians away. I couldn't blame her, but they weren't our priority. I would've left them to shift for themselves.

Taking a few deep breaths, I readied myself for the next part of the idiotic plan I'd just concocted on the fly. I rose, kept low, and raced towards the stone wall no more than ten metres from my location. More dirt sprayed up, this time just behind me. He was a good shot, but either had the wrong firearm to enable him to cover this kind of distance, or he'd never been a sniper. I wouldn't be able to take a man down under these circumstances if I were Hess. I'm a good shot, but I'm not a sniper. The breeze coming off the sea didn't help him zero in on me.

Two more rounds. The second hit a stone, and it exploded. Shards of rock slammed against my gear, one slicing into the back of my hand. The pain was immediate, making me gasp. It was my left. Liquid and heat trailed over my fingers. I hit the wall with my shoulder first and dropped to my knees.

"Sitrep," I barked.

"Civilians safe," Megan reported.

Marvellous. Well, that really helps.

An unfair thought. She was alone down there with complex priorities.

Then she said, "Approaching the house. Firearm live."

"Megan, no!" I yelled, trying to assess the damage to my hand. It hurt like a bastard, but by some miracle, the stone shards had grazed over the thin skin, not penetrated it.

Several more shots were fired, but not near me. The bastard was—

I heard a scream. Sharp in my right ear. Soft in my left, the distance muting her pain.

"Megan!" I yelled.

Nothing.

I heard cars leaving the area. The tourists? No, wait. I heard children.

"Get off me, you bitch." Then, "Megan!" screamed a young voice.

"Matty," I muttered.

Damn it. I switched direction. Vaulting over the stone

wall, I raced into the thick bracken behind the cottage. More rounds came downrange. I was visible but not clear in the undergrowth from this distance. I slid and tumbled down the sharp slope, my left hand protesting as I used it to brace me, the right controlled my weapon. The back of the cottage loomed up, and I dropped the two metres that separated the hillside from the door. My boots hit flagstones, and I was running around the side. Just as the Micra pulled out.

Matty pounded on the rear window. I lifted the rifle, took aim at the rear tyre on the right. The stonework on the cottage shattered by my ear and it sliced into my face and neck. My helmet rattled, and my head was knocked sideways. I stumbled, and the Micra roared away.

With my ears ringing from the contact, I ran through the front garden, and over the wall. A window burst behind me, and something in the house exploded as the round buried itself inside.

I saw Megan's dark form crumpled on the ground, separating the parking space for the tourists and the short driveway attached to the cottage. She lay on her side. Nothing dark stained the ground behind her back. Skidding my knees. I pushed my hands into the shoulders of her ballistic vest and lifted, pulling her backwards. My arse hit the low stone wall of the front garden, and I dragged us both over it.

Only then did I roll Megan over. Her eyes were still closed. Her breathing was shallow. A glint of metal in the centre of her chest covering made my shoulders drop. Megan twitched, grunted, coughed.

"Steady, you took a round to the chest. You're okay." I released the straps on her vest and eased it away, but not off. Shoving my hand up there, I began to grope and poke at her sternum and ribs.

She coughed again. "If you want to cop a feel, you just have to ask."

I chuckled, feeling lightheaded. "No blood." For the first time since I'd heard her go down, I took a deep breath. Tears pricked the backs of my eyes. I'd almost lost her. For long moments there my mind had been one long scream of terror, even as my body moved to do its job.

"The children?"

"Don't. I'm going after Hess. Stay here," I said.

"Griffin." She reached out, but I was already slipping from her grasp. With no members of the public in the way, I fired three rounds into the hillside. By now, I had Hess's location pretty well pinned down. He was on the high ground above the cliffs, between the coastal path and the edge. Almost nothing would protect me as I headed up there except he'd expended a lot more rounds than I had. With my firearms being legal, and his not, I was gambling on him having limited capacity for another volley. He'd have to be careful.

My three-round strategy worked. A man in a full Ghillie suit, tatty fronds of camo fluttering in the wind, broke cover. He held a long-barrelled rifle in his arms and, rather than run away, Hess raced towards me.

Well, okay then.

I stopped on the top side of the narrow beach and lifted the semi-automatic to my shoulder. Dropping my eyeline to the scope, I took a moment to control my breathing. My finger, under protest from the wound in my hand, squeezed the trigger. It held at the halfway for a nanosecond before I pulled it all the way back and…

Click.

I blinked. Went again.

Click.

The fucking gun had jammed. Why? I dropped it from my shoulder while moving out of the line of sight from the man running down the hill, who appeared to be heedless of danger. I cleared the barrel, released the clip and inserted a fresh magazine. Time to move back into position…

CRACK.

My head snapped back with such force, I hit the ground hard. The air rushed out of me. My vision went black. My brain yowled in pain. A sensation like ten million ants made of lightning rushed through my body from toe to fingertip. The sun rolled through me. Flashes of colour hit my eyes and vanished. Bubbles popped in my brain.

"I'm going to fucking kill you!" someone screamed.

Who? Me? Why? What the hell is going on?

Heavy boots crunched over the stones and sand under my head. I heard everything. Then nothing. Ringing. Oh yeah, lots of ringing. Bow bells in my brain. Jangle, jangle.

Boots.

Move, fool! Move.

I rolled. A foot stamped where my face had been. Why was a bush trying to stamp on my head?

Not a bush. Man. Kill him. Now.

Instinct. Training. Self-bloody-preservation. I don't know what made me able to do it, but I rolled again, pulling my knees to my chest, and rose. Even as I reached for my sidearm. I yanked the weapon clear, and a boot smacked into my arm. Everything went numb. I rocked sideways. Hit the ground again. Mouthful of sand.

"Griffin!" came a shout.

The bush turned. My right hand scrambled for my belt, and I felt the dagger's hilt. That would do. Flicking the popper open, I pulled it and slashed, not able to focus.

The blade made contact. A cry of pain. Shots rang out,

small calibre, coming inbound. I slashed again. Made it to my knees. Saw my Glock. Left arm moved. I overbalanced again, feeling seasick, and hit the ground. My right hand dropped the knife, picked up the loaded weapon and, *click.*

This wasn't happening.

The knife came back to my hand with surprising ease considering how complicated I found being alive. Once more, I slashed at the bushman.

"Adrian, you are under arrest," Megan's voice rang out.

Don't say that, just shoot him!

Hess dropped his rifle and began to run.

I tried. Damn, I really tried to get up, but my limbs wouldn't get their collective shit together. They and my eyes just kept wandering off target.

Megan knelt beside me, her breathing ragged. She undid my helmet and yanked it off with some effort. I, *ooffed*, and the pressure on my brain eased back.

"My God, that was close," she murmured, sitting her arse down on the hot sand. "Look." She pointed to the battle helmet. An impact point over my right eye and a long score down the side made it clear how close to death's call I'd come. He'd hit Megan in the chest, me in the head. Hess was playing for keeps.

"My weapons misfired. Both of them," I said, holding up the Glock like it was a venomous snake.

I aimed at the sea, squeezed the trigger and when the round discharged, the recoil took me completely by surprise and I almost punched Megan in the nose.

She removed the weapon. "Let's not do that again."

After stowing the weapon safely in the holster on my left thigh, she asked, "What do we do now?"

I blinked a few times, spat sand out of my mouth, and wondered when my brain would stop ringing. "We go find them." Flexing my left hand, rolling my shoulder, I struggled to my feet. "How are you feeling?"

"Like a donkey kicked me in the chest," she said. "Nothing broken, but the bruising is going to be a masterpiece of modern design."

I picked up my weapons, including the dagger. "I'll kiss it better." We tried to walk quickly back to the cottage. "What did you tell the tourists?"

"That we had a mentally ill farmer letting off his shotgun at the woman who broke his heart in the cottage. The rest of my team were on their way."

"Clever."

She shrugged and winced. "Terrorist threats to cover DoPI activity doesn't help. We need better lies for Cornwall. It works in cities, but it won't hold for rural communities forever. It also won't help the tourist industry and we all rely on that."

Having made it to the car, I stripped the assault rifle down. "No way this failed."

"Could it be a spell?" Megan asked.

Huh, I hadn't thought of that. "Maybe. Who's driving?"

"You've just been shot in the head. I'm not letting you do it. Besides, I know the fastest route to Truro."

"You think that's where she'll go?" I asked, pleased not to be in operational control for a while.

"I don't think we've left her with any other option. She'll be there tonight. We just have to find them."

"Among twenty-one thousand residents."

"And the tourists."

I groaned. "Best I call Sid for some help."

Chapter Twenty-Five

By now, we were battling the traffic going home from the beaches. Families with tired children stuck behind caravans being towed through narrow lanes once meant for ponies and fishermen. A thirty-five minute, sixteen-mile journey took us another two hours. Our only consolation was that Dr Grove would be having the same problem. At least our car wasn't stuffed full of scared children. Somehow, I doubted Matty would be happy with endless rounds of *Old MacDonald Had a Farm*.

Matty had been privy to all our conversations, and he wouldn't be hiding any of the gory details from the other kids. Despite knowing their 'mother' for years, I'd lay money on them not making life easy for her right now. Or maybe she'd given them a sleeping draught to keep them under control.

As we'd woven through the slow-moving roads, I'd been on the phone to Sid and Blyth. It turned out Megan had called it right, my firearms had likely been spelled.

"You might've warned me this was possible," I snapped at the DoPI sorcerer.

"I assumed you knew, Corporal. Isn't it standard teaching that certain spellcasters can affect explosives due to their control of the elements?"

It was true. I'd done the seminar, but it had been years ago, and I hadn't faced a sorcerer of this calibre before. "Next time, remind me of what they're capable of, please." I heard the testy tone, but I didn't care. The headache I had wasn't being helped by the total failure of the Vectra's ageing air con to keep the temperature down in the car. "What are the odds Dr Grove goes straight to the cathedral?"

"Slim. She'll want to do the ceremony tomorrow if possible."

"If that's not possible?" I thought of the squat the teenagers had lived in. Would she go there to hide for a day?

"Then yes, she'll go to the cathedral."

I said goodbye and ended the call. Next came Sid.

"It's not good news, I take it," he said.

"No, bad misjudgement on my part. Hess was up on the headland with a rifle. We're lucky to be alive."

"Not luck, mate. Blyth's been here in full witchy mode. We have candles and wands and magic circles all over the floor of the office." He sounded as if he were outside. "The man's terrifying, Griffin. I'm glad he's on our side. He was pushing threats away at a distance."

"That's impressive," said Megan, who had heard the conversation. "I'm not sure that I believe it's possible, but if it is, then wow."

"Can you track the Micra that Grove is using to move the kids?" I asked.

"Truro doesn't have great CCTV coverage, Griffin. I'll do what I can with the ANPR cameras, but if she comes in on one of the small roads, which she will, I'll struggle to find her. Drones are of no use for the same reason. I don't know what route she'll take."

"Then we head to the cathedral and wait for her," I said. "I need to talk to the bishop. I think we could use his help."

"There's something you have to know," Sid said.

A plunging sensation in my stomach told me I really didn't need to know. "Go on."

"Today is the beginning of art and literature festival in the city. It's really popular, very busy. The entire city centre gets involved. Special services at the cathedral, the whole thing. And get this, the special service is for children. Griffin, there are going to be dozens, if not hundreds, of kids running around."

Seriously? See, this is what happens when you take the piss out of Sod's Law? I did warn you.

Rubbing my head, I had vague memories of seeing leaflets on the desk of the office receptionist in that bug-ugly building in the cathedral grounds. I just said, "Understood." The weight of the dagger on my belt grew heavier by the moment. "Can you meet me in Truro?"

"Of course. Do you want me to bring anything?" Sid asked.

"Don't suppose we have a *sorcerer-catcher* among our stuff?" I asked, leaning my head back to ease the stiffening muscles in my neck. Even a glancing blow from a bullet can cause serious damage. Megan sat at an angle behind the wheel, her upper body obviously twisted as she tried to cope with the growing stiffness.

Sid drew me back. "No, but I'll go and check the inventory, just in case we have something that might help the more human element. How are you both?"

Just fucking peachy. I've totally failed. Again.

"Fine," I lied.

"Okay. I'll head for the cathedral and see you there."

We ended the call.

Megan glanced at me. "That didn't sound good."

"No, it isn't." I explained about the festival. Megan just sighed and nodded. We both slumped into silence.

I watched the countryside trickle past. The dry landscape looked decidedly bleak and unwholesome today. The trees, many alone among the hedgerows, or standing like sentinels in a field, took on the aspect of lonely warriors, lost in a desert, far from water and desperate. The grass shrank back, appearing frazzled, and I couldn't help but imagine little tiny mouths opening and closing like beached fish, desperate for water.

"You alright?" Megan asked, her voice quiet.

"Not really," I said, rousing myself. "I don't know how to solve this problem. I just can't see a path where the good guys win."

"What will happen if this sorcerer succeeds?"

"In theory, the children will become the four horsemen of the apocalypse. Or the angels will bring about the end days. Rise of the Anti-Christ—"

"Okay, I get it. Do we really know that's going to happen?" she asked. Ever practical.

"No. The ceremony might not work at all. It's not the kind of thing she can practice like some of the other stuff we've encountered."

"How do we ensure the ceremony fails? I mean, before she starts it with the children?"

I thought about this. We could lock the cathedral up, but

she'd probably go to another church, and I'd never find her. "Let me call the bishop."

Megan frowned, wanting an answer. A nuts-and-bolts response to an ethereal threat.

I pulled up the number for the bishop's office, and it rang twice. "Anna Price, how can I help?" came Anna's civilised voice.

"Hi, Anna, it's Griffin Woodbury from—"

"Hello. How can I help?" she asked.

"Can I speak with the bishop?"

"I'm afraid he's very busy today."

Yes, well, I'm trying to stop the fucking apocalypse.

"It's rather urgent, Anna. I need his help." I felt her wanting to give me more excuses. "Please," I added.

She puffed out a breath. "I'll have to put you on hold." The line held still.

Megan managed a crooked smile. "Good to know the Church is here to battle evil at the drop of a crozier."

I was too exhausted to reply.

"Griffin, dear boy, what's going on?" Bishop Chadwick asked a few minutes later.

I'd been drumming my left hand on my thigh, trying to keep the fingers from stiffening. The entire hand was turning black from the bruising, and the shrapnel's graze was raw and blistered; the wound leaky. Trying to keep the impatience out of my voice, I said, "Bishop, I think we need your help."

"Mine?" he chuckled. "I'm fairly sure I'm past the point I can chase down bad guys. The situation we've already spoken about has accelerated?"

The vision of Bishop James Chadwick chasing Adrian Hess caused my brain to misfire for a second. He broke the silence.

Softly, Bishop Chadwick dropped an info bomb in my lap. "I used to be a Forces' chaplain about a hundred years ago, Griffin, you can talk to me. There is very little I haven't seen in the field."

Well, that might help. At least he'll understand my actions a bit more. "I'm happy to do the chasing if I can find the people to chase. Bishop, we know you have a children's service at the cathedral this evening. Is there any chance you can cancel—"

"I'm sorry, they are already arriving. The school is acting as a hub. It's a choir made up of children from churches all over the southwest of England. Buses are arriving all the time." He sounded genuinely contrite, which helped me keep my temper.

"If we send you images of a woman, a man and one of the vulnerable children involved in this case, can you ask your people to look for them among the crowd? Share my number and Sergeant Ackley's?"

"Of course. We can send it to the parents involved in our child safety team as well. That's what it is there for."

"We also have reason to believe they'll be heading for the St Mary's Chapel in the cathedral. Can you make sure to have people posted there? Do not engage, Bishop. The woman involved is very, very dangerous and desperate. If she arrives, pull your people back, inform me, and we'll do the rest."

"Yes, of course." Now he sounded worried. "Perhaps we should cancel the service…" His voice faded away.

Megan glanced at me and shook her head. "It'll just alert her, she'll go to ground, and we'll never find her in time. If anything, having her inside the cathedral will help. I can have uniforms in there, covering the exits and monitoring people coming in and out of the area."

With this in mind, I said to Bishop Chadwick, "Don't cancel. We'll have a strong police presence in the area. Don't worry, the children will be safe." At least the ones in the choirs would be safe, if not Dr Elena Grove's victims.

The congestion in Truro's narrow streets almost finished off what was left of my patience and sanity. Megan took every backstreet she could to avoid the heavy traffic heading into the centre. By now, twilight wanted to shoulder daylight out of the way so it could have its glory moment before night took over for the long haul. I glanced up at the sky, despite the pain in my neck, and sure enough, the first of the planets had started to become visible.

Megan broke our shared tense silence. "You know, there's a Methodist church right next to the cathedral. What if that's important? We've never considered it."

"It won't have the same heft as the Bishop's Seat. We don't have to worry about any other church except Kenwyn's. That might be a problem."

Megan focused as we hit the one-way system around the cathedral. There were people everywhere, but as I cursed the chances of finding a parking space, I received a text message. Anna had reserved a parking place for us inside the grounds.

I wiggled my phone at Megan. "See, miracles do happen."

"Parking fairies."

"What?" I asked.

"I have parking fairies working for me."

"So you can believe in parking fairies but not God?"

"I created parking fairies. They work for me. God was created by old men to control everyone, but mostly women. So, no, I don't have much time for that." She swung the old

Vectra onto the cathedral grounds. I saw a piece of paper stuck to a post with my name on it, and we parked.

Getting out of the car, I looked at the sky. There were no clouds. The hard blue of the day had softened, the eastern sky beginning to turn to indigo. Above us, the perfect line of the planets shone bright. From our angle, it looked as if they were pointing right to the centre of the cathedral's transept. How had this strange alignment happened? The architect of the building couldn't have known almost two centuries ago. I wondered what it would look like from the ancient sites Sid and I had visited further south. Oh, how I wished we were down there enjoying the free light show.

We left the vehicle. I couldn't use the assault rifle here, and we didn't have a police armed response unit in Truro. However, I could carry the Glock under a t-shirt. Using the car as cover, I changed into a pair of jeans I'd packed just in case, and ditched the ballistic vest. Megan and I placed her Velcro POLICE badges on the patches of her vest. The number of people milling around was overwhelming. We stayed together, weaving through the crowd towards the main doors, but neither of us saw four small children with an adult female.

The heat of the day reverberated around us, making people's tempers sharper. The smells of cologne, perfume, and body spray leaked over us, making my senses spin.

My earpiece crackled to life. "Griffin? You on this channel?"

"Sid?"

"Your phone isn't working."

I pulled it out. How the hell hadn't I noticed? The battery was dead. What kind of incompetent operator was I? "It's dead. What's up? Megan's on comms as well."

I saw her touch her ear. "I'm here, Sid," she said.

"I've sent the images you requested to the appropriate people. We have as many eyes as possible looking for Grove and the children. I've distributed… Oh, I see you. Turn around."

I did as asked and Sid, with Luce, were coming towards us through the crowd. He lowered his comms unit on approach.

"Fuck, Griffin, what happened?" he asked, taking me in.

"Got shot several times. Blyth saved my life. He here?" I asked, eyes still scanning the crowd moving around us. So many children.

"He's at our place. Whatever he did for you knocked him on his arse. He has a migraine so bad he can't see straight. You alright, Megan?" he asked.

"Well, you know, shot in the chest. Lost the bad guys. Feel like crap. Wanna go home and have a good cry." She managed a grin.

Luce was watching the crowd. "This is impossible. We've the south transept entrance as well."

"It's not open," Megan said. "We've already checked."

"Let's split up and quarter the crowd out here. If we don't see anything, we'll go into the cathedral, but the bishop's people have most of that covered," I said.

"Hang on a second," Luce said. "I just need to say this. If I don't, I'll regret it. Dr Grove's plan is so complex, right from the conception of the children, I can't believe this woman would leave anything to chance. Something about this isn't right, Griffin. She's led you a merry dance over the last few days. There is something we're missing."

"I agree. I have no idea what's going to happen, when or where, but this is the best we have right now. So we look, we check, we muddle through."

'Muddle', not a word I should use when I'd been trained as an operative of the highest calibre.

The anxiety, the self-doubt and recriminations, the sense of failure — they all jostled for the number one spot in my head. The hope and optimism of just a few hours ago had fled into the long grass and vanished. I'd handled this one badly. Sanchez should've given me a team, sent Blyth sooner, and an experienced exorcist. I had a single police officer, a tech guy and an academic trying to help me piece this together. Yes, we now had others looking for Hess, Grove and the children, but right from the off, we'd been playing this wrong. Despite all those extra pairs of eyes, only four of us knew the terrible truth we were facing.

If I didn't stop this in time, I'd have to kill four innocent children. A burden I knew I couldn't carry.

Chapter Twenty-Six

Tension rippled through me as we watched the large plaza and grounds around the cathedral emptying of our last hopes for an easy victory. Another hot night had its sweaty grip on the city. The planets overhead glowed, with Mars, Venus and Jupiter being the most obvious. The line of those planets above the spires of the cathedral felt like an accusing finger pointing at my failure.

I had to force myself not to pace as we gathered in front of the large doors to the building. Megan completely failed to hide her exasperation. We'd had her police colleagues posted at every conceivable entrance and exit to the cathedral, and the surrounding streets. Nothing. Zero. A few near misses, women with four children in the right age category being spotted, but they all presented as legitimate. Each one of those call-ins came over my comms unit and made my pulse jump into my throat, they sent me running to attend, only to be disappointed and forced to apologise to a worried parent or carer. To wide-eyed children.

This horrible, sickening anti-climax to the murderously

hot evening, made me twitchy. What the hell had we missed? I wanted to claw at the sky. Howl at the moon. Scream at those fucking planets. Those great, bright orbs of inconsequential rock and gases that had caused so much death and misery. What possible effect could they realistically have on events here in Truro, on planet bloody earth? They had no more control over our thoughts and actions than God.

Ooo, we are being Mister Cynical tonight, aren't we?

I grunted, opened my mouth and tried to wriggle the tension from my jaw.

The bishop came out of the building towards our small group. His round belly pressed against the purple t-shirt he wore, stretching the graphic on the front. It read: *I don't have to like you, but God does. Count your damned blessings.*

Bishop Chadwick was full of surprises.

"Well, Griffin, it seems tonight we dodged a bullet," the portly man said. His words were jovial, but his expression remained tight. He'd obviously seen missions go awry because of dodgy intel, and he'd placed a great deal of faith in me. Not only had I let Matty down, I'd failed him as well.

"Perhaps, sir." What else could I say? We'd even had police posted at Kenwyn, and she hadn't been seen there. With the weight of tourists in the city, we'd been told our overwatch of the church was no longer a priority, and they'd been pulled back. Truro's security monitoring station hadn't seen anything on the cameras. The Micra had vanished from the roads. Even Sid hadn't found any trace of the damned thing.

All these thoughts tumbled and rushed around inside my head as I tried to grasp at a straw spinning out of control down a flooded river.

"I think it's time we stopped," Bishop Chadwick said. He patted my arm. "Come on, son, you all have to sleep."

"It's not over, sir. It can't be. She's spent more than a decade planning this event. There is no way she just gives up." My voice felt tight in my throat.

Luce and Megan looked exhausted. The stress and heat of the day had taken their toll. We'd been non-stop since before dawn. Still, something gnawed at me. Luce had called it right, this was all too elaborate for Grove to give up so easily. What were we missing?

Maybe you aren't meant to win this one, soldier boy.

Yeah, right, fuck that. I wanted Matty back. I was a Royal Marine Commando, we never give up.

Bishop Chadwick placed a hand on my shoulder. "I'll leave you to it. If you need me, ring. I'll be spending the night in Truro."

"Thank you, sir. I apologise for the heavy hand and disruption."

"Son, you are trying to save the lives of four children from a disturbed woman. I think I can afford a little forgiveness." He smiled, but I saw his disappointment. Nodding to the rest of the team, he left us alone.

"Megan, can you go home with Sid? I'll bring the car back soon, I just..." I made a growling noise. "I can't let this go." Rolling my shoulders, I felt muscles snark and bitch. The headache and whiplash from the headshot Hess had tried were making themselves known again.

She shook her head. "Griffin, you can't do it alone." Despite her exhaustion and the pain she doubtless felt from being shot in the chest, the woman wasn't going to give up. My admiration for her rose once more.

I breathed out in a puff and stole a look at my boots. They were hot on my feet. Everything felt sticky and uncomfortable. I couldn't think straight, didn't have a strategy, and I wished all the decisions didn't sit on my shoulders. If I called this wrong, children were going to die, and we'd be ushering in chaos.

Where the hell was Grove and those children?

"One more patrol through the area. Then that's it. I'll do one more and follow you down the road to home," I said.

Megan pushed off the car. "*We'll* do one more. I'll take the inner cordon, you do the outer. Put those long legs to use." She managed a tired smile.

Luce shook her head. "I don't like this, something feels off." Her eyes drifted to the cathedral. Glancing at her watch, she added, "It's the fifteenth now. Everything is in place. I can't believe she'd change venue. We've missed something."

"The cathedral is locked up tight. An army can't get through those doors," I said pointing to the large wooden barrier between the world and Christ's house within.

Luce didn't appear to be convinced. She looked at Sid. "Is there anything else we can do?" She sounded desperate. I realised, she'd witnessed the kidnapping and attempted murder of her house guests. The people she'd tried to help us protect. Naomi had almost died on Luce's pavement. This must be horrible for her and I had no way of making it easier.

I added Luce to the people I'd failed tonight.

Sid shook his head. "Sorry, love. I can't think of anything else. You and I are of no use in a fight. It's best we go home, and come back with fresher minds. Maybe my spiders will have found images of Hess, the children or Grove on the servers, and we'll know where they are hiding." As his final act, Sid handed me back my phone, now charged from one of his many battery packs. He didn't bother saying anything, but I gave him a grateful nod.

I pushed my earpiece back in place, Megan did the same. We looked at each other, gave a single nod and set out for one more patrol. She'd circle the cathedral, going clockwise, checking the many nooks and crannies in the building. Also, the doorways and windows of the houses and businesses immediately surrounding the large stone edifice. I'd go anti-clockwise and check the next layer of streets, car parks, municipal buildings and anything else. We were looking for the unusual among the usual. Having done this six times already, we knew what was usual, so anything else should stand out.

Tiredness kept us quiet on comms as we patrolled. I felt the stiffness in my legs from hours of standing, pacing the city, the wild flurry of action first at Luce's, then the beach and now this… emptiness. The horrible anti-climax of failure. What had we guessed wrong? All the signs Grove had left in her wake were there, we should be in the right place, at the right time. Wesson knew it would happen tonight, even if he hadn't known who.

I heard Sid's Mini pull away, the sound unique to the small car. After midnight, the streets were quiet, but not empty. Some of the venues for the arts and literature festival were still open, with people drinking wine and pints in the street. Unsurprisingly, I didn't have to dodge piles of vomit or screaming fights between pissed couples. Arts festivals aren't known to be inhabited by the types of people who cause street fights. With the weather still hot and heavy, this felt more like southern France or Spain. Civilised drunkenness. I scanned each crowd, but didn't expect to see anything.

The narrow streets were darker, and I quickly filtered

through each one, feeling like a white blood cell looking for something to destroy in the arteries of the body of Truro.

Unable to help myself, I pressed on the pretzel of the comms unit. "Anything?"

Megan's voice came back in my right ear, "Nothing. All quiet. Luce is right, though, this doesn't feel good. Something is off here." Her tension rippled through me.

"Yeah, I just don't know—"

"Griffin! Aghhhh…" Her voice died in my ear.

"Megan? Meg? Fuck. Report. Send location." I was already running towards the cathedral. Why the hell hadn't I just asked her location ten seconds ago? That's basic unit protocol when in the field. Why hadn't I done it? I knew the reason, we were too damned comfortable with each other, we both ignored the rules. We always had done, even as kids. My mind did some rapid calculations, and I guessed she'd be in the southwestern corner.

The line crackled and popped in my ear. "Hess… Griff… F…" The hot air wheezed out of me as I rounded a corner and saw an Audi pulling away. I had no chance of reaching it. Instead, I pulled out my phone and speed dialled my only hope. "Sid?"

"It's me," said Luce.

"Hess has Megan. He must've been waiting somewhere. Fuck!" I screamed in frustration, pulling the phone away from my mouth, bent double, stamping my feet as useless power surged through me. "Luce, I need you both back here. Hess must've changed his number plate, he used his car to take her from right outside the cathedral. We should've picked it up."

I was running back to the car park. I'd need toys for hunting Hess. Taking him down would be a pleasure, a grim, dark delight.

"Griffin," I heard Sid on speaker. "This is what he wants. For you to go after Megan. We have to think."

"What else am I supposed to do?" I almost screeched. "I can't leave her to face him alone."

"Do your job," Sid said, with a level of calm I'd never reach under these circumstances. "Your job is to protect the cathedral. I'm dropping off Luce, you need someone at your back who understands what's happening, she'll act as support. I'll go after Megan. We know where they're likely to be. Trust me, Griffin, this is the best option we have."

I stared up at the night sky, the planets cut off from me by the height of the buildings. "Why? Why take her?" When I focused on ground level, I saw the small, round headlights coming towards me. The tangle in my belly made breathing hard. I wanted to get into the Vectra, go after them, rip Hess's face off and make him wear it on his arse.

The Mini pulled up, Sid spoke through the open window as Luce climbed out. "Griffin, we don't understand this ritual. If he's driven away, maybe he's gone to Kenwyn. We've all thought the place was important. I'll head there. Stay here. If I see Grove, or the children, I will ring. If I don't, I'll go after Megan and Hess. You're just going to have to wait."

"Sid…" I wanted to…

What? He was right. I had a job to do, and it wasn't saving Megan, it was stopping Grove. The damned sorcerer was the problem. Her Renfield was there to act as a distraction, to weaken the team, to take me away from this damned place. I wanted to rage and weep all at once. This is why romantically involved operatives should never work together, it smothered priorities.

A long-fingered hand reached out and gripped my wrist. I glanced at Sid. He said, low and controlled. "I'll find her."

I gave a brief nod. His words didn't reassure me. He'd find her alright, I trusted him with that mission, but would she still be alive? Never in all my years had I been so afraid. I thought the scariest thing I'd done was walk across a pebbled beach in Somerset with a suicide vest draped over my shoulders. How wrong was I? This feeling, this terrible sense of helplessness, this was worse. Far, far worse.

The Mini drove away, and Luce approached. "Griffin?" she asked, a brief touch to my shoulder showing her deep concern.

"I'm okay," I squeezed out of a tight throat. The lie writ clear in every line of my body.

Luce silently handed me a bottle of water. It was such a random act under these conditions that it snapped me back to reality, to *my* mission.

Opening the bottle, I said, "I need you to think about how Grove could get into the cathedral. Is there anything we haven't considered?" I stared into Luce's big brown eyes and pushed my desperation into the poor damned woman.

Luce rocked back a little under the force of my anguish and closed her eyes. "I've been here a lot, even as a child. Dad would let me run around loose after it was closed to the tourists. I liked the small chapels..." Her voice trailed off, eyes snapping open. A look of wonder passed over her face.

I grabbed at it. "You have something?"

"It's a weird thing, Griffin. I don't even know—"

"Just tell me." I refrained from shaking her, but I was tempted.

Luce began to hurry towards High Cross Street, one of the places Megan had just patrolled. I followed, confused. While she jogged, she said, "There is a tiny doorway. It's barely four feet high. Old, medieval old, not Victorian like the rest of the building. It's a remnant of the original St Mary's Church."

"I've seen it. Deacon Archer said it was kept locked. One key, which is in the office. No one has used it in decades."

"Doesn't stop it from being a door, though," Luce pointed out. "And I don't think it's on the plans."

"What do you mean?" I asked.

She slowed. "Shh."

The hulking mass of old carved stone and glass on our left made the narrow street dark despite the street lamps. I pulled Luce behind me and removed the Glock from the belt holster under my t-shirt. "Tell me," I whispered.

"I've been studying the plans of the building. Making sure everything lines up." She spoke into my ear, making me shiver. "The door isn't there on the plans. We've all seen it, though, but because it's not a normal door, none of us have registered it as a potential threat to the building. It doesn't lead anywhere, but I've also seen on one set of documents from the library catalogue that when they dismantled the original church, they had an argument with the locals about the crypt. The cathedral builders wanted it filled in because of the weight—"

"Yeah, okay, Luce, I get it complicated historical stuff, just tell me," I hissed.

She flicked her head, re-organising her thoughts to give me the pertinent details, not a history lesson. "The crypt's entrance was on the side of the original church. That doorway might well be it, which means it'll go under the cathedral, under the south aisle, the site of the original St Mary's church. Grove's preferred saint."

"Grove doesn't need to get inside the actual cathedral building? She just needs to get into the original church?"

Luce nodded. "Well, we can't know for certain, but it would be a best guess."

My earpiece spluttered to life. "Megan? Can you hear me?"

"Griff…" her voice sounded faint and slurred. "In boot. Go up ill."

"Say again?" I pressed the earpiece.

"Ill," she managed.

"Hill?"

"Rogder tat. Uck. Azer. Can't eak…"

"Understood." Though I didn't. "Sid is coming to you. Meg, I can't… I'm sorry…"

"No, oo, 'elp dere. Call po-li-ce," she enunciated slowly.

"Roger that."

I heard her grunt, a shout, and something bash. "Megan?"

A heavier grunt. "Is that you, Marine?" hissed a man's voice through Megan's comms unit. "I have the whore now. She will serve my mistress and me. As was promised."

"Let her go, Hess. They'll be coming for you now," I growled.

"It'll be too late. You are all too late." A muffled thump, then, "You fucking bitch." A squeal of noise, afterwards nothing. Megan was fighting Hess. She was alive and strong enough to hurt him.

I tried to control my breathing. Luce reached out and took both of my hands in hers. I glanced up at her. The beauty of her sculpted bone structure and smooth skin, many shades darker than mine, held me still. If ever an angel wore a human face, then it could be Lucinda Carmichael's.

"Griffin, trust your team. Sid will make sure the police reach Megan in time. No one else can go down into that crypt and save those children but you. That's where Megan would want you to be, doing the job to which you are both committed. Save those children. Bring Matty back to us."

I matched her calm breathing, feeling the panic reduce until I could push it back. Suddenly, thankfully, the switch inside me flicked. I stopped being Griffin Woodbury, lover and friend, I became Corporal Woodbury, Royal Marine Commando and Special Forces Operative.

Luce watched it happen. She released my hands and stepped back. "I'll call the bishop. Let him know we have a problem." Her voice had become detached, distant. She didn't like this version of me.

I didn't care. "Roger that." I was already moving away, down the side of the cathedral, towards the small door.

Along this side, there were narrow, heavily decorated buttresses separating each wide stained-glass window. The small door stood in the centre of the penultimate colourful storyboard. I approached on silent feet.

The door really was only about a metre and a half tall and extremely narrow. The stonework surrounding it looked far more weathered than the decorative bosses on either side, and the door itself had a sense of age the rest of the cathedral lacked. A plain knob and simple lock were on the right. The door itself had unadorned decoration of iron beams running downwards with smaller beams going crosswise at the top, making them resemble elongated crosses. Despite its narrow width, there were four of these laid into the wood. It made me think of the apostles. Let's hope they were listening now.

I crossed the doorway, kept my body angled away from the small entrance, put my Glock into my right hand and reached for the knob with my left. It felt cold, as if the relentless heat of the summer had never reached this spot. I had no doubt the sun struggled to touch this old door, the street was so narrow. This tiny portal had guarded the lonely corner of the building for centuries. I turned the knob and, on silent hinges, it swung inward.

Air released from my chest in a heavy puff. We'd found the place I'd needed to be all damned day. What fools we'd been. How many times had we passed this door? How many people ignored it over the years? And yet, Grove knew.

I licked my lips, mouth dry. Would I be in time to stop the ceremony? It had only just become the fifteenth. Suddenly, I felt the weight of the sacrificial dagger at my right hip. Thoughts of Sanchez's desire for a demon chased my mouse-like fears of DoPI having four children each with monster inside them. Blyth wanted them dead. Sanchez wanted them for DoPI—preferably with a demon. I wanted them alive and unhurt. Especially Matty.

Time to push all those cat and mouse games out of my head. Now, I needed to act.

First, I scanned the narrow entrance. Left, right, up and down. I saw no wires, nothing to indicate a trap. Nothing conventional, nothing *para.* No markings on the walls of the interior. I removed my smallest Maglite from a pocket and placed it under the barrel of the Glock, which now nestled like a lover's hand in my left. During the last five minutes, all the aches and pains I'd collected, vanished. Each of my senses pinged.

I bent almost double to slide into the narrow space sideways. My earpiece crackled. I held my breath.

"Griffin?" Megan's voice came over clear.

I backed away from the entrance. "I'm here."

She spoke quietly, "I'm hunting him through Kenwyn church. I think he's hurt. He didn't check me for weapons. I managed to get a shot off. He's out of his mind. Not following protocol."

"Megan, back off. A team is inbound. Sid is there somewhere."

"No, I can bring him in."

The line between us crackled and died. Cold air rushed up the stairway, and a smell of damp stone and old death mixed with something sickly sweet.

I tried to reach Megan on comms. Then I tried my re-energised mobile. Nothing. Too much stone between us? Or something more sinister preventing our communications from working?

Regardless, I couldn't control Megan's actions from here. I had to trust her training. It wasn't easy, but I refocused on my part in this mission. I stepped onto the first of the stairs. They were worn, ancient and descended steeply into the gloom. The walls and ceiling here were of dressed stone, but not as fine as you'd find in an old church. This was rougher, and my back made a soft hushing, as I walked slowly downwards. I had to keep my knees bent to save my head on the arched ceiling. The steps curved slightly. As I rounded the bend, the flickering light became obvious. I switched off my torch and returned it to my pocket. Keeping the Glock raised but close to my centre of mass, I kept going down.

Chapter Twenty-Seven

When I reached the ground level, I stood still for a moment as I listened. I'd reached a small antechamber, the low ceiling only a few inches over my head, with simple but impressive fanned barrel vaulting in the Romanesque style. Either side of the small room were three layers of chambers set into the walls. At one point, they must've contained coffins, but they now stood empty. Whoever had been buried here, held money and influence, but not enough to be in the main chamber, which was ahead of me.

I heard low-level chanting from a single voice. The smell of whatever she was burning was stronger down here, cloying, and it made me feel sick, a bit dizzy. Was she using hallucinogens? The atmosphere lay on me like a suffocating duvet, and rather than the cold I'd felt at the surface, the air had become tropical.

Slowly, I approached the next medieval archway. No door this time, just a simple metal gateway, the kind of thing you'd expect in a dungeon. Again it had a lock, but this time, someone had set about it with a blowtorch. Grove must've been down here working on this for weeks, maybe years. No one in the cathedral would hear her, or see her coming and going from that small door. The street held no CCTV. If it were after hours, the shops would be ignorant of her comings and goings.

Taking care, I popped my head around the thick wall and took in as much of the room as possible in three seconds.

With my back now pressed against the smoother stone of the antechamber, I gave myself a moment to assess what I'd seen.

The barrel vaulting continued over the ceiling. The space was long and wide, it surprised me. Grove had done some work on it. Several sarcophagi that had probably filled the centre of the space were smashed flat, the rubble, bones and medieval cloth discarded in the corners of the room. There were three tiers of coffins around the walls and the odd plaque of bronze or brass. At right angles to my left side, a pile of rubble had been formed into a rough mound and on the top, Grove had placed several planks of wood. The surface held an effigy of the Virgin Mary. Flanking her, two on each side, were similar statues of angels. They weren't the lesser ones either. I instantly recognised the warrior stance of Michael. Surrounding them stood tall candles of white, offerings of flowers and beautiful silver bowls, either filled with what was probably blessed water or wine, I couldn't be sure. Behind the figurines rose a simple wooden cross.

On the opposite wall rose another mound, maybe eight metres separated them. This one held four figures. The only one I recognised was a statue of Andras, Marquis of Hell. Grove must've had them made from the images I'd seen in the *Ars Goetia*, the others would be equally powerful demons.

Surrounding them were black and red candles, bowls made from bronze, maybe, or gold. Inside each sat an organ—not the piping kind. Blood and viscera leaked from a liver that was too large for its container. Another held the mound of a large heart. Were those kidneys in a third? I examined the image in my memory. I thought: pancreas? They had to be too large for a human body. I suspected a cow or bull. Somehow, I doubted they came from the local butchers or supermarket meat department. Hess would know how to butcher an animal.

Knowing I'd allowed my mind's eyes to remember the easier parts of the chamber, I then forced my memory into new areas of the room. It took me to the centre. The bit I didn't want to have seen or acknowledge even now.

A complex pattern had been drawn on the floor. It really didn't matter what, I just needed to destroy it. In the centre stood Dr Elena Grove, inside a pentagram for protection that was surrounded by a circle, all in white. Her long brown hair trailed over a simple gown of white cotton. Naked feet were spread wide, her arms were covered to the wrists. Her face was clean of markings.

Not so the children.

Each knelt on their heels, heads raised towards her, inside a smaller circle. No pentagram this time. No protection. A channel of white lines ran from a break in each circle to the next and the next until the final child, nearest the dark altar. That one contained the same lines going up to the platform holding the dark deities of Hell. I knew what it meant. The energy from the summoning would run between the lines and hit each host seeking the one designed to keep its demonic form inside human flesh. I guessed a demon sigil was under each of the children.

They wore simple white robes as well, but their faces

were decorated. Each had white paint of some kind over their round features. Their eyes had thick black circles covering them, making their innocence appear demonic. Lips were widened by scarlet pigment. Over their foreheads, covering what many considered the place of the third eye, was a sigil. The children were at the compass points. Matty's small figure was north, the one nearest the altar. His hands rested on his thighs, slack and unresponsive. Those bright and curious eyes were glazed, empty of everything. Perhaps a mercy considering the circumstances.

Was I too late? Had she been down here all day? None of us had checked the door. This ceremony might've been happening for hours.

My right hand went to the dagger at my belt. What should I do?

"Fuck it," I murmured. I'd shoot the bitch and be done. We'd deal with the children afterwards. I wasn't cutting their throats. Not now, not ever. Blyth could not ask me to be that man. I didn't deserve it. And Sanchez would not be getting her demon. An image of my DoPI predecessor sat at his desk, beside mine, flickered through my mind: his terrible, haunted, blank-eyed stare during the moments he thought himself alone.

Grove's voice rose and fell in hypnotic phrases. I didn't recognise them. She'd call the demons in, then beseech Mary to summon the angels. The air crackled and pinged. Over the smell of heavy incense rose the stink of sulphur. It wasn't too late. My heart lept at the thought. The demons weren't in the children. I could stop this catastrophe from happening.

I took a deep breath, sent a thought to Megan, and stepped into the doorway, squeezing the trigger the moment I had Grove in sight.

Click.

Oh, for fuck's sake. Not again.

Eyes like agate turned on me. "Did you really think it would be that easy?" she asked, breaking her chant.

Well, yeah, I had some hope that you might be a bit distracted from your madness and the good guys would win.

Replacing the useless firearm, I drew the sacrificial dagger from the sheath.

The woman *tsked* at me, waved a hand, and I felt a sledgehammer hitting my chest, sending me back against the wall. I smacked into it and fell in a crumpled heap.

Gasping for air, I struggled to rise, but nothing happened. A weight sat on me. The dreadful heaviness was building. Each time I struggled, it grew stronger. I floundered under its terrible constraint, my back and ribs creaking, the muscles in my arms bulging as they fought to lift my torso. I had no chance of moving my legs. Every vertebra in my neck creaked each time I tried to lift my head. Sweat poured off me as the heat in the crypt built with every loop of Grove's chant.

Only my eyes worked, and my mouth. She began to sway, her power building, making the air crackle and hum like the inside of a firework.

I did the only thing I could think of to do, I began to pray.

The sorcerer's eyes flickered to mine, and her chant dropped away.

"You are damned annoying," she snapped.

I screamed as pain ripped through my back, then over my chest. Blood sprayed. What felt like a boot smacked into my thigh, and despite the weight holding me to the hot stone floor, I jerked hard, hitting my head against the wall. Another slashing pain ripped over my hip, and my clothing tore open along with my skin. They weren't deep cuts, but much more of this and my body would just give out. Breath heh-hawed through me, my heart pounded. I began to shout the prayers.

They were babbling almost nonsense, but each time I called on God and the Holy Spirit, the sorcerer flinched.

Something struck me in the back. How it happened considering I was pinned to the wall, I had no idea, but I arched again and shot forwards over the grey flagstones.

I stared at Matty, willing him to wake up, to defy the sorcerer. Then my eyes flickered to one of the girls, Emyla, by my guess. I'd seen photos of her mother. She'd been with Grove the longest, since she was an infant. Her big blue eyes weren't trapped like the others. She wasn't vacant. Whatever she'd learned over the years at Grove's side, she now understood the horror of what she and the others faced.

Tears dribbled over her eyelids, leaving trails through the black paint and making grey streaks in the white. Her gaze was beseeching. Begging. Desperate. I had to help.

Another slice down my back. I screamed. The blood was hot. Burning hot, but the weight lifted a little with each attack. Grove couldn't keep all her controls in place as the ceremony continued. I was splitting her concentration. If I could reach the edge of just one of the circles and smudge the white line to nothing, I had a chance, a small one, of saving the children, even if it meant the demons would escape the summoning circle. That might just be sufficient to save them, and we were under a cathedral, so surely it would be enough to control a demonic presence. Prevent the Marquises of Hell from escaping.

I inched my hand over the burning floor. As the stink in the air grew stronger, I tried to cough, but it hurt. The ground below the building trembled. My eyes flickered to the altar. Each of the statues began to writhe. Arms and legs stretched. Mouths opened, and eyes came to life. Was this real? Or did the incense Grove used contain a toxin, and I was imagining this?

Please, God, let me be imagining this!

In a croak, I managed, "Our Father, in Heaven, I beg you to look down on your children and summon the Holy Ghost to…" Coughing racked my body.

Oh, shit, you're actually dying.

I was. I really was dying here on this floor.

Then, from behind me, I heard something that changed all of Grove's dreams.

A strong male voice cried out as if called across two-thousand years and endless generations of righteous power, "In the name of the Father, the Son and the Holy Ghost, I command you to stop."

The power holding me to the floor vanished. I twisted around, gasping at the pain.

Bishop James Chadwick, Anna Price, Deacon Jayne Archer, and several others were crammed into the antechamber. All in full regalia. The bishop held his staff of office. Jayne held the thurible as it billowed sweet incense, forcing the sulphur back.

I hardly recognised the bishop. The rage on his face and his stance made me very aware of his background in the armed forces. This man had seen conflict somewhere in the world, he'd witnessed war.

His eyes flickered to mine, then to the markings on the floor. I understood. On trembling limbs I rose. Despite knowing I risked a full possession by more than one demon, I stepped over the line separating me from Matty.

Grove screamed. The air between the bishop and the sorcerer wavered, vibrating with power, pushing it this way and that. I felt it nudge against me, but no longer able to stop me. I bent, placed my arms around Matty and simply lifted him off the floor. His head lashed back into my chest, eyes going full white, mouth opening too wide, and the tormented noise of the damned poured forth from his small body, layering over the demands of sorcerer and bishop.

I held the boy to my chest, and with my boots, I rubbed hard over the stonework. Grove had painted the designs on the floor, but the soles of my boots were tough, designed to march me over moors and deserts for countless miles.

Matty's small body began to shake and quiver in my arms. I glanced at the effigies on the altar. They writhed as I stamped and rubbed at the first sigil. The grating sound of my boot on the stone floor began to form a pattern with the bishop's rising voice. I sensed his presence filling the room, filling me, and I stared at the statues as they writhed, twisted, and gradually began to crumble.

Glancing over my shoulder at the altar designed for the Virgin Mary and the archangels, I witnessed something that would be one of the most baffling, marvellous things I'd ever see in my life. A blue light pulsed from the demure effigy of the Virgin. Her downcast gaze and pale hands, clasped in prayer, seemed to lift and open. The angels also lifted their faces to the ceiling, where the cathedral towered over the city, a monument to faith, to God, to humanity's wish to become a better version of itself.

I turned to look at the bishop and his people. Tears stained their faces. Their voices cracked with emotion as they watched their faith made manifest, probably for the first time in their lives.

Matty flopped in my arms, head dropping forwards, limbs going slack. Each of the children did the same, falling on their faces, or sideways, hitting their heads on the ground, making me wince. I hooked my left arm under Matty's dangling legs and stepped out of the circle. His small chest rose and fell in short puffs, but he felt so light, as if the weight of his soul had left with the demon, and I carried nothing but a shell.

"Griffin!" yelled Jayne.

I turned. Elena Grove, bleeding from her eyes, nose and ears, rushed towards me. In one movement, I crouched, tumbled Matty to the ground where he rolled away. At some point during Grove's attack I'd released the dagger, but crouching, turning, in one impossibly fluid movement, I scooped it up and rose, turning into Grove's attack.

The blade slid into her body as her clawed hands reached for my face. Her eyes, vivid green, widened, her snarling mouth turning into an 'Oh' of shock. Heat and a viscous liquid poured over my right hand. Her breasts pressed against my chest as I held her tight around her shoulders and drove the sharp dagger further into her body, twisting, wriggling, tearing at her insides. I did not want this woman to live. I did not want DoPI to have her. Sanchez would not control her.

Watching the light in Grove's eyes fade was eerie. I'd never killed someone so close. Never seen life drift away in pieces as their heart failed. Her left hand reached up, and I thought she wanted to touch my face. I reared back slightly, but instead, she grabbed an old quartz pendant around her neck, and as life ebbed away, her hand turned into a fist, snapping the chain, but not releasing the crystal.

A far meatier hand squeezed my shoulder. "She's dead, Marine, let her go."

I looked into the bishop's face. So grave, patient and full of wisdom. He gave a nod. I released my grip on the corpse and the dagger. The body dropped at my feet, its blood pooling around us.

"The children?" I asked him.

"Safe. I think. They are waking."

I glanced at the altar that held the Virgin Mary and the angels. "She… She came to save them."

The bishop's smile could only be described as coy. "Perhaps she came to save us all."

"Megan. I have to leave. I have to find Megan. Can you…?"

"Go. We'll get the police here, some ambulances."

I nodded, pushing through the crowd of people, storming up the stairs to the twenty-first century pavement and road outside the crypt. Somehow, I thought it should be dawn. Hours should've passed, but they hadn't. Hardly any time had—

My comms unit crackled to life in my right ear. "Get off me!" screamed Megan.

I started to run northwards. Or maybe hobble would be a more apt description.

In my ear, I heard Megan fighting for her life. A horrible series of grunts, yelps and cursing. Then: "No, Adrian. Don't! Please don't let go, for fuck's sake. I can hold you. We just have to wait. Adrian! Hold on…" A pause. Megan, calmer, "No, don't, please don't say that. We'll find a way through this. I'll help you. Just hold on." It sounded like her arms were being ripped from her sockets. Each word a gasp of torment. "I'm not letting go! No!" Then, in more panic. "No." A whispered denial.

I stopped my run. "Megan?" Her name was more of a pant than a word. "Megan? Can you hear me? Meg?"

"Griff…" she sobbed.

"I'm right here. I'm coming to you, love. Just wait." I

glanced around, frantic for a better form of transport than shank's pony. One of the city electric bike stands came into view. I fumbled for some change in my pocket, released it from the holder, and slung a leg over the saddle. I hadn't ridden a bike for years, and never an electric one. It took me a full minute to figure out what needed to happen, but before I knew it, I was being propelled northwards without any discernible effort on my part. It felt as surreal as the rest of the night.

As the wind dried the blood and sweat on my body, I kept talking to Megan. She was incoherent.

Then I heard Sid's voice. "Mate, she's in a bad way. I'm calling an ambulance."

"I'm coming. Five mikes max."

"Okay, I'll try to get her down from the tower."

The what now?

Chapter Twenty-Eight

When I reached the church, white lights bobbed about everywhere. Strobing blue and red dashed through the thick yew and holly leaves, bouncing around like those fucking lights at the incubus' parties. My stomach had so many knots forming, I could barely breathe past them. In the narrow lane, I wove the bike through the stand of vehicles and saw the steps for the graveyard. Dropping the city's swanky machine to the tarmac, I began to run.

"Sid!" I bellowed over the crowd. "Sid!"

"Here." A shadow rose from among the multitude of people, all of which had big labels on their backs declaring their jobs. I dodged around the graves.

At Sid's feet sat a huddled mass. Her blonde hair had long since sprung loose of her usual braid. It hung like limp seaweed around her pale face. Those big blue eyes had turned into saucers, diffuse and unfocused.

I knelt before her, brushed hair off her face with my too-big hands. She shivered, and I pulled the thin, shimmering foil blanket more tightly around her shoulders.

"I'm right here, Megan. I'm right here. Meg? Can you look at me? Megan?"

Sid couched beside me. "She's in shock, Griffin."

"Is she hurt?"

He nodded. "She won't let the paramedics look her over. I told them to wait a bit. Christ, mate, you're bleeding everywhere."

"Yeah, it's been a night. I don't know where Luce is, I'm sorry."

"Don't worry. She's at the cathedral, helping the children and explaining everything to the bishop."

I breathed out. "Megan? Love? I need you to look at me. Come on. Look at me, Sergeant Ackley."

That did it. Her eyes tracked slowly away from the wall of the church building and focused on me. "Megan? Speak to me."

Her earpiece lay on her shoulder. "He died," she whispered. "He tried to kill me. He died."

Someone approached. "Sir? We need to get her in an ambulance. Can you help with that?"

I looked up and saw the same paramedic we'd met at Wesson's place that first night. The air was so sultry and thick, I could hardly suck in a breath without drowning in humidity. "Hi, yeah, I can help." Returning my focus to Megan, I said, "We're going to move now. I need your help. The medics want to check you over." She had blood on her face from a head wound, and bruising was changing the colour of her skin.

"He died, Griffin. I couldn't hold him." Her eyes didn't focus, and one of her pupils looked wider than the other. Not good.

"I know, love. I know. I'm so sorry. But right now, we have to deal with the living. That's you and me. I have to go to the hospital with you. I'm bleeding badly, Meg. We have to move. Understood?"

She nodded. Small, rapid movements. Suddenly feeling every one of my bones and muscles, I struggled upright with Sid's help. Then, we both helped Megan to her feet. In the light of someone's torch, I saw the side of her face more clearly, the bruises were blooming like wicked, bloated flowers. Her throat looked red. She swayed.

Sid wrapped an arm around her. I trailed behind, my right leg finally giving up its fight for life and showing a disinterest in being cooperative. The three of us shuffled towards the path down to the waiting ambulance, four paramedics herding us like ducklings. When I had Megan inside one of the vehicles, the paramedics pounced. Stripping her of the ballistic vest and the silver blanket, I realised why they'd wanted to move her so badly. They rolled up her t-shirt, and I saw that Hess had kicked her badly. The bruise across her belly was thick and black already.

I was pushed away as the doors closed, and I heard: "Internal bleeding, head trauma. Unresponsive pupil in the right eye…"

I turned to Sid. "What now?" I swayed alarmingly.

He put a hand on my arm. "Now you go to the hospital. Let me deal with this. I'll come when they release me from the scene. Right now, I'm the only witness. What happened at the cathedral?"

"The bishop turned up and did some magic," I managed.

My friend chuckled. "Magic, huh? Good for him. The children?"

"Not sure. Alive. I hope they're okay."

"I'll find out. Come on. Ambulance."

I felt a small arm encircle my waist. The female paramedic again. “This way, sir. Come on. We need to get you cleaned up.”

She guided me to the second ambulance, and I walked up the steps like my skin had become glass. Slowly, she coaxed me onto the bed, and when I lay down, my mind just switched off. The journey to the hospital and my admission were a blur of bright lights and noise. I answered some important questions, and the doctors decided I needed full sedation for them to tackle the long wounds covering my torso and back. After that, time pissed off to do its own thing for a while, not needing me to keep an eye on it.

It took three days for me to come back to myself. There were moments of lucidity, but most of the time I slept, or screamed. Apparently, there was a lot of screaming. The hospital shrink was called in to help. I managed a half-arsed explanation about being a Royal Marine and operations overseas, bringing past trauma back due to current events. I promised I was seeing a private therapist in my role as a government field operative for Rural Security. The nice man was all too willing to believe me, he looked harried to the point of tears himself.

I had staples and stitches. Almost two hundred in total. It was nothing compared to Megan. Hess had kicked her down the nave of the church, rupturing her bowel. Her organs survived due to her ballistic vest and a huge dose of luck.

Sid filled me in on the details during day three. I came to wish he hadn’t.

“Hess had copies of the keys to the church. The local plod discovered Grove had become part of the congregation up there and at the cathedral over the years. She’d managed to worm her way into the offices, and she'd taken copies. No one suspected her. Everyone on the cathedral's regular staff recognised her. The woman's long-term planning is terrifying, Griffin. Anyway, Megan chased Hess into the nave. They fought. She managed to get a shot off, but it didn't slow him down much. I tried, mate, really—"

"Don't," I said, placing a hand on his where they rested on my white blanket. "Not your job. Never your job, Sid."

He didn't look convinced, but he continued. "He grabbed her, threw her into the lectern, and then started kicking her. Megan lashed out, but it was clear she was dazed. He ran to the tower's entrance. She scrambled after him, telling me to get outside. We could hear the sirens coming. It was my job to show them where to go."

"She did the right thing," I said.

Sid just grunted. Not convinced. "Then I heard her and Hess screaming at each other on the roof. He went for her. Megan slipped sideways, or down, or something. She vanished behind one of the crenellations. Hess toppled over her, I think. Then she was lunging for him. In the lights on the church tower, I saw Hess holding the stonework, Megan grabbing him. She was sliding off the roof as well. I ran for the door, meaning to go up to help, when I heard the body hit the ground, and she screamed." He took a deep breath. "When I reached her, she kept saying, 'He thought he could fly', I guess he was caught in a spell similar to the one those kids from the car park thought would protect them."

God, that felt like months ago rather than days.

"I need to see her," I said.

Sid shook his head. "She's in ICU, mate. They aren't going to let you in there in this state. Her family is with her. They want to come see you as well, but, well..."

"She's their priority. Besides, they aren't really my family anymore," I said, feeling desperately lonely and sad. It hit me like a tsunami, and the sudden pressure behind my eyes was almost too much.

My friend rubbed my arm. "No, mate, it's not that, trust me. Iris will be in later. She's really worried about you. Nice woman. No, it's just…" He sucked in a breath and puffed it out again. "Griffin, it's touch and go with Megan."

I searched his eyes and saw the pity. "She'll be okay, right?" My throat felt like I had rocks inside it, and they were growing.

"I'm sorry, mate. It's fifty-fifty. The head injury. It's really bad." Sid was struggling to get the words out.

They refused to register. Each word sat on the surface of my mind and just floated there in shades of grey. Nothing would make sense without Megan. The world would just be a jumble of faces and noise that had no discernible meaning.

"Griffin?" Sid asked, rising from his chair. "Do you hear me, mate?"

"Go away," I mumbled, my throat too tight and dry. "Go away. No more. No more." I rolled onto my side.

A chair creaked. "I'll be back later," Sid whispered. "I'm sorry, Griffin."

The earth turned. I breathed. Images swam about inside me, all of me. I felt some in my heart: that first kiss, her small hand at mum's funeral, her laughing at the river's side as I puked on too much cider aged fourteen, the love in her eyes as I pulled a lad off her at the summer dance, her damned bravery. We hadn't been given enough time.

Hey, she'll get through this. Fifty percent is better than nothing. A lot better.

But everyone I loved left me.

Oh my God! Really? Your mother died. All the other women in your life before Megan, they just left you. None of them died. Get over it.

Get over it? How? I felt cursed. All I'd ever wanted was Megan in my life. I'd stayed away from her because we were cousins, and when the truth came out, it was like the dawn breaking in both our lives. A new start. A beginning of something special.

Hess took it from me, and that fucking Grove woman. I wish I'd left her alive and given her to Sanchez. I could've gone up to London and demanded some 'alone' time. It was the least they fucking owed me.

Then the tears began. When they stopped, I found the hospital blanket scrunched up against my battered face, the screams and sobs trapped in the folds of cotton.

I had money put aside. Enough to buy a small house down here in Redruth, nothing fancy, but if I found a job as a security guard, or even joined the police, I could pay a mortgage and care for her. I could build us a life. She just had to live. It didn't matter what state—

The door to my tiny room opened. "Griffin?"

I whimpered. It was Iris's soft voice.

"Oh, my luver," her Cornish accent turned the word into something tender. "Don't fret, son. She'll be alright. You'll see."

I looked at my mother's adopted sister. "Sid said it was—"

"I know the odds, but we both know our girl. She'll come back to us. Do you want me to explain? Or do you just need a good cry and a hug?" she asked as if I were ten again.

I loved my Aunt Iris. "Got any biscuits?" I asked on a sniff.

She laughed. "Cheeky, boy. As it happens, I've some

shortcake I'll leave with you. Now, let's talk about our girl." Her hand was hot, but trembling as it lay on mine.

It turned out Megan had swelling and a small bleed in her frontal lobe, where the impact had been worst. Her bowel had split, her liver was swollen and bruised, and she might lose her spleen; the next day or so would confirm. They'd operated, stitched her up and put her into a coma to give her brain a chance to heal. She'd had several MRIs, and the bleed wasn't getting any larger in the last twelve hours. This was all good news. She had septicaemia from the bowel split and how long she'd been on her feet after the event, but the antibiotics would knock it into submission.

I confessed to Iris that she'd waited until I reached her before allowing the ambulance to take her away. Apparently, that wasn't my fault. I couldn't have known. Sid had explained the events at the church to the family on the first day. I owed Sid.

"It's important that you get well, Griffin. She'll need you."

"I'm not sure she'll ever want to see me again."

Iris laughed. "Don't be daft, son. She loves you. I think you both need to consider your life choices regarding your jobs, but I've never had any sway with Megan over that. Or any other part of her life, if I'm honest."

Was that an unspoken referral to keeping my mother's adoption a secret for so long, therefore keeping me away from her daughter? It's a Cornish way of approaching a difficult subject, going around all the houses, farms and bushes, before getting to the bloody point. I wasn't going to push. Iris had done her best, and any decisions she made weren't out of malice. I'd pounded a lot of miles to reach that conclusion over the summer.

"I don't think any of us have much of a say in Megan's life," I said gently.

Iris looked at me. "That's not true. You do. If she could've gone into the Marines, she would have. That girl would follow you to hell and back."

"She might march beside me, but I can't imagine she'd follow me," I pointed out.

A smile lit Iris's face, making her look just like her daughter for a moment. "Well, you're probably right. The problem is, Griffin, that your job, whatever it is, seems to be getting my daughter into serious trouble."

Now I couldn't meet her gaze. I started smoothing the creases out of the blanket, releasing the screams and sobs. "Yeah, I know. I'm sorry."

"Let's just see if we can make a few changes in that department, for Megan's sake."

I glanced at her. "I'll try, Aunt Iris, but she's been offered a full posting with the department. The money is excellent. Generally, better hours and the holiday allowance can be generous. We just have to be on call at all times."

Iris did not look pleased. She left soon after, and I was alone to ponder the events. Eventually, I fell asleep.

Chapter Twenty-Nine

The blackness of sleep shifted. One moment, I had no awareness of my place in the world. Next, I was fully aware of my reality. I stood not in familiar surroundings, but inside the deep nothingness of the veil. At least I wasn't in free fall this time.

Nothing lay beneath my feet. I had a sense of solid ground only because that's what my mind told me I had to be standing on, more from ingrained habit than a real idea of a location.

A hot wind blasted my face for a second. It smelt the same as the crypt under the cathedral. *"Think you can escape me?"* hissed a woman's voice. It surrounded me, coming from the tempest.

I swallowed hard. "I was hoping too, yes." Despite wearing full fatigues, I carried no weapons. "Besides, isn't it you who needs to escape from us?" I asked. "We won."

The wind hit me again, and this time, I stumbled back, gasping in pain. The blast felt as if it contained a billion grains of sand. I'd pissed her off.

"You cannot escape me in this place. I can leave you here and take your body, little sailor boy. I bet your rotten old sorcerer didn't tell you that, did he?" The words were no more than a hiss.

No, no, he hadn't, but I doubted even Blyth could've seen this coming.

Another blast hit me, and I grunted in pain as the skin on my hands and face felt like I'd mistaken a scouring pad for a flannel, and I'd used it for several hours. I had nowhere to run, so I crouched, tucking my face and hands into my knees. The wind started to swirl around my body. My clothing began to shred. The sorcerer, formerly known as Dr Elena Grove, screamed and howled as she bore down on the part of me trapped within the veil.

How had this happened? *Not the question to ask, Marine.* Great, my inner critic was here to lend a hand.

What is the question? *Let's start with how we get out of this?*

Yeah, okay, how do we do that then? *You're asking me? I'm just your self-doubt and misery, mate. Oh, let's not forget the paranoia, I'm that bit as well. You're the brains of the outfit.*

I blocked out the voice, it was right, I had to find a way of escaping. The skin on my back began to burn as my shirt frayed under the assault. What was her endgame here? She'd dragged my consciousness into this place, which meant…

Oh, shit.

Yeah, oh, shit, indeed. It meant my body was empty. When I came into the veil, it was a kind of astral projection. A shell awaited me in the hospital bed. That meant only one thing. If she destroyed my mind here, she had access to my body. If she managed to perform such a feat, and I had no doubt she could, considering her other accomplishments to date, I was royally fucked. A sorcerer would wake in my place, have access to all of DoPI's files and buildings, never mind the weapons and my training.

The only option was to find a way back on my own. I had to leave the veil. All well and good, but I wasn't standing on an oily rainbow. The Dru had thrown me back the first time, the second…

Trying hard to keep the wind off my face, I forced my hand down my shirt, and I grabbed the witch's stone. Bringing it up to my eye, I tried to look through the small hole, to think of Megan waiting for me in the hospital.

The storm surrounding me laughed. *"You think I'll let you go back to that murdering bitch?"*

"No!" boomed a new voice. "But I shall contain you, sorcerer, agent of demons. I call you by your real name, Elena, bringer of light turned to dark. Elena, named for the moon Selene. Elena, harbinger of curses, as Helen was to Troy. I summon you, ethereal being, to me. I summon you and compel you to my command."

The wind screamed and tore away from me, knocking me flat in the process. I glanced up and, damn me, I saw Blyth standing in the veil, still wearing his trench coat buttoned and belted. He held a square object, opaque and black, about the size of a shoebox.

A torment of words and screams began, but Blyth held his box up, as if offering it to some nameless god. A horrible realisation coursed through me. DoPI, and therefore Sanchez, was about to get their mucky paws on a sorcerer able to summon a Marquis of Hell.

Blyth called out, "I command you to enter. You must obey." The force of his will, even here, in this nothingness place, dominated me. I'd have crawled into the box if he'd ordered me to do it. The man's eyes and voice held more power than I'd ever witnessed in a mortal. He looked akin to that damned djinn I'd glimpsed the first time I'd stood on the edge of the veil in Somerset.

The wind began to spiral, twist and twist, and again, until the base of it was a needlepoint hovering over the box.

"I compel and command you," Blyth roared.

The wind screamed, but found itself pulled down into the box. It bucked, shivered and twisted in Blyth's hands.

Then, nothing. Utter silence. I remained on the ground.

"It's alright, laddie, you can stand up now." Blyth's voice, soft, Scottish, calm.

I lifted off the ground. "What's happening?" My back felt like it had been turned into hamburger meat.

Rather than making me move, Blyth came closer. "I've been waiting here for you. I knew she'd find you and drag you into this place. Trouble is, laddie, she had no idea you've walked here before. All I had to do was wait for you to turn up, then the creature to make itself known, and the rest is here." He patted the box under his arm. "Well done, the witch's stone helped me locate you. That was the bit I couldn't predict, but everything turned out well in the end."

"Well?" I asked. "I can't move." The pain had started to register.

"Hush, laddie, hush, I'll have you right in a moment. Don't you worry. This'll be one injury you'll not carry into the real world. Give me the arm with the dryad's mark and I'll send you home."

"How will you get her back to our reality?" I nodded at the box.

"That's my business, Corporal."

I didn't want to argue, not here, he could leave me stranded, but we'd be seeing about that conclusion in the real world. I held out the arm with the odd tangle of knotwork running up on the inside. Blyth grasped it hard, muttered a few words I didn't catch, and the image flared.

When I opened my eyes, I stared up at the ceiling of my hospital room, but I wasn't on the bed, I'd hit the floor. In the process, I'd torn the IV from my right hand, the left was covered in bandages—blood had steadily leaked out. The nurses would not be pleased. Slowly, I managed to gain my feet, though I was moving like a lamb who'd just plopped out onto spring grass.

Getting my arse back on the bed, I took a few steadying breaths. The last time I'd been thrown out of the veil, I'd had Megan there to ground me. This time, I was alone. It didn't feel great.

"Time to take action, Marine," I murmured, attempting to stem the blood still dripping from my hand. My head felt woozy, and I realised I hadn't eaten enough in days. Hospital food was better than some of the crap the navy fed us, but the portions were too small, and it wasn't enough to keep me on my toes for long.

I had dressings covering the burns on my legs, arm, face, neck and more dressings on the long slash marks caused by the sorcerer's attack in the crypt. Still, I wanted to reach Megan. At least if I saw her, I might not feel like I'd been cut adrift in the world.

"Christ, what if she doesn't forgive me?" I muttered, feeling the reality of that thought slash at my emotional self-control—or lack of it.

Trying to focus on the present, I took a few more steadying breaths and stood up again. The room was unsteady for a bit, the pain flared, then sank, and I made my way to the small bathroom in the corner of the room. After that, I shuffled barefoot into the corridor.

It took me a while to find the ICU, and I stood outside the doors watching the desk. I doubted they'd let me in to see Megan, so I needed to pick my moment. The noise and smells of the hospital wove around me, but my memory still held firm to the smells in the crypt. The heady incense from the bishop's thurible, the sticky-sweet scent of whatever Grove had burned, the underlying horror of sulphur. I wondered what it would take to override the visceral memory.

After a few minutes, I saw the nurses at the station out front leave and an orderly came through the doors. Before the doors closed, I snuck inside and went hunting. Shuffling along like a geriatric, not entirely a disguise, I looked through a few windows and on the fourth try, I found her.

I pushed open the door. She had tubes and a mask covering her pale face. The summer freckles were stark against the pallor, and she was tiny and so still. Even in her sleep, Megan's life bubbled around her, taking up more space than her physical body. When we hugged, I was often surprised by how small she felt in my arms.

Gently, I lowered myself into the nearby chair. The machines blipped and hissed.

"I'm so sorry, Megan," I whispered.

Being tender in a way that she'd scoff at if she were awake, I wiggled my hand under hers. The soft fingers were unresponsive and cold, but her palm held a little heat.

With my objective attained, I just sat there, staring at nothing, thinking too much and wishing for different outcomes. Time became meaningless. Eventually, I started to talk to her. Regrets, plans, ideas, dreams and wishes. I probably covered them all. Mostly, I apologised for not being there to save her from Hess. For not having killed him. For not being a better Marine.

I don't know how long it took, but eventually a nurse found me. I explained, and she took pity on me.

"Don't worry, she'll wake up soon. This is a medical coma. The swelling has gone down considerably, and the bleed really was small." She assured me that Megan's body was already absorbing the blood. Then, I was firmly escorted back to my room.

Later that day, Sid returned.

"They said you'll be discharged tomorrow." He brought a huge pile of food with him. "Stress cooking," he admitted, plonking it on my bed.

I delved in. Who needed to be polite at a time like this? I found pasta with sun-dried tomatoes and tuna. "I had a vision-thing," I muttered. "It was nasty." I went on to explain.

Sid grunted. "That makes sense."

"It does?" I asked around a mouthful. My skin may hate me, but my stomach became my new best friend.

Sid nodded. "Blyth took off for London this morning with barely a goodbye. He's been holed up in our spare room for days, I've hardly seen him."

"He was in the veil, waiting for me to be summoned by the sorcerer," I said.

Sid rubbed his face. "God, that's fucking weird and a bit dark."

"You're telling me. He's taken her back to London in a box, hasn't he? I don't want Sanchez to have whatever remains of Elena Grove. It feels like a bad thing."

For a long moment, Sid stared out of the small window. The weather had broken, and rain had moved into Cornwall. It felt like closure.

He said, "I fear you may be right."

"They have a powerful, incorporeal being trapped in a box that's been inside the veil. I'm not happy with not knowing what's going to be done with the thing. With her. I don't trust them, Sid." I found some olive bread in the bag of goodies.

Sid's dark eyes sharpened on me. "You want to go to London, don't you?"

"I think it's wise to have this out with Sanchez once and for all. Megan's been badly hurt because we didn't have the right operational control. We didn't have enough boots on the ground, and I made some bad judgement calls."

"No, Griffin, you can't take that on board. It wasn't your fault."

I really looked at Sid, holding his gaze. "If not mine, then who's? It's easy to blame Hess, or the magic, or the demons, or Grove's intense drive to destroy the Church. Ultimately, this is on me. I made operational decisions that led to Megan being in that church alone with a Renfield."

Sid dropped his gaze. "I should've gone in after her."

"No, Sid. You'd have been hurt as well. You aren't trained to fight, and you can't use a firearm. Maybe she shouldn't have gone in after him, but she did, because I needed him stopped. That's on me. What I don't want to happen is DoPI dropping us in the shit again, especially not with demons involved."

"I won't argue with that. When are we leaving for London?" he asked.

I grinned. "When I get out of here and cleaned up a bit."

Chapter Thirty

It took another two days before the hospital let me go, and I felt able to travel the four-plus hours it would take to reach the capital. In that time, I'd written a full report for Sanchez, detailing everything. Megan would need to fill in the blanks, but without the bishop and his people, I made it clear, we'd have failed. Luce had been the one to bring him in and that one action saved us all. I needed to thank him personally at some point.

I'd also managed a brief visit with Megan and another with Naomi, who remained in hospital. Megan's went considerably better than Naomi's.

Megan woke from her coma and, despite still being in a critical care unit, they'd removed her from some of the machines. There may have been tears on my part when she told me she loved me.

"I killed him, Griff," she murmured, clutching my hand.

"No, love. Grove killed him long before we came close. He wouldn't have survived."

"She picked him because of me. Us." Megan's eyes shone like deep pools of lonely water.

"Yes, she did, but Hess's obsession with you made him an easy target. That was on him, Meg. Not on you, not on us. He wasn't a well man. He wasn't a very nice man. Remember that."

"I tried to save him."

"He almost killed you. I should've done better. I'm sorry." Now I couldn't meet her eyes.

Her thumb rubbed over my knuckles. "I want to work for DoPI full time, Griffin. I would like to understand the world you move around in. I'm of no use to you like this, with no background, no training and no education. If I have to believe in the weird shit to be good at my job, then I have to go all in. I can't pick and choose. We're a team."

I should've been elated, but instead, I felt glum. "Your mother is never going to forgive me."

"Yeah, she will. She might not like you much for a bit, but you really are her favourite son."

We both managed a small chuckle, injuries permitting.

For a while we remained wrapped in a soft silence. Megan might've dozed. I just stroked the soft skin of her hand, desperate to maintain contact. When her eyes opened again, she murmured, "What happened to Grove? The children? No one has told me."

"You don't have to worry about that," I said to her, trying to divert her from the truth. She needed to know, I had no intention of keeping it from her forever, but for now, I just wanted her to heal.

"Don't do that, Griffin. Don't hide from me. It doesn't suit you."

Lifting her hand, I kissed the back. "You don't need to know now."

"I wouldn't have asked if I didn't want to know," she said.

Slowly, I explained what happened in the crypt. I also told her about the vision I'd had the night before and Blyth's actions.

"He's returned to London with this box?" she asked, looking more alert.

"Yep. He basically has the sorcerer's energy form trapped. It's like something from Ghostbusters."

Megan laughed, then groaned. "Don't make me do that, it hurts." She paused, catching her breath. "She could have killed you in the veil, couldn't she?"

"Yes," I admitted. "I don't understand the place. How it works, what its rules are, why I seem to slip into it with such ease."

"Then we need to work on that. Trystan will help, right?"

I nodded. "I'd trust him over Blyth. I can't believe he used me like that."

"I can. We're the pointy end of the spear, aren't we? That means we're expendable. Our role is to fight and die for the rest of DoPI to maintain their hold on the *paras* leaking into our world."

"Christ, that's bleak, Megan."

"I know. It's something we have to change. We have to protect ourselves while doing our jobs. It's going to be difficult. I'm not planning on dying for DoPI. Now, tell me about the children. Is Matty okay?"

"Sid's been monitoring progress—"

"What aren't you telling me?"

Oh, I really didn't want to tell her. "Three of them have gone to London. DoPI's providing safe foster care for the moment. Those that were with Grove the longest are basically behaving as if we stripped them of their birthright. It seems to be cult-like programming. Sanchez is worried about their long term mental health, not because she's worried about them per se, more that she's concerned demons will find them easier to climb into and use. They're concerned the children will be versed in the occult deeply enough to try to repeat the ritual themselves."

"Jesus, that's terrible," Megan murmured. Her horror at the thought made her cheeks pink a little. "What about Matty?"

I allowed myself a smile. "Yeah, well, they tried to take Matty. However, Sid was copied into the email by accident, as was I, apparently. When he saw it, he mobilised Naomi and Glendower. She is still here, but Glendower came to the hospital and took Matty away. When the DoPI operatives tried to stop them, he threatened them with the press, citing kidnapping. Then Naomi said she'd keep DoPI's secrets only if she had her son back. Otherwise, it would be a full WikiLeaks-type affair. The medical staff got involved and told DoPI we had no right to separate family members without the police and the Social Services being informed. One of the nurses told me it all became a bit savage."

"Wouldn't DoPI just dump Naomi in a hole?" Megan asked.

"She'd already put it all online, with a timer. They'd never have closed it down in time. Sid pointed out that even he couldn't stop it from happening. They released Matty into her and Glendower's care with the proviso that DoPI be allowed to monitor the boy's behaviour. Which means we get to go to Grumbla for tea and cakes whenever we like. Though Naomi's not too happy about that, so we might have to take our own cake." I smiled. "Which means it's not all bad news."

"I feel so sorry for the others, though," she whispered, her gaze far away.

"Yeah, me too. Sid's checked out the foster home, it seems nice. They have other children to play with who've come from cults. They'll be moved to a decent place, out in the Cotswolds. Horses, dogs, and a small farm they run. A local school. It'll help them reintegrate, maybe forget much of what's happened to them."

"I hope they find some peace."

"Yeah." I found myself staring at the floor.

"What is it?" she asked.

"I'm worried about what DoPI will do with Grove. What Sanchez's plans are."

"You think they'll use her?"

"I'm sure they will," I confessed.

"Then you need to go to London and talk to Sanchez. You can't keep tying yourself in knots over this. You are running the first remote station for DoPI in its entire history, so it has to give you some kind of authority. Challenge her. Learn more. Persuade them that DoPI can't keep killing and containing. We need allies in the *para-world*."

I smiled. "We?"

Where bruising allowed, Megan nodded and smiled in return. "We."

I shuffled off soon after that and went in search of Naomi. Not a job I wanted, but I felt I couldn't escape it. She was on a general care ward. The moment I shuffled down the corridor between the beds, and she saw me, she scowled. This was a full-on three-year-old's 'I'm about to lose my shit' kind of scowl. I almost backed out. Instead, I forced myself to remain standing beside her bed, despite being desperate to sit down.

"Hi," I opened with something simple.

"Hi?" Her hazel eyes sparked and spat fireworks at me. "Is that it? Hi?"

"No, but I need to sit or I'm going to faint," I admitted, lowering myself into the visitor's chair. I puffed out a breath. "I can't remember ever feeling this bad before."

Naomi huffed. "Try being stabbed."

"Yeah, sorry." I could point out I'd been stomped on by a sorcerer, but I didn't think it would help. "I hear you managed to keep DoPI under control. I'm glad."

That surprised her. "You are?"

"If I'd known, I'd have been down here backing you up. Matty needs to be with you. How is he?"

Naomi's eyes filled with tears. "He thinks you're a bloody hero. Someone told him that you nearly died to save his life."

I felt my cheeks grow warm. "It wasn't quite like that, but… He was my priority."

Naomi studied her hospital blanket. "Thank you. For saving him."

"I'm sorry we placed you in danger."

She managed a short shrug. "Who knows? They could've found us. Probably would have, and we'd all have died. That fucking doctor was…"

"Yeah, she was." I didn't think mentioning the woman still existed inside a black box taken to London would help matters.

"So, how is he? Matty, I mean?" I asked.

A tear slid down her cheek. "He's… Not himself. Nightmares. Anxiety. Fear. He doesn't like going anywhere alone. He's afraid of the dark. Says he can hear things in it."

I nodded. "Okay, I'll talk to the bishop. He's a good bloke. Maybe he'll help Matty in a way we can't."

"I don't want Matty indoctrinated." Her anger flared briefly.

"It won't be like that, Naomi. Bishop Chadwick really will just want to help. It might offer you some comfort as well."

The suggestion was met with a flat glare.

Or maybe not.

"At least you know Matty's safe now. You don't have to hide him away." I tried a smile.

She didn't say anything. I decided it was time for me to leave. Lifting myself out of the chair, I turned to go.

Softly, Naomi said, "Thank you, Griffin. Thank Megan for me as well. Glendower and Sid explained you both almost died to protect my son. That was selfless. So, thanks."

I gave her a brief nod. "You're very welcome." It took a long time to shuffle back to my small, box-like room in a different part of the hospital.

The next day, they released me with strict instructions to rest. Which is why I let Sid drive us to London. Unfortunately, he wouldn't allow me to hire a car, so we both squashed into the small Mini. By the time we reached Stonehenge, I had to stop. Sid helped me out, and my back screamed as I tried to straighten.

"Sorry," Sid mumbled. "I'm just not comfortable driving a modern vehicle."

I refrained from commenting. It wouldn't help to snap at him. After walking around for a few minutes, I stood and took in the ancient monument. It always surprised me how small it was, and yet, it dominated the entire plain. Even the frantic A303 was diminished in comparison. Despite the damp summer day, one with a glowering sky and stickiness I could've done without, an odd sense of peace seemed to flow upwards from the ground. I moved from the tarmac to stand on the grassy verge. The sensation became stronger, almost a tingle in my legs. Healing, calming. The crows wove overhead, the cacophony louder than the chattering families, barking dogs, engines and more. I closed my eyes and breathed in. The scent of petrol and diesel diminished.

For a few seconds I felt the tug of the veil, the thin, bubble-like oily rainbow beckoning. My hands bunched into fists, not to fight, but to remind me that the world existed on two planes. *I* existed on two planes of reality. If I pushed, would I see the ancient world and its ceremonies, like I had at the old monuments in Cornwall? Would I learn what so many archaeologists and esoteric believers were desperate to figure out? Perhaps. Or it could be the unfiltered imaginings of one mind.

Opening my eyes, I found Sid watching me from where he leaned against the snubby nose of the Mini. "You alright?" he asked.

I pushed the desire to travel into the veil away. "Yeah. I'm fine." With my eyes on the ancient stones, I added, "This place is special."

Sid glanced over his shoulder. "Gives me the creeps. I'm happy to stay away, to be honest."

We climbed back into the car, and the stitches down my back pulled alarmingly. From Stonehenge to London, we remained quiet, the both of us wrapped up in thoughts related to the last few days, months, all of it since moving to Cornwall.

Sid drove with practiced ease through London. His only comment was, "I'd forgotten how bastard bloody busy this place is." We made it to the head office in Whitehall Place, and due to the diminutive size of the vehicle, we found a parking space without a problem. The Mini looked incongruous among all the larger, branded new cars and taxis of this rarefied area of the capital.

After the rich air of Cornwall, trying to breathe in the city's scent made my nose flinch and my head spin. The sultry late August air dominated the metropolis. It felt like everything in it had a thin coating of something sticky and unwelcome.

"Good to be back?" I asked Sid.

"Oddly, no," he said with a frown, checking the street, eyes narrowed. "I feel all the old paranoia returning."

"Like what?" I asked.

"Like being pulled over because I'm black. Oddly, that just doesn't happen in Cornwall."

I didn't know what to say. It wasn't an experience I'd had; nothing in the normal world of Britain made me feel that kind of vulnerability. I wasn't a woman or a minority. I was a fit, healthy, big, white man with money. It gave me freedoms and protections I took for granted.

"We'll be home soon enough," I said.

"Or sacked," Sid added.

"Or black sited."

He glared at me as we headed for the office. "Thanks for that, Griffin, it really helps the paranoia."

"You're welcome," I grinned.

Sid shook his head, and we began the laborious process of gaining access to the office. The buildings here were made of white stone or pale gold of sandstone, the exteriors heavily decorated, the windows triple glazed and bulletproof, spy proof, and you'd have a hard time throwing yourself out of one. Internally, they were sleek, modern, high-security buildings. We were near the heart of government and the Security Services, but also slightly separate. DoPI predated the modern world by several centuries.

When we reached Sanchez's floor, I paused before heading into the office space I used to occupy just a few months ago. "This feels weird."

"Yep. It does, like back to your old school. We need to figure out what's happening."

"Springing the visit on her won't be appreciated."

Sid shrugged. "Fuck her." He pushed open the door and strode in.

I stifled a laugh. Sid's mouth was going to get us both in trouble if I wasn't careful, but still it would be fun to watch.

Markin sat at my old desk, and he looked up as we entered. "What the hell are you doing here?"

"Good to see you as well," I said. "Is she in?"

He rose. "You can't just go in there."

I strode past him and knocked on Sanchez's door.

"What?" came the irritable response I knew so well.

I opened the door.

She looked up from her screen. "Woodbury." Her gaze slid to Sid and turned to ice. "What are you doing here?" Her expression was one I'd never seen before. Actual surprise. Markin began to babble something, but she waved him away, and he closed the door.

"Always a pleasure, Pilar," Sid said, plonking himself down on a chair without being asked.

Sanchez's eyes returned to mine. "I thought we agreed you'd keep him contained in Cornwall?"

I shrugged. "I needed a driver. I'm taking a lot of medication. I also need to sit, sorry, ma'am." With more care than Sid managed, I lowered myself into a soft and comfortable office chair. "Oh, that's better." When I next looked up, my eyes were drawn to the mind-melting artwork behind her chair. I almost let my opinion of the piece slip out of my mouth. Fortunately, Sanchez spoke first.

"What are you doing here, Corporal?" she asked. "You're on medical leave since sending in your report."

"I felt it was time for a catch-up, ma'am," I said, trying to meet her gaze and not look over her shoulder as I would a commanding officer. My mind babbled that I ought to be standing at attention. My body told me to forget it.

"A catch—up?" She spread the words out, as if she were a snake pondering whether to eat the mouse that had just been placed in its cage. A slight curiosity about it as a concept.

"Yes, ma'am. I felt it was time we discussed plans." I felt my palms begin to sweat. Facing off with a sorcerer was easier than this conversation.

"Plans?" she asked. "For what, exactly?"

I took an air-conditioned breath. "Mostly for the entity previously known as Dr Elena Grove. Next, I'd like to know what your long-term plans are for our work in Cornwall. It's clear the veil down there is thinning. Grove wouldn't have achieved her level of skill with the occult practices without being in Cornwall. I want to know why we are there? The veil is thinning in several places, but you chose that peninsular."

Her manicured eyebrows rose. "I thought you'd like the country air?" she suggested.

Sid chuckled. "I know it's a punishment for me, but you were basically sending him to the only home he's ever had, so what's going on? We want to know what the plans are, because life down there is scary. We had to deal with a demon summoning alone. Griffin was facing a Renfield with the training given to a paratrooper. Blyth saved his life and Megan's."

"That's why I sent him. He came out of retirement to help you."

Blyth hadn't mentioned that. Interesting.

"If it hadn't been for the bishop, we'd have lost," I pointed out.

"He was fully briefed."

"I wasn't," I snapped.

An amused smile lifted one corner of her mouth. "I see." Her dark eyes narrowed. "What do you want me to tell you, Corporal Woodbury?" She leaned back in her chair. "That your commitment to your work is exemplary?"

Sid muttered something I didn't catch, but I heard the next part. "Stop blowing smoke up his arse. We all know he's one of the best operatives you've had in the field. Griffin's more human than most of your spear points. He gives a shit. He's always looking for the right solution, not necessarily the easy one. You can trust him. Now that we have all that out of the way, tell us what you plan to do with Grove. She was bloody dangerous contained in flesh, God knows what she'll be like in spirit. Griffin being pulled into the veil by her and ending up acting as bait for Blyth, is another level of weird. We need help."

Sanchez stared over our heads for a moment, pontificating. "Alright, come with me." She rose. Her summer pantsuit and flat shoes were expensive, elegant and understated. Her hair, as always, nestled in a tight bun at the back of her neck. She was about Megan's height, but with a slimmer frame. Just like Megan, she took up considerably more room than just the physical space she occupied.

Sid and I trailed after her, puppies following mummy dog. I felt Markin's eyes on me until we left the room. Sanchez took us to the lift and waved her ID at the little window of dark glass where a button might be for a more normal office. When the lift arrived, she walked in and turned, remaining at the front. Sid and I were forced to move around her. He rolled his eyes at me and slumped against the wall. Sanchez pressed a button on the console that was marked -4.

This time we shared a look and a frown. Neither of us had been to the underground levels in the building. In silence, we descended. When the door swished open, she stepped out.

"Don't get lost," she warned without looking at either of us. The lift opened into a concrete corridor. The ground had a simple vinyl floor of misty blue, with three thick stripes painted on. Red, green and yellow. They went in separate directions down three different corridors. The walls were painted a soft green, and the lighting also had a muted feel to it.

"We find keeping this area in a half-light helps to maintain calm for the occupants. Too bright, and it agitates some of our more aggressive… inmates." She strode off along the yellow strand. "The colours are just designations of beings. Grove has no form, the yellow line indicates this. We have powerful poltergeists, a few lesser demons, spirit entities conjured from the veil many centuries ago, and humans who have done stupid things and lost their biological form. Also, a few other species who've been known to do the same thing. Red is for those beings who are physically present in this world and have strong psychic abilities. Be they human or otherwise. Green indicates those we are trying to reintegrate. Powerful cult leaders, for example. Those who know how to manipulate and tap into the world's energy strands, making them able to control the weak-minded."

I thought of Watchet and Hinkley Point, though I didn't say anything.

"Despite the rumours, we do not send these creatures, humans, beings, whatever you want to call them, to black sites overseas. That would be very foolish. We just build more cages. The city itself helps to keep a damper on the energy produced by these beings. As you know, the more rural the location, the more likely we are to have an outbreak."

"So if I'd been forced to fight the Dru and won, which was unlikely, it would've ended up here?" I asked.

"If it had survived the destruction of the woodland, then yes," she admitted.

I couldn't imagine a worse fate for the noble warrior. The corridor began to have doors on either side. I found my skin starting to prickle, and a near constant tickle of raw power shivered up my spine.

"I expect you find this place uncomfortable, Corporal?" she asked.

"You could say that," I muttered. Something flared in my gut. A reaction to… what? I stopped walking and approached a door.

"Interesting," Sanchez murmured.

Sid hung back.

I peered through a small window full of security glass. The room contained a bed, a desk, bookshelves, artwork, though without frames, and a woman sat on a chair. I realised it was screwed to the floor. As my face shifted the light coming into her room, she looked up. Long black hair was tied in a braid down to her waist. Her eyes were the colour of old granite, a deep grey I'd never seen before. She wore an Edwardian-looking nightgown, and her small feet were in dainty slippers.

When she saw me, she smiled. Her lips were a fetching rosebud. As she stood, some instinct inside me made me pull back from the glass. At no more than five foot two inches or so, she posed no physical threat to me, but that finely honed DoPI created fear prickled and pinged through me.

The young woman pressed something on her side of the wall. "Hello stranger." Her voice came from an intercom I'd not noticed. It sounded tinny and flat.

"We modify her voice as it comes out, or she'll ensnare you," Sanchez said, keeping a distance from the door.

I pressed the button, intrigued, despite my instincts. "Hello. Who are you?"

"Anne," she said simply. "That's what they call me."

"It's a pleasure to meet you, Anne," I said, confused. This young, doe-like creature didn't seem dangerous to me. What could she…?

A sound like nothing else I've ever heard erupted from the small speaker. The young woman's face flickered, her mouth opening wider than a snake's as it devours its prey. Her eyes turned black and huge. Her skin lost its soft, youthful appearance, and she became a hag from a nightmare.

I backed off, eyes wide and staring.

"A banshee," Sanchez said. "Don't worry, her voice is contained in the cell, she won't kill you. Until I took over DoPI, she was kept bound and gagged, in something similar to a scold's bridle." She glanced at us to see if we understood the definition. We both nodded. Sid had paled considerably.

Sanchez continued. "We captured her just before the riots of 1917. It's probably fair to say Ireland has more than its share of monsters. They don't help the stability of the place, especially in the north. This one was found just outside Belfast. I want to see if she can be educated, civilised and eventually tamed. Her voice is powerful, a useful tool in the right hands."

"You want to turn her into a weapon?" Sid asked, horrified.

"I want her to become an ally, just like your Dru and the dryads," Sanchez clarified. "I know you don't trust me, Sid, but I am interested in the *concept* of allies. When Griffin suggested it after the events in Madron, I decided that allies could, perhaps, be formed inside the veil, not just here."

Sid and I stared at her in astonishment. Eventually, I said, "Where is Grove?"

Chapter Thirty-One

We continued along the corridor, but neither Sid nor I risked looking through more windows. About six doors down from Anne, the banshee, something slammed against a solid metal door, the kind of thing I imagined any prison used. A small hatch on the outside, closed, secure.

"What the hell is that?" asked Sid.

"A powerful poltergeist," Sanchez said. "It was part of Warwick Castle. We contained it during the Great War, brought it here. Several priests lost their minds in an effort to exorcise it. The damned thing won't leave and won't settle. It's been banging around in there for over a century."

"How?" I asked.

Sanchez shrugged. "The latest theory is that it's not a true poltergeist, but some kind of ghostly demon." She sighed. "Who knows? If it ever settles down long enough for us to communicate with it, we might find out how to set it free, or kill it. At the moment, it's in a lead-lined room with silver coating the surface."

The budget all this took must have been huge. I knew

DoPI had deep pockets, but this was out of my experience. How much did we take from the taxpayers?

As if reading my mind, Sanchez said, "We create many of our own resources. We have our black budget from the government of course, but much of what we do comes from private investors." She raised her hand. "And before you start, Sid, we do not allow them to set our agenda. They get to be a part of our great experiment, and our history. They are informed of progress, invited to give their opinions, and we are very selective about the types of people invited to invest. We also drive innovations that wouldn't be possible without our extensive studies of the *para-world.*"

"Like what?" Sid asked.

"At the moment, we are looking into the veil as an inter-dimensional portal we could use for exploration."

"Seeking resources?" he asked, still suspicious. "Like bloody Columbus and the rest?"

"Like DoPI, not like Columbus, and no resources, Sid, knowledge. We, the Department are seekers of knowledge. The more we have, the more protected our world. With that come resources, but I'm not interested in trying to take coal from a world inhabited by fairy folk, or the dryads, for example. I am interested in learning how their worlds interact, how they are one layer of our reality. It's a form of quantum entanglement. We are the base level, the heaviest matter." She held her hand up in a tight fist. "The elementals like Anne—they are beings that move through our dense world, interact with it, but they aren't part of it, and yet they reflect it, change it, alter destinies." Here, she used her other hand, tippy-tapped over the fist. "They can affect us, we can ruin them, it's all entangled."

Sid frowned and came to a stop. "Investors will want more than just a cosmic post office."

"Bus stop," I said. Sanchez and Sid looked at me and I felt my ears and cheeks grown hot. "That's what Trystan calls the veil, a bus stop." My companions ignored me.

Sid repeated his demand, "Well? What other little nasties do you have stashed down here to sell to the Illuminati or whoever?"

Pilar Sanchez actually rolled her eyes at him. "Please, the Illuminati? I'm sure you can do better than that, Sid."

"I can, just answer the damned question."

Why was this important? I had no idea, but I trusted Sid far more than Sanchez, so I kept my mouth shut.

"Fine, if you really want to know, here's another titbit for your paranoid musings. In the blue corridor we have an area for experimentations." She held up a hand. "We don't dissect aliens before you start mithering about that, but we have a number of operatives who have rare abilities we wish to harness."

"Just get on with it," Sid muttered.

"Telekinesis, Sid. If we can find a way to use a natural gift, harness it, amplify it, we could learn to control something like a drone. Currently, these vital machines are fragile. They can be defeated by targeted pulses to fry their electronics. If we protect their electronics, they become too heavy to be useful. However, if a swam of them can be controlled by a single mind, they no longer have electronics to fry. Imagine how much that would be worth? Imagine the control Great Britain would have on the world stage if we owned such power? Then there are the firebugs, pyrokinesis, these practitioners are inherently unstable personality types, but if we can harness their abilities we have a potential weapon. We are examining DNA of people like these to find out if we can separate genes so they can be—"

Sid's face twisted in horror. "Put into people, like soldiers? Like him?" He jerked a thumb at me.

"No," she said. "What we can do, if we find the genes, is find more people who have those genes, and when we do find those subjects, we can offer them a future without fear of their abilities. Sid, you're a savant at what you do, but if DoPI hadn't found you, where would you be?"

He glowered but didn't say anything.

"Exactly. Prison, or dead. We gave you a safe future. In other areas, we have people with particular skills at communicating with animals. Dogs, horses, dolphins—though we don't keep them here. We can send an animal into a specific location and our 'readers' can see through their eyes, hear things we'd never be able to without a fly on the wall. As it were."

We all paused for a long moment to take in this revelation. There'd be more questions, I had no doubt. Sid was caught. DoPI had saved him, used him, and he knew he saved lives because of it. Did that make their commercialisation of the *para* abilities people showed good, or bad? Was it a white hat, black hat situation or more nuanced? Oh, this would take some thinking about.

Personally, I wanted to find out a bit more about my problems. So, I brought us back to basics. "The veil, then, it's a portal?" I asked for clarification.

"We think so, though few have ever travelled it the way you do." She eyed me as we stopped in front of another door. "You have unique abilities, Griffin, just like many who work with DoPI. You always have had. It's why, once you became a commando and saw active service, we brought you into DoPI. It's why I've placed you in Cornwall, and it's why I used you when Lorne Turner needed help. Now, let's see what we have in our mysterious new guest. In the process, I hope you'll learn to trust us a little more."

Pilar Sanchez knocked on the door. A plain wooden affair with safety glass in half of it, but nothing more solid than a Yale lock on the outside.

"Door's open, Pilar," came a voice I knew.

Sid looked at me and mouthed, "Blyth?"

I shrugged and followed the boss into a large room.

It felt like walking onto a film set of a medieval polymath and alchemist. Blyth wore his charcoal suit, but no coat. It was hanging incongruously on a modern coat rack just to my right. The rest of the large space was filled with bookshelves, ancient-looking tables covered in stains and burn marks, braziers that sat alongside modern Bunsen burners. A mortar and pestle that looked to be made from wood had an aged quality to it, but it stood next to a laptop. The room smelt of herbs and spices. Jars stood between books, some of them filled with things my brain did not want to think about. Any spare piece of wall not filled with shelves held images on everything from parchment to modern, slick paper. They were charts, diagrams, trees of knowledge and more.

I focused on Blyth. "Hello again." After my experience in the veil, trusting this strange man felt impossible.

"It's good to see you, Griffin. I'm glad you made it out alive and sane," he said with a bright smile. "I must say, Pilar, I'm very grateful you kept my room as it has always been."

"We both knew you just needed a long holiday, Blyth. People like you don't retire." She looked at him with an expression of benign indulgence, like one would a favourite, but batty uncle.

"Perhaps. We'll see. For the moment, I'm intrigued by

our Dr Elena Grove," Blyth said, waving a hand at the box I'd seen him holding in the veil.

He looked so peaceful, almost blasé about what had happened to me in that empty nothingness of the veil. The fear and the pain. My total inability to escape. It pissed me off.

"Never fucking mind about the fact I almost died," I snapped, stepping in front of Sanchez to loom over the smaller man. "You used me."

He blinked his strange, round eyes. "I saved you."

"I was bait."

"That's your job," he pointed out, refusing to step back, despite my growing frustration.

"Corporal," Sanchez said quietly from behind me. "Step back. Blyth did what was necessary to contain Grove. We didn't warn you because—"

I rounded on her. "You knew?"

Her face twitched.

My breathing increased. "You have no idea what it's like in that place. How fucking terrifying it is. Pilar," this was the first time I'd ever used her first name, "it's a place where nothing exists. Nothing. I have no control. I've never entered it willingly. I've never escaped it on purpose. Nothing exists there. It's a vast emptiness. A place where the soul is lost forever." My hand swept out, and Sid caught it before I dismantled a series of glass tubes, beakers and something bubbling in a gin still. I felt my chest rising and falling.

"He's right," Sid said. "Whatever that place is, it's dangerous, and not the kind of dangerous an operative should have to deal with. Each time he enters, his body goes into some kind of shock, and when he comes out, he's a mess."

"It's your job, Corporal," Sanchez pointed out, echoing Blyth, her expression cold.

"Fuck you," I snapped for the first time. Never in my career had I spoken to a commanding officer in such a fashion. She had the right to have me up on charges for the outburst. "Thanks to this idiot," I gestured to Blyth, "Megan now wants to become part of our merry band of lunatics. She wants to join despite lying in a critical care ward, having had the shit kicked out of her by a Renfield." All my frustration, the physical and emotional pain of the last few weeks, began pouring out. "We are hundreds of miles from a crack DoPI team. We are alone down there, and we've already had three incidents this year. Three! And you used me without having the respect to warn me that I'd be bait for a sorcerer who wants to destroy the Church of England." I was shouting. I rarely shouted. It reminded me too much of my father.

Breathing heavily, I sucked down the rest of the words and backed off, turning and walking to the other side of the long room. Silence chased me, thick and rippling with other unspoken words. Where would they lead us if I let them out?

I leaned on the old stone sink, and gripped it hard, allowing it to anchor me to this world. "For fuck's sake, ma'am," I tried to put some respect back into my voice, but even I heard the sarcasm. "I don't even know who I am anymore." The shame and confusion of that ten-year-old boy, looking into the grave of his dead mother. The woman who killed herself rather than be with him.

With me! My internal voice wailed. *She left me!*

The quality of the silence changed as it drifted over my shoulders.

"Griffin?" Sid said softly. "They know something."

I turned, feeling like each one of my bruised and battered bones, every stitch, hurt. I stared at Sanchez. Her eyes were dark, shadowy in the soft light of this weird-arsed chemistry lab. Blyth should never try to play poker. He stared at me with pity and, wait, was that—shame?

"What do you know?" I asked, biting the words.

Sanchez started, "You wanted answers about Dr Grove, Corporal. One can't have—"

"Oh, for goodness sake, Pilar," snapped Blyth, throwing his arms in the air. "Give the lad what he needs. If he doesn't know the truth, how do you expect him to trust you? We've talked about this. You can't go on alone. DoPI has to change." Blyth pointed at me. "He is the future."

I was? It felt like the right time to keep my mouth shut.

Sanchez licked her lips, and her soft-soled shoes shuffled just a little. I'd never seen her express so much emotion. "Do you remember the reports about the Winter Sun Project, Griffin?"

Sid and I exchanged a look. He nodded. I glanced back at the boss.

Silence. The weapon I'd learned to deploy since working for her, and this time, *I* held my finger on the trigger.

She drew in an audible breath. "Your mother received treatment from the Winter Sun Project."

"But that was closed shortly after the war, right?" I asked.

Sanchez walked to a chair and sat. "Yes, but the scientists involved moved some of it to another site in Porton Down. We didn't have all the details. It was a difficult time in the sixties with the Cold War. Successive governments weren't happy about our presence, when they had Russia threatening our borders. Your maternal grandfather was working on the Winter Sun Project as it was closed down. He was a junior scientist at that point, but was quickly promoted when things moved location. He married your grandmother, but they didn't conceive your mother until late into their marriage. He…" She no longer had the courage to look me in the face. "He was not a kind man. He injected your grandmother with the same chemicals they gave the airmen and soldiers in Somerset to try to rid her of her depression while she was carrying your mother. No one sanctioned it, no one knew until it was too late. After the birth, your grandmother went crazy. I mean, her mental health collapsed completely." Sanchez ran a hand over her hair and shook her head. "There is no easy way to say this, Griffin, I am sorry. She killed your grandfather and tried to murder your mother. My predecessor stepped in and saved Hazel. It was… It was all rather violent."

"My mother had Winter Sun inside her as a foetus?" I whispered. I'd read the reports, many of them written by Lorne Turner. Due to his psychic abilities, he'd stumbled over an abandoned hospital on Exmoor. It's where they'd been trying to find a way to cure shell-shock during WWII. Servicemen were, and still are, expensive to train and losing them to mental health issues isn't helpful during a conflict. In the process of creating a cure, the scientists killed many, many men. Their spirits became tied to the land. Lorne found them, and eventually freed them, but in the process, others came looking for the secrets of the Winter Sun Project. I'd been there in the final act, but only after Turner killed those trying to escape with what, we thought, were the final remnants of the project.

Sanchez nodded. "Placing your mother with the Ackley family, who were looking for another daughter, seemed wise. A good upbringing on a farm in Cornwall. It was deemed safe. If she hadn't met your father, who knows, maybe she'd have survived. But his behaviour turned whatever she carried in her DNA into something too painful for her to carry. He triggered latent abilities she never understood. We didn't know about them. She never sought medical advice in a way that triggered our processes. If we'd known something was wrong, we'd have stepped in. She could bear whatever was happening up here." Sanchez tapped her head as if that explained why my mother felt she had to kill herself. "Hazel passed this on to you, but not your brother."

"Passed on what, exactly?" I didn't recognise my voice. I sounded like I'd been dipped in a glacier and carved from the bedrock of granite underneath.

Sanchez glanced at Blyth as if beseeching him to take up the story. He shook his head. "Oh, no, I'm not getting involved."

Pilar Sanchez squared her shoulders and stared at me. "When you were a boy, well, a teenager I suppose, I took over here, at DoPI."

Sid and I looked at each other. She didn't appear to be any older than me, and I'd never seen her take enough time off work to visit Harley Street's version of Doctor Frankenstein.

She continued, "Griffin, there is no nice way to put this, but I had your grandmother, and your mother, exhumed. I wanted their DNA tested against yours and that of your older brother. He carries none of the markers that you do. How that's possible we have yet to figure out, maybe something happened in Hazel's life, or she ate a different brand of cereal. Something woke up the dormant genes while you were… um… Well, you know."

My brain had started to spin, and I really didn't understand what the fuck was happening. "You did what?" I whispered. That switch—the one the commando training planted inside me—flipped to the 'on' position. I stalked forward, my boots silent on the wooden floor. "You dug my mother up?"

Sanchez backed up a step. "I needed to test her DNA. When she died, no one thought it important, but after reading your later school reports, about the night wanders, the screaming, the haunted—"

I snarled.

Sid manoeuvred himself between me and our boss lady. "Steady, Griffin. Hear her out. We need this intel."

"Move," I growled.

Blyth stepped neatly around me and Sid, pulling Sanchez away. "He's right, Marine, you need to hear this."

"Fuck you," I barked. I really needed to smash something. I was one of their damned experiments. A thought flickered through my mind, and I headed for the door.

"Don't do it, Woodbury," Sanchez snapped out.

"What the fuck do you know?" I asked, shoulders hunched, body primed for attack.

"You're going to let Anne out. Don't."

That gave me a reason to pause.

Sanchez sighed. "Maybe you aren't the only one touched by projects down here. You broadcast your thoughts when you're angry with me. It's not hard to hear."

This was too much. I wanted to go home. The wide-open skies of Cornwall. The tumble of the sea. The endless patchwork of fields. A sense of peace I'd never had anywhere else in the world. Also, my Megan and the family that had adopted me as one of their own.

"We're leaving," I said to Sid.

"Fair enough." Though he didn't move. "But don't you want to hear the rest? It might be important to Megan."

"Why?"

"Kids, Griffin. Kids." He sounded sad and just a bit scared.

A wave crashed into me and suddenly the medication, the stress, the exhaustion—it tumbled my mind sideways and I stumbled. Sid caught me, lowered me to the chair Sanchez had been using. "Steady, soldier boy. Steady."

"What's happening to me?" I asked him.

He glanced at Sanchez. "You'd better tell him the rest."

"When we found the DNA markers that matched in three of the four test subjects, I knew we had an opportunity."

A fucking opportunity? Is that what we are? For fu—

I tried to listen, but a high-pitched whine had started in my ears.

Her words washed over me, and I hoped Sid was paying attention. He'd handed me a glass of water and kept a hand on my shoulder.

"What was the opportunity?" he asked.

"Another person able to move between worlds," Sanchez said.

"Another?" Sid asked.

"Hazel was able to slip between realities, just as Griffin does. We didn't know, or we'd have taken her in, cared for her, guided her. I promise. Your father… He kept her under too much control. In those days we had no electronic surveillance. With private medics caring for her, we had no access. It was all too late for Hazel, but when I saw it in Griffin, I knew I had to act. He needed to be stronger, so joining the Royal Marines seemed wise. Then a gradual indoctrination into DoPI's methods and ideology—"

"You designed me?" I asked.

"We as a team guided you." She glanced at Blyth. Obviously one of her co-conspirators. "You will be in the vanguard of DoPI's evolution as we negotiate with the *para-world*. You are the intermediary we've been waiting for. They need you. We need you. Griffin, you are pivotal—"

I rose. Sid slipped a hand under my elbow. "We're leaving. I'm going home."

Sanchez opened her mouth, those usually unreadable dark eyes full of emotions I didn't have the bandwidth to interpret.

Blyth placed a hand on her forearm and shook his head. "Let him go."

Chapter Thirty-Two

The drive back to Cornwall was a strange one. I sat in the Mini's small seat, feeling every pothole in the road, scrunched up and staring out of the window as the city petered out and the countryside began. Sid sat in silence next to me, throwing anxious glances in my general direction here and there, but mostly leaving me alone. It was a wise move.

By the time we reached Stonehenge twilight had shouldered the apathetic light of a muggy August day to one side. It glowered over the rolling plains, turning the sky the colour of a gothic drama. I refused to look skyward and see the planets, now shifted slightly, overhead. Seeing them point at the ancient monoliths wouldn't help my frame of mind.

"Need to stop?" Sid asked.

I gazed at the stones. "No." Then added. "Thanks."

"Wanna greasy truckstop dinner?" he asked.

At that, my stomach rolled, making as much noise as a wooden barrel on cobbles. It didn't care that my mind was a frayed piece of tapestry, undone at the seams and full of threadbare patches.

"Yeah. Why not?"

A little further down the A303, we pulled into a layby with a mobile greasy spoon café parked up. The place did a roaring trade for the regulars of the main artery from London to the South West if you didn't want to take the motorway heading to Wales. I groaned as I tried to pull myself out of the tiny car.

Sid was already ordering bacon and egg baps, tea in huge china mugs, and walnut cake. The woman behind the counter chattered with him about the Mini, one of his favourite subjects, and I watched the crows settling down for the night in a nearby wood, even as I listened to the traffic swish past.

We ate at a small bench set on the verge. Sid said, "It'll rain soon." As he put down the tray full of food.

"Yep," I agreed.

He looked at me over the top of his huge sandwich. "You know, it's not all bad."

"Is that right?" I asked, warning him with my tone to be bloody cautious.

"Griffin, we stopped what might've been the beginning of a religious war on British soil. Can you imagine how it would've played out if Grove had managed to manifest demonic or angelic power in those children? We'd not only have the Christian community tearing itself apart, but I can't imagine our Muslim brothers and sisters being very happy about it either. It would've spread through Europe and beyond. That's without whatever harbingers of doom intended to bring to the party. Proof of God's existence, actual proof of Satan's existence? It would've been a hellstorm. We did good." He was focused on the win with Grove. Somehow, that felt like a lifetime ago.

"Yeah, I guess we did good. Go team." Pancakes weren't any flatter.

Sid reached over the table and poked me. "Stop it, Griffin. Maudlin self-indulgence doesn't suit you. Try a different perspective."

"Oh, I'm really bloody sorry that I'm not bouncing with joy over being manipulated by a government department who wants to use me as an experiment. They dug up my mother. They helped hide the abuse my grandfather perpetrated on the women in his life. No one stopped my father's cruelty. And they didn't fucking save her!" I banged the table, making the mugs jump and tea slosh.

Sid sat back a little to avoid any more explosions. His expression was kind. "No, they didn't, and they deserve all the shit you want to serve up for that. But," and here he tapped the table, "it won't bring her back, Griffin. It won't help you heal. As dark and complicated as your world has just become, you need to find the positives."

I glared at him. "What would those be? That whatever genetic freakery I have in my body I get to pass on to my children?" To be fair to Sid, he kept his expression passive, calm, like a therapist might in the face of a rage-filled teenager wielding a knife.

Sid's mouth quirked. "You might want to talk to Megan about that. I'm not sure she's the breeding kind."

"That's beside the point."

"No, that is one of many points. Did you want kids?" he asked.

I hadn't given it a moment's thought. "Don't know."

"Then let's shelve that disaster and move on to the next. We now know for certain that your mother's mental health problems were not your fault. Not that they were anyway, at age ten, how could they have been, but this gives adult Griffin some kind of perspective. A new window through which to view the past. It helps you understand your own issues. We can lean into this knowledge and learn to use it to help you. Yes, Sanchez wants you to bounce in and out of the veil at will, but she can't *make* you do it. If it comes down to it, quit DoPI. Go back to the Marines."

"I'm not doing that. I can't go back."

"Then you know you want to move forward. It's a good place to start. We can talk to people outside DoPI. Hell, even that royal pain in our arses from Anwen's Children might be able to help. Trystan certainly will."

I nodded. The pressure behind my eye grew heavier the longer Sid spoke. He was more than I deserved right then.

A single tear rolled down my cheek as I examined the tabletop in the last of twilight's efforts to stave off the demands of its big brother, night. "Sanchez stole from her dead body, Sid."

"I know, buddy."

I glanced at him. "Is that why she keeps calling me to her grave? Why she can't rest in peace?"

"Maybe. We'll talk to that vicar friend of Turner's. Maybe she'll come down to Cornwall and do a special ceremony for you. Better yet, I'll talk to Luce, her father can come down. You like Dilly. He's a good bloke, and he knows you better than… What's her name?"

"Ella, Ella Morgan. She's up in Northumberland now."

"Then Dilly it is. We'll get him down and say a proper goodbye. It'll help you and your mum." He rubbed my fist where it rested on the table. "You aren't alone, Griffin. I know this is a strange concept for you, but you have family. Let us help."

I sucked in a slow breath and nodded, relaxing my hand on the table's surface and feeling its rough and weathered grain. "Yeah, thanks, mate."

"It's a lot to deal with, Griffin. Don't think I'm not aware of that, but you can't let DoPI's shit swallow you whole. We have to be smarter than that. I've watched too many operatives burn out. Let me deal with Sanchez until we have you on an even keel."

I nodded. "What if Megan does want kids, Sid?"

"Then you talk about it and make decisions. Just like everyone else does when they know they have a genetic problem in the family. Somehow, I don't think it'll be an issue."

We drove back to Cornwall, and around Yeovil I fell asleep.

Picking Megan up from the hospital meant a tussle with Iris. She wanted her daughter home, but Megan wanted to convalesce at Turpin Cottage, and I wasn't going to argue. Every other day it seemed I needed my stitches checked by the practice nurse at the local GP's centre. Megan also needed to be seen by a doctor to make sure she continued to recover. In between all this, we wrote more reports and talked.

After a drive to the coast and a walk along a random beach, the heat finally relaxing its hold on Cornwall after some spectacular storms, we stopped for tea and cake.

I had something I needed to say before I grew too used to her living in the house.

To start with, I just enjoyed the sound of the sea's gentle murmur as she spoke to the sandy shore. The background chaos of the gulls as they teased aerobatics out of their wild and savage frolics. The pale blue of today's sky dipped almost to white on the horizon, and wind-torn clouds tried to hold their forms together overhead. They reminded me of ghosts.

"Something's bothering you," Megan said.

I huffed a small laugh. "You could say that."

"I meant above the usual." She seemed fragile, as if Hess's pounding on her body had fractured something in her mind. It's why I'd been delaying this conversation.

"Can we talk about the future?" I asked, feeling all squirrelly and weird in my gut.

Her right eyebrow rose. "Okay. What have you got in mind? A holiday somewhere lovely for Christmas so I can avoid the usual family drama?"

I laughed. "No, I want in on an Ackley family Christmas, thank you very much. It's the least I deserve. I might even arrange a punch-up with your brothers."

Megan laughed. "I might just let you."

I took her hand, and she frowned, saying, "It's that serious, is it?"

"I've told you this Winter Sun Project stuff altered my DNA somehow, right?"

She nodded.

"It's genetic. I've never thought about having kids. It was never on the cards with the other women in my life, but you're different."

She held up her hand. "I need to stop you there, Griff. I don't want children. If that's a game changer for you, I understand. Adrian," she tripped over the name and swallowed hard. There had been plenty of tears about his death, which confused me. "He wanted them. Told me I didn't know what I was missing. That the time to be fertile was…" Her voice faded, her eyes became distant, then snapped back as she forced herself into the present. "Well, that doesn't matter. What matters is I've never wanted children. I enjoy my life the way it is. I like my career, and I don't want to compromise."

Her eyes stared right into mine, searching for the truth. She was nervous about my reaction.

Rubbing her knuckles, I smiled. "Then we don't have children. I've never wanted to be a father. The idea of it terrifies me."

"I would like a dog, though."

I laughed. "I can commit to a dog, but I don't think it would be fair to have one in your flat."

"No…" Her look became coy, which, if I was honest, Megan didn't do well.

"So," I said, "this is my second question. Come live with me? Don't leave Turpin Cottage. I love having you there all the time."

"It's too small for the three of us."

"No, it'll be alright. Sid's spending more time at Luce's anyway."

"He won't want a dog… All his stuff is too nice."

"Then we move out and he can have the cottage. We'll find somewhere further out in the country. Save up, buy something."

She snorted. "Buy something in Cornwall? What've you got? A magic money tree I don't know about?"

I felt the smile on my face deepen, warm, and spread throughout my body. "No, but you've just agreed to move in, which means I have you. That's more important than anything else."

Megan laughed. "No marriage, Griff. Don't want to get married either."

I felt a pang of disappointment at that, but fair enough,

and she might change her mind down the road. "We don't have to get married, Meg."

She breathed in, and her smile softened her face as she closed her eyes against the sun. "I'm happy."

My chest ached with joy. "So am I."

Releasing my hand, she lifted her delicate plate with the cake on it. "Here's a toast to our future."

I laughed and lifted my plate. They gently clicked. "To our future."

The seagulls wove overhead. The breeze tousled what was left of my hair after the fire at the caravan. While we ate our cake, our free hands entwined and spoke in a language our words would match in that future.

More by Joe Talon

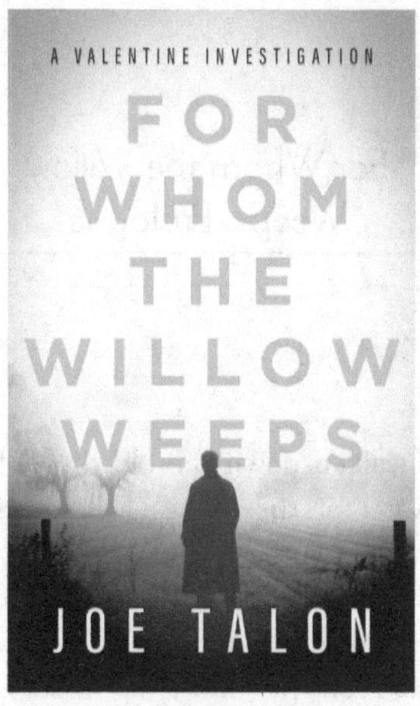

vinci-books.com/forwhomthewillowweeps

Two bodies. One willow. And a truth rotting beneath the roots.

Two bodies beneath the same willow, twenty-five years apart. Linked by poison pen letters and buried secrets, ex-cop Dale Valentine digs through Glastonbury's rural quiet to expose a tragedy no one wants unearthed. But the truth here doesn't just destroy lives—it devours them.

Turn the page for a free preview…

For Whom the Willow Weeps: Prologue

Together they walked down the old drove, beside the dull and slinking water of the rhyne. The soft light of a midsummer evening made the twilight sky wide and deep over their heads. The scent of the damp earth rose after a day of blessed sunlight. Now the damn festival was over, the rain released its hold on the low-lying moors around Glastonbury.

"Water's high," stated Backman.

A man built from the strictest verses in the Bible. He had mouse coloured hair, cut short by his wife, who didn't know what a straight line looked like, and eyes that mirrored the ditch water they trudged alongside.

"Arr, it's too high for good drainage in the winter. We'll both need to keep the heavy cattle out of these fields, or the banks will fold," said Douglas.

He stood over six feet, his frame made from freshly mowed hay bales and too many of his wife's scones. His hair shone white and stuck out in tufts from under his ever-present flat cap, and his eyes mirrored the sky during a bright dawn in the moments just after the pink has gone. He didn't want to trudge. His natural gait would see him bounce through the farmland, sometimes picking flowers for his family to enjoy at the kitchen table.

Duty bound him to Backman and therefore to these quarterly walks along their borders to check hedges, fences and most especially the rhynes. Too full of summer water, they'd never flow quickly enough into the rivers to drain the land after the inevitable storms of the next three seasons. These peaty soils might raise good, fat stock, but if they became waterlogged… Well, you only had to see what happened to the land over Pilton way to know the damage that could be done.

Backman stirred himself enough to speak again, "How you doin' with them travellers?"

Douglas sighed. "It's not easy, right enough. I knows we all have to find a place and way to live, but they ain't like the gypsies we used to get down this way when we was nippers. It's the kiddies my missus worries about."

"Godless folk to be sure," Backman pronounced.

Douglas eyed him. The temptation to take the mickey out of the old sod rose strongly, but he resisted the urge. The thought of Backman praying for his sarcastic soul and offering him forgiveness for his sin of—well, anything really—proved to be enough to still Douglas's tongue.

"Now the festival's over there seems to be more than ever. I guess they want to be here for the solstice." He realised his mistake the moment the words hit the warm summer air and bounced into his ears.

Backman inhaled heavily through his large and hairy nose. "It is not a Christian festival and the Church in that heathen town should not allow it. St Michael's was once consecrated ground…"

The rant continued. Douglas listened with half an ear, alright, a quarter of an ear so he could nod in the right places. As far as he knew, hanging a bishop from the tor's summit probably de-consecrated the hilltop, but it didn't do to dwell on history, especially old history.

He peered along the drove, the soil heavy and thick on his boots, to the old willow tree that marked the official border between his land and Backman's. Randel Cottage stood between the rhyne, the tree and Folly Farm, a sizeable plot.

Douglas frowned, puzzled by the flash of red among the tall grass. The willow's undulating branches parted for a moment, the breeze fluttering them away. Red and white. Dark red, bright white.

"Oh shit," he said unthinkingly.

"Profanity is the solace of the untutored mind—"

"Bugger the untutored mind, some bastard's had one of my sheep," Douglas said, breaking into a run.

He gathered speed like a steam train, trying to see beyond the thick, deep screen of green leaves. The tree, for its part, seemed to want to keep its secrets from the observer until the moment Douglas reached out for their whip-like branches.

Not a sheep.

"Oh my God," he whispered.

"Oh, have mercy. Jesus Christ, our Lord and Saviour, have mercy on us all," cried out Backman.

"Go, call the police, call everyone," Douglas ordered.

Backman hesitated.

"Now, man, before night falls!"

Backman stumbled, but raced towards his bleak home.

Douglas stood alone in the field with the willow tree and

felt a tear scorch his sun-browned cheek. "You poor lad, what happened to you?" he whispered.

The boy was clearly beyond his help, the wide eyes opaque, the lips blue not red, the skin grey, not flushed with health and life. Douglas dropped to his knees, only now noticing the vast swathe of picked summer flowers. He frowned and lifted one, a yellow flag iris. This is why the banks of the rhyne didn't look right. He kept thinking something was off, but couldn't place it until now. Someone had stripped the banks of flowers and the prettiest grasses.

"It's Freddie, isn't it?" he whispered to the lad. "My missus, she feeds you and that other lad. She's going to be heartbroken over this. I'm so sorry, boy, but the police will be here soon, and they'll take you back to your family. They'll find out what happened. You'll see." He paused for a long time, trying to seal his pity and sorrow behind a wall of manliness. "You'll see," he murmured, hands between his knees, head bowed, tears falling heedless of his efforts to contain them.

The gentle fronds of the willow tree cloaked his shoulders as twilight dissolved the last of the mid-summer light.

For Whom the Willow Weeps: Chapter One

The summer light warmed the inside of the Green Man café. Today, it even reached the back corner of the large room where Dale sat enjoying his guilty treat of veggie burger and chips. Carbohydrate heaven. The very long day, spent sorting through the hundreds of images he'd collated, left him hungry and faintly depressed. His latest client, Mrs Thompson, might need to dig the dirt on her errant husband, but she wouldn't be pleased when she realised he'd replaced her with a carbon copy. One twenty years her junior. He didn't want to make that house call.

Being a private investigator in a small, rural town made him see his neighbours in a very different light.

A brief flicker in the sullen sunbeam hitting his laptop's screen warned him of impending disaster. A hand appeared, and a chip vanished.

"That one was bad," said a female voice.

Dale looked up from his laptop. "No, Milly, it wasn't."

The wide grin and bright green eyes of his self-appointed assistant made him sigh. Another chip dematerialised off his plate.

"You're late," he said, pulling the plate protectively towards him. Sharing didn't come naturally after spending four years in a cell with two other men and eating prison food. Stealing nosh would get you broken fingers, or worse.

Milly waved half the chip at him. "And you're grumpy. Again. The sun's shining, you can't be grumpy. It's the kind of day you should celebrate."

Dale felt his teeth clamp together. "I'm grumpy because you're late."

"To be fair, Guvnor," she said in her terrible mock Cockney, "I cracked the case."

Dale fought the desire to smile. It never paid well if he rewarded Milly's attempts at humour with too much appreciation. It encouraged her to think they were friends. Acquaintances, okay, employees and associates too, he'd handle them. But friends? No.

"Not so much cracked, Milly. You went at it with a sledgehammer, and it happened to work out for you. This time," he said, a hint of warning rumbling through the bass notes of his voice. "The images are good, though."

Milly peered over the screen of his laptop, and grinned again, showing teeth a little too crowded to fit correctly, but well-maintained. "They're good piccies, right?"

"Yeah, they're good. Though, I'm sure the client won't like 'em too much. I've selected the ones that Mrs Thompson can hand over to her solicitor without giving her panic attacks over ageing," Dale said, noticing another chip vanishing off his plate. He dragged it even closer. The girl had chip magnets on her fingers. "You want a plate? Go ask your mum."

Milly pulled a face. “She’s got me on a diet. No more chips.”

He chuckled. “She did warn you.”

The young woman sat back with a heavy sigh. “I know. I know. It’s not good for my diabetes.”

“It’s not good for my sanity either, Milly. You scared me.” Dale pointed one of his chips at her. “I don’t like finding young women passed out in my hallway. It’s not a good look.” How she’d fainted with type 2 diabetes, he’d never figure out.

He watched her twirl one of her mass of red ringlets around her finger. “Yeah, I know, sorry.”

Dale refrained from yet another nag. She had enough people in the town to do that to her. It kept them professional if he didn’t care too much. “Right, do you want to come with me to show Mrs Thompson these photos and to give her the report?”

He watched with a sinking feeling as Milly shook her head. “No, Guv. I very much don’t want to do that. Mostly because I think Mrs Thompson would cut my face off if you didn’t go alone.”

“If I promise to sew your face back on, will you come?” Dale asked, aware of that fact he was pleading.

The glint in those jade green eyes turned merry. “Oh, no. You can deal with the succubus all alone.”

“Who’s a succubus?” asked an older, more faded, though just as friendly, version of Milly.

“A client, Mum,” said Milly.

“That’s not nice, Milly. Succubi are dangerous demons. You shouldn’t refer to real people as demons. They’ll hear you.”

Dale opened his mouth to question the logic on this comment, but Milly placed her hand on his to force silence on the subject. Her pale, youthful skin stood in contrast to his own, olive wood dark and well-worn hand.

"Don't," she said. "Mum has a thing about sex demons."

"Do I want to know?" Dale whispered, long having learnt that Daisy Wolfe had ears sharper than a fox when in her domain of the Green Man café.

Milly shook her head. "No. You don't. And if you think you can't protect your virtue, then I guess I'll go with you to see Mrs Thompson. These pictures will go a long way towards her goals in the divorce settlement."

Dale closed his laptop. "So long as she pays her final bill, I'll be happy."

Milly pushed his phone around on the table, looking pensive.

"What?" he asked.

Her green eyes flickered to his. "Don't you ever get bored with this kind of job?"

He sat back, crossing his arms over his broad chest. "Chasing lost spouses?"

"Yeah, I mean, it's..."

He allowed his amusement to show. "It's what? Beneath us? Seedy? Feeding monsters in court?"

Milly shrugged. "I guess." Rather than twenty-five, she suddenly looked about twelve.

He leaned forwards, his elbows on the table either side of his laptop and food. "Listen to me. It's more important to me to help people with small domestic issues, moving them through a difficult transition in their lives as smoothly as possible, than tackling the things you listen to on those true crime podcasts you love so much. I've had more than my fair share of drama in my life, and I didn't move to

Somerset to find more. I enjoy being a small-town detective and I like my humdrum existence."

He wanted to say more. He wanted to confess he was lonely. That he knew this small life cost him the connection to humanity that he craved, but he couldn't seem to let go of the past. Holding on to it kept the memories alive, and memories were all he had left.

Milly gazed at him. Her eyes full of compassion, even though she had no idea what his past contained. The girl had a gift for climbing under his skin and connecting to the pain of his secrets.

His phone rang, making them both flinch. Number unknown. He slid to green and pressed loudspeaker. "Hello, this is Valentine Investigations, Dale speaking. How can I help?"

Milly smirked at the way he always softened his voice when talking to clients on the phone. He gave her a scowl. Dale knew his hard, South London accent needed toning down for the countryside clients he courted.

A woman asked, "Hello, are you? Are you a private detective?" Her voice sounded fragile, expensive, and distinctly *not* from Somerset.

"I am. How can I help?" Dale pushed back in his seat.

"My name is Mrs Penning, and I think I'm in terrible danger."

Dale's eyes met Milly's. They both heard the edge of panic in the caller's voice.

The doorbell to the café chimed, and a crowd of young people came inside. He turned off the speaker and put the phone to his ear, switching his attention to the voice on the other end.

Milly watched him become absorbed by the call. She knew from experience that even when he appeared to be totally focused on a client's needs, he still knew exactly what was going on around him. Right now, his gaze had slipped into the distance as he listened to the woman on the other end of the line. Milly's ears didn't have her mother's penetrative skills, so she reverted to watching his body language. He always sat with his back to a wall, aware of his surroundings even if his attention remained fixed on his laptop. She'd never been able to surprise him. Right now, he remained still and just listened, allowing the woman on the other end to say her piece.

Milly slipped away to the counter, helping her mother serve the new customers. The movements mechanical after years of working in the café.

While she helped out, she watched Dale's expression shift from his usual mild irritation and grumpiness to surprise. Not an emotion she was used to seeing on his face. Though, she'd learned over the last six months while working for Valentine Investigations that Dale didn't give away his emotions lightly. She planned on it being Valentine and Wolfe one day, but she had a lot to do to make Dale accept that plan. He wasn't so much a closed book, as a locked book buried in a treasure chest you'd need a map to find.

When he'd started using the café as his alternative office to the one he had in his home, she'd soon made herself useful. Being from London, Dale had no knowledge of the local area. The gossip, the people, or even the basic premise of what Glastonbury was all about mystified him. Pun intended. Milly had spent the first few weeks explaining as much as possible, between his bouts of bad temper, and the sense of necessary isolation he carried around like a suit of implacable, bitter armour.

Dale's size alone made him stand out in the town. Built like a prop-forward that even his designer clothes couldn't mask, the combination of his father's Scottish heritage and his mother's Italian beauty, made him big, dark, and burdened with movie-star bone structure. Only the horrible scarring from adolescent acne ruined the effect. Dale Valentine also hailed from Peckham, South London, meaning every time he opened his mouth, he sounded foreign. Although Milly only knew a tenth, maybe less, of his past, whatever happened to him made his natural good looks too bitter. It's why she'd had the courage to talk to him in the first place. Handsome men made Milly deeply uncomfortable. Dale, with the close-cropped black hair going silver and pockmark scars, wasn't quite handsome.

She'd liked him the moment he'd growled his first order of veggie burger and chips over the counter while she'd been serving in the café. He gave the impression of being a displaced giant in a town full of farmers and hippies.

He finished the call. "We have a new case. Come on. She's upset. I think I'll need you." He picked up his laptop, stuffed it into his leather messenger bag, and made to move towards the door.

Even as Milly tried to gather her scattered thoughts, she scrambled after him.

"Eat something sensible," yelled her mother as the door chimed their exit.

Milly almost jogged to keep up with Dale's long strides. He walked straight over the High Street, the crawling traffic as seemingly insignificant as flies, and up the steep hill on the shaded side of the road.

"You parked in Butts Close?" she huffed, trying not to sound like an asthmatic train.

"Yep. We have to go to a place called Folly Farm, on…" he glanced down at her, almost a full twelve inches separated their heights. "Is there really a place called Splotts Moor?"

Milly laughed. "Yeah."

"You know the farm?"

"Not sure, but I know where Splotts Moor is, so it can't be far." It sounded familiar, but the memories drifted away when she grabbed at them. They'd come back. She usually needed a visual reference to access her mental database.

They found the sleek, midnight blue, Audi A7 Sports Back and Dale pinged the locks from a distance. She'd asked him why once, why he always did it from the furthest distance possible. He'd told her it was for security. Milly often wondered what made him so paranoid.

He eased himself with effortless grace into the low-slung leather seat, and Milly collapsed into the passenger side like a small elephant might. The car started with a purr of potential and Dale, who always parked nose out in a car park, pulled away smoothly, and they joined the afternoon traffic. Once clear of the town, he switched on their agreed playlist. Simon and Garfunkel's *Sound of Silence* called mournfully through the interior. Dale loved prog rock, Milly loved folk, they'd found a middle ground when together.

Dale considered, for the thousandth time since moving to Somerset, why he didn't trade in his beautiful Audi A7 for a tank. The mud currently lashing at his paintwork, while he followed a tractor around the back of the odd shaped hill forming much of Glastonbury's fame, broke his heart.

Overtaking, even with the Audi's swift response time, wouldn't end well in the narrow confines of the lane.

"I should have taken us the other way," muttered Milly.

He glanced at her and registered the glum expression and high colour in her round cheeks.

"So why'd you choose this way?" he asked, trying, and failing, to keep his voice neutral.

She glanced at him. "It's the safest and quickest way to cycle."

He gave up hiding it. He smiled. Milly hadn't learned to drive. She hadn't learned to do many of the things he'd taken for granted by the time he'd hit twenty-five and had an exciting career in the Metropolitan Police. There were moments when he wanted to ask why she'd stayed in her hometown, so close to her parents, but that would stray into the personal. They didn't have a personal relationship. Dale made certain of that. The last thing he needed was someone in Glastonbury asking questions about his old life in London.

"Don't worry about it. I'm considering taking out shares in the local car wash." This time he failed to keep the irritation out of his voice. Then the irritation transferred to himself, as he watched Milly sink further into the plush leather seat. "Seriously, without you, I'd never find anything around here. Satnav just isn't that good." The blatant lie made her relax a little. "Right, what I'm going to need you to do is soften my edges, take notes and keep Mrs Penning on track. From what little she told me on the phone, her family is new to the area and their country idyll is turning to dust."

"So they bought this farm and expected everything to be like an episode of Country Life?" Milly asked.

Dale, right hand resting lightly on the steering wheel,

glanced at her again. "Not all incomers are bad people. We create valuable income for locals."

Milly scowled. They'd had the argument many times over the last six months, and it had never resolved itself. The unanswerable question of local versus incomer was a nasty many-pronged conundrum Dale couldn't see a way to resolve. Fleeing London for Somerset, being able to buy his old cottage outright, had rendered him a privileged status in the countryside that he'd never have had in the city.

"Just play nice. It's what I pay you for," he said.

"I will. It's not her fault. You need to go left here," Milly pointed.

The tight confines of the lane opened out into the next narrow artery, just about wide enough for two vehicles, but it didn't qualify for a white line in the middle of the road. Dale continued at a sensible pace. After moving down here, he'd soon learned the locals travelled at two speeds, crawling and way too fast to avoid. Well used to city traffic, he preferred the former. The advanced driving courses he'd done with the Met had no place in this quiet life he'd adopted.

They trundled along, the early summer sun dazzling on the wet, bright emerald of the hedges and verges. White flowers, cow parsley according to Milly, waved their bright umbrellas and the Mendips in the distance, were a high, green barrier made hazy by the sun. Dale relaxed as he gazed at the mass of farmland rolling away. It tugged at his heart in a way a cityscape never had, and he was learning to love the moods of this new world he occupied. A gift after the endless shit he'd suffered and caused.

Milly interrupted his mental meander.

"Up here on the right, there's a turning into a farm track."

"Wonderful," Dale sighed, wondering how the low-slung vehicle would cope.

Fortune smiled on the sleek car, however, because Folly Farm had a well-maintained gravel lane, with fewer potholes than the council-maintained road, and little mud. The house itself, when he parked, looked typical of the area.

For Whom the Willow Weeps: Chapter Two

Folly Farm
The timbers of your home are cursed and will lay their foulness inside you.
The stones of your home hold the screams of the innocent and they will ruin you.
The rot inside that place will end you.
Run. Leave. Go back to your safe life in the city. This is not the place for you.
That house is damned, and so are you.

Dale breathed out, and he heard Milly gasp in shock.

"Well, that's different," he said.

Mrs Penning's eyes looked a little glazed. It made Dale think that she probably hadn't eaten all day. The wine must be pumping pretty quickly around her slight frame. "Can you see why I'm worried?"

He nodded. "I can."

"Who could do this? We… I… I wanted a fresh start. We used to have a place in the Cotswolds but… Well,

Lucinda isn't easy, and we needed to change schools. Again." Her eyes shone with emotions the wine would knock loose if Dale didn't take precautions.

Milly finally felt able to speak. "Mrs Penning, we can see what a problem this is for you, and we can help. You aren't alone. It's always scary moving to somewhere new. I've not seen you in town. Do you come into Glastonbury?"

Dale hid his smile. As always, Milly acted as a distraction. He'd noticed her gift the first time he'd met a pair of terrified parents in the Green Man. They'd needed help to find their drug-addled and missing son. Dale had struggled to control the mother's rising terror that a murderous cult had swallowed her son. Milly sat with her and within ten minutes, the mother gave up information that would've taken Dale an hour to uncover. He'd found the young man and returned him to the family.

While Milly did her magic, Dale went through the folder. The messages were odd, even for poison pen letters. Each one seemed to be aimed at warning the Pennings away from the farm, rather than attacking the family.

"Mrs Penning," he said, interrupting Milly. "Have you or your husband any reason to think this is a personal attack?"

The woman shook her head. "No, that's just the thing. We don't know anyone in this area of Somerset. What happened with Lucinda in the Cotswolds… that…" Her voice bled off and her colour rose in splotches up her neck.

Dale wondered if it was worth pursuing whatever happened in the Cotswolds. Could someone have chased them into Somerset? He had the feeling that if that were the case, Mrs Penning wouldn't be withholding information. Her total mystification at the hate in the letters wasn't faked.

"When did you move here, Mrs Penning?" he asked.

"We bought the house six months ago. A building firm had taken it on as a project after they won an auction. Apparently, it was in quite a state. They had an architect design the interior, then the final touches were made during the purchase period under our instruction."

"And these letters started arriving?"

"Four months ago. Just one in the first month, but they've slowly been coming more frequently. This last week I've had three." Tears rose in her eyes, and she retreated to the fridge for more wine. "I dread the post arriving."

Dale and Milly shared a long look. Another bucket of wine wouldn't help them retrieve more information.

"Well, if you're happy, I'm sure we can find out something about what's happening."

"I don't care what it costs. I just want these letters to stop. This is too much. I don't deserve it." She gulped down another mouthful of wine.

Dale thought about where he'd grown up and all the terrible things he'd witnessed in South London. The poverty, the crime, the drugs, the fear and hate. Many of the people he knew didn't deserve that either, but they had no escape. No giant fridge full of wine. Just needles laced with their favoured brand of escapism.

Forcing his prejudice to one side, he said, "Milly will send the details of our rates—"

"No, I want you looking now. Send whatever you have to, and I'll backdate the payments. I can't afford to move to Somerset time. Do you understand?" Her blue eyes cleared, and the woman who walked into expensive restaurants and expected instant service stared at him.

He swallowed back his immediate retort, taking orders rubbing against him like savage sandpaper. He managed a polite, "Then we'll take this folder with us, and I'll report back in a week on progress, or sooner, if we make a discovery. How does that sound? You'll be welcome to phone or email during the investigation, and if any more letters turn up, don't open them. Just phone and I'll come to pick it up. Alright?"

She nodded. Dull now after the flash flame of a moment before. "Yes. Thank you. You've been more comfort than the police."

Dale held his hand out. "That's what you're paying for, Mrs Penning. A professional approach."

Her limp hand vanished inside his paw.

When they left the house behind, a forlorn Mrs Penning standing in the doorway with her wine, and returned to the car, he heard Milly breathe out nice and slow.

Dale chuckled. "I'm bloody glad you came. Thank you."

She looked at him and her expression made him frown. "What is it?" he asked.

"Dale, that farm. I remember it now. It used to be in a terrible state. Almost condemned. The family that lived there, they..." Milly puffed out her cheeks, obviously looking for the right words.

"Spit it out."

"The body of a boy was found here about twenty-five years ago. I only know, because we used to tell each other ghost stories in school. His drowned spirit would return to claim a victim, because he was lonely."

"Nice," Dale murmured.

"Not really. It gave me nightmares. So Dad told me the truth. A boy had died here, laid out with flowers all around him, under a willow tree. It was beside the footpath running across Folly Farm's land, down by Twelve Foot Rhyne."

Having lived in the area for a couple of years, Dale now

knew a rhyne was an artificial river built to drain the Somerset Levels of water, much of which was below sea level. They'd started the process during the Middle Ages, but the landowners of the eighteenth century did most of the work, or their peasants did.

"So it was murder?" he asked.

She nodded, looking sad. "They never uncovered the truth. Many of the locals thought it must be the farmer. They were a strange lot. An old Somerset family, but they chose not to be part of the community, so they had no trust. Dad, he told me all this because he wanted me to understand how stupid and dangerous false assumptions could be. After the death of the boy, the family cut themselves off even more."

Milly's local knowledge gave Wikipedia a run for its money.

Dale glanced at her as he navigated a less direct, but more Audi-friendly, route back to the town. "Does your dad know more?"

"Probably. You want to talk to him?" she asked.

"A good place to start. I'll read through the letters again, take some notes, and talk it over with him."

"You don't seem to think she's in danger?"

He shook his head. "The letters aren't directed at her. That's the thing I need to think about. The envelopes aren't aimed at her either. They're sent directly to Folly Farm."

"So it's someone who hates the farm?" Milly asked. "What's that all about? Why would someone hate a farm?"

"Why indeed? I think that's the place we need to start. Who would hate a farm?"

They turned right onto the post rush-hour A361.

"It's busy. Tourist season," Milly stated.

Dale said, "This isn't busy." Being used to London traffic, he'd never understand how more than twenty cars in sight on a main road constituted busy.

When they reached the edge of town, Milly said, "I can walk down from yours. It'll add to my steps for the day and keep Mum happy." She waved her wrist at him, the machine flashing to life.

"Sorry, Milly, it's almost dark, I'm not letting you walk home alone," Dale stated.

She huffed. "For God's sake, it's Glastonbury, not Peckham. It's nowhere near dark. It's almost mid-summer."

"You've just told me a boy was murdered and ritually placed in a field. You're not walking."

He glanced at her, slowing for four young people crossing the road dressed like rainbows and carrying an acoustic guitar, digeridoo, and a set of bongos. Instinctually, he knew they'd be heading for a night on the Tor, smoking weed, taking some acid and watching the stars while playing their version of music. With pale skins, blonde dreadlocks, and general good health it was equally obvious the bank of mummy and daddy fed the machine that kept them fuelled.

He drove slowly down the main High Street, the shops gradually becoming more eccentric. The steep hill rose from Glastonbury Market Cross, the octagonal nineteenth century gothic stone monument, a natural gathering place. This evening young people covered it, enjoying the warmth of the early summer evening. On the other side of the market square, outside the medieval George and Pilgrims Hotel, a crowd gathered. Two men yelled at each other, and the shoving began.

About the Author

Joe Talon tolerates reality by escaping on a regular basis into strange worlds and spaces that appear from a muse who likes to take the darker path. Be it murder in Glastonbury, or monsters on the wilds of Exmoor and Cornwall, Joe feels the tug of words and enjoys the company of many invisible friends. Mostly, Joe really likes seeing the bad guys suffer.

While living a small life in rural Spain with far too many rescue dogs, Joe battles demons, slays dragons, and imagines what the apocalypse will really be like when it comes and are there enough lentils in storage to make it through.

With an addiction to stories, collecting dogs, and trying to grow vegetables (mostly unsuccessfully), Joe really hopes that the darker paths those stories take aren't real. Though, in the quiet of the night, when the moon is bright, the air is still and a fox barks as an owl screeches, Joe's fairly sure they offer adventures that cannot be resisted forever.

Joe has a degree in medieval stuff, grew up on the edge of Exmoor, managed to survive gaining martial arts black belts in three disciplines and loves to walk. Which is just as well with all the dogs.

www.ingramcontent.com/pod-product-compliance
Lightning Source LLC
LaVergne TN
LVHW030915080826
845145LV00013B/2907